WITH THE ENEMY

Other books by Susan Curran

Novels

Communion with Death
Mine
Mrs Forster
The Heron's Catch
The Mouse God

Biographies

The Marriage of Margery Paston
The English Friend

With the Enemy

Susan Curran

CURRAN
PUBLISHING

First published 2015 by Curran Publishing
an imprint of Curran Publishing Services Ltd
2 St Giles Terrace, Norwich NR2 1NS

www.curranpublishing.com

ISBN 978-0-9931603-0-1

Typeset by Curran Publishing Services
Designed by Susan Curran

England, 1998

For Paul

1

On the morning she discovered the Beaver's corpse – which was also the morning she met James Connaught for the first time, two things which were inevitably linked from then on in her mind – Eliza Stannard spent two hours in the old print room at St Jude's House in Costhorpe, waiting to be interviewed by the police.

There were perhaps thirty people there, not counting the two uniformed police constables who stood near the door, and asked them every now and then not to talk to each other. It was not, Eliza had noticed, a random cross-section of those who worked at St Jude's. No wonder: the people who were in the office before 7 am were not a random group, since apart from the shift workers, few people below grade 6 or so (as they had used to call it) ever came in that early. There were a couple of security guards, a clutch of people she recognized as IT support workers, and the rest were mainly managers like herself. No board members, she noticed, although Frank Mills at least had been in the office not long after the discovery. And James Connaught (whom she had met shortly before being directed to the print room) was not there either. He had mentioned he was to be interviewed by a detective chief inspector, if she remembered right. He had been given a name. It occurred to her that the police must be even more grade and status conscious than the civil service, or its privatized equivalent (of which the RUS Group, her employer, was an example). That was probably why she and these others were waiting so long: the police would sort out somewhere more comfortable for the big bosses to wait, and talk to them first, regardless of who had actually seen what.

She sat with Mitchell Jones and Genevieve Bush, the two other section leaders from her department, on the low chairs, upholstered in prickly purple cloth, that the police must have brought in from somewhere else on the ground floor. The dusty equipment – the in-house printing operation had been closed down three or four months earlier – loomed silent around them in the flat neon light. Obediently she barely talked to either Mitchell or Genevieve, though they exchanged vague smiles from time to time, and once Genevieve reached for and squeezed her hand. Most of the talk

she overheard consisted of requests to smoke (politely denied
by the police) and for cups of coffee (provided, though slowly).
Howard Nkolo, who had discovered the corpse with her, was
across the room, sitting with Sandie Masters and Hugh Worning.

Sandie was one of the first to be called for interview, as was
Geraldine – Eliza could not fathom how the order was determined
– and Howard was called before she was summoned herself. He
detoured past her on the way to the door. 'Courage, mon ami,'
he said cheerfully. Then he added, in a low voice, 'We never saw
Sandie or Hugh.'

But we – oh. It had not occurred to her before then to say
anything but the truth.

Except that – hell, thought Eliza, he's right. No one tells the
police everything, and there was no point creating trouble for
Hugh or Sandie. She would not, of course, have lied to protect a
murderer. But it stood to reason (to her) that none of the people
in the room with her could possibly be a murderer.

It occurred to her then that she could have spent this waiting
time – although she had not expected to have to wait as long as
she had – sorting out the story she would give. But it was too
late now: barely a minute after they asked for Howard, a woman
appeared and told Eliza to follow her.

2

She was interviewed in a small ground-floor room that she had never been in before. Room 1K, it was called. Someone's office, she assumed, although there was no name on the door. Maybe it was another office (there were quite a few) that had been used by someone who had now left RUS. It was not even vaguely grand, not like the offices in the senior management suite. There was a desk (its surface bare), a metal cupboard (closed), a leather chair of the kind that tilts and swivels which had evidently been pulled out from behind the desk, and a couple of purple cloth chairs like the ones that had been brought into the print room, all crowding the space between the desk and the door. A police officer who introduced himself as Inspector Crane (and introduced his silent companion as a detective constable) told her to sit in the leather chair. He took one of the cloth ones, and the constable took the other and got out his notebook. Didn't the police record interviews, she wondered? She supposed they had brought nothing to record them with.

Inspector Crane was a sturdy man, maybe five foot eleven, with receding fair hair and features slightly too sharp to rate as handsome. His nose was small, his chin angular, his eyes a deep grey. He told her to start by telling them what she had seen and done that morning.

Eliza gave this account.

It was a Thursday, April the sixteenth. It had begun early for her, earlier than she would have chosen. She had always liked to wake after seven, to get to work after eight (although these days she had copied the other managers, and shifted that forwards to half-seven or so), and to work late if it was necessary to get a job finished, or to show her dedication.

It was a morning of burnished aluminium, damped with a pearlized mist-cum-drizzle. When she turned the corner into Blackfriars Street low cloud truncated the sudden close-up of the cathedral spire. Her car was a red K-reg Lotus Elan. It was her biggest extravagance. She loved speed, and the power that promised speed. She loved her car.

She turned on to, then off, the inner ring road, and parked

as usual in the multi-storey above Ham Road Shopping Centre,
where the RUS Car Park Club had a season ticket scheme. She
remembered checking her watch before she got out of the car.
She was edgy even then, before the first murder. Most mornings
she checked her watch two or three times before she settled at
her desk, and she would usually look at it again at least every
half-hour through the day.

In April, early to work – Eliza's early, which meant 6.28 when
she checked her watch in the carpark – did not mean dark. That
she did not see Howard Nkolo until he spoke was down to the
rain, her hunched posture to ward it off – her coat was volumi-
nous and fastened only with a tie belt, which she never tied – and
her preoccupation.

She reckoned she remembered their conversation verbatim,
although it hadn't impressed her particularly at the time. The
entire sequence from meeting Howard to finding the corpse played
like a black-and-white film in her memory – David Lean perhaps,
a director from the mid-twentieth century whose characters spoke
clear precise English. As Howard did.

'Let's play it again. Good morning, Eliza.'

'Uh? Oh, hi, Howard.' She said this half-turning, with her
weight already on the handle of the heavy glass door to St Jude's
House. She had to release it, since her other hand held her
briefcase, to brush a damp lock out of her eyes. She smiled. She
took in Howard's familiar appearance. (He was six-one or so, slim
verging on thin, with crinkly brown hair, pockmarked chocolate
skin and a cocker-spaniel face: limpid eyes, bags beneath them, a
downturned mouth. His suit was conservative, his tie blue tweed.)
'Sorry, didn't mean to ignore you.'

'No sweat. You're no one's idea of a morning person,' Howard
said as they proceeded through the door. They had been inside
the brightly-lit reception area, surely – a recent innovation, with
low sofas grouped around a coffee table, and a security guard in
a blue uniform behind an expanse of limed oak and visitors' signing-in pads – when he went on, 'And no one, but no one's a 6.30
person, me included. You've a meeting with the Beaver?'

'We really oughtn't call him that.'

'Whyever not? He's not listening. Morning Bill. Bloody inconsiderate swine anyway, calling us in at this hour, and I was here
till gone eleven last night. You heard about Bill, by the way?' He

can't have said this until they had flashed their security passes and gone through the inner door of the reception area and into the lobby. Here the lights were dimmer.

'Heard what?'

'He's on the list for this Friday. They told him yesterday, him and all the other security guards except Alf. They're not in keeping with the new corporate image apparently. They want babes to man the desks. It's compulsory so he'll get the six months, but he hadn't been expecting it. He has an elderly mother at home. He's devastated. I don't think he's dared tell his mother yet.'

'Oh dear. That's tough.' Trust Howard to know: he had been at RUS all his working life, knew everyone, and took an interest in everyone's business. Eliza herself was hot-blooded but cool-mannered, and not blessed with Howard's chatty ease. 'Absolutely terrible,' she added, feeling as if she was giving a mediocre performance as someone appalled. She hadn't known, and objectively she did think it was appalling, but she did not recall actually being appalled. You have to realize, she had explained to Inspector Crane (although without going into these niceties, which would not, she assumed, have interested him) that this was eight months after the takeover. First we had all been nervous during the bidding rounds, then we had been cautiously hopeful, then we had been slashed. Again and again. We were (are, at the time of her speaking to him) pretty much dulled by it all. This had not seemed like the right moment for dramatic gestures, fierce refusals, industrial action. Anyway, this was Regional Utility Services – sorry, the RUS Group Limited. Things like that didn't happen at RUS.

Her next line embarrassed her each time she replayed it in her head.

'So many corpses.'

'In a manner of speaking. Fourth floor?'

'No, I'll go to my desk first. Second.'

'Mind you, if there's to be a real corpse out of all this metaphorical bloodshed I'd not be surprised if it was Bill. He's not a man of inner resources, I've always thought. More fragile than he looks.'

'You amaze me sometimes, Howard. Living proof that it's possible to be an intuitive accountant.'

'Most accountants are intuitive, but about money rather than souls.' The lift jerked to a halt at 2, and he added, 'I'll see you there.'

'You're in the same meeting? Sorry, I'm being slow today.'

'Yes, it's on the budget, right?'

'Oh. Right.' Eliza found herself flustered. She had spent half the night worrying what could have prompted Harding to summon her. In person. He had called her at home. Her section's work – the organization of office space and services for government departments and agencies with temporary needs they couldn't fulfil in-house – didn't generally merit much attention from senior management, and she hadn't been aware of any major crises brewing, or any great new projects on the horizon. The mood at RUS being what it was, she had pretty much assumed he had uncovered a disaster, even though there had been nothing in his words or his telephone manner to signal one. Discovering it was the budget was a relief, much as she hated the bloody budget. At the same time it was thoroughly annoying. Hauled into the office at 6.45 for another bleeding set-to on the figures?

It was only a week since the last round of budget projections. Surely he didn't want another set of figures? Didn't he realize they would never make their sodding impossible targets if all normal work was permanently suspended while they worked on endless spreadsheets refining this bloody fictional budget?

There was no time to unload her thoughts on to Howard, and by the time she shouldered open the swing doors to room 2B they had mutated into fury. Hell, if only there were other jobs in Costhorpe. If only she had been there ten more years, and in line for a hundred K if she took the redundancy deal.

Ceiling spots shone from the near end of the room, although it was dark at the far end, where the building made a turn to the right. She dumped her umbrella in a black plastic stand and her briefcase on the carpet. She opened the grey metal coat cupboard that served her section. (It had six staff: she listed them for Inspector Crane.) Her camelhair coat, its close-woven surface beaded with damp, joined a solitary black mac. Inspector Crane made a lot of this, but he never managed to prove its significance. Eliza believed all along that it had none. It was a law of RUS life, indeed of all office life as she had known it: whatever the hour or season, coat cupboards always contained at least one dark mac. She did not know who owned this one, and nobody subsequently laid claim to it.

Her desk was set just off parallel to the wall, with her chair behind it and a bookcase at right angles against the partition. It was neat but crowded: computer at one end, telephone at the other (with miniature red squeezy plastic telephone next to it, good for pummelling to let off frustration), manila files bowing a four-high stack of plastic trays and covering all the remaining surface. A row of books and binders and the section fax machine sat on top of the bookcase. On the windowsill above the radiator (which was prone to rattle) was a row of pots containing a couple of ivies, a spider plant, a zebra plant and several pelargoniums. These were Eliza's own, RUS didn't furnish its offices with plants.

A manila folder was propped against her keyboard, with a sheet of plain paper tucked into the elastic band around it. She bent to read it. The writing was John Donaldson's – her boss for the last four months.

'Nkolo tells me we've failed on this tender. Please give me a full explanation in writing by Friday 12 noon.'

Asshole. They had failed because he had insisted they up the price to include the compulsory new profit margin of 24 per cent. How many words was she supposed to take to tell him so?

No time for that now. The budget file. Hell, where was it? What a way to work. Dashing into meetings without proper preparation had become the norm since the takeover, but it wasn't a way of working that suited Eliza. Colleagues like Mitchell had the knack of improvising on the hoof, but she didn't. She liked predictable meetings with written agendas, but even meetings arranged well in advance didn't have those any more.

It was 6.35 already so there was no time to check the papers through. Eliza's memory-film, although not her police statement, showed her taking a moment to comb her hair. The fringe was sticking damply to her forehead, so she used a tissue from the box on her desk to mop it. Her hair was fair, shoulder-length, naturally wavy, and prone to frizz into a cloud that on all but her worst days she thought attractive, and men – so they told her – thought sexy. However, it didn't readily flatten to fit a neat corporate image. To have it cut would be too great a sacrifice. Thank God Harding hadn't suggested it – although he'd had a go at Hugh Worning the week before about his stubble, if the rumour was to be believed.

Small sigh. An uneasy thought that she had been grumpy to

Howard, whom she both liked and valued as an ally. For all his flippant and not-so-flippant noises of dissatisfaction, Howard was in a good position. He not only had his old allies, he had done better than most at making contact with the enemy, as Eliza still thought of them. Harding himself was said to value him. In other companies, with other bosses, this would not have meant much, but for RUS and the Beaver it was practically unique. It struck her as logical, however. Barking-and-growling managers tended to gravitate to the everyone's-friend types, and it stood to reason Harding and his cohorts would need to keep a few managers who had been there long enough to know what was on the backup discs; plus, no sane CEO paid redundancy money to a competent, honest accountant.

She could suggest a coffee later, maybe; plead the need for some extra budget tuition, and pick his brains in the Courtyard. Howard's friendship was more easily kept than lost.

She was back by the lifts now, and they were taking an age to respond. She would be late. Perhaps Howard would distract Harding till she arrived, or perhaps there were other attendees – the other sector managers in her division, Genevieve and Mitchell? Someone else was in, presumably, or the lights wouldn't have been on in the office. Genevieve had always been a dawn type, but Mitchell wasn't, although he would have obeyed a summons just as she had.

Harding had probably asked senior managers from the Professional Services Division too, since there were lights in room 2A on the other side of the lift lobby. As the lift rumbled up to her floor she glimpsed a figure passing from one bank of metal cabinets to another, but he (the figure was trousered) was too far away to identify, and not coming her way. Anyway, she was late: the other attendees were probably all in 4B1, waiting for her.

By seven o'clock half the managers would be in. It was a depressing thought; worse than depressing, corporate lunacy. If you had kids, or aged parents – God, Bill the security man. It was, it really was a shitty thing to do. Easy to say he was better off without all that crap, who wants to work for lousy bosses like these etcetera, but Bill would have even less chance on the outside than she did: he was fifty-five maybe, and had been at RUS forever.

The lobby on 4 was lit, a blue-white strip illuminating lift doors, stairwell door, and a notice board half-filled with old notices from RUS societies: the Civil Service Motoring Association, the Golf

Society, the Christian Union, the Half-Term Playgroup Committee. Eliza gave them barely a glance as she went through into room 4B – no need, none of them had changed in six months.

She had thought the meeting was in 4B1, a conference room that was towards the far end of the 'B' side of the lift lobby. (Between it and the lobby came an open plan office, while 4A on the other side of the building held the senior management suite, with an open-plan area for the secretaries, and a row of closed-off offices for the directors.) But although the overhead lights were on in the main office, no lights shone from behind the frosted glass upper walls of the conference room partitions. Damn, had she got it wrong? She had written the room number on her phone pad at home, but she didn't have it in writing at the office. There was no one at home she could phone to check. If she was wrong she would face an embarrassing few minutes ringing all the meeting room phones to see which one the Beaver answered.

It was worth being certain. She nudged the door handle down with an elbow and shouldered her way, file-laden, into the darkened space.

No Howard, no Genevieve, no Mitchell, no Beaver. Nobody. No; one of the chairs at the far end was turned away from her, and had an occupant who was looking out of the outer window where, through vertical blinds that hung open, a couple of early lorries could be seen swinging through the roundabout on the inner ring road.

'Mr Harding?' The thin grey hair marked out the seated man as the Beaver. Obviously it was a more intimate meeting than she had anticipated. 'Sorry I'm late,' Eliza rattled on, dropping her file and notepad on the conference table. A scatter of papers already lay across the smooth surface at the far end. 'I got caught up in a conversation downstairs. Howard Nkolo isn't here yet?'

No reply. Not a good sign. She thought of switching the lights on, then opted for caution, since the Beaver had been known to chew people to bits for doing as little as that without his express permission. 'Shall I put the lights on?'

Still no reply. Could he actually have a reason for sitting in the gloom? She inspected his back, or what she could see of it. It conveyed no clear message. 'Well, when you're ready,' she added, feeling a little foolish, and sat down at the near end of the table. Damn, where was Howard?

He burst through the door several long, silent seconds later. 'I thought you weren't here for a moment. No lights? Sir, shall I ...?'

Eliza put her finger to her lips, then spread her hands. She looked at the Beaver's back, and so did Howard. He looked at her. He flipped his head to one side and linked his hands under his lower ear. She was slow to read the mime. Oh – asleep. It was obvious now he had suggested it: only her paranoia could have read it as biding his time before swinging round and firing them. She even had the impression now that his head had slid to a nod-off angle.

Howard grinned, as if delighted at this proof that the Beaver actually had weaknesses. It was, Eliza assured Inspector Crane, a beguiling grin. It was genuine, she could swear. She did not believe Howard could have grinned like that if he had known.

Then he glanced at the Beaver again, and swinging back to Eliza, frowned. Do we wake him, was the message Eliza read? She tried to convey that she didn't know. Most likely he would be livid if they did and furious if they didn't.

Howard decided for her. 'We'd better get started.' He moved swiftly, flipping switches.

Reacting automatically to the change of mood and lighting, Eliza scrambled to her feet. 'I'll get some coffee if you'd like some, sir.' She was conscious of having raised her voice, and briefly wondered whether the Beaver would think her tone insulting. God, they crept round him so carefully. It was difficult to explain to an outsider why this small, ageing man inspired such – fear, that was the only word for it.

She could feel the fear each time she replayed the scene. It was her strongest emotion, stronger than anything that followed. She had never been in the Beaver's company without being terrified she would step over some invisible line. Her muscles had been tensed as if in anticipation of a blow. A shout. The Beaver didn't hit his staff, of course, but he did shout frequently. Senior men whom she had thought imperturbable had been left visibly shaking after the Beaver shouted at them.

'Black with two sugars, isn't it?' She hadn't met him often, but no one forgot a detail with him.

'And mine's white without,' Howard added.

There was a long embarrassing pause, like the kind that slowly makes it apparent to an audience an actor has forgotten his cue.

The trouble was, neither Eliza nor Howard felt confident about doing anything else. They couldn't actually go for coffee, and even less could they start the meeting. They couldn't do anything until the Beaver woke up, swung round and took charge.

Tungsten lights tipped down on to the pale oak table with its stacks of files, the grey carpet and the three figures.

'Sir ...' Howard said again. He took a couple of strides towards the Beaver, who still had made no reaction. 'Excuse me, sir.'

3

'Then he realized,' Inspector Crane interrupted her. (She needed to be interrupted: explaining about the uncomfortable pause had pushed her into a gabble, as if she was trying to neutralize it.) 'What had happened.'

'No.'

'No?'

'No, he didn't. Not yet. Not then. I suppose I'm being pedantic, but you need to have it clear, and Howard didn't actually take it in till he'd come right up to him. He was facing away from us, you see. You couldn't tell at all from where we were.'

'So you hadn't realized yourself.'

'Oh God no, I was really dense. Not that I'm normally slow on the uptake, but it was early, and it wasn't what I was expecting, or thinking about. I didn't twig to the situation till Howard spelled it out to me.'

'And you think Mr Nkolo was dense too.'

This irritated Eliza. She had been gearing herself up to tell the last bit of the story, and she couldn't understand why Inspector Crane didn't let her get to it. Not that there was much to tell really, now he had interrupted. Just the fact that they realized. Saw. Phoned the police.

She supposed Inspector Crane saw Howard (and herself, come to that) as a suspect. It seemed to her a trite assumption, man finds corpse therefore man equals murder suspect. Sometimes she thought the police got carried away by statistics. OK, so many murder victims are killed by the person who reports their discovery. It didn't follow that this was the likely scenario in the Beaver's case.

Mr Harding's case. Now he was dead, it felt inappropriate to use his nickname.

'I don't,' she said carefully, 'think Howard – Mr Nkolo – is a dense person. In the sense of thick or stupid. Obviously he's not, he's very intelligent, and not only in an accounting way. He's not one of those scientific types who can only relate to pages of figures, he's a sociable sort of bloke. He's intuitive.' (She recalled the comment about Bill he had made earlier, thought of repeating it, and censored the thought. There was nothing to it, obviously, but it didn't seem diplomatic to mention that someone had a reason for being mad at the Beaver. Mr Harding. A specific reason, that was: in a general way they were all mad at the Beaver.) 'But you – there are some people whose minds you can read, and Howard's one of them. I'd have known if he was hiding something, and he wasn't. He didn't know what had happened when he came in, and he didn't know even when he was walking over to Mr Harding.'

'What else might he have thought?'

'That he was asleep. It was the obvious answer.'

'It wasn't so obvious, surely. You haven't suggested you'd ever known Mr Harding fall asleep in public before.'

Eliza frowned. 'All right, it was odd. But when you find a reason for something odd, you tend to stick to it. You don't look for another reason. If Howard had suggested he was dead I might have bought that, but he didn't. It didn't come to mind.'

'To your mind.'

'I suppose it might have come to his mind. That Mr Harding had died in his chair, you know, peacefully. But I don't think so, honestly I don't. The way he walked over to him wasn't like he was hiding the fact he suspected something awful had happened because I was there. It was like, we were both wondering, was the Beaver – sorry, Mr Harding – playing games with us, and what was he going to come out with when he moved, and most likely it'd have been something we didn't want to hear, and we were trying to think of the possibilities and plan a way to cover our backs.'

'The Beaver?'

'That's what we called him, not to his face of course. I'm not sure who thought it up. I think it was partly because he looked like a beaver, if you've seen photos, little and stocky and slightly buck-toothed, and partly because he worried away at things. You know, gnawed.'

'Gnawed.'

His habit of repetition was starting to grate on her. The interview process was wearing, even at this stage. There was more than an hour to go, but fortunately she didn't guess this at the time.

'Yes. He was a compulsive personality, I guess. Extremely thorough.'

'Like Mr Nkolo.'

'In a way. More aggressive, though, and not so patient.'

'Are you like that too, Miss Stannard?'

'I'm methodical, because you have to be in my job. I wouldn't call myself compulsive, and I'm definitely not aggressive in the way the Beaver – Mr Harding – was. He'd yell at people, and I couldn't do that sort of thing. I think we were very different personalities.'

'And you and Mr Nkolo?'

'Different too, differently different. Mr Nkolo's easy-going and sociable. I'm not really like that, and Mr Harding wasn't like that. At least, I didn't see him like that. I didn't know him well. Maybe there was another side to him that I didn't come across.'

'You didn't like him, did you?'

'Nobody liked him. I suppose it's the circumstances. Taking over an organization like RUS that had never been commercial, and turning it into something that was going to make lots of money for its backers. Firing people, as I guess you know. Making them redundant. I don't know that anyone would expect to be liked in that situation.'

Inspector Crane leaned forward. He looked so hard at Eliza she would almost have called it a stare. 'Would you say,' he said slowly, 'you had a tendency to think of other people as very much like yourself?'

'In character? No. I thought I'd just made that obvious. I think I and Mr Harding and Mr Nkolo are all very different.'

'In their reactions. Do you think it's possible – I don't mean to criticize you, it's a very natural thing to do – but possible that you're assuming Mr Nkolo was thinking the same things as you were thinking, when in fact he wasn't at all?'

It came across as a criticism, and Eliza was not a woman who took criticism kindly. She didn't mean to, but she bridled. 'No,' she said, too quickly. The renewed thought that he was trying to set up Howard as a suspect came next, and that annoyed her too. She wrestled the annoyance down.

'I see what you mean. I guess we all impute thoughts to other people on the basis of what we'd think ourselves, because there's no other way to make sense of the world. I don't think I do it to excess, but I wouldn't deny that I do it. I think when you feel you have an empathy with someone, when you think you're reading their mind, it's usually true. There are people I can't read at all, can't anticipate. The Beaver's a good example. It's one reason we found him so disconcerting, because we never knew what he'd come out with next.'

'We,' Inspector Crane said, with satisfaction.

Eliza recognized the trap, and silently cursed. 'Most people,' she amended. 'I mean, the Beaver was particularly hard to read, and I can't think offhand of anyone who read him well. Maybe his wife did, if he had one, or Janine, his secretary. Maybe Howard read him a bit better than I did, but on the whole he was hard to read. Howard isn't. He's one of those people whose body language conveys his thoughts. I think,' she added rather inconsequentially, 'that's why people feel at ease with him.'

'Most people.'

'Most people.'

'Do you think you read me well?'

The question surprised her. She looked at him. She realized she hadn't thought of him as an individual, merely as a functionary with whom she was briefly interacting. She mentally reviewed the interview. He seemed a civil, even a civilized bloke in his way. He had put some thought into his questions, although she didn't think much of their trend. She had not been trying to anticipate them.

She said, 'I think there's a tendency people have to underestimate the police. I'm generalizing again I know, but like I said, some generalizations are valid and necessary. Maybe it's because of fictional detectives usually being so stupid, at least the writers call them clever but when you look at what they do, they're not. Also I think your job encourages you not to give much away, and the interview situation. I haven't been trying to read you, to be honest. I've been concentrating on answering.'

'I know,' he said, and smiled. She felt acutely at a disadvantage. 'Do you think I'm capable of lying?'

'Without my noticing? Probably. I don't know you well enough to say. And before you ask me, Howard isn't. He can just about do the your-cheque's-in-the-post bit if it's over the phone, but he's not a devious type. Anyway, why would he pretend not to have realized Mr Harding was dead, assuming he had nothing to hide, and I'm sure he didn't? Howard's not a murderer.'

'You're probably right,' Inspector Crane said.

Eliza relaxed a little.

'But I'd like you to consider the possibility that he realized what had happened at a much earlier stage.'

4

The emphasis on when Howard realized the Beaver was dead seemed strange at the time. Later, she began to understand why Crane had focused on it.

He also focused on timings. This was more understandable, not least because Eliza's tidy account became less tidy when she tried to piece the events together. She soon wished she had not told him so readily about looking at her watch in the carpark: 6.28, it had been. She had prided herself on recalling it exactly.

It was just past 6.35 when she headed up to 4B1. She had looked at her watch again, shortly before the lift arrived.

According to Crane, it was 7.20 when she walked back into 2B, stopped at Genevieve's desk and told Genevieve, 'Harding's dead.' He had this from Genevieve, she assumed, although he could have had it from several people. Russell and Helen from her team had been in the office by then, and Genevieve's senior account handler Ahmed was there too. It was too early for phone calls and the office was quiet, so half of them heard her and the other half knew within ten seconds.

It was ten minutes past seven when the emergency calls were logged. Howard had phoned, but she had been with him. He had used the phone on the floor in the far corner of 4B1, perhaps five feet from the chair which held the Beaver's corpse. She had stood close to the door, and left the room as soon as the call was over. Howard had said he would stay there so she needn't do so.

That left twenty minutes or more when she must logically have been in 4B1 with the Beaver. It seemed too long. Asked by Crane how long she had been there, she had answered without thinking, no time at all. Well, ten minutes max: five at the most before Howard arrived, and less than five from when he arrived to when they realized.

Her watch was always accurate within a minute. She hadn't used the office clocks.

So what had she done, Inspector Crane demanded? What exactly had she and Howard done for those twenty minutes?

The only answer she could give was, nothing.

It wasn't enough. Crane and the previously silent constable

both told her so. That was understandable, only doing their job, etcetera. She put her head in her hands and thought. She felt quite unreasonably calm, but as her friend Rachel pointed out afterwards, that was probably shock.

'I suppose,' she said slowly, 'it all took much longer than I realized. I was in a daze. God, I'm a hopeless witness, but I do see it clearly, standing there with Howard. He was all hunched up on the chair, so dead, so unmistakably dead. He had on this white shirt and a very loud tie, he went for loud ties, turquoise blue with pink palm trees on it. It was skewed to one side and there was blood all over his shirt front. Really red blood. No blood on the palm trees, I remember thinking that. I suppose .... I suppose we stood there for ages.'

It was true. Freeze-frame. She knew even then (when he didn't press it) that he didn't believe her, but it seemed unfair because it was true, the palm trees and all.

5

Genevieve said, 'He's what?'

She was a short woman, with neat features and greying reddish-brown hair which she refused to dye, but did have cut into a stylish bob. The fringe was short and vaguely aggressive. She was slim, although she didn't seem it, being so short, and big-breasted. That day she was wearing an olive-green jersey two-piece, with a yellow and orange leaf-patterned scarf at the neck.

'Dead,' Eliza said. 'Killed.'

She saw the blood drain from Genevieve's face, turning it as pale as the ruled pad on her desk. Genevieve's jaw sagged open for a moment, making her look all of her forty-seven years.

'What, in a car crash?'

'No. Murdered, I suppose.'

'He's what?' Ahmed said.

'He's upstairs dead.'

'I don't believe it,' Genevieve said. 'I can't believe it.'

'I've just seen him. Me and Howard. Howard and I,' she corrected herself automatically. 'We had a meeting with him but he's dead.' The word dead, repeated, seemed to echo against the flat windows and the maroon-cloth-covered partitions.

'You had a meeting with him,' Genevieve said. She shook her head. 'No, this is all wrong. It can't be.'

'I know it's all wrong, but it's what's happened. There's blood on his shirt and he's, well, obviously dead.' She paused and frowned. 'Shot or knifed or something.' She felt she ought to be able to say precisely how he had died, but in fact she had no idea. There had been no dagger hilt sticking out of his chest, no gun tossed on the carpet. Would there have been more mess if he had been shot, or was that just a Hollywood notion?

'Shit me,' Ahmed said. 'Have you told anyone?'

'We've phoned the police.'

'Anyone else?' Helen asked. She was Eliza's senior account handler, a stolid woman in her early thirties with curly black hair and puffy features.

'Who'd we tell?' Eliza glanced round the gathering group. Genevieve was still sitting at her desk. Ahmed, tall and lithe, hovered at her side. Russell was within earshot too. Immediately it struck her as an unwise question. She ought to be asserting her authority, not asking her colleagues and subordinates for advice. 'Frank Mills, I guess,' she answered her own question.

There was a short but significant silence, which Eliza, at least, peopled with unspoken protests that it couldn't be Frank who would take charge.

'We ought to tell Marjorie Bergman as well,' Russell said, while Helen said at the same moment, 'Hugh Worning, and David Summerfield.'

Other voices chimed in, and a petty argument began its self-orchestration. Eliza left it behind, went back to her own desk and leafed through her old RUS directory for Frank Mills's extension.

6

Inspector Crane said, 'Frank Mills used to be the RUS chief executive, right?'

'The director, we called him. You don't have chief executives in the public sector,' Eliza said. 'Or at least, you didn't use to.'

'And now he's ...'

'They've changed his title a couple of times. I think he's director of development now.'

'And Harding was chief executive.'

'That's right, of the RUS Group. Limited.'

'What about James Connaught? You didn't think to tell him?'

'I'd never come across him before,' she said honestly. (It was then 11 o'clock. She had met James for the first time less than four hours earlier.) 'Until this morning I'd never heard of him. So it wasn't an option.'

'What's his role?'

'You probably know as much as I do. I'm not aware that he has an official position in RUS. He turned up this morning and said he was from the Saturn Trust. He seems to have taken charge now, but it's not what any of us expected.'

'Did you think Mills would take charge?'

'I ...' Eliza stopped and flushed. It was a question she found difficult to answer.

Crane said softly, 'Tell me.'

'There's nothing to tell, really. It's just that it's hard for me to say. I'm not particularly senior here, I'm not on the board, and I don't really know what's going on. I wouldn't say communication has been the top priority over the last few months. There are lots of new directors and I've never even met some of them. I know Frank, obviously, but I don't know how he fits in these days. Maybe there's someone else who'd be the natural – well, obviously there was. I didn't even know this James Connaught existed, and now he seems to be in charge.'

'Mills didn't say anything to you? Do you think he anticipated that?'

'Does it matter? What's it got to do with Mr Harding's death?'

Crane gave her a thin look, as if she was being stupid.

Eliza said slowly, 'I know he's dead, but it's so hard to imagine that anyone killed him. Anyone I know. It couldn't be, it just couldn't.'

Crane sat back in his chair. 'I'd advise you to start getting used to the idea that it was.'

7

Frank Mills answered Eliza's call himself, since it was too early for Annie, his secretary, to be in the office. It wasn't news to him that Harding was dead, because he had just been phoned by Howard. She offered to come to his office, but he told her not to. They would send home the junior staff as they arrived, he said, but no one already in the building should leave. He told her to get a cup of tea. No, there wasn't anything she could do. 'I'll sort everything out,' he said. 'Don't worry, dear. Leave it to me.' She bridled at that 'dear'. Frank had a tendency to misjudged chumminess with his inferiors.

She had a cup of tea since Helen had brought her one, from the machine, and indecently sweet. (Eliza did not generally take sugar in her tea, as Helen knew.) She mulled over the events of the morning, as far as she knew them, and couldn't think what she ought to do. It seemed inappropriate to switch her computer on and get to work. Nobody else appeared to have started work. They were standing around in knots, muttering. Eliza felt disinclined to knot or mutter.

Genevieve came over. She took the spare section chair, which had been by Helen's desk, and dragged it to Eliza's side. 'Are you OK?' she asked.

'Perfectly OK. I'm not in shock, even though Helen seems to think I ought to be.' In fact Genevieve looked worse than she felt herself.

'Look, I need to know. What was this meeting you had with Patrick Harding?'

Eliza shrugged. 'Howard thought it was a budget meeting, but Harding didn't say anything in particular to me, just that he wanted to see me at 6.45. Why, did you have a budget meeting lined up with him?'

Genevieve hesitated. 'I .... Yes, we had a meeting lined up.'

'On the budget.'

'He didn't say.'

'Oh well. It's irrelevant now.'

Genevieve frowned. Eliza caught a trace of Shalimar, the older woman's usual perfume, as she leaned closer. 'The thing is, I had a meeting with him at 6.30.'

'I'd thought you and Mitchell might be coming. But where were you?'

'Waiting in room 3C2.'

'Both of you?'

'Just me. I haven't seen Mitchell yet this morning.'

'You must have got the room wrong. The meeting was in 4B1.'

'I didn't get it wrong,' Genevieve said. 'I printed out the email Janine sent, so I know I went to the right place.'

'The Beaver must have got it wrong then, or Janine.'

Genevieve shook her head again. She seemed – she doubtless was – upset, distracted. She looked down at her hands, then back at Eliza. 'What did your email say?'

'I didn't get an email. Harding phoned me at home last night, around nine.'

'He phoned you in person?'

'Yes. Unprecedented, at least for me. I was up half the night worrying about it.'

'And he said the meeting was in 4B1.'

'Yes. Obviously I got that right, because that's where he was.'

'But he was dead.'

'True, but he must have come there before he was dead. I suppose. I can't imagine he'd have been killed somewhere else and then coincidentally dumped in the room he'd arranged to have a meeting in.'

Genevieve's neat features crumpled into a frown. 'It's all so confusing. So weird. It didn't seem like him to send me that email. Very blunt, it was. And telling me to meet him in one place when he'd told you to meet him in another, why would he do that?'

'I've no idea.' Eliza could only agree it was weird. She didn't doubt Genevieve had gone to the place she had been told to go to. Genevieve wasn't the sort of person to confuse meeting arrangements. Anyway, she had said she had it in writing.

Genevieve said, 'I suppose I should tell someone.'

'I suppose so. They'll want to piece his movements together. Although it's not got much to do with his movements if he didn't turn up.'

'Lizzie, when did he die?'

It seemed to Eliza a strange question. It was not, she supposed. It was the sort of thing the police would want to know. Maybe it was just that Genevieve was acting oddly. She didn't seem her usual self at all. Normally a briskly elegant woman, she was sitting awkwardly in the low-backed chair, back hunched, hands twisted together, wrists resting on the edge of Eliza's desk. Her eyes were lowered. Genevieve was someone who looked you in the eye. As a rule she acted swiftly – sometimes too swiftly, when caution would have served her better – surely, and with no apparent qualms.

When had he died? Eliza couldn't say. The tableau she had stumbled on had been so still, posed almost. Whatever violence had taken place, it was over by then. If there had been signs of a struggle, they had been tidied away. Perhaps there hadn't been any struggle.

Even if she had touched him, she would have been hard pushed to guess the time of his death. She was no pathologist, and she possessed no information on the temperatures of corpses or the progress of rigor mortis. Anyway she hadn't touched him.

Perhaps he had died hours before. After a meeting in the room the night before. He could have died only minutes before, though, and she would have been none the wiser. Seconds before. Just time for the killer to escape before she pushed open the door from the lift lobby to room 4B.

Which meant –

'Excuse me,' a deep male voice interrupted.

8

He was standing at the far side of her desk, close enough to block out the light from overhead. Her first impression was of a very tall man – true, although their height difference (six inches) was exaggerated since she was sitting and he was standing – with strong, almost harsh features and a shock of dense black hair. He looked to be in his mid-thirties. His hair was verging on untidy (a natural failing, rather than his barber's) but his clothes were immaculate. His suit, a classic dark grey, hung perfectly from broad shoulders. A half-inch of white shirt showed at each cuff. He wore a Rolex on his left wrist. His tie had an abstract pattern of triangles in dull shades of red and orange. He looked expensive, successful, metropolitan – all the things that RUS types, as a rule, were not.

Frank Mills had a reputation as a natty dresser, but in comparison he seemed almost down at heel, his floral waistcoat faded, his suit a trifle rumpled. He reached her desk three seconds later, stopping at the stranger's left elbow.

'This is Eliza Stannard,' he said, gesturing at her. He did not bother to introduce Genevieve.

'James Connaught,' the stranger said. He reached out a hand over the desk, obliging Eliza to stumble to her feet to take it. His grip was cool and firm. He did not smile. 'I'd like to talk to you in private.'

'We'll go up to my office, James,' Frank said.

'I don't want to stop you working. Janine can find me a room. Excuse me.' He reached across the desk and picked up Eliza's phone.

'You'll hardly do that. It's my priority to –'

'Just a minute, Janine.' Connaught put his hand over the mouthpiece and half-turned to Frank. 'There's no need to stay. Miss Stannard can show me the way.'

'But I'd be glad –'

A wave of the hand dismissed him. Eliza and Genevieve watched him take a step backwards. Eliza thought he swallowed a gulp. 'You'll call me when you need me,' he said, but Connaught paid no attention.

Eliza and Genevieve shared a quick glance. Genevieve's eyes

flicked over James Connaught, still taking to Janine on the phone, and her neat mouth pursed in a 'Mmm.' It was a very Genevieve gesture. If she had been shaken for a few minutes she was recovered now, maybe miffed into it by Frank's unaccustomed rudeness and Connaught's forcefulness. She touched Eliza's sleeve. 'Talk to you later.' By the time Connaught put down the phone, after a ten-sentence conversation, Eliza was facing him alone.

'Janine suggests I use Ken Thursby's old office. She seemed to think you'd know where it was. I'll have her come down and guide us if you don't.'

'Of course I do.' Eliza was unintentionally curt. 'Do I need a pen and paper?'

'No. Shall we go?'

They went. He didn't speak at all as they waited for the lift. Ken Thursby's old office was in wing 4A, in the senior management suite, although the rumour was that Harding had been planning to move the directors' offices. There hardly seemed the need, to Eliza: most of them spent the majority of their time in the London office rather than the Costhorpe one. At any rate, it appeared no one had bothered to claim Ken's room. His name was still on the door, and a musty smell of cigarette smoke greeted them as Eliza opened it. There was no dust on the desk (pale oak like most of the office furniture, but twice the size of Eliza's), but the notices on the pinboard dated from RUS pre-privatization, and an internal phone directory of the same era propped up a sheaf of faded memos in the top tray of a three-tier stack. His computer was still on his desk, a laser printer on a table at right angles to it.

James Connaught strode over to the window that made up the whole of the far wall. The blinds were pulled to the left of the glass, providing a clear view out over the ring road, a few yards along from the roundabout that could be seen from 4B1. He gave no more than a cursory glance to the rain, heavier now, and the stream of traffic, before swinging round and taking the chair behind the desk.

'Who was Ken Thursby? Shut the door and sit down,' he said without pausing.

Eliza's fur was up, as her father used to say. 'More to the point, who are you?'

There was a short but ominous pause. She realized she had

been brusque, verging on rude. She expected for a moment that he would retaliate.

He didn't. 'I'm a director of the Saturn Trust,' he said. 'For the time being at least, I'll take charge here. Will you answer me now?'

Clearly a man to be obeyed, however little she liked it. She went to shut the door then returned to the desk and sat down in the visitor's chair. She looked at him. Ken Thursby, she thought. She had expected him to ask immediately about Harding, since that was doubtless why she was there. Maybe this was the sort of first-of-interview question he didn't care about the answer to.

'He was the personnel director,' she said. 'You didn't meet him during the privatization negotiations?'

'Not that I recall. Did he jump or was he pushed?'

'Oh, pushed. He came in one morning and there was someone else sitting behind his desk.'

'Not literally, I assume.'

'In every sense but. So it looked to us, anyway. All we ever got was a five-line memo saying Marjorie Bergman was now the human resources director. It was the first big firing,' she added after a second.

'Did he deserve to go?'

She met his eyes. It was the moment she realized their attraction was mutual, although it was evident to her afterwards that he would have behaved differently from the outset if she had been Genevieve.

She was the first to break the contact. Her eyes lingered on his mouth, which was wide and thin-lipped. She had an insane urge to touch it.

She dragged her mind back to Ken Thursby. 'Nobody deserves to go like that,' she said. 'He'd worked for RUS for, I think, twenty-nine years. He was in his fifties, looking forward to an honourable retirement, presentation, speeches and all the rest of it. I wouldn't say he was a cutting-edge professional, but he did a decent job on his own terms. He knew everyone, and everyone liked him.'

'Maybe that was the problem.'

'All right, he probably wasn't the person to handle a major redundancy – although he'd seen off plenty of people over the last few years. You realize we lost a third of our staff before you ever took over.'

'The Saturn Trust didn't take over, we provide venture capital for the RUS Group. There's a difference.'

'James, you've made it apparent already that you head the heap.'

He smiled slightly in acknowledgement of her use of his name. 'So I have. Is there anyone here who isn't hostile to the new management?'

'There's Frank Mills,' she said.

He gave a short curt laugh. 'Point taken. The usual complement of ass-lickers. Well, you sure aren't one of them.'

'Do you want me to be?'

He held her eye again. There was a plump silence. The complicity between them sat on the desk, like a sleek long-haired cat on the polished surface.

'I don't know that I want you in any way at all.'

He'd stressed the word 'want' slightly but noticeably. Otherwise his voice was flat. The brutality was in the words, but his manner did nothing to counter it. Eliza felt herself curl up inside her skin.

After a pause he said in a barely changed voice, 'I'm sorry, I'm being inconsiderate. You had a hell of an experience this morning, by all accounts. Would you like some hot tea?'

To her annoyance, she had to make an effort to keep her voice level. She said 'Yes thanks,' not out of thirst, since Helen's sugary tea was still on her tongue, but to give them both the pause it would provide. He had to – he did – phone Janine and place the order. They waited in silence. Janine did not stoop to machine tea, so it took maybe five minutes. He looked out of the window, she looked at the notices on the pinboard. There was a copy of *The RUStler*, dated the previous October, with a front-page story about the appointment of Patrick Harding as chief executive of the RUS Group, and a list of members of a Safety at Work committee. (Of ten of them, only two remained with RUS.) Also a notice about training opportunities, signed by Rachel Morecambe, training manager, Eliza's best friend. All training had been stopped when the RUS Group took over. They had said it was temporary at first, then they had fired all the in-house trainers.

There was a knock, and Janine came in to James's curt 'Enter'. A sweet-faced but gawky woman with thick legs – and an inexplicable fondness for short skirts that showed them at their worst

– she had joined the company with Harding. Apparently she had worked for him before, at Lime Street Associates. Eliza scarcely knew her.

Janine was walking stiffly, as if all her instincts had deserted her and she had consciously to make each move. She and Harding were reckoned to have been a close team. If anyone in the company was likely to mourn him, it was this girl.

'I'm sorry, Janine,' Eliza said. 'It's the most terrible thing.'

Janine looked up from the tea tray. Her lower lip trembled. Her face crazed like a mud-pack. Pain oozed from the cracks. 'It's not ...' she began. Then came the shaking sobs.

Eliza came to her feet without thought. She reached out and put her arms round the other woman. Janine was sturdier, but three or four inches shorter than she was. She felt hot and soft, her bones hard-edged beneath the cushion of flesh, not resisting the comfort but not relaxing into it.

Eliza did not look at James. She had no sense that he moved or reacted. For several minutes neither he nor she spoke, Eliza because she couldn't think what else to say.

Janine recovered in gulps. Eliza loosed her hands and Janine took a step backwards. She did not look directly at either Eliza or James. She fished out a tissue and mopped her eyes. 'Sorry about that,' she said. 'It's just ... unbelievable. He was a good man. You didn't know him, but he was. A good man. Good boss. I can't imagine how anyone could –'

James stood. 'Some psychopath,' he said. 'We'll find them, Janine, and get them put away forever. You ought to go home. Is there someone who can go with you?'

Eliza felt obliged to offer, and Janine obliged to refuse to go. James cut through their protests, and sent for another director's secretary to escort her. It appeared she was staying at the Mornington Arms, the most expensive hotel in Costhorpe, where Harding too had had a room. In the months since the privatization neither she nor her boss had found houses in the Costhorpe area.

As Crystal was coming to fetch Janine, the phone rang. James answered it. He sat again, the receiver in his left hand, swinging the chair right round and turning his back on the desk, Eliza and the business of getting rid of Janine. Eliza waited till Janine and Crystal had gone, then poured the stewed tea and half-listened to his end of the conversation. She reckoned his manner with the caller was less abrasive, more impersonal than his manner to her. He said nothing more informative than 'Right', 'Mmm', and finally, 'Do that.'

Swinging round again to replace the phone, he said, 'One has to admire the police ability to assemble a team at short notice. Apparently they'll have the manpower to interview everyone who was in the building first thing this morning in the course of today. Briefly in some cases, I imagine. I'm seeing a Detective Chief Inspector Foxton in half an hour. You'd better tell me whatever will be most useful.'

Momentarily, she had no idea what to say. He prompted her. 'Apart from the directors, I don't know a soul at RUS. You can start by telling me where you fit in.'

She took a breath. 'That's easy enough. I've been here twelve years, and I'm a sector manager in the Office Services section. I head a small team who liaise with the clients, set up facilities for them and so on. I report to John Donaldson, the office services director, if you know him.'

'We've met. How much contact did you have with Harding?'

'Next to none. There are fifty, sixty budget holders like me. I went to the pep-talk rally at Teddington, of course, and I've been in a dozen or so meetings when he was there.'

'One to one?'

'No, none of them. This morning's would have been me, him and Howard Nkolo, one of the accountants. Every other time there've been at least half a dozen people. Budget meetings, mostly.'

'And was this to be a budget meeting?'

'So Howard thought. Harding didn't say to me.'

'What did he say?'

She told him, nothing, and he frowned. She added, 'He phoned me at home last night. About nine o'clock. He'd never done that before.'

'Janine didn't make the call?'

'I suppose she'd left work by then.'

James frowned again, as if it was unreasonable of a secretary to have quit by 9 pm. 'So there's a crisis in your section, I take it.'

'Not that I know of,' Eliza said. 'We've been set impossible targets and we don't expect to meet them, but unless you call that a crisis ... .'

'We'll discuss that another time. I take it that as far as you're aware, there's no connection between this meeting and Harding's death.'

'I can't think of one.'

Silence. There wasn't even the humming of a computer fan, or the whirr of a fax or printer. Dead silence.

'Let's try again,' James said. 'Off the top of your head, and completely off the record, what was your immediate thought? Who did this?'

Stunned, she said, 'I've no idea.'

'You must have thought something when you realized he'd been killed.'

She had, of course. She was not a woman whose mind was often still. But her thoughts had been inconsequential, trivial even. They had not included any speculation on the killer. They were none of them thoughts she could imagine sharing with this man.

She said, carefully, 'I've no inclination to list all the people who've said they'd like to kill Harding over the last few months. Lots of us have said that, me included on occasion. I've never thought any of them planned to carry it out.'

'Would you like to tell me why they've said that?'

'That's obvious, surely. He's wrecked their lives.'

James gave a short bark that might have been intended as a laugh. 'For heaven's sake. Redundancy's hardly an excuse for murder. Anyway you haven't been made redundant.'

'True, but a job I enjoyed has turned into one I hate. I've seen colleagues I liked and admired thrown out in the most brutal and inhumane way, and others breaking under the strain. The workforce has been cut so far that the systems are breaking down. We can't do a good job for our clients any more. They complain when they see the quality drop and the prices rise, and I don't know what to say to them. I was proud to work for RUS and I'm ashamed to work for the RUS Group. Did I hate Patrick Harding? Yes, I did. Did I kill him? No. I know a great many people whose friends would think it understandable if it turned out they'd done it, but I find it hard to imagine that any of them did.'

'You blame Harding for all of that?'

Her voice had risen, she realized, during this little rant. His was still level. He was sitting forward on his chair now. He had taken a silver biro from his jacket pocket and was turning it in his fingers, although he had no paper in front of him.

She sat back, and took her time answering.

'I'm not naive, and I'm under no illusion that he's the only one at fault. For what it's worth, I've heard colleagues say they'd like to kill everyone from the prime minister to our local union rep. It's a bad situation and they're all to blame in some degree, I dare say. Harding has his name at the top of the letterhead, well, just below Sir Anthony Thrussell's, but he's too much of a nonentity to inspire much hatred. He's – he was – a free man, he can choose to say yes and he can choose to say no. You can say the system put him in a position where he had little option but to do these things. He could have done them differently. He didn't have to stay in that position at all. He destroyed people's lives and he's profiting from it. Was. Of course I blame him. We all do.'

'Do you blame me?'

'I try not to be too indiscriminate. I don't know what you did. If I did know, most likely I'd reckon you deserved a share of the blame.'

'Most likely you would,' he said crisply. He got to his feet. 'Is there anything practical I should know? About what you and Nkolo saw?'

It took her a moment to adjust to his change of direction, and to realize that in his eyes, the meeting was over. A part of her was relieved, indeed longing to be away from him. Another part of her regretted the dismissal. She was used to exercising more control over her meetings, even when they were with her superiors. She felt she had made a mess of this encounter, and there would be no chance now to retrieve it.

She stood. 'I don't think so,' she said. 'I'm afraid I don't even know how he died. There was blood on his shirt, so he had a wound in his chest, I guess. There were no signs of a struggle. It was all quite ordered, almost staged. He was angled so it looked from the back as if he was still alive. I don't know if that happened naturally. There weren't any obvious clues.'

'That's unfortunate.' He sounded indifferent, or perhaps disbelieving. He had come round the desk and was standing a foot or two from her, near enough for her to feel the heat of his body, but in spite of his closeness the earlier sense of intimacy she had had was gone. He did not touch her; she did not think he was tempted to. 'We'll speak again soon.'

'I can't think why,' a final aggressive instinct made Eliza say. She left the room without waiting for him to show her out.

9

She was hauled off to wait for her police interview when she returned to her desk, and after the long wait and the long interview, it was past midday when Crane finished with her. She asked him if she could leave St Jude's House, and was told she could.

No one from her team was there when she returned to room 2B, but she didn't feel she could leave without telling someone from RUS, and the logical person was Genevieve, sitting at her desk a few yards farther along, on the phone and gesticulating wildly in her usual manner. Eliza headed for her, and arriving at her desk noticed that Mitchell, shirt-sleeved, was at his desk too, in his section which was located on the far side of Genevieve's.

'Tomorrow. Yes, fine,' Genevieve said, and put the phone down. 'Coffee?' she added to Eliza, without pausing. 'Or a sandwich even?'

'I was thinking of going. I suppose sending everyone home didn't include the managers.'

'Nobody would mind if you did, I'm sure. I thought of going myself after the cops finished with me, but I was enjoying the peace; no, that's not true. I intended to enjoy the peace and wrap up those bleeding March figures, but the phone's rung non-stop and there's no one else to answer it.' It rang again that moment, in stereo. 'Damn.'

Mitchell caught Eliza's eye, and signalled to her to come over. Over Genevieve's brisk voice addressing her caller, from down the largely silent office Eliza could hear a message being broadcast from the answering machine that served her own section. There was a note of exaggerated concern, and it was this more than the timbre of the voice that marked it as her ex-boyfriend Phil. She ignored it and went over to Mitchell. He was a soft-bodied man in his early forties with thinning ginger hair and pale blue eyes behind small round gold-rimmed glasses, and a style that matched his desk, which was loaded with files piled to chest-height, crumpled memos and curling heaps of faxes. His team missed half their deadlines, but the clients adored him.

'High drama,' he said.

'Bloody horrifying,' Eliza agreed.

'Poor old Beaver. Much as I hated him, I wouldn't have wished murder on him or anyone. But it's fascinating all the same in its alien way, like those small ads in the *Sunday Sport*.'

'Mitchell!'

Mitchell gave a sheepish grin. 'You must admit it. We know it's in terrible taste, but we're all desperate to hear the details. So tell.'

'There's not that much to tell. I saw him dead, end of story.'

'How dead? Did the police tell you anything?'

'Not sure, maybe stabbed, and no, they just asked questions. Honest, Mitch. He was just sitting there dead. You know, blood on his shirt and not alive. Everyone seems to think I should know who did it, but I haven't a clue. There wasn't a label stuck on him saying "Joe Bloggs did this", and if there were fingerprints I wouldn't have seen them, would I?'

'A nice observant girl like you,' Mitchell mourned.

'Some things I'd rather not observe.'

'I dare say. Poor lass. Sit down.'

'I think I'll get off home.'

'Give me a minute and I'll update you first. You know, what we've found out since the police let us out of the print room. They didn't interview me for long, so I've had a while to ask around.' Mitchell gestured at Harry's empty chair. Intrigued despite herself, Eliza went to drag it over. Mitchell waited till she was sitting, then said, 'My meeting with the Beaver was in 3B7, except it wasn't. We still haven't worked out why you got the short straw.'

'What? You had a meeting too?'

'That's right. It was fixed by email, one of seven we know about so far. Maybe there were more, I dare say the police know by now, but they didn't tell me much either.'

'Mitch, tell me that again, but slowly. You're saying seven people had meetings set up with the Beaver?'

'Eight including you, all at 6.30, and we've only asked around Office Services and the IT Department.'

'Then it's nine including me and Howard Nkolo. Although we were told to come at 6.45.'

'And yours was the only one with more than one person invited. You didn't get an email either, Genevieve said?'

Eliza explained about Harding's phone call. She had thought it remarkable, and it seemed it had been, since everyone else summoned to a meeting had received an identical email message. Mitchell produced a copy of his:

Message from: Broughton J, Central Admin
Date: Wednesday 15 April
To: Jones M, Office Services
Copies to: (blank)
Re: Meeting Thursday 16 April
Please attend a meeting with Patrick J Harding, Chief Executive,
at 6.30 am on Thursday 16 April in room 3B7. No confirmation
is necessary.

Terse, but that was the usual style of the Beaver's summonses. Eliza looked up from the sheet of A4 printout. 'Have you asked Janine what was going on?'

'I tried, but she's gone home, prostrate with grief apparently. We'll ask her tomorrow, but I can't see what kind of an explanation she can come up with that'll make any sense. I mean, eight meetings at the same time. Harding wasn't God, even if Ms Broughton acted like he was. He couldn't be everywhere at once. Actually I don't think he had a hand in this at all, I think the murderer set it up.'

Eliza jumped. 'You what?'

Mitchell smiled. 'It's quite clever when you think about it.'

'You've lost me, Mitch.'

'I'll take it slowly. Someone wanted to kill Patrick Harding, right?'

'So it appears.'

'In cold blood, and without getting caught, obviously. So they made plans. They aimed to do it at a quiet time, because you'd hardly take a knife to someone in an office full of people. That wasn't so difficult, because when he was in Costhorpe two days running Harding usually started at fishermen's hours on the second day.'

'I suppose he did.' She hadn't ever bothered to plot the Beaver's movements, but it fitted his reputation.

'But though they didn't want an office full of people, neither did they want to be the only person around apart from Harding and the security guards and maybe the odd bunch of IT types all huddled together over some dicky terminal. I'd guess they didn't come sailing in through the main door flashing their pass, but even if they found some other way in, say they had a key to the goods entrance, there'd have been a risk of someone seeing them and marking them out as the prime suspect. So to make sure the police had a nice big choice, they fixed it so there was an assortment of other possible murderers in St Jude's House at the same time.'

'By having them come in to meetings.'

'Exactly. They set up one meeting per person, so all us poor suckers were left sitting in rooms on our own.'

'So you and Genevieve and the rest were asked to come in at 6.30, just so you'd figure on the suspect list.'

'That's about how the Mars bar melts. Genevieve's OK, though: she made a phonecall about 6.35. We don't know when he died yet but I'd guess the timing was fairly tight, so with luck it puts her in the clear.'

Eliza shook her head again. 'It seems too ...'

'Logical?'

'Risky, I was going to say. What if people compared notes?'

'I guess it was done so there wasn't much opportunity for them to. The emails definitely went on the system after two o'clock, because I sent an email to the DoE then and mine wasn't down as unread mail. I suspect it was more like four or five. You know most people these days check the bloody things first thing in the morning and last thing before they leave, just in case the Beaver wants them to turn up to some sodding breakfast meeting minus the breakfast. I read mine at 6.30, Genevieve read hers at a quarter to 7. We've been trying to narrow it down still more.'

'Janine wasn't in the office yesterday afternoon. She was at that client get-together with Harding.'

'That fits too. It means she'd have been hard pushed to send the messages, wouldn't she? And it must have been someone else who did that.'

Eliza frowned. It was unnerving to think of a murderer making this elaborate plan. It was unnerving to think of a murderer at all. In the hours when she had been waiting for the police to interview her, she had not seriously asked herself who could have done the deed.

'And of course,' Mitchell went on, 'it also means that if you did find out someone else was supposed to have a meeting with him at the same time but in a different place, you couldn't check with Janine what was going on. Not that you were very likely to find that out, because I reckon the murderer picked people who weren't best mates. Most of them are spread pretty thin across the building. Genevieve and I work in the same room, true, but you know I can't stand all her "I know this" and "I know that" so we hardly ever talk. We didn't realize it till afterwards, and even if we had realized in advance, what could we have done? Most likely Genevieve would have gone to one room and I'd have gone to the other, and we'd have agreed whoever found the Beaver would phone the other one.'

'You're talking someone who knew just how the systems work here.'

'So it looks. But that covers most of RUS.'

'True.' Even after the redundancies, there were plenty of people around who had been at RUS for twenty or thirty years; and newer arrivals too who had been absorbed into the dark-brown stew, and could predict without thinking how their colleagues would react.

'Anyway,' Mitchell continued, 'it seems to have gone precisely according to the someone's plan. I haven't ticked off all down the card yet, but everyone I've talked to reacted the same way. They all turned up on the dot at 6.30. They all waited like wallies in different meeting rooms, then come a quarter to 7 they all started phoning round to see where they ought to be. Me included, of course. But it was too late by then.'

Eliza went over it again in her head. She thought of asking Mitchell if he had a particular reason for wanting the Beaver dead, one that she didn't know about. If he was right, it stood to reason that the murderer would have picked likely suspects, but Mitchell didn't strike her as a likely suspect at all. Nor did Genevieve.

Good friend though he was, she couldn't bring herself to ask. She said instead, 'I don't see how I fit into the pattern. Me and Howard.'

Mitchell shrugged. 'All I can think is, it's random noise. Not part of the game at all. If the Beaver asked you himself, I suppose he genuinely did want a meeting with you. Maybe the murderer knew nothing about it. You're lucky he'd done the deed and cleared off before you turned up.'

Her mouth sagged open.

'It's all right,' Mitchell said, not very reassuringly. 'You're still alive.'

10

Eliza thought of phoning Phil back, then decided not to. In the abstract the thought of someone fussing over her as if she was an invalid was appealing, but in reality her first reaction to his voice had been irritation. In person he would irritate her even more. He wouldn't make demands, but he would not make them in a way which was itself intensely demanding. It would be putting back her campaign to extricate herself from their relationship, which had been going too slowly as it was.

She turned down Genevieve's renewed offer of a sandwich, and retrieved her coat. It was still damp, but the mist had almost evaporated and the rain eased back to a thin drizzle, so she didn't really need to wear it. She slung it over her arm. She didn't take her briefcase home.

As she was passing through the lobby she saw James Connaught again. He was standing by the foot of the main stairs, talking to David Summerfield, the new (at least, post-privatization) finance director. Summerfield looked short and bewildered, Connaught tall and angry. He saw her; she saw him pause in his sentence and look her over. She looked back. Although they were twenty feet apart, it felt as if their eyes connected. She sensed a little surge of adrenalin, a renewed awareness that she at least was definitely alive.

She wondered if he expected her to come across and speak to him. But she had nothing to say, and he made no move to come to her. She half-nodded, feeling she ought to make some acknowledgement of him, and hurried out of the double doors and over to the multi-storey carpark.

As she drove along the river a thin wind tongued the pale new leaves on the oak and hawthorn by the side of the road. Browning Street where she lived was a beech-lined street of late-Victorian terraces, a mile and a half from the office. She drove first to the newsagent round the corner, where she bought a *Guardian* and a Maverick bar. As with the abandoned briefcase, she had a half-articulated sense that she deserved indulgence. There was nothing cosseting, though, about arriving home to still-drawn curtains, a sheaf of brown envelopes on the mat relieved only by the plastic bag containing a copy of *Current Archaeology*, and the grounds-crusted coffee mug and cafetière in her living room at the back of the house.

She meant to wash up, open the windows, put on a load of washing. Instead she sat on the sofa. She wrapped her hands around her upper body and felt herself shaking.

Any death, even the Beaver's, has its own resonance. She could hear his voice – a light, surprisingly attractive one – as it had come over the phone the previous evening. 'Eliza Stannard? This is Patrick Harding.' The rest had gone. She tried to reconstitute his phrasing, but his voice wouldn't echo her thoughts. All she could hear was Rachel's much-repeated imitation (only slightly marred by her Antrim accent): 'Miss Morecambe, you surely don't imagine I'm a believer in the stakeholder enterprise.'

She sat for a while longer. She fished the Maverick out of her bag and ate it, quickly, realizing she was hungry. She threw the red and yellow wrapper on the coffee table, which was, she noticed, dulled with dust. Her notes and calculations for a job the team was to quote on, providing temporary offices and backup facilities for a public enquiry that was expected to last a year, lay in a jumbled heap. She had been meaning to take them back into the office for a fortnight. It had started off as a routine job, but now it would be a scramble to get the quote ready anywhere near the deadline. Helen had reminded her the day before, and she had scribbled *Bring in Wigan* on a Post-it, but left it stuck on her computer.

Two of the Clarice Cliff patterned coasters had wine-rings on them. When had someone last been round with a bottle? Rachel? No, Mitchell and Val, the previous Saturday, or was it Friday? There had been a time when she had tidied every morning, emptied the wastepaper bin, watered the plants, even dusted the picture frames sometimes. Then it had fallen to a Saturday skim before she went shopping, and God, last Saturday she hadn't even done that. There had been forward planning meetings with John Donaldson and the other sector managers all morning, and in the afternoon the shopping, washing and bed-making had finished her off.

'What a life,' she said out loud. The words echoed round the empty room. She slipped off her shoes, swung her legs on to the sofa – feet on the arm – and contemplated the print above the television. All her prints featured flowers, without being dryly botanical: this one was of a shack in the West Indies, with bougainvillaea trailing over rusty corrugated iron.

The decay it showed was more real to her than the life and hope the flowers symbolized. A life that had six months before seemed reasonably satisfying felt now as if it was crumbling at the edges, and not only the edges. She had been conscious ever since the privatization of the intensifying disintegration of people and systems at RUS, but the murder had crystallized it brutally. 'The centre cannot hold,' she said. 'Mere anarchy.' The phrase obscurely pleased her.

She thought about Mitchell, his busy little investigations, the guileless glee with which he had retailed them to her. Surely that proved he was as innocent as she was? She wanted to feel it was so. She didn't exactly have a list of suspects, but even so she wanted to cross Mitchell off it.

She tried to imagine being the murderer, making those elaborate plans and taking a knife into the office to kill the Beaver. If it had been a knife. The image assumed no weight in her mind. It'll be real to me later, she told herself, but what could be more real than the sight of a corpse?

She swung her feet off the sofa, went upstairs and stood for some time under a cool shower.

Feeling clean restored some energy; toast and a can of tomato soup completed the job. She spent the afternoon cleaning the house. She hoovered, dusted, threw out four plants that looked beyond resuscitation and left the rest absorbing saucers-full of water. She drove to the big Tesco on the edge of the city and bought milk, bagels, Philadelphia cheese, brown rice, aubergines, broad beans, courgettes, beef tomatoes, a hunk of brie, two bottles of Nottage Hill Cabernet Sauvignon and a large bunch of pink carnations.

She arranged the carnations in a shallow Singalese brass bowl, and put it on the coffee table, replacing the Wigan documents which she put in a carrier bag in her car. She brunched on bagels and Philly, half a litre of orange juice and two mugs of fresh coffee. It was nearly half past four. She put Enya's *Shepherd Moons* on the stereo, changed it after one track for Ella Fitzgerald singing the *Cole Porter Songbook*, and sat down to read about evidence of a Bronze Age ritual landscape on the Isle of Thanet.

Somewhere around 'Night and Day', sleep took over. The phone woke her.

'Lizzy?' It was Rachel. 'I just saw the *Evening Star*. My God, and you found him. What a terrible thing to happen.'

Eliza received Rachel's sympathy with unstated gratitude, and gave her the obvious information and the predictable reassurances. She had been a bit shaken at the time, but she was OK now. Yes, she had taken the afternoon off, and felt much better for it. Would it change things at RUS? Too soon to say, but she doubted it.

'Kill one obsessive capitalist bastard and another one takes his place,' Rachel said.

'You sound like Jez.' Their (Rachel's former) RUS colleague frequently caricatured his own perfectly sincere far-left views.

'I feel like Jez. I can't be sorry about Harding getting killed, only for you getting caught up in it. That man destroyed RUS, everything that was good about it. God, I'm so glad I got out. I'd be more glad if I'd found a new job, of course, but there's hope on the outside at least. I've another interview next week, I must tell you about it, but not now, you won't want to hear it all now. Which reminds me, you're coming to Fem-Man tonight?'

'Tonight?' Eliza said without thinking.

'Lizzy, I sent you the newsletter. You did get it, didn't you?'

It would have been pointless to explain. She had tried before, and met not just incomprehension, but an unwillingness to comprehend. Rachel – like all the women in the Fem-Man group who were not at RUS any more, which was most of them – was obsessed with RUS, but at the same time uninterested in knowing what it was like. To her it was a soap story now, a tale told by the *Daily Mail* of furtive affairs and small-time cheats. Being too tired to do the washing-up before going to bed was not something she empathized with. Told about it, she would say, how awful, and forget immediately. She would phone at 11, 11.30, although Eliza had said three or four times that she was usually in bed by 10.30 these days. Once or twice she had phoned mid-afternoon and left messages on the answerphone, half-apologetic, half-angry because she had forgotten Eliza was not home during working hours.

'Of course I did,' Eliza said, knowing she had not even opened the envelope with Rachel's neat schoolgirl writing. 'But to be honest I'm a bit fagged for that. Maybe I'll take a raincheck this time, but I promise I'll make the next meeting.'

'It's at the Golden Grape. And you missed the last supper.'

'Nice venue.' Eliza tried to sound reassuring without implying that she would change her mind.

'Oh Lizzy, you're tired, aren't you? But I don't want to not see you this time. We hardly seem to meet up at all these days.' Rachel paused, to silence from Eliza. What could she say? They still had their regular Sunday lunches, but it was true that she saw far less of Rachel than she had in less frantic times. 'I tell you what, why don't I skip the meeting too, and you can come over here for supper. We'll have a girl's night in. I could nip out and get a bottle of Aussie red.'

'I've just bought some, and been to Tesco's. Why don't you come over here?' She said it on auto, but it sounded OK once it was articulated, appealing even. She didn't really want to spend the evening alone, which was as well, because Rachel agreed immediately.

11

'He's rung three times? God, Lizzy, that man is still *keen*.'

'Obsessed is more like it,' Eliza said wryly. They were sitting in her kitchen-cum-breakfast-room, at a pine table with a stained-glass lamp shading it. On the wall at the side was a large painting of a fig tree in an overgrown garden, done in an expansive style in brightly-coloured oils. The Nottage Hill was poured, a baguette crumbed the blue and white cloth, and the rich smell of vegetable moussaka wafted from the oven. 'Today especially. I almost feel I ought to be grateful, you know, for his concern, but I'm not. It really irritates me. I suppose it's flattering, but I don't want him to keep on pushing at me.'

'Are you sure, Lizzy?' Rachel eyed her seriously. 'I mean, I know you're off balance and you don't want him to pressurize you right now, but are you sure you'd feel better if he hadn't phoned at all? If he took your word for it and never phoned again? I know you said you wanted out, but it's not as if there's anyone else for you to move on to, is there? And you're not making much of a job of ending it, you know. I wonder if you really do want to, deep down. I know Phil's not perfect, but what man is? He's got his good points, hasn't he?' Rachel waited for a reply, didn't get it, and went on. 'He's house-trained. He wears decently cut suits and no floral ties. He showers every morning, or at least he looks like he does.'

'Oh, every day and sometimes twice a day. You're right, he's very presentable, very hygienic and thoroughly nice. But would you go out with him?'

Rachel's eyebrows flickered. 'You know he's not my type. But he must have been yours once, or you wouldn't have got together with him in the first place.'

True, he had been: not Eliza's dream man, but someone she had seriously considered settling for. She had told herself it was time to be realistic. She was thirty-seven (Rachel was thirty-six), still hoped to have children, and there was a limited pool of potential partners in Costhorpe. She had a slim figure, and a face her friends called intriguing and her lovers beautiful, but even at twenty she had not seriously aspired to catch Harrison Ford.

Rachel in contrast was classically stunning. Her dark brown hair fell almost to her waist, slick and shiny as a newly washed Ferrari under the light from the lamp. Her limbs were fragile, her legs endless, her lashes long over liquid dark eyes. She did not go out with men like Phil Curtin.

But then, Rachel was not going out with anyone at all. It was six months or more since she had split with Owen, and she had had two years on her own after her divorce and before the affair with him. Eliza wondered sometimes if she felt that itchy need for a man, for his smell, his touch, the release he brought, which to her had made Phil – not exactly irresistible, but necessary. She had half-phrased the question sometimes, but Rachel had never completed or answered it. No need: she knew the answer. Rachel had never had a liaison with a workman with a neat grin and a pert bum; she had never come to a discreet arrangement with a pleasant colleague whose marriage had mutated away from desire. When she lusted, it was after a Missoni suit or Blahnik pumps. Her emotional needs were real and strong, but sexual passion did not seem to colour them.

So she did not get into tangles like Eliza's with Phil, and understood them only as far as rationality could take her; although that was far enough for at least a degree of sympathy.

Eliza did not try to explain the (to Rachel) inexplicable. Privately she knew she could have lived with the computer-nerd edge which (she sensed) made Rachel herself rule Phil out. It was not that he was boring: although he was not artistically inclined, he had a variety of interests and a judgement of others that she had found to be both acute and generous. But he didn't ... tame her. He didn't make her content. He didn't give her the kind of charge that – for example – she had felt from James Connaught that morning. It annoyed, even upset her that her sexual needs were so fundamental, but she knew herself well enough to accept that they were. It was nothing kinky she wanted, no handcuffs or whips; but she wanted some essence in a man which there was not in Phil. Lewis had had that essence: she had been content with him, right up to when he had left her for Kate. Now she needed a man who would make her forget Lewis, and Phil had not succeeded in that. She had found herself thinking more and more often that if she tied herself to him she would end up cheating, hurting him, wrecking herself.

'The trouble is,' she said to Rachel, 'I don't know how to make it *not serious*. If only he was less keen. If I could see him on a casual basis and keep looking, I'd do it. But that's not what he wants. I've given it a good try, more than a good try, and I never managed to stop looking. It's not fair to him to keep on with it.'

'I suppose not,' Rachel said. 'No, I know not. It's not that I'm trying to persuade you to settle for second best, Lizzy. I just want to see you happy, and you're never happy on your own, are you?'

'No. Never.' She said it with a smile, but it hurt to know it.

They ate. Rachel asked Eliza's opinion about the latest job she had applied for – admin assistant at the Castle Arts Centre. Only £11,000, but it'd be fun, better than the dole surely? It would wreck her CV, Eliza said practically. Rachel said she wasn't sure she cared.

They talked about old friends, books Rachel had read and Eliza had meant to read, films Rachel had seen and Eliza had meant to see. Rachel was waspishly funny about Tom Cruise and Bruce Willis, deep-space monsters and sad comedies about lonely divorcees. Eliza laughed out loud several times. She was surprised to find herself enjoying Rachel's company more than she had for some time. She realized why: they were not talking about RUS. Rachel had sensed that she didn't want to discuss Harding's murder any more, and was steering so far wide of it that she didn't mention the company at all, or even the Fem-Man supper they were missing, with its coterie of past and present RUSers.

Eliza was opening the second bottle of wine when the phone rang. There was an extension in the room at the front of the house that she used as a study, as well as one upstairs. 'Number four,' Rachel said.

'Sod him. Perhaps I should just not answer it.'

'No, tell him we're all round here, all of Fem-Man. That'll put him off.'

'It would too.' Eliza pushed back her chair, went into the study and picked up the receiver. 'Hi.' She said it cheerfully, half-meaning to take up Rachel's suggestion.

'Eliza? James Connaught.'

He was the last caller she had expected. She said, abruptly, 'How did you get my number?'

'Crystal. I told her there were some more things I needed to ask you.'

'And are there?'

He paused. Eliza had the impression he had expected a different reception from her, though why, she couldn't see. Then he said in a careful voice, 'I think so. Not particularly about Harding.'

'Oh.' She was conscious of Rachel, in listening range, if she wanted to listen.

'Assuming you want me to,' Connaught added.

'To ask me.'

'Yes. Well, assuming you want to see me.'

'What else did Crystal say?'

'Nothing. I'm not that indiscreet. Frank Mills mentioned you were single, only by the by, as a reason you'd be particularly upset by finding the corpse. He thought you'd need some company, not that he was suggesting mine. But I guess I am.'

'Suggesting yours.'

'Yes. No obligation. I'd like to see you. I'd like to talk to you.'

'Tonight.'

'Yes.'

It was the weirdest, most abrasive proposition she had ever been made. She had no doubt that it was a proposition. She couldn't have been more sure if he had said out loud, 'I want to fuck you.' She realized she wanted to fuck him. She had wanted it from the start. All the tension that the evening with Rachel had only thinly suppressed had bubbled to the surface. If he were to come they would fight, and fuck, and afterwards she would lie in a pool of tranquillity. She wanted all three, the fighting, the fucking and the aftermath.

'I've a girlfriend with me.' She went to the door and glanced down the hall and into the kitchen. She could just see the corner of the dining table, where Rachel had evidently taken over the task of opening the second bottle of wine. She put the bottle on the table and began unthreading the cork from the corkscrew. She glanced up at Eliza. 'Not Phil?' she queried. Eliza shook her head. She heard James say, 'Can you get her to leave?'

'Work?' Rachel hazarded. 'Bloody hell.'

Eliza put her hand over the receiver. 'Sorry. Give me a minute,' she said to Rachel. She retreated into the study, out of Rachel's sight, and moved her hand again. 'You've a bloody cheek,' she said.

'You're not saying no.'

No, she wasn't. It hadn't come out angrily, although she had perhaps intended it to. A complete stranger, or as good as. His brass nerve turned her on, and he knew it. 'Hold on,' she said. 'I'll see what I can do.' She went back to the door, and looked at Rachel.

Rachel looked sympathetic rather than irritated. 'Sorry, I never thought. The police?'

'No. No, it's someone from work.'

'But about that.'

She meant the murder. 'Sort of,' Eliza said. 'I'm sorry.' She knew she would manoeuvre Rachel into offering to leave, and she felt guilty, but not guilty enough to not do it.

'God, so am I,' Rachel said. She put the cork down and came through to the study. She slipped an arm round Eliza's waist and rested a cool cheek momentarily against hers. Eliza wanted to feel empathy, but she was conscious mostly of the intense sexual tension she didn't want Rachel to sense, and of a nervousness lest James say something that Rachel would hear.

Rachel said softly, 'Shall I wait or shall I go?'

'It's not really fair to send you off early.'

'No sweat, I'll pick up the end of the Fem-Man meeting. I'll get my bag.' Rachel loosed her arm and padded barefoot towards the sitting room. Eliza stood for a moment, unmoving, then loosed the hand she had clamped round the mouthpiece.

'Eliza?'

'She's going.'

'Shall I give you half an hour?'

Rachel reappeared in the hallway, in her blue silk jacket and low-heeled pumps. She blew a kiss.

Eliza blew one back, then turned back to the phone. 'Do you know how to find me?'

12

He said he would come by taxi. He didn't give her half an hour, it was a bare twenty minutes after Rachel left when she heard the doorbell ring. She had been in the kitchen, washing up after their supper. She had not combed her hair or tidied herself; not quite consciously refusing to prepare for him, but not quite unaware that she hadn't. She was not unconscious of her clothes, a loose-fitting safari-style trouser suit in a heavy figured yellow silk, worn over cream lace-trimmed briefs and bra. She could smell the faint traces of her herbal shampoo, and of the perfume – Oscar – she had splashed on after her shower.

He hadn't changed from his business suit. Even barely knowing him she could see his weariness, in the faint hollows under his eyes, and the slight droop of his shoulders as he fell back against the wall just inside her front door. He had been at St Jude's House since a quarter past seven that morning, if not earlier. It was then half-nine.

'You have green eyes,' he said.

'True.' She leaned against the wall opposite him. It was a narrow hallway, with a hundred-watt bulb above them. Her posture suggested distance, but she was within touching range.

'I'm glad you let me come,' he said.

'That's OK.'

He reached out and touched her hair, her eyebrow, then her cheekbone. His thumb flickered, light as a daddy-long-legs, across her eyelashes. He traced the lobe of her ear. She didn't move, but her entire awareness was within each nerve ending as it traced his touch. This was and wasn't what she had expected.

'Do you want me to make love to you?'

She hadn't been sure how they would navigate the bit before the sex, but it hadn't occurred to her that there would be no bit before the sex. It appalled and pleased her. After all, she thought, if we talked we would only argue.

'Yes,' she said.

13

She woke alone, to a warm bedroom still smelling faintly of semen and sweat, to rumpled sheets and a radio alarm she had forgotten to set. The red numbers spelled out 7.47.

It was months since she had arrived at work later than that, but she could engender no sense of urgency. She got up slowly, and showered at length. Her body ached, inside and out. There were a couple of faint bruises on her wrists. James had not been sadistic, though; she had had no sense that he enjoyed inflicting pain. What he enjoyed, she thought now, was being in control. The sex, orchestrated from start to end by him, had both been and not been what she had expected, much as a film you watch is like and unlike you expect from the synopsis. He was a very good lover – at least, for a woman who was willing to fight and then submit. She had been.

He was also married, or as good as. They had not talked much – not before, not during, and only briefly after – but she had felt obliged to ask him that. Not that she had really needed to ask, she had been all but certain he would be. Nine years with a partner he had not named. Two children with her. She had not asked, and he had not told her, whether it was a happy relationship. Nor had she asked if it was by his choice they had not married. She did not know if he cheated on this unknown partner on a regular basis.

Did she want to know? She told herself not. A part of her, a large part, wished it had not happened. Not just the cheating – although that was something new for her, she had always been careful to pick unattached men, and she was aware of the grubbiness of the situation – but the politics of it. Nor was it only that it is rarely a good idea for a woman to start an affair with a more senior married colleague. It was more that in some way, Harding's murder had accentuated the divide between the two groups at RUS. Us and them, she thought. Mitchell, Genevieve, Howard, all her old colleagues – and to some extent the people who had left too, like Rachel and Lewis – set up against the people who had taken over, stepped on their bowed backs like conquerors, and proceeded to plunder the organization.

She had no friends among the newcomers, no dealings with

them more intimate than her regular, and usually brief, meetings with her boss, John Donaldson. In time, if she stayed with RUS, that would have to change, she supposed. But for now, it seemed to be true of all the old hands that she talked to. And they would close their circles tight against Harding's colleagues now; this was not the time to start fraternizing, beyond a bit of token sympathy. She would be stepping out of line in more ways than one if she let this turn into any kind of continuing relationship.

Still, that was probably not what James intended either. Anyway, most likely he would leave Costhorpe very soon, and she would see no more of him. It was a reaction to the morning's horrors, uncharacteristic, something she should forgive herself for and forget.

It was 8.32 when she reached St Jude's House. Everything seemed normal: Bill was at his desk in the reception area, there were no police in evidence, and the usual people milled across the lobbies. When she came into room 2B, and headed for the area occupied by her own team, she found Genevieve perched on the corner of her junior account handler Martha's desk. As Eliza approached, Martha glanced in her direction.

'Don't mind me,' Eliza said, although it would hardly have been like Martha to do so. She looped her suit jacket over the back of her chair. She hadn't worn a coat: it was a still, sunny morning.

'Actually I was only chatting to Mattie while I was waiting for you,' Genevieve said. 'No problems, I hope?'

That made you so late, Eliza assumed she meant. 'Delayed reaction, maybe. I'm fine now.'

'So. You talked to him, so tell us: who exactly is this James Connaught?'

'He didn't tell me much. Apparently he's a director of the Saturn Trust. I don't know why he was up here, but I got the impression he'd take charge now, at least until he fixes on someone to take over permanently.'

'Well, that hasn't happened,' Genevieve said. 'The email's up this morning: David Summerfield will be acting chief exec until further notice.'

'Summerfield?' She remembered seeing James with him the afternoon before. She barely knew the recently appointed finance director, and her main impression had been of a small retiring man, devoid of charisma. Had James planned this, or had he been overruled? She wished at that moment that they had talked more, not about their personal lives but about work; that she had taken advantage of the situation to ask him lots of questions. They were told so little by the new managers, and she imagined Harding's death would only make communications worse.

'They say he's a brainbox,' Martha said.

'That's fine for a finance director, but chief exec?' She said it without thinking, then checked herself. Criticizing the bosses among her fellow team managers was questionable enough; she knew she should have been more professional than to do it in front of her subordinates.

Genevieve, however, seemed to have no such inhibitions. 'True, a natural figurehead that man is not. But it makes you wonder if there's a piranha lurking under the wet cod. I mean, if you'd asked me a couple of days ago, I'd have said that in a situation like this, it'd be Frank Mills who'd be back in Room 4A1 before you could blink. Then when Connaught turned up, I thought, oh, perhaps it'll be this guy. So what I'm really wondering is, did Connaught choose Summerfield to cut Frank out, maybe? Or does Connaught have the opposite problem? I mean, he seemed the alpha male type, but maybe he's secretly so lacking in zap that Summerfield managed to knock out both of them?'

Martha laughed. 'Hell, Genevieve, you do this politics stuff so well.'

To a point, Eliza thought. Genevieve gossiped and networked plenty, and she was bright and hard working. But she was still only a team leader, on a par with Eliza herself and Mitchell. All that politicking hadn't enabled her to do well out of the takeover. Indeed, none of the old staff had. Even Frank Mills: they might grumble that he had clung on and found himself a comfy corner when most of the other directors had been shoved out of the door, but it didn't alter the fact that he had had to swallow a demotion when Harding came in.

She said, with care, 'It's an interesting theory. You make me wish I'd looked harder at Summerfield. I guess we'll all have to study him now.'

'But Connaught didn't say anything to you?'

'About Summerfield? Zip. He didn't give me a briefing, he asked questions.'

'So is he going now?' Martha asked. 'Or d'you think he'll be around for a while? 'Cos to tell you the truth, I rather fancied him.'

'God's sake, Martha,' Genevieve said.

Martha grinned. At twenty-two, she still had a spoiled daughter's belief that she could get away with being outrageous. She treated bosses and messengers with the same breezy charm. 'You mean you didn't?' she asked. 'I bet you did, Eliza.'

Eliza sometimes felt that Martha needed a put-down, but the means of delivering it were not in her armoury, and this was definitely not the moment. She felt too vulnerable on this territory. But she had to make some kind of response, bring the conversation to a close. 'Well, he's the alpha male type all right', she said warily. 'But I kind of miss the old civil service days. You know, when the bosses talked to us? When they all dressed just as badly as Mitchell does? It seems like alien territory up on the fourth floor now, all these sharp types in their Armani suits. And to be honest, I guess we'll still see most of John Donaldson. Which reminds me, I have to get a report wrapped up for him, so maybe we should get back to work now.'

'*Back* to work?' Genevieve could rarely resist digging her colleagues in the ribs. 'Well, I think you've got the right idea in a way, Martha. It's no good carrying on forever treating everyone new like an enemy. Perhaps we can all watch you cross no man's land and hook up with Connaught.'

'If I wasn't in love with Tibor, I might.' Martha seemed to think she had won the exchange. She grabbed the team tray and went for coffee.

Unsettled by the conversation, Eliza sat down and turned on her computer. When Windows had loaded she logged on to the diary and mail utility. She always got a lot of emails overnight, but the list of new messages that filled the screen and reached down past the end of it was even longer than usual.

She flicked down with her mouse. She told herself she was looking for the email Genevieve had mentioned, though the word at the top of her mind was Connaught. The two were not necessarily mutually exclusive – was it he who had posted the message about Summerfield?

No, it wasn't, and nor was there any other message from him – not that she had expected any personal one. Anyway, there had been no time. She double-clicked on F Mills's 'P S Harding'. '*You *may already have heard the tragic news of the death earlier today of our chief executive, Patrick Harding,'* it began, and went on to exhort members of staff to keep calm and continue to work as normal. *'For the time being, please refer to me all requests that would have been referred to Mr Harding,'* it continued, before concluding with a comment that funeral arrangements would be advised later.

You blew it there, Frank, Eliza thought coolly. Never wise to celebrate before you're over the finishing line. Above and below this sadly revealing message was a stack of the kind of message she had reviewed by title on Wednesday night but not had time to delete: endless variations on famous last lines and twelve o'clock at the Jugged Hare, interspersed with desperate pleas for particular varieties of toner cartridge, for overhead film, one for window envelopes. Most departments had lost their old ordering clerks, and the system now for getting approval for new stationery orders was so slow and cumbersome that people were perpetually running out of essentials. And the leaving parties were a perpetual feature of Friday lunchtimes.

C. Canning's 'Interim arrangements' was timed three hours after Frank Mills's circular. It was a terse announcement that D. Summerfield had been appointed acting chief executive, signed 'on behalf of the board of the RUS Group Limited'. C. Canning was Crystal, David Summerfield's secretary. Janine would have posted a board message normally, but presumably she had not returned to the office the previous day.

Even here there was no mention of James Connaught, so perhaps he had kept well out of the jostling. No – that couldn't be true, judging by her sight of him with Summerfield the day before. Plenty of others must have seen them too, and Frank Mills probably had a very good idea of who had gone for Summerfield and not gone for him. If she saw James again, she maybe should warn him that Frank made a nasty enemy.

'No sugar today, OK?'

'Oh? Thanks, Martha.'

'Only you didn't half bawl out Helen yesterday.'

'I'm sorry. I wasn't myself yesterday. Helen's not in today?'

'She's in London at that meeting with the DRMS group, you know, the ones who wanted temporary filing clerks. It's still going ahead, obviously, and she thought you'd want her to go.'

'Fair enough.' Eliza watched Martha move on, then her eyes drifted back to the screen. There was nothing else in the email list that drew her eye.

She turned to her in-tray instead. The note was on top, a folded sheet in a sealed envelope marked 'Personal. Eliza Stannard.' It was brief and unsigned. *'Supper tonight?'* Still, she was smiling as she picked up the plastic cup of coffee.

14

A few minutes later, Inspector Crane rang. 'Just following up and cross-checking statements. I wanted to know, the security guard in reception when you came in yesterday morning. You said it was Bill Downs?'

'Bill, yes. I don't know his surname, but I'm sure it was Bill.'

'You're sure? It wasn't his colleague Stew Harker?'

Eliza thought it had been Bill. Surely Howard had called him Bill? She knew him by sight, had seen him in the lobby a thousand times, had always nodded to him and sometimes had a brief conversation – about the weather, the carpark, a parcel she was expecting. She could describe him to Crane, a shortish man with a thick head of grey hair and a chiselled profile. She knew his voice, his thick Norfolk accent, although he had not spoken that morning as far as she recalled. The only thing she was not sure about was his name. There were five or six security guards. She knew Jack, the young one; and she knew one of the others was called Bill and one Stew, but she could not have matched their names to their faces, or named the other guards at all. This ignorance embarrassed her. She was sure Howard, for instance, knew all the guards by name.

'Howard Nkolo called him Bill.'

'But Mr Nkolo told us it was Harker.'

'Then one of us got it wrong. Me, most likely. It's the kind of thing it's easy to misremember.'

'Well, one of you definitely got it wrong.' He rang off leaving an echo of that 'wrong' behind him.

15

James rang her at eleven. Eliza had just put the phone down on a conversation with Howard Nkolo. She wanted to talk to him – talk properly, not on the phone – for all sorts of reasons, the mix-up that Crane had mentioned being among them. And normally Howard was perfectly happy to meet up and chat with her. But he had turned down her suggestion of coffee in the Courtyard, and she had had to settle for his offer of a chat over a drink at the lunchtime leaving do for the security guards. That wasn't at all what she had intended, and she couldn't understand why Howard had been so obtuse.

So she was feeling irritable when the next call came, and although she recognized James's voice on 'Eliza?' there was nothing in his tone to restore her cheer.

'Yes, it's Eliza's phone and Eliza here.'

'Having a shit day like all of us, I take it. I need you to do something for me. Janine Broughton hasn't come in this morning, and she's not answering the phone in her hotel room. Go over there and see what's up.'

'Me?'

'It's you I'm talking to, isn't it?'

'Yes, but it's not my –'

'Your job,' James interrupted her, 'is to do what needs to be done to get things straight around here. You seem to get on with her. Bring her back if she's in a half-reasonable state, the police want to see her.'

'James, you maybe got the wrong impression. I barely know Janine. If you want to send over some friend of hers, then Crystal, I should think –'

'I can't spare Crystal. If she can't come with you, ring me as soon as you're back here. This side of lunchtime, that means.'

'You expect me to drop –' Eliza was left protesting to an empty line.

'Something up?' asked Genevieve, passing.

'Uh? Not really.' She couldn't explain to Genevieve why she was annoyed; she didn't even want to tell her what she had been told to do. Genevieve would latch straight onto the fact that

James had picked on her for this task, and make mountains of the reasons. 'Just an everyday crisis of office folk. I've got to go out.'

'Lucky you,' Genevieve said dryly.

16

The sun twinkled like a gold button on a blue satin sky. The air was lukewarm tea, the traffic fumes like tannin thickening it as she made her way down the narrow curved streets between St Jude's House and the city centre. Shoppers, bags drooping, tramped back to the ring-road carparks; grey-suited executives pushed past her. On the Cut a couple of swans paddled amid discarded cigarette wrappers, avoiding a half-submerged super-market trolley. She stopped on the bridge, turning an unfocused gaze on them.

What a mess. What a total, total mess. Harding's death was terrible, of course, but having barely known him, what concerned Eliza more was her own position. It hadn't exactly been great two days earlier, but everything that had happened since seemed to have made it worse, her own stupid actions not least. She hadn't even had a chance to say no to supper with James, so she supposed he would turn up on her doorstep that evening. He wouldn't risk a public meal out with her in Costhorpe, or anywhere near it, not if he had a partner and two kids, and there were people at RUS who knew that. And even if there weren't, it could hardly fail to be a disaster if people learned that the two of them had become involved with each other.

But she could hardly slam the door on him, and she wasn't even sure – even now, with hindsight – that she would want to do so, when it came to it. It wasn't the sex, great though it had been. It was the sense of connection. The end, however momentary, of feeling frighteningly alone.

Oh, get a grip, Eliza. Go hang out with Rachel, or Mitchell, or any of a dozen other good old friends. Get a grip on your career, come to that. If you didn't know before, you surely know now that RUS is not a place you want to be any more. Start looking for another job. So if there's nothing else in Costhorpe, think about leaving Costhorpe. True, RUS is not the only good organization that has been wrecked in the dubious names of privatization and efficiency, but there must be some decent jobs left somewhere, surely.

The voluntary redundancy list was still open, as far as she knew.

It moved slower now than it had done six months earlier. They had stopped letting anyone go who chose to, and started firing the people they didn't want to stay. Like the security guards. It was against the agreement with the trade unions, but then, almost everything the new management did was against the agreement with the trade unions. Andy Dormand, the joint unions rep, sent forlorn circulars protesting. One had been on her email list that morning.

Martha Chmielewski was on the list, with maybe 500 others – the numbers were never released. Putting herself on the end of it wouldn't achieve anything unless John Donaldson or someone else with clout decided they would like to see the back of her. No, that was an excuse. She remembered repeating that argument for the umpteenth time to Arthur Atchison at Ted Hawley's party. According to rumour the new bosses had wanted to keep Arthur, who had been director of IT, but he had taken a month off with stress, then quietly been let go. 'Don't be daft, girl,' he had said to her. 'If you don't want to stay there are plenty of ways of giving 'em the message.' Like fucking a director of the Saturn Trust, she thought. Like discovering the corpse of the chief exec. How had he died? 'RUS Boss Found Murdered,' the A-board outside the newsagent on the corner of Gilroy Road had said, but she hadn't stopped to buy a paper, so she still didn't know.

Death and sex. The core of life, and at the same time a pair of old clichés. It was too facile to blame her behaviour with James on Harding.

'Gosh, you don't change, Eliza. There's a little cloud round you sometimes labelled "thinking".'

The voice, close by her left ear, made her jump. She swung round to the creased face and mouse-brown eyes of Ted Hawley, who had headed Office Services before John Donaldson replaced him.

'Sorry, Ted. So I've been told before. It's congenital. Actually I wasn't thinking of much at all.'

'A study in pink and purple.' Her suit was purple, the scoop-necked jersey top beneath it a deep cyclamen. 'River scene with swans. Pissarro?'

'Oh, Sisley, I should think, or even Whistler.' She felt her muscles loosen. Even when he had been her superior, she had found Ted relaxing company. 'What brings you this way?'

'The usual circuit: Job Centre, Reference Library, the Six Bells at lunchtime for Jez Barnard's leaving do. One more bites the dust.'

'Gosh, Jez is going today? I didn't even know.'

'They must be insane to let him.' He swung round, falling into step with her as they walked on past the Cut and towards the red Gothic bulk of the Technical Institute. 'Jez has so much talent. I told them so, of course. You know I had to do this list right after we were privatized, my stars they called it. Who are your stars, who should we hold on to? You were on it, Lizzy, I've always rated you, and obviously Jez ...'.

'Sure. But he ...'. She tried to phrase an explanation, how the radically left-wing Jez didn't fit, would never fit the new RUS, then decided it wasn't worth it. Ted didn't want to know the new management's rationale, he simply wanted his own verdict reinforced. 'They honestly don't look for talent, Ted. Not among the old staff. We're all civil servants with "Public Service" stamped in indelible ink on our brains, so we can't erase the message and get our heads round the profit ethos instead. No shareholder values for us. At least, that's what they reckon.'

Ted was pursuing his own thoughts. 'Alice Brown, Carla Ngumbe. Eight people I listed, and there's only two of you they've held on to. And they haven't promoted you, have they, Lizzy?'

'They haven't promoted anyone.'

'Frank Mills seems to be doing all right. The bastard. Christ knows what deal he did behind our backs before it all went through.'

'Director of development? It's like minister without portfolio, Ted. Nothing in the in-tray.'

'Mandelson's thriving on it, though. Similar character if you ask me.'

She had no wish to pursue this line. 'Maybe so. Am I to take it you're not exactly loving your life of leisure?'

Ted shrugged. 'For a week it's a novelty to lie in, but even then the wife wakes me every morning. She grumbles if I do too much round the house, and I never was into gardening. I go to the lunchtime concerts at St Philip's, they're pretty good, and the Pipe Club still meets up. Twice a week now, a drink at lunchtime, and we're planning a trip to Antwerp next month.'

'Keeps you up with the gossip.' The Sherlock Holmes Pipe

Club had been RUS's most powerful drinking clique, with a dozen members including four or five directors.

'More or less. Howard still comes, Howard Nkolo. We don't get Hugh Worning very often these days.'

'He's pretty busy at the moment. I wouldn't take it personally.'

'Oh, 18-hour days. I've heard all that. 'Course he's young.'

'That's true.' Therefore, regarded even by the new owners as promotable. And male, of course, Eliza thought a little sourly. In their early days she and Rachel had ranted at the Pipe Club, the Expensive Masons as Rachel had called them. They had both manoeuvred to join, been politely turned away (and Rachel less politely, when she had persisted), and eventually set up Fem-Man as a female counterpart. The Pipe Club had one woman member, Audrey Smith, but in the ten years Eliza had watched from a distance it had never accepted another. That sense of exclusion still rankled faintly, underneath her pity for Ted. He was only 46, but he wasn't the type to adapt readily to changed circumstances. For him the euphemistic VER might well mean retirement for ever.

Thinking this, she went on, 'Any plans for the future, Ted?'

'Work, you mean? I've one or two ideas I'm looking into. Early stages.'

'Still, you have to start somewhere. I'm glad to know you're working on it.'

He squinted sideways at her. 'Why, might you be interested?'

'Something in the procurement field? I'd like to hear what takes shape, certainly. It's not as if I'm committed to RUS for life.'

'I'll keep in touch. You're going up to the city?'

'Mornington Arms.' Eliza cut behind him to his left-hand side. 'I'll see you.'

'You won't be there at lunchtime?'

''Fraid not. I promised to be at the security guards' do.' And Jez hadn't asked her to his, she silently added, although to be fair he had most likely put a general invitation on the email system and since she wasn't motivated to go (he was a close friend of her ex-husband, who would doubtless be there), she hadn't taken it in. 'Take care.'

'And you.' He caught her arm before she could step away. A slight man, he had to look up to meet her eyes. 'I mean it, Eliza. It's nasty these days from all I hear, not like it used to be. This terrible business yesterday, all right, no loss that man, but even so. What I mean is, you never were the best at watching your back.'

Which is why people like Jez blind-sided me, Eliza thought. And for all this stars business, you let him. In the five years Ted had been her boss they had scarcely had a cross word, but she hadn't been given a single promotion. That hadn't all been Frank Mills's doing.

She smiled anyway, and said 'Thanks for the warning', before heading off down St Asaph Lane.

17

Eliza didn't give Janine a thought until she was within sight of the Mornington Arms, when her irritation at the assignment resurfaced. She had no idea how to play it. She had done her best with sympathy in Ken Thursby's office, but she was no nurse manqué, and anyway that scene was over with. She would have to move on, but to what? She felt sorry for Janine, but she didn't share her grief, and couldn't imagine exchanging happy memories of Patrick Harding. Nor did she feel inclined to make a brusque demand that Janine pull herself together and come back to the office.

Hell. If the police wanted to interview her, they should have come. If James wanted her to get back to work, he should have known better. Surely one day off was allowable after the murder of her boss.

She would say she had been sent by James to make sure Janine was all right, she decided; and mention the request from the police, but without applying any pressure. Actually that was what James had asked of her, as far as she could recall his words. Acutely conscious of his ruthless streak, she had read his demand in that light, but he hadn't said in so many words that Janine would have to get back to the coal face pronto, or else.

She rarely went into the Mornington, but she knew it, of course; all Costhorpe did, although few locals ate, drank or sent their friends to stay there. In a city too small and remote to attract the five-star chains, too prosaic to be a major tourist centre, it was the nearest thing to a grand hotel. From her last visit, a good year earlier, she recalled its public rooms as sedate, quaint in places – the place was 300 years old, and did not let its punters forget it – and slightly faded.

The lobby surprised her. It oozed white flowers, carnations, orchids and heavy-smelling hyacinths, their beds of fern and ivy frothing over the sides of stepped bronze planters to greet an expanse of deep red carpet. This carried on through to the lounge beyond, which had new-looking blue leather chesterfields and buttoned armchairs arranged in 'conversation groups'. 'The Mornington, an Inns of England Hostelry,' an easel proclaimed.

What had it been last time, TrustHouse Forte? She couldn't remember. Behind the polished reception desk three of the genre of babe RUS presumably intended to hire to replace Bill and Stew were gossiping in a bored manner, leaning against the pigeonholes that held the keys of vacant rooms.

One of them reluctantly came over to deal with her. Eliza apologized that she didn't know Janine's room number, and the babe looked it up – room 352. She rang the room, but Janine didn't answer. Sorry, she said, and turned away.

Eliza was irritated enough to persist. Had Janine gone out? The receptionist said she had no idea. She wasn't prepared to check to see if Janine's key had been handed in, because the hotel didn't give out such information on principle. Eliza asked if she could be paged. The receptionist said, sure, but the bar and restaurant aren't open yet, and you can see from here that she's not in the lobby or the lounge. OK, said Eliza, I'll go up to her room. Sorry, said the receptionist. We can't allow that.

Eliza thanked the girl more politely than she reckoned she deserved, and returned to the street. She was tempted to go straight back to RUS and report failure to James, but conscience interposed: she knew perfectly well how to reach the upper floors unobserved. She walked round to a side door labelled 'Anglia Carvery'. There was a passage beyond it. She ignored the glass inner door to the carvery, through which she could see waiters setting tables, continued down the corridor to the back stairs, and made her way unchallenged up to room 352.

Janine answered on her second knock. She was fully dressed in a short grey skirt and a navy blue chenille jumper with a shirt collar. 'What the hell do you want?' she said.

'I'm here officially, as it were. Sent to see how you are.'

Janine glared for a moment, then her features smoothed into the professionally aloof expression Eliza was familiar with. 'I see. Excuse me, I've had a rather wearing morning. You'd better come in.'

The Mornington had a few celebrated 'historical' rooms, but this was not one of them, it was straight off the four-star-business-hotel pattern book. There was the usual narrow corridor past the bathroom. In the rectangle beyond, two orange-cover-letted double beds filled most of the space. A formica range of wardrobe, desk, false-fronted fridge and television nudged their feet. At the far end two tub chairs upholstered in a greenish tweed squatted either side of a small round marble-effect table which held a dirty ashtray, a pack of Marlboro Lights and an orange plastic disposable lighter, a glass of what looked like water, and an upturned paperback. This was the only sign of occupation in the room. The squat outline of Costhorpe Castle was faintly visible through the nylon net that swathed the window.

'I can't offer you coffee unless we go down to the lounge,' Janine said. 'I've used all the sachets and we don't get an allowance for room service. There's mineral water in the fridge.'

'I don't need anything, thanks.' Eliza took the chair farthest from the ashtray, glass and paperback. It was a Silhouette romance, she noticed, *Surrender to Love*. 'James Connaught sent me. He's concerned about you.'

'That's, er, thoughtful of him. You can tell him' – Janine hesitated, choosing her words – 'I'm recovering, but I need a day or two. I'll come back to the office according to my contract, obviously, and by then I suppose I'll have some idea what I'm going to do. I won't need a sick note for just a couple of days, will I? I haven't been sick for years, I don't know the rules. And I haven't got a doctor up here.'

'No; no, you shouldn't need a sick note.' Although she would have no trouble getting one, Eliza thought, looking more carefully at the younger woman. Janine's hair, a mid-length brown bob with blonde streaks, was rattier than Eliza had seen it before, and her eyes had the puffiness of recent tears. Her manner was brittle, and she didn't quite meet Eliza's eyes.

She ran over Janine's words, and added, 'I didn't realize. Will you leave RUS?'

Janine's gaze just caught hers, and flicked away again. 'I don't want to commit myself to anything yet.'

'I wasn't asking officially,' Eliza said. 'I was just concerned about your situation. I'm sure no one would ask you to leave. Far from it, really: you must be the only one who knows a lot of what Mr Harding was up to. I'm certain Ja—' – she stopped and corrected herself – 'David Summerfield will want you to stay.'

'There's plenty of people who won't.'

There was some truth in that, but Eliza could hardly agree out loud. She was still trying to phrase an honest but polite response when Janine went on, 'And I've had enough, to be frank. Don't pass this on to Connaught, but what the hell does he expect?

Patrick gets murdered and a dozen people come down on me and he thinks I'll soldier on uncomplainingly? As if I want to stay in this godforsaken hole. I keep telling myself, don't do anything when you're off balance, but I can't imagine I'll change my mind about that. He'll be lucky if I work my notice out.'

'I know you were very close to Mr Harding,' Eliza said. 'I can see it's an awful shock. And I can understand it might seem there isn't much here for you now that –'

'Don't start that crap. You're not another bloody one who thinks I was having an affair with him.'

'That's not what I meant,' Eliza said, trying hard to hold on to a remnant of sympathy. 'Of course I don't think that. I just meant you had a very good working –'

'Oh sure,' Janine interrupted her. She hadn't sat down, and now she took a step backward and swung round to the window. 'Well, at least you don't think I killed him.'

'Gosh, no one thinks that!' The embarrassing contrast with her response to Janine's last accusation sunk in a moment later. She blundered on. 'Janine, I do sympathize. It's a terrible situation. And ...' And even more terrible if she was suspected of the murder, she had been about to add, when she it struck her that it was a bizarre comment for Janine to have made. No one did suspect her of the murder, surely? Why should it even have occurred to her that anyone might? Unless ...

An explanation came to her.

'And if the police have been coming down heavy on you, it's no wonder you're feeling done in. I had a long session with them myself yesterday, so I know what it's like.'

'It's not the police,' Janine said shortly. 'It's just about everyone else. This emails business. What on earth do they imagine, I signed on to some crappy scheme to set things up for my boss's murder?'

'Other people are on edge too. We're all a bit shorter-tempered than we ought to be.'

'Huh. The cops can go and chase these other people then. I haven't got anything to say. I wasn't involved. Whatever got done with these bloody emails, it wasn't me that did it.'

'I believe you. But I think you have to tell that direct to the police, if you haven't yet. As for anyone else coming the heavy with you, I can't see why they would, but if they are doing, it can be stopped. If you tell me who's –'

'Jesus, no!'

Her vehemence astonished Eliza. She said slowly, 'Janine, are you afraid?'

'Afraid!' Janine couldn't have been more sarcastic if Eliza had injected a taunting note into her question – which she hadn't. 'Of course I'm not bloody afraid,' she threw out, spinning back to confront Eliza. 'I'm angry, that's what I bloody am. All you pathetic little shits. You've been trying to wreck everything Patrick's done since the minute he came here, and now you've finally got him, you've done the worst you can possibly do, and you're snivelling around trying to blame other people and cover it all up.'

Eliza's temper went. '*I* haven't been doing anything, thank you!' she retorted, getting to her feet. 'Except working my bloody arse off for your fucking boss. That's what we've all done, all of us, and much bloody thanks we've ever got.'

'Huh!' Janine spat. 'You can't come that one on me. As if I don't know what you're like. I've seen a barrelful of it, thank you, from his shitty little mistress to the arse-licking idiots who used to run the place to the stuck-up fucking secretaries, so called, who won't give me the time of day. You're all mean and pathetic and as jealous as hell. Toads, that's what you are, slimy horrible toads. You haven't the slightest fucking clue how to run an organization and when someone comes in and shows you how you just can't handle it. Mean little crybabies. Don't have any skills, any qualifications half of you, and you grumble because Patrick didn't want you. Christ, have you seen yourselves? Grumbling all the way to the bank with your half-million payoffs. Falling over each other to get to the door because you can't face doing a real day's work. He despised you, you know that, and I'll tell you what, you deserved to have him despise you, because you couldn't see what he was, you were just too twisted and jealous. And then some twisted jealous little fucker sneaks in and kills him. God, do I hate you. I hate you, I hate you, I hate you!'

Eliza, frozen at first, found the use of her limbs halfway through this tirade. By the time Janine raised her fists and slammed them down on the last 'hate you', tears cutting a motorway down her cheeks, she had got to the door.

18

She was breathless by the time she reached the street again. She hadn't been running, but the scene had leached the air from her lungs. She paused till she was breathing steadily, then thick with emptiness, she crossed the road. She was halfway up St James's Street before any kind of rational thought returned.

She stopped, and looked around. St James's Street was at the castle-and-cathedral end of the city centre, cobbled and charming, its shop windows gleaming in the sunshine. She had come to a halt outside the Cutting Edge salon, between the Cozy Corner Tea Shoppe and H Soothing, Newsagents and Confectioners. Across the street was St James's Church, redundant for fifty years or more, and kept open by a small charity as a meditation centre. A tiny churchyard, mown grass hemmed by upright gravestones and a wisteria hedge, surrounded it.

She ducked into the newsagents and bought a *Morning Record*. Then she paused again on the pavement, glancing across at the church. She hadn't been inside since taking her mother on an open-day tour of Costhorpe churches five or six years earlier. She crossed the street and went through the open wooden gate.

The gravel path was weed-crusted, the porch silted with dirt in its corners, the notice board punctuated only by a couple of rusted drawing pins. But the heavy latch turned under her hand, and the oak door swung smoothly inwards. Inside it was cool and shadowy, with a faint smell of damp stone and long-forgotten incense. A handwritten notice propped against a vase of bluebells and Michaelmas daisies invited visitors to sign a book and make a donation.

There were no visitors apart from her. There were no pews, but there were rows of hard chairs. Eliza subsided onto one and closed her eyes.

She was looking for – not religion, but whatever the irreligious can use to bring the same peace into their lives. Or perhaps she wasn't. She opened her eyes again and read the headlines on the *Morning Record*. The story took up most of page one, and carried over on to pages two and three. Patrick Harding had been stabbed, it said. The weapon had not yet been found. A shaded box summarized the history of the RUS takeover and stated that Harding had single-handedly turned the organization from disastrous losses into a situation where a good profit was expected in the current financial year.

That casual comment was all she needed to tap her anger. Damn him, damn him. As if he had done anything remotely admirable at RUS. It was all a fake, a facade. She was no accountant, but Howard had explained to her the pathetically simple manoeuvres which had written down asset values almost to zero, shunted costs backwards and profits forwards. Bloody bastards, buying cheap in a corrupt auction, and set to make millions out of it.

Twisted jealous little fucker, Janine's voice echoed in her head.

The hellish thing was, it was true. It was all distorted but it was true as well. They were jealous, of course they were, of the fat salaries and the share options and the jobs advertised only in the *Sunday Times* that were so clearly not for them. It did anger them that the new bosses took no account of their years of experience, as if ten years doing a job was overshadowed by the three years of university that – also true – quite a lot of the older staff had never done. (Not Eliza: her history degree was perfectly respectable.) They had been beastly to Janine: of course they had, they hated her. No wonder, Harding and his sidekicks had made dozens of secretaries and administrators redundant, dumped them, compulsorily some of them, and then this girl had skated in and taken the top PA job. Rumour had it she was paid £25,000 a year, almost as much as Eliza. Oh, how they had sworn at that, Genevieve and Marshall, Mattie and Helen and the whole damn lot of them. Everything they had thought belonged to them had been given to Patrick bloody Harding and his cohorts. How could they not hate the man, his secretary, everyone and everything he had brought with him?

And yet she hated the hating, hated her own black feelings. This was not how anyone should live their life. Admittedly things hadn't always been wonderful in the RUS days; all right, the old management had not all been cutting-edge brilliant. But they had been pretty good people on the whole. Men like Ted Hawley had been a pleasure to know. Going to work had been enjoyable. It hadn't made her rich, it hadn't protected her from the anguish of divorce, but life had been OK. Life now was shit.

It makes you want to kill someone. The sentence came into

her brain and she froze around it. Because the chilling thing, the horrendous thing that was only now becoming real to her, was that someone had killed someone. Patrick Harding was dead. Detestable shit maybe, but even so he was dead. No wonder Janine was going barmy: her boss had been murdered.

And Inspector Crane was, depressingly, almost certainly right. Someone she knew had killed him.

Who could have done it? She had no idea.

Her mind skimmed through the people who had been in St Jude's House at 6.30 the day before: Howard Nkolo, Mitchell, Genevieve, Bill the doorman. They were all as angry inside as she was. She had plenty of reason to know that, there had been more than enough nights of bitching down at the Six Bells. But how could any of them have reached the pitch of murder?

She couldn't see it, not at all.

Did Janine see it, she wondered? Was that why she was so upset, because she knew, or at least guessed, who had done it?

Or was the explanation even more chilling? Janine had protested hard enough, but it looked to Eliza as if the emails for the false meetings had been sent from her computer. Had she really been as ignorant of them as she had tried to make out?

19

Eliza did not relish reporting back to James. The scene with Janine embarrassed her. She had handled it poorly, she knew, and made an enemy in the process. She decided to say as little as possible, and hope he wouldn't be in the mood to ask questions.

He wasn't. 'OK,' he said. 'If she's in that much of a state the police will have to wait. I don't suppose she has much to tell them anyway. Thanks for trying.'

She rang off quickly, and let out her breath. Only then did it occur to her that she had said nothing about supper. She had meant to ask him not to come; she really did not want to spend that evening with him. But she hesitated to ring him straight back in order to say so.

Perhaps he would forget, she told herself. Even if Summerfield was now acting chief exec, it looked as if plenty of problems were pitching up at James's door. With luck he too had thought better of their seeing more of each other, and the problem would go away of its own accord.

20

It was now 12.30. Phil Curtin had rung her four times, Martha said, and Howard had come round to her desk while she was out of the office, and left a message that he was going on to the pub without her. 'Damn,' Eliza said. 'Still, I agreed we'd go at ten past, so I suppose I'm to blame. I'll set off now and try to catch him.'

'Mind if I come too?'

'Is no one else around?' Eliza glanced around the deserted section.

'Nope. What d'you expect, there are about a dozen leaving dos this lunchtime.'

Martha's insouciant manner irritated her. 'I expect cover,' she said tartly. 'You know, cover? Like we used to give? Somebody manning the phones to take calls from the clients? Remember the clients?'

'Dimly,' Martha said.

'Mattie, for heaven's –' Eliza began; then she bit her tongue. It was an old exchange, Martha too flippant, Eliza too quick to boil into irritation. But there was no drive behind it: it occurred to her quite suddenly that she didn't care.

She fell against the back of her chair, and looked up at Martha, who was as cheerfully unabashed as usual. 'That's about it, isn't it?'

'Yeah. Collapse of stout institution.'

'You know what got me really, really angry this morning? A bit in the paper saying what a bloody marvellous job Patrick Harding had done of turning round RUS.'

'Oh, he's turned it round all right. He's got all our clients heading away from us.'

'But it doesn't show on the accounts, that's the thing. They're living on last year's contracts, and the profit and loss account's manipulated in every way known to the City.'

'So you've said before.'

'And life revolves around a completely fictitious budget. I cannot get together the inclination to hack over those unbelievable projections one more time. There's no one left to do the work anyway. Where do they think we're going to get a 20 per cent increase in turnover when there's no one to do the work?'

'Search me.'

'Let's go.'

'OK.' Martha went back to her desk to collect her jacket and bag. 'Which reminds me,' she went on, rejoining Eliza, 'talking of no one left. Now things are shaken up again, sort of, d'you think this is a good time to see if you can get some movement on my redundancy? You know I really, really do want to get it.'

'I don't know.'

'It's nothing against you, you do know that? You've been fine as a boss. It's this bloody place.'

'Then why don't you just quit? You wouldn't get that much money from the redundancy anyway, would you?'

'£4,290 plus my three months' notice, which they don't usually make people work out, do they? And rising each day I stay. It's not much compared with Jez's payoff, but it's about £4,289 more than I've got in the bank. I could go freelance on that.'

Martha had trained as a graphic designer before resigning herself to admin. 'And you couldn't without?'

'Nope.' Martha's brown curls bounced as she shook her head. 'I'd have to get another job without, and I'm working hard on it, but there's nothing in Costhorpe, and I don't want to leave Tibor.'

'Working hard on it.'

'Not in office hours. Well, not much. I'm not that behind on my work, am I?'

'Less than I am,' Eliza agreed. 'I'll see what I can do, Mattie.'

They reached the end of the street, and automatically set off in different directions. A couple of paces along Eliza stopped, turned back, and saw that Martha had done the same.

'The Six Bells, right?' Martha said.

'Oh, you're going to Jez's. Sorry, I'm going to the security guards' do.'

'But you can't not go to Jez's, Eliza. How long have you worked with that man for?'

'Less time than I've said hi to the guards each morning. And I'm meeting Howard at the Brown Cow.'

'Call in later then,' Martha said. 'They'll be there all afternoon, I expect.'

'Jez and his inner circle? I dare say.'

It wasn't a direct answer, but it was enough for Martha. 'See you later then,' she said, flashed a smile, and tripped off on her high heels.

Eliza stood watching her for a moment. Martha Chmielewski, aged twenty-two. Five foot five, brown curly hair just short of her shoulders, brown eyes, freckled face, merry grin. Bright, enthusiastic, not always tactful, and inclined to bouts of petulance when she didn't get her way. Innocent. Undamaged.

Unlike Eliza. She knew it wasn't just the clash of leaving drinks parties that was causing her to miss Jez's. She didn't want to go because she thought Lewis would be there, and she didn't want to see him. Damn ex-husbands. Damn – oh shit. Just as Lewis was odds-on to be at Jez's do, so Phil Curtin was odds-on to be at the Brown Cow.

She couldn't stand up Howard, albeit he would doubtless not miss her. She had to make an opportunity to talk to him before the police approached her again. And she would have to say something to Phil, she supposed, if she was to stop his endless phonecalls. With a sigh, she turned her feet towards the Brown Cow.

21

A blast of loud conversation and glass-clinking greeted her as she opened the door of the Brown Cow. It was a low-ceilinged early Victorian pub only five minutes from St Jude's House, crammed from door to cellar to Gents with the familiar and half-familiar faces of RUS personnel.

'Hi, darling.'

'Hi, John,' she greeted an accounts clerk who was a long-standing, if casual, acquaintance. 'Is Howard Nkolo here?'

'Heavens, is he leaving too?'

'You know he's not. Is this all the security guards' do?'

'You want the back bar. This bit's Ellie Gordon's do, and I think some guy from Facilities is having one too.'

'I'll go find Howard in the back then. See you.' She began to inch her way through the crowds that blocked the door to the rear bar, only to find herself hard up against a familiar back. It turned before she could edge away again.

Phil Curtin was solidly built, just under six foot, with dark brown hair cut short at the back and black-framed glasses dominating regular, if undramatic, features. His suit was navy blue, the choice of a man who cared for tidiness and convention but not for fashion. His frown lightened as soon as he recognized her.

'Liz! At last I've found you. I couldn't get Martha to say where you'd be this lunchtime, so I had to guess that you'd come here.'

Eliza forced a smile. 'Of course Martha couldn't say because she didn't know what my plans were.'

'Anyway, no matter, you're here now. How are you, Liz?'

In fact it did matter. He would have to get it into his head that she couldn't tolerate his harassing her staff. This wasn't the moment to tell him so, though. 'I'm fine,' she said.

'I've been so worried, so terribly worried. To think of you in such danger.'

'Phil, please. I wasn't in danger.'

'You were, you must have been. A few minutes earlier and you might have walked straight in on a murderer. In the act. My blood runs cold to think of it.'

'Then don't.' He was being even more melodramatic than she

had feared, and it was irritating her just as much as she had anticipated.

'You need to be looked after, Liz. I was so worried last night, when I couldn't get through to you. Your phone must have gone on the blink. I tried reporting it but they said the report had to come from you.'

'There's nothing wrong with my phone, Phil. I took it off the hook when I went to bed, early.'

'But you didn't phone me back.'

He was fishing for guilt, and she was damned if she would oblige him by succumbing to it. She was under no obligation to return Phil's calls instantly. Their relationship was over: she had told him that as plainly as she could three or four times now. She hadn't been out with him on a one-to-one basis, or slept with him, for over a month.

'I know.' It came out harsher than she had intended, harsher than was justified, she realized as his face crumpled with pain. Phil was a kind and thoughtful man, and it wasn't his fault if he was unable to turn off his emotions to suit her. He hadn't changed, she reminded herself: it was only her perception of him that had. 'I'm sorry, Phil,' she added. 'I do appreciate your concern, but I just didn't want to discuss what had happened last night.'

'Oh. I'm awfully sorry, I never thought of that. Still, here you are. What're you drinking?'

'I'm afraid I'm only here in passing. I've come to meet Howard Nkolo, and I'm late already.'

'Oh no, Liz. I can't let you go that soon.'

He was right, she reluctantly conceded. In the circumstances she would have to have one drink with him. 'OK, just one. At least Howard's not the type to be sitting on his own in a corner waiting for me. I'll have an orange juice, thanks.'

'You can manage a proper drink. They'll hardly fire you for it, when half the office are here with you.'

'True, but I don't fancy one.'

'You're sure? A glass of white wine, maybe?'

'No, orange juice.'

'If you're certain.' To her relief he accepted her insistence and headed for the crush round the bar. Eliza slipped into the group of people he had been with. She knew them all, though none of them were close friends.

They were talking about the Beaver's murder. She learned quickly that a police incident room had been set up in room 1E, which had been deserted since an internal printing operation had been closed down. Several people had been pumping the officers for information, and others had been making their own enquiries. They wanted to know who the killer was, and assumed it was someone from RUS. Who else, as they said, would hate the Beaver enough?

But so many people had had cause to hate him, and it seemed plenty of them had had the opportunity to kill him. Pat Shorten was waving a list of the twenty-one people who, he had discovered, had been in St Jude's House by 6.30 on the morning of the murder. Four of them were computer services staff who had been working together, and everyone agreed they could be put out of contention. They courteously decided that Eliza and Howard were in the clear too. Two others were the security guards. Most of the group ruled these out as well, but two girls who worked with Phil began to argue whether anyone would have told on them if they had left their desks, and whether anyone could have got in without their noticing. There was no signing-in system for regular staff, only for visitors, and there were no security cameras.

'Come to that, there are three doors without a security guard,' Pat pointed out. 'But you've got to draw a line somewhere. The West Door isn't opened or manned till 7.30. The fire exits can only be opened from inside, and the goods entrance was definitely locked. I had that from a detective sergeant, and he told me they'd treble-checked it.'

'That doesn't mean anything,' Phil said, catching the tail end of this discussion when he returned with Eliza's orange juice and a pint of Abbot for himself. 'There are umpteen keys for it, so someone could have sneaked in that way and locked it again afterwards.'

'Are there?' Pat said. 'Why, who d'you know's got one?'

'All the directors, for a start. Allan Mark's got a list of twenty keyholders, but that's not including the unofficial duplicates.'

Allan was the building services manager, a tight-faced Scot who had a reputation as a heavy drinker. 'Allan would hardly give out duplicates,' Eliza said.

'I'm not saying he did, I'm saying there are duplicates he doesn't have listed.'

'For instance?'

'Only for instance. I know one of the old directors had a copy made before he handed his in when he was given the shove.'

'Why'd he do that?' a girl asked naively, while half a dozen others said, 'So who was it?'

'I'd hardly name names. It's putting him on the list, isn't it?'

'Oh come on, Phil, don't be a tease,' a thin girl called Anthea said. 'Now you've told us that much you have to tell us who.'

'No. Anyway I don't agree with all this private investigator crap, I think we ought to leave it to the police. Liz, there're some seats over there.' He set off through the crowd, both drinks in his hands, leaving Eliza to follow, which she did.

A chorus of pleas and grumbles followed them. As soon as they had claimed the cramped corner table Eliza said, 'Phil, why on earth did you tell them that? You must have known they won't let it rest now till you've given them a name.'

Phil gave her a defensive look. 'I didn't start anything, I just joined in the conversation. Everyone's talking about it.'

But she hadn't expected him to join in. And he had cut in so quickly that she knew he had been discussing it earlier, developing the scenario. He had been stupid to hint at a new suspect. Then that cheap line about the private investigator crap, designed to annoy everyone who was listening, and completely inconsistent with the curiosity he had evidently shown himself: why had he said that? It was crass, and crassness was not one of Phil's usual faults.

He was off balance, she supposed, like her; like everyone. She said carefully, 'I suppose so. I guess I ... don't like it. You were right, we ought to leave it to the police. You have told them, I take it?'

'Told them what?'

'About this guy who had the key.'

'That's not the point, Liz. The point is that lots of people have keys. They won't be able to pin this thing down that easily. In fact I wouldn't be surprised if they didn't manage to pin it down at all. Anyway, let's forget it. How are you?'

'I told you, I'm fine. How are you?'

'Missing you. Last night especially. And worrying about you, as I said. You pretend to be strong but I know you're not. Have you seen a doctor? You ought to get counselling after something horrific like that.'

So much for changing the subject. Eliza said, 'I'm not traumatized, Phil. It wasn't that big a deal. And I wasn't on my own last night, Rachel came over.'

'That's good, you need all your friends at a time like this. Now tonight you must come over to my house. I'll cook us supper.'

'That's kind of you, but I'm busy tonight.' Although she wasn't, she added silently to herself. She had no intention of cooking supper for James Connaught. If he did come to her door, she would turn him away again.

She drained her orange juice, a tricky business since it was loaded with ice cubes, and stood. 'Phil, I really must go now.'

'Tomorrow then. I don't want to push you, Liz, but I need to know when.'

'You are pushing me.' He had risen from his seat too, and was standing close to her, in her private space, making it difficult for her to escape through the crowd without touching him. 'Please, Phil. I'll give you a ring soon, but supper's not on, not at the moment. You know that.'

'It'd be good for you.'

'I honestly don't think so. We both need to give each other some space.'

'That's not true, Liz. I love you. I need to be with you.'

'Phil, you have to let me go.'

'I can't. Not like that.'

'You must.' Being so forthright with him made her uncomfortable, but she knew she was right. He had to realize the relationship was over for good. She took his arm, using his weight as a fulcrum to ease herself past him. There was no charge when she touched him: there never had been, with Phil. Feeling the lack, she knew she had always found it difficult to believe in the depth of emotion he professed, but there was no mistaking the anguish in his face as he caught her by the elbow and pulled her back.

'Not now, Liz, not when you're upset. This isn't the time to lose me. Cry off tonight and come round to mine. I'll do your favourite Irish stew.'

It was his favourite, not hers. Liz was his choice of name, not her chosen nickname. Phil might be mild-mannered, but he had a stolid streak of selfishness. 'No,' said Eliza, her voice rising, pulling free of his grip and retreating rapidly. He didn't follow her, and in any case would have found it difficult to guide his bulk through the narrow gaps between clumps of drinkers.

By the time she had battled her way to the back bar, Howard had gone. 'Maybe to Jez's do,' one of his colleagues suggested. 'You could catch up with him there.'

'I guess I could.' She didn't want to, though. And what would it gain her? A ten-minute dash, and a brief whispered conversation with a reluctant Howard in another heaving pub where she could not realistically raise any of the issues she wanted to talk about. Better to make the best of where she was, and try to get hold of Howard later. He couldn't really be avoiding her, surely. It was in his interests too for them to talk.

She fought her way to the far end of the bar, where the guard she thought was called Bill was holding court to a group of IT technicians.

'Ah, Mrs Stannard.' He raised a hand as she approached. 'What're you having?'

'Orange juice, but I'll get it, thanks.'

'No need, there's a kitty.'

She hoped he was telling the truth. Half the office seemed to be in the back bar, and it would be expensive if he and his colleagues were paying for them all. Six months' pay and a TUPE lump sum, generous though it was by most standards, wouldn't last him and his elderly mother forever.

'Hello gorgeous.'

It was Jack, the youngest of the guards. A gangling lad with a high forehead, receding hair and a thick blond moustache, he had always been cheerful, whatever time she had come into or left the office. He was cheery now; he was also so sozzled he could barely stand up.

What the hell; he had just been given the chop. He had every right to get blotto if he wanted to. Eliza smiled back at him. 'Well, hello,' she echoed. 'You're looking pretty gorgeous yourself.' She let him drape a heavy arm across her shoulders, and returned the damp kiss he planted on her cheek. 'I'm sorry you're going, Jack,' she added, and squeezed him round the waist. Heavens, he was heavy leaning on her shoulder. Six foot four or so, maybe fifteen stone of flesh and muscle.

'I'm sorry too, but what the fuck. Bloody shits who gave us

the push. Fuck 'em all, that's what I say. Kill 'em all.' He focused hazily on her face. 'Eliza Stannard, the lady with the stiff. Fucking Harding dead. Bloody good thing if you ask me. Kill 'em all, that's what we do. We made a start, eh?'

Camaraderie or not, this was too near the edge for her. She moved her feet, gave him a slight push, trying unsuccessfully to ease his weight off her, and said uneasily, 'Well, yes, but that won't do much good, Jack.'

'Bloody good if you ask me. The axeman dieth, that's what Hugh said. The axeman dieth. Quote, isn't it?'

'Something like.'

'The knifeman got him. Right here.' He jabbed his finger under her ribs. His aim was uncertain, but there was force behind it; Eliza gasped. Jack meanwhile was maundering on, 'Stuck it right in, right in his heart. Great guy doing that. The knifeman.'

'The knifeman?'

'The killer.' Jack hiccupped and grinned. 'All them cops running after him. They won't get him, won't get the knifeman, 'cos we'll stick together, us against the enemy. Eh, Liza? You're with us, aren't you?'

'This lad bothering you?'

With difficulty, Eliza turned her head. It was Bill – or was he called Stew? – who had brought over her orange juice.

She didn't want to be mean to Jack, so she said, not quite truthfully, 'He's all right.'

Bill said anyway, 'You watch it, Jack. Watch your mouth, eh. No swearing in front of ladies.'

'Liza's all right. We're con-shpiring, aren't we, Liza?'

'Sort of.' She met Bill's eyes. He seemed pretty sober: hopefully he would read her message and help her head Jack on to safer ground.

Instead he gave her an intent look and moved a step closer, drawing her into a triangle of himself and Jack. His voice lowered. 'You were there that morning, weren't you?'

Her stomach turned over, and not only because of Jack's stab. 'Sorry, but I don't want to talk about it.'

'Don't you worry, that's all I want to say. We're not telling nothing. Me and all the rest of us, including Jack here, he's a daft lad today but he's not stupid, y'know? We're not telling nothing that'll get no one in trouble.'

He held her eyes again. At that moment she felt close to him. Her unease dissolved. He was someone she could trust, she reckoned. And she could see the sense in what he was proposing.

'Sounds good to me,' she said in a low voice.

'Me too,' Jack said. 'Not stupid, yer old fucker.'

'And you haven't said nothing, have you?' Bill said.

She wasn't sure what he meant. But she said, anyway, 'No. Nothing that'll get anyone in trouble.'

'That's good. Sometimes things look bad, y'know, but you hunker down and they sort out all right. Bloody bad business that. Shitty bastard but I didn't want him dead. Nor did Jack really, it's just high talk, weren't it lad?'

'Oh, I want 'im dead,' Jack said belligerently.

'Shut it lad. This is it, gal. You know, I know, Jack knows, we all know, it wasn't none of us what did it. Some psychopath, some nutter, that's who it was. Got in somehow and went for him.'

'Could be.'

'It was. You tell yourself that, gal. It wasn't no one we know.'

'Bill, hey, say hello to us.'

They swung round together, to find a group of girls from the IT department at their shoulders. Marie Moss was pulling on Bill's arm, and they were chorusing Hi Bill, don't want you to go, you're lucky to be out of it, and all the rest. Bill caught Eliza's eye, grinned sheepishly, and let them lead him away.

Definitely Bill, Eliza thought to herself. That was the man who had been on the desk the morning before, and everyone was calling him Bill.

'Come sit with me, Liza. Got a bench over there,' Jack said.

'Sure, Jack.' She barely kept her feet as he stumbled, arm still round her, towards a table in the corner. He flopped on to the bench that ran along its near side, tossing his head forward and narrowly missing the full pints of bitter lined up along the edge of the table.

Eliza followed, smiling awkwardly at the other men around the table. Another guard whose name she didn't know was sitting opposite Jack, and between them, in the shadows at the edge of the back room, was the saturnine, newly clean-shaven, slightly chubby figure of Hugh Worning. She nodded at him, and he nodded back.

'Not at Jez's, Eliza?'

'As you see. Nor you?'

'I came on from there.'

'Oh?'

'Lewis was there, Ted Hawley, quite a lot of the old crowd. Good to see them all.'

'Ted Hawley at least.'

'Oh, of course,' he said, taking in her omission of Lewis. 'Well, most of them. And some of the directors turned up too. Or at least, Frank Mills did.' He smiled as if she would know what he meant; and she did, more or less. Hugh wasn't an intimate friend of hers, Lewis's or Jez's for that matter: he was a few years younger than all three of them, and worked in Major Sales, where none of them had ever worked. He was a sociable man, though, the kind you saw at every leaving do. Or so his friends said; his enemies called it obsessive networking. He was always pleasant, but he always left the faint impression that he had an agenda, one involving the advancement of Hugh Worning.

Still, Eliza thought with half her mind – the other half was still on Bill, and what he had said to her – Hugh wouldn't have got that much out of a few words exchanged with Frank, and it sounded as if, as usual, none of the new management had gone along. They generally kept well clear of all the presentations, drinks parties and so on. Hugh's nose was always sniffing, so it would not be lost on him that Frank had fouled up over the handover of power, and would be in no position to give a boost to anyone else's career for a while. Most likely he really had gone along simply for old times' sake, and it was just habit that had made him cast around for useful contacts. And there was no mileage at all in coming from Jez's do with its complement of retired directors, some of whom would not want to retire completely and would be working on plans for the future, on to this lower-level piss-up. So she shouldn't be cynical: he must have moved on purely to say goodbye to guys he had grown fond of.

It was Jack, stirring out of his stupor to take another gulp of beer, who offered her a different reason. 'Hugh an' me're con-shpiring, aren't we, Hugh. An' me an' Liza. All con-shpiring, that's what we've got to do.'

Her eyes flickered to Hugh's; and his currant-eyes met them. Hugh was not drunk, not like Jack. What she read in them was a warning.

She couldn't help remembering he had figured on Pat Shorten's list of people who'd been in St Jude's House at 6.30 the previous day. She had no idea what he had seen or not seen; what he had done or not done, for that matter.

Was it Hugh that Bill had been trying to protect? She searched her body for a shiver, some reaction to the thought that he might be a murderer. There wasn't one. She couldn't believe he was a murderer. Not him, not Jack, not Bill. Not anyone.

But her rational mind knew it had not been an outsider, a psychopath.

Hugh looked past her to Jack. He said calmly, 'We're just mates, Jack. Getting pissed. No one's conspiring, and you don't want to say that, someone one might misunderstand you.'

'You unnerstand me, Hugh.'

'Of course I do. Have another drink. I'll have a toast with you. To liberty.'

'Yeah, liberty.' The other guard raised his glass. 'Liberty, equality, fraternity.'

There were worse things to drink to, Eliza thought. She drank to that.

22

Eliza left the Brown Cow once she had drunk her second orange juice. The budget called; plus the note Donaldson had demanded, her team member Russell's report on his meeting with an Office Services manager at the DoE, and three or four job costings, all of which had to be checked and approved before being passed upwards to Donaldson for further approval; or if they were sizeable, to the board as a whole. This was apparently what the new management regarded as doing away with unnecessary bureaucracy. Par for the return of proposals sent to Donaldson was running at five weeks.

She worked solidly till seven, and even then she had barely explored the foothills of her mountainous action tray. She had heard nothing from James Connaught. That was clear enough, she reckoned: he would hardly expect supper with her without some kind of confirmation, so he too must have thought better of the idea. He would almost certainly be working late, probably sending out for a takeaway or settling for a room-service meal at the Mornington when he got back there. At least she assumed he was staying at the Mornington, not that it was any of her business.

Seven felt late enough to her. Her mind hadn't really been focused on the work anyway, and she was approaching the point of tiredness when she would start to make stupid mistakes.

Back home, she checked her post – only circulars and the weekly postcard from her sister Amelia in Sydney – and made the bed she had left rumpled that morning. She wanted to shower and then hang out in her dressing gown. But there was a small chance James would turn up on her doorstep, and she didn't like to undress in case he did so. He might read it as the kind of invitation she did not intend to give him. So she settled for staying in her work clothes, and rummaged in the fridge for something effortless she could make for supper. An omelette and salad felt about right.

It was a day she would be happy to put behind her.

It occurred to her as she was breaking the eggs into a bowl that she had forgotten to chase Personnel about Martha's redundancy

application. She ought to do that, it would be good to feel that
she had done something positive for someone that day. She left
the half-prepared meal, went through to her study, and made a
note on a Post-It which she stuck to the inner flap of her handbag.

The doorbell rang when she was back in the hall. Damn. How
was she to play this? He had probably seen her moving shadow
through the glass of the door, so it was no good pretending not to
be at home.

But when she opened the door it was Phil who stood on the
doormat. Phil, to whom she had not given a single thought since
she had left him in the Brown Cow. She was so surprised that he
had shouldered his way past her before she could move to prevent
him.

'I know you said no, but I worry about you, Liz. So I'm going
to take you out for supper, give you a chance to relax a bit.'

She was more embarrassed than angry. Relieved, even. Breaking
up with Phil might be turning into a slow tedious business, but
that at least was something she knew how to deal with.

'Phil, I told you I was busy tonight.'

'But you're here now. You haven't eaten yet, have you? Come
on, get your coat.'

'Shall I say it again? No means no. I'm sorry, Phil, but I'm not
going to do that.'

Phil stared at her. He did not glance at her clothes; he focused,
a little too obsessively, on her face. Although that had its advan-
tages, she thought silently. He was not the kind of man who
would notice whether she had changed for an evening out. So
long as she kept him out of the kitchen, with its evidence of her
planned omelette, she would be able to fake an appointment,
leave the house and go – it didn't matter where, so long as it was
somewhere he couldn't follow her. Circle round, and come back
to collapse in peace.

Whatever Phil read in her expression, it was enough to puncture
his brief moment of confidence. She could see him taking it in that
he would have to rethink his plan.

'What're you doing, having a drink with Rachel? Or is it the
Fem-Man meeting? You can spare me a few minutes first.' He
headed on into her sitting room and sat on the sofa. Knees spread,
hands clasped between them, he was less the belligerent lover than
the forlorn one.

'It's warm in here,' he said. He took off his glasses, which had misted up, and proceeded to polish them on a handkerchief. Eliza stood watching him. Phil didn't look remotely like someone who could help her relax. He looked more like he was in need of help himself. What a shitty business it was, breaking up with someone who didn't want to let you go. But she wasn't tempted to relent. Most of all he irritated her, with his sheer neediness, his obtuseness, his awkwardness.

Phil put back his glasses and blinked up at her. 'Sit down,' he said, patting the cushion next to him.

'Phil.' She took a breath. 'I really do appreciate your concern, but it's not necessary. I told you that. I'm perfectly OK. I know you're sorry we've broken up, and I'm –'

'Liz, honestly.' Phil scrambled clumsily to his feet, and grabbed her hands, tightening his grip as she tried to pull free. 'You must stop talking like that. You've been feeling a bit off colour, I know, but that's no reason to muck up our relationship. Now why don't you phone Rachel and tell her you can't make it, and –'

'Phil!' She yanked sharply, and her hands came away from his, making Phil take a step backwards in reaction. 'I can't have this. I don't want you coming round here uninvited. And right now I'd like you to leave.'

'Liz, you haven't listened to a word I've said.'

'Yes I have. I've listened to every word, but I wonder if you've heard anything I've said.'

'You need someone to love you, someone to care for you. And that's me. You know it is. You'll never find anyone who –'

This unpromising sentence was broken into by the doorbell ringing again.

Oh my God. It was all too likely that this would be James. Phil had paused in his outburst, but only for a couple of seconds. He ignored the bell and started up again. 'What I mean is, we're so good together, you know we are. And I know that when you're not off balance you –' He was pursuing her steadily across the room, she retreating to avoid his grabbing her, and she was now caught in the alcove not occupied by the CD player, her legs backed against a small Victorian button-backed chair.

Another long trill on the bell was matched by her own loud 'Phil!' He hadn't stopped talking, but she put out a hand to the centre of his chest, and gave a sharp shove. Momentarily, it unbalanced him, and she pressed on quickly. 'In case you didn't hear it, that was the door. I'm going to answer it. And you're going to leave.'

Phil's heavy brows lowered behind his glasses. 'Who is it?'

'That's none of your business.'

'Of course it's my business.'

'No it is not.' Oh God, what a mess. Was there any chance it was someone other than James? Not really, unless the Jehovah's Witnesses had picked that moment to call on her. Was there any chance Phil wouldn't recognize him? That was possible, she thought frantically. But he was clearly going to react badly to any other man coming to her house. It would be worse, though, to turn James away. That would make Phil think he had won, and as for what James would think ...

A third blast on the doorbell decided her. She pushed Phil again, and managed to scramble past him and go to open the door.

'Hi,' James said. He was carrying what looked like a bunch of service-station flowers and a couple of carrier bags, one of which smelled of curry.

'James. I'm afraid this is a really bad moment. I –' She was aware Phil had followed her, so it was no surprise when he interrupted.

'Who the hell are you?'

'Phil, for Christ's sake!'

Raising her voice to him might have been necessary, but it wasn't helpful. Phil, already agitated, upped his volume too.

'For Christ's bloody sake indeed! What the hell are you doing, Liz? Are you cheating on me?'

For an instant Eliza was too horrified to react. She could feel her face burning. James took advantage of the silence.

'Eliza, what do you want to do? Do you want me to go, or do you want this guy to leave?'

'Phil's leaving right now.'

Phil stared at her, then he turned and stared at James. James was in his business suit, his tie a white flash of lightning on midnight blue, his shirt a slash of white too in the light of the porch. Eliza glanced from him back at Phil, with his nondescript jacket and slacks, his too-short hair, his thick-framed glasses. It was a painful contrast, something even Phil seemed to take in.

'Liz, please ...?'

'We'll talk soon. Now, go, please.'

'I don't like this.'

Well, that made three of them, Eliza thought. She could think of nothing more to say that would not make things worse. So she stood there in silence as James stepped aside to let Phil go past him. A slightly hunched figure, they watched him make his way down the path, down the street.

Eliza breathed out.

'I'm sorry', James said. 'Mills told me you were single.'

'Actually I am. I split up with Phil a month ago. But for some reason he seemed to think I'd want him to come and support me.'

'Support you?' For a moment he looked blank. 'Oh. Post-traumatic stress, or something?'

'Or something, perhaps.'

'Are you in need of support?'

He sounded more curious than anything else; she wouldn't have called it concern. And she didn't sense that support was something he intended to offer. Fair enough, maybe: that was what you looked to old friends for, not new lovers. But it was a little – cold, she felt. Putting that together with his assumption that he would be welcome at her house again, when he hadn't bothered to confirm before turning up there, it made her wary. The James Connaughts of this world take women for granted, she thought, in the way that the Phil Curtins cannot afford to do.

She said, carefully, 'I think I'm a pretty strong woman.'

'I don't doubt it. But it's a situation when you need to take a lot of care. You ought to call the police if he does that again.'

'It won't need that, I'm sure.' It would have felt disloyal to Phil to do so. She might not want him, but nor did she want to humiliate him, let alone to make an enemy of him. 'I'll give him a ring later and square things.'

'Sounds wise.' They had been talked in the corridor, but as he spoke James hefted the carrier bags in his hand. 'Take these,' he said, handing over the flowers, red carnations. 'Through this way?'

It occurred to her that she could ask him too to leave. But she took the flowers, and led the way through to her kitchen cum dining room. 'I'll get some plates.'

'Oh,' James said, putting the carriers on the counter and taking in the bowl of whipped egg. 'I guess you really weren't expecting me.'

'I wasn't expecting either of you. But we'll eat, now you're here.'

'Well, that's a relief. I've had nothing since breakfast. Wine?'

'Not for me, thanks.'

He gave her a narrow look. 'Are you pissed off with me for getting you to look up Janine?'

'Not especially. I guess I was just thinking all this is pretty unwise.'

'Probably is. But even if you don't want any support, I could sure do with some. I need someone I can trust around here. Nobody else comes to mind. Bloody Summerfield's already shaping up to be a disaster, and I can't see there's anyone else who's remotely capable of taking charge, so I'm going to be stuck here for a while at least. Unless you can suggest someone?'

'I wouldn't suggest Phil,' Eliza said dryly.

'You mean that guy works at RUS?'

She paused, squatting by the door of the cupboard that held her dinner plates, and turned to him. 'This is a small city. RUS is a big employer. Everyone knows everyone. Everyone knows everyone's business.'

'How glad I am I don't live in one of those. I get the message. Or part of it. Should I read that as meaning you actually know who killed Harding?'

'Christ, no!'

'But you'll find it hard when the police get them.'

True, she thought, but did not say. She straightened up and put the plates on the table. 'Perhaps I'll have some wine after all,' she found herself saying.

'Toss me a corkscrew,' he responded, drawing a couple of bottles out of the second carrier. 'You can dish up while I open it.'

'I'll put it all in the oven for a minute to keep warm while I sort out these flowers first.'

They did these tasks in a silence that was not quite uncomfortable, though it was definitely not cosy. Eliza was thinking that Phil clearly had not recognized James. But what were the odds he would tell someone of the encounter, ask around, find out who he was? She thought they were not overly high. Phil had plenty of acquaintances, but he was the kind of man who confided rarely in others, and what would he say, even if he had someone to say it to? It was not an incident any of them would choose to boast about.

These thoughts straightened in her head, she considered passing them on to James. No. He could sweat a little.

She put the flowers in a white china vase, and set them on the table. The flowers she had bought the day before were in her sitting room. Too many flowers, she thought. Almost funereal.

They had almost finished the chicken dansak, sag aloo and dal, and were on their second glasses of wine, when the phone rang.

'Leave it,' James said.

'I will. It's probably Phil anyway.'

After a few rings, the answerphone cut in. Eliza had forgotten it would do that. Now James would have to listen to Phil maundering on. Except it was not Phil. It sounded like a woman. A few words Eliza couldn't catch, then a sudden shout of 'No! I w–'

Scuffling noises. Then more shouts in the woman's voice. 'Oh God, help me, help me, help me! A high thin wild insane scream of sheer agony; then a kind of liquid choking sound; then a heavy silence. And the click of the phone being disconnected.

'What in God's name was that?' he said.

23

The supper forgotten, she replayed the tape. And again. From close up they could hear more. The woman had started by saying, 'I bloody am. I'm telling her now.' And there was a breath or two, sharp as if indrawn, after the woman's scream, in what Eliza had taken at first for silence. She had the sensation for a moment that this was a piece of play-acting. But she knew it was not.

'Who is it, do you know?' James asked.

'I'm not sure.'

'But you think?'

She turned and met his eyes. 'I think it was Janine Broughton.'

He considered a moment. 'I think you could be right. I'd better phone the police.'

It was her phone, but she did not quibble. James rang 999 and tapped his hand impatiently on the oak desk on which her phone sat as he waited for the operator to put him through. He gave the details cleanly and tersely. 'Yes, screams. No, I've told you we can't be sure. I'm telling you to check.' Telling you, she thought. A pause, in which she could half-hear the voice on the other end of the line. 'Yes, we'll go there ourselves. Right now.'

He put the phone down. 'Let's go. I'll drive.'

His car turned out to be a dark green Mercedes E320, sleek, shiny, almost new. It was little more than a mile from her house to the Mornington. He drove fast, but not recklessly, and parked on the double yellow lines opposite the hotel. The lobby was cluttered with suitcases, and there was a queue at the reception desk. James shouldered past it, saying firmly, 'Excuse me. This is an emergency.' Eliza envied his certainty. She felt certain of nothing, not even of what she had heard. It was unreal, a nightmare; the whole evening seemed unreal.

'No, no,' James was saying. She could hear him over the murmur of the waiting guests. He was not shouting, but he spoke with loud confidence. 'I called them, they should be here.'

The door to the street swung open, and two uniformed police officers came in. 'James,' Eliza called out.

'Thank God.' The reception area had gone silent; the people in the queue stepped aside for him. He glanced over to her. 'Eliza, what number room is it?'

'Now let's take this slowly, sir.'

She thought for a moment James would lose his cool; but he did not. And what was the rush, she thought wildly? If she had not been dreaming it, then the woman who had called her was past needing them to run to her. He must have realized that too, as he calmly gave the police the minimal details they possessed.

The policemen exchanged glances, then one said, 'To be honest, sir, I should think it was just a lover's quarrel. But as you're so concerned I'll have the receptionist ring up to the room.'

Everyone in the lobby watched as the officer made his request, a red-haired receptionist dialled the internal phone, and over the silence, they could hear its distant ringing.

'There's no answer, sir.' Perhaps she was talking to the policeman, but she was looking at James.

'I'm sorry, sir,' the other policeman said.

'I want you to check the room. Now.'

'Sir, we don't normally –' the receptionist began.

James cut in sharply. 'This is not normal, this is an emergency. I am seriously concerned for this woman's safety. Now please give me a key and if the police won't, I'll check the room myself.'

The second receptionist behind the desk said quietly, 'I'll get the duty manager.'

'Look, can't you just –' one of the waiting guests began, but his voice faded away. They waited, all of them, until the duty manager arrived. A slim woman in her thirties, she listened as one of the policemen repeated the story. Eliza reckoned James would have preferred to tell it himself. It did not occur to her to say anything.

'We don't like to embarrass our guests, but in the circumstances I think we'd better check. Can I have the spare key to 352, Lorraine?'

Lorraine handed it over. They all set off for the lift – the duty manager, the two policemen, James and Eliza. The duty manager led the way to room 352. The corridor was quiet and anonymous. Eliza thought, we must have imagined this. Both of us. We're on edge, we misheard. And it can't have been Janine. Why on earth would Janine have rung me, anyway?

The duty manager knocked, but there was no reply. She called out that the police were there. Again, silence. She put the key to the lock. James took Eliza's hand. They were only three or four feet from the door. She saw the door to Janine's room swing open, right open, banging against the outer wall of the bathroom. A streetlight shone through the net curtains at the far window. She could see only the bathroom wall and a narrow strip of window and bed beyond, but immediately she knew the worst had happened.

She pulled free of James's grip, pushed past the duty manager, and half-ran, half-stumbled down the narrow passage between the bathroom and the wardrobe. She did not stop till she was at the foot of the far bed.

Janine lay on its orange counterpane. She was on her back, her arms flung out. Her sightless eyes bulged up at the ceiling. Her mouth was open wide. A scarlet ring circled her neck, and there were dark red stains clogging the ribs of her chenille jersey. Blood pooled on the counterpane and spattered the cream-papered walls. The room stank of shit and fear and death.

'Oh my giddy aunt,' one of the policemen said.

24

Eliza woke with sullen heaviness the next morning. Slowly she became aware that she was in a strange room, in a strange double bed. She sat up, and took in an orange counterpane.

There was a black moment until she came to her senses. Orange, orange and the red pool of blood.

James, naked, was holding her tightly to him. She was on her knees on the bed, and he was standing by its side. 'Lizzy. Lizzy, gently. Gently, Lizzy.'

She took a deep sobbing breath. And another. It occurred to her that she had been screaming. Her throat felt tight and sore. Her hands groped, found the broad warm flesh of his back, and knew he was real. They stayed there for a moment, then she slowly loosed him and he loosed her, keeping his hands lightly on her shoulders.

'I didn't dream it.'

'I'm afraid you didn't,' he said gravely.

'The counterpanes are like hers.'

'I didn't think about that last night. Maybe I should have taken you home, but it was so late by the time the police let us go.'

I could have noticed it myself, Eliza thought. It wasn't his job. Not his job to take her home either. But it was, evidently, his room. In which she too had stayed. She glanced around it as he removed his hands from her shoulders and padded over to the desk. It was not a plain rectangle like Janine's, it was one of the hotel's historic rooms. A couple of heavy oak beams drew wavy lines across the low ceiling. A diamond-paned window looked out onto grey sky. The furniture was carved black oak, the beds higher and narrower than standard hotel king-size. A laptop computer, lid open, sat on a desk against the wall opposite the two beds.

She watched James take a kettle from the desktop, and go to the bathroom to fill it. These prosaic details, the beams, the grey light, the practical way in which James, oblivious to his nakedness, plugged in the kettle, brought her steadily to clear wakefulness.

James tried to switch on a table light, realized he had unplugged it for the kettle, and went to the door to turn on the dim central light. Finally he came to sit by her.

'How much do you remember?'

'Oh, I remember it all.' What did he imagine, a fit of amnesia? She didn't doubt she was in shock, but every detail was sharp in her memory. She could even taste the chicken dansak on her unwashed teeth. She could see Janine's slightly ratty unwashed hair, though her mind shied away from the details of her wounds.

'Except the police interview,' she added. 'That's a bit vague in my mind. I don't think I can have been much help.'

'They'll talk to you again today. Last night you were pretty obsessed about her picking you to call. You didn't know her that well, you said?'

'No. Hardly at all. And we – we didn't get on, when I came over her to talk to her. That's still mystifying. Why on earth did she ring me?'

The kettle was hissing. James ignored it. 'Well, if you don't know, I sure don't. But it's revealing, I guess. If it's any consolation, I'm sure they'll get him. The Harding killing I had my doubts about, because it was so bloody clinical, not a fingerprint, not a stray hair, nothing apparently, but this was a messy job. He'll have left traces. You know how sophisticated it all is these days. It might take them a while, but they'll track down who it was.'

These comments percolated into her brain, which still seemed to be functioning only intermittently. 'You mean – you think – whoever killed the Beaver ...?'

'The Beaver?'

'Sorry, Mr Harding.'

'Not a bad name for him.' He rose and went to make the tea. 'Did he know?'

'About the name? Heaven knows.'

'He wouldn't have taken it kindly. I liked old Patrick, he was a real buccaneer in his way, but even his best friend couldn't pretend he had a sense of humour. Sorry, I'm drifting. Do I think the killings are connected? Yes. Don't you?'

To her they had been quite different. The bizarre posed revelation of the Beaver, dead; the blatancy of Janine's warm corpse. The terrible immediacy of the screams on their phone, and their terrible distance, the inability to do anything, stop it. Howard, shocked in a calm kind of way. James – she could not really figure out how James had reacted. Pretty well, she supposed. It was unnerving how readily she had let him take control, but at the

same time it was reassuring that he had. He was evidently not one
of life's panickers.

Slowly she said, 'I suppose they must be. But why? The Beaver
I could understand, sort of. But Janine?'

'You could understand?'

The incredulous note in his voice was mirrored on his
face as he turned to her. That was a dumb thing to say,
Eliza thought vaguely. If she had had an illusion for a while
that this man was her ally, that comment had definitely
shattered it.

She looked down at her hands, and the bare thighs on which
they rested. She glanced across at the other bed. The coverlet was
smooth, the surface strewn with male garments, plus her own
purple suit and her sleeveless top. Clearly it had not been slept
in. Ergo, this man and she had slept naked in each other's arms.
He was, she thought – not with fear, but with some surprise – a
stranger.

And he was a stranger with whom she had been mad, mad
to share her uncensored thoughts. Any one of her longstanding
colleagues would have known what she meant in an instant.
Indeed, what she had meant, and what she had said, was pretty
mild compared with many of the comments she had heard in
the pub the day before. But that did not excuse it. Harding's
colleagues, the newcomers, had not been in the pub. Nor had
the police come to that. In those circumstances, it made a kind
of sense to talk of the whole thing like an interesting puzzle in
an Agatha Christie novel. In the wider world, all, all of them had
to talk as if it was a horror, an outrage that the B – no, *Mister*
Harding had been killed.

She was conscious that James had not moved, that he was
standing across the room, still staring at her. Instinctively she
slipped back under the sheets, pulling the orange coverlet up over
her breasts.

She spoke slowly, hesitantly, quietly enough that he had to
come closer to hear her.

'I can't imagine how anyone could kill someone. It's just – not
something that happens to people you know. I can understand
getting upset, getting angry, making a bloody idiot of yourself,
like Phil last night.' And us. You and me, she thought, that's
pretty idiotic too, and did not say. She went on, 'I can understand

being ambitious and being willing to do others down to get on, not because I've done it, because I haven't, but because I've seen people do it. I can understand why people wished Harding would disappear down a black hole, because he messed up their lives. But I can't imagine how any of those could lead to something as ... stupid as murder.'

'I think you can,' James said coolly. He retreated to the desk, and she was half-aware, although she did not look, of his tearing open a couple of foil-and-plastic cartons and adding milk to the tea. He brought two cups over, set them down on the small table between the two beds, and sat on the second bed, facing her. 'So can I, to be fair. It's not so bloody unimaginable when we see it on the telly every day. Harding was hated, wasn't he?'

'Yes.'

'Generally hated. By lots of people.'

She nodded.

'I didn't really take that in.' He took a gulp of his tea. 'The psychology of the takeover.'

She nodded again.

'So this is all to do with the redundancies. You'll have to forgive me if I'm being bloody stupid, but I just don't fathom it. It's not a power thing, it can't be, there wasn't any management buy-out bid. And OK, he's been letting people go, but from all I heard they were queuing up to take the money and run.'

'You don't understand,' she said.

'Evidently not.' She was conscious of him looking steadily at her. 'I realize you said something of the kind to me on Thursday,' he went on. 'In a way I didn't take it seriously, which I suppose was very obtuse of me. I thought, I don't know, that you were building up the antagonism as part of the thing between you and me.' She didn't reply, and after a moment he went on, 'I'm trying to be honest with you. I'm being blatantly honest and indiscreet or tactless or whatever because I want you to be honest with me. I want there to be honesty between us, because in all this shit I'd like to have someone to trust, and that someone is you. Do you understand?'

Slowly, she nodded.

He did not speak again for a moment. He leaned over and touched her shoulder where it crested the orange coverlet. Her skin prickled, but she did not move. His fingers caressed her, then withdrew.

'So. You're an intelligent and open-minded woman, you've got everything to gain from privatization or so I'd have thought, and you still understand why –' He stopped, then resumed, 'No. You still hated Patrick Harding.'

'True.'

He made a short noise that in other circumstances she would have taken for a laugh. He stood, pushed the covers back, and got into the pristine bed he had been sitting on. He leaned back, hands behind his head, and said to the beamed ceiling, 'Foxton actually suggested an Orient Express type thing. You know, everyone taking a hand. A conspiracy. I'm afraid I laughed.'

'That didn't happen, I'm sure.'

'No. This Janine thing makes it more obvious. Poor girl.' He paused. 'I think I need you to tell me what happened yesterday.'

'When I saw her, earlier?'

'When you went to the hotel, yes.'

'I'll try.'

Once she had started to speak the words came readily. She outlined the whole incident more or less as it had taken place, pausing only to concentrate on remembering all their conversation. She did not try to censor it. It seemed necessary to her that he should know the truth, or as near to it as she could come. He listened intently.

'Being bullied,' he said, into the silence that followed.

'That's what she said, I'm sure, or at least that's the impression I was given. Oh, and she said – well, not quite said, but implied – that Harding was having an affair.'

'With her?'

'No, with someone else. She didn't tell me who.'

'But you thought she knew.'

'Secretaries usually do.'

'True.' He was still staring at the ceiling. She watched his profile. His nose was long, his chin strong, the lines of his face and neck clean. She would not have called him handsome, his features were too coarse for that, but it was a beautiful profile, at least to her. It occurred to her that he was probably younger than her. Not by much, but at thirty-seven she was very conscious of her own age.

'I wouldn't know who, in case you were wondering,' he said. 'If he'd had a mistress in London I might have heard about it, or met her even, but not if it was someone up here. We weren't bosom buddies, just business contacts.'

'So you did the financing of this deal?'

'More or less.'

'It was a good organization in the civil service days, but not one that was easy to transfer over. By the time they'd finished slimming it down for privatization it was a mess, and he hasn't turned it round, in fact he's made it worse. I know you got it cheap, but there's nothing secure. We don't make anything, we're just middlemen. We're losing contracts; it could all go down the plughole.'

He gave his short semi-laugh again. 'You're quite likely right, but it's not particularly relevant to us. You look at it from the point of view of an ongoing business, but we don't see it like that. It's a transaction, three-year funding maximum. On that basis we'll make a good profit.'

'That's obscene.'

He turned to her now. 'My dear, you're too earnest. You talk as if life ought to be fair, and it isn't. There are legitimate opportunities to make a killing, and we take them. If we didn't, someone else would. I don't think it would have added to the sum of world happiness if the Saturn Trust had nobly stood back on this one. Anyway, as I said, there wasn't a management proposal.'

'That was Frank Mills's idea,' Eliza said. 'Apparently. And a bloody bad idea too, so it's generally reckoned. Not that I'm high enough to be in with the decisions.'

'Then blame him. Blame the government, or the last government. Don't blame Saturn, and don't blame Patrick Harding. He was just working to the targets we set him, and they were pretty tough targets too.'

But I do blame him, she though. She knew her reasons would not win over this man.

'We ought to get up,' he said. 'I said I'd get you to the police station by 10. We'll have breakfast up here, shall we? I didn't order last night, but I can phone down now.'

'I don't know that I'm hungry.'

'Rubbish. You didn't get to finish your supper last night. You need to eat, and I do too.' He leaned over and picked up the phone.

Eliza watched him. When he put down the receiver she said, 'You're not going back down to London?'

'Today I will, but I'll have to be mostly up here for the next week or two at least. It's a bloody pain, but there's not much alternative. As you so wisely say, RUS isn't in the strongest shape at the moment. It needs someone to make sure it doesn't sink under the waves, and as I mentioned yesterday, I can't see that Summerfield is the man.'

'We all thought it'd be Frank Mills. Not that he's popular with everyone. He's a pain in lots of ways. But he's been chief exec before.'

'You're not that dumb, Eliza. There is no way I'm letting the organization go native again.' He stood up, and reached for her hand. She let him pull her out of bed. To her surprise he didn't let her go, but pulled her to him. She felt the length of his naked body against hers. He kissed her, briefly but hard. She felt his cock stir.

'You can shower first,' he said. Then, 'No. Later.' He guided her back down to the bed, followed her on to it, his body on hers, then bent to kiss her again, twining his fingers in her hair, so they were hard on her scalp as he pulled her to him.

We didn't fuck last night, she thought with sudden clarity. Until then she couldn't have said, but she knew now that they had not. And she didn't want – but almost before the thought was articulated she felt what he must have felt. The smell, the feel, the chemistry that is the only thing strong enough to drive away death, or its shadow. The sharp fierce incomprehension, the anger he needed to exercise, or to exorcise. He was not rough but he gave her no time, one more kiss, her hand drawn by his to his cock, the feel of it thickening and hardening under her fingers, his fingers testing her readiness, then he came in to her.

He was briefly motionless, filling her. Then he moved, swiftly, rhythmically, building fast to a climax. His teeth were set, his lips drawn back over them, his eyes fixed on the wall and not on her. She clutched his shoulders, pulling herself into his rhythm. She chased him to the finish line, did not reach it in time, and was still moving around him as he gasped and stiffened. At least he did not despise her need. He held himself in position as she screwed him into her, rotated her hips around him, found the pressure point she needed to open the door and fall through.

'Yes,' he said only, as they lay spent together. Half a minute, and he was up. It was he who showered first; again, she followed.

25

They breakfasted rapidly and in near-silence – a roll for her, a croissant for him – then he drove her to the Central Police Station. She had asked to be taken home so she could change, but he had refused: no time, he had said.

It was 10.10. He did not stay, did not get out of his car. 'Thanks for the lift,' she said when he drew up outside the station.

'No problem.' He did not kiss her; somehow she did not expect it. As she waited in the interview room to which she had been ushered, she thought mostly of the sex. He was rougher than the handful of other lovers she had had; much rougher, if she was honest. It unnerved her that she had responded to that in him.

She thought of his dark green Mercedes. They shared a taste for fast cars, clearly, although she could not have afforded one like his.

Phil drove a Land Rover. He was passionate about Land Rovers, he belonged to an owners' club and went to rallies. That was not a passion she shared. Her ex-husband Lewis had no interest in cars. He had bought whatever caught his eye, a Volvo one year, a Renault 9 the next.

She thought also about Bill the security man, and what he had said in the Brown Cow. She supposed he knew something; something she didn't. But she didn't know what it was, which eased her conscience, since she wouldn't have pointed the police in his direction.

She knew she was not thinking about Janine, and yet she was; the screams were with her all the time.

She waited ten minutes perhaps, then the door opened and Inspector Crane came in with a young woman dressed in denims and a grey sweatshirt.

'Getting a bit of a habit, this.'

Eliza had taken a chair at one side of a brown Formica table. Crane and the woman sat down opposite her as he spoke. His belligerence shook her. She even felt herself jump.

'Sir,' the woman said.

'It's true. If anyone's in the thick of this bloody mess you are. You told the officers last night you hardly knew this girl. So how come she picked you to phone?'

'Sir!'

'Don't worry, I'm not going to break the rules. But I want this bastard, and I'm not going to let anyone get in my way. So now that's clear, let's start the interview properly. Carol, switch the tape on. You know me, Miss Stannard, Inspector Crane, and this is Detective Constable Joyce.' He went with a kind of half-controlled aggression through the routine of spelling out the date and time for the record, of warning her. She could have a solicitor with her if she wished, he said, though he added that he didn't think she'd killed the girl herself.

Very reassuring. What he probably thought was that she knew who had. It occurred to Eliza that it might actually be wise to ask for someone to be with her. Not necessarily a solicitor, since she thought Crane was telling the truth, and she was not a serious suspect. A friend, perhaps – but she couldn't think of a friend she could ask, any more than James Connaught could think of a decent new boss for RUS. Not Rachel. She thought – she knew – the police would ask her things she didn't want Rachel to know. Not anyone still at RUS. They probably wouldn't allow that anyway, since everyone at RUS was presumably to some degree a suspect.

'I'm sure you didn't,' DC Joyce said.

With her scruffy clothes and tousled shoulder-length brown hair, she seemed relaxed and open, in spite of the hostile situation. I could get on with her, Eliza thought. In different circumstances. Meanwhile, in these circumstances, DC Joyce would probably do as someone to keep Crane in line. She didn't know a solicitor she could call on a Saturday morning, anyway. She hadn't spoken to any solicitors since her divorce, and she wouldn't have asked for the man who had handled that.

She said slowly, 'It's OK. I'll do without.'

'Good choice, it'd only hold us up. But let's get this clear: we need to know everything. None of this crap you gave my colleagues last night. None of these timelines that don't check out. D'you want a coffee, then we'll get started.'

'Yes please,' Eliza said. DC Joyce phoned for it. She did not go for it herself, and the three of them waited in silence until a uniformed PC brought in three thick white china cups in which khaki liquid slopped.

Eliza was thinking, I never got to talk to Howard Nkolo. I

should have done that yesterday. I should have made bloody sure
I did it yesterday. It was too late now.

When he had gone Crane said, 'So let's start with Ms Broughton,
how you come to know her.'

It was simply told. Janine had come to work at the RUS Group,
Eliza already worked there, and they dealt with each other on
mostly – no, entirely, as far as Eliza could recall – routine matters.
Janine fixed meetings, primarily. Sometimes she requested reports
and briefings. She had only been with the company for six months.
Eliza had made no effort to become friends with her, and they had
had no lunches or coffees together. She knew next to nothing
about the other woman, she realized now.

Crane sat in a hunched position, elbows on the Formica table
that separated them, hands clasped, eyes on her, listening carefully.
'Let me get this straight,' he said when she paused. 'You didn't
want to leave RUS.'

Eliza shook her head.

'So you meant to stay, to make a career there. Didn't you ever
try to get thick with the chief exec's PA?'

'Get thick?' Eliza repeated.

'Is that such a weird idea?'

Yes. No. She groped for the words to explain. 'I wouldn't have
tried to make friends just to get influence, not unless I'd got on
with her, and I didn't. Not that I disliked her particularly, but we
didn't really hit it off.'

'So who did hit it off with her?'

'I don't know. You'd have to ask the other directors' secretaries, Crystal Canning maybe. I think she was quite friendly with
Janine.'

'She says not.'

'Oh.'

'So this girl came up to Costhorpe, staying in a hotel on her
own, and nobody put themselves out for her? No one asked her
round to supper or anything?'

'I don't know that anyone did.'

'Wasn't that bloody awful?'

Riled, Eliza said, 'It was an awful time. She came in the middle
of it. Right at the start we'd tried being nice to Harding and
it all backfired, he was vile to everyone, he fired lots of people
and didn't promote any of us and brought in all these outsiders.

Janine came six weeks, two months later, and she was another sodding outsider getting a job one of us could have had, and overpaid for it too. Did I fall over my feet to be nice to her? No I didn't. She wasn't my responsibility anyway, she was a secretary, a director's secretary. I have a section to run, I'm nice to them. I have colleagues, and they're other sector managers. I don't see it as my job to hold secretaries' hands. If it was anyone's job, it was Crystal's. If she didn't do it, how was I to know?'

'What a shit awful place you seem to work in.'

'Hole in one.'

'So did this Janine hate you?'

It stopped her. She closed her eyes. Janine's distorted face, ribboned with tears, was brutally drawn on her eyelids.

'Yes,' she said on a whisper.

'You're uncomfortable about that.'

She opened them again, and met Crane's cool grey stare. She could see black depths in the centre of his pupils, unplumbable black.

He was just doing his job, she supposed. And she did want to cooperate. She had no problem with seeing whoever had killed Janine caught and locked up for several lifetimes. But she did not want to open her soul to him. She wished he hadn't asked her those questions, and she wished even more that she hadn't given such honest answers.

'Not personally,' she said, more evenly. 'I don't want you misunderstanding. It wasn't simply that she hated me. It was generic, all the new people, all the old. I think – I'm trying to say – in some way Harding and his people hated us just as much as we hated them. Despised is maybe a better word. I saw it in Janine, but only yesterday, never when she was at work. At work we just – didn't connect. There are 800 people at St Jude's House; up till last December there were 1,200. You can't connect with all of them, however sociable you are. I didn't have any real reason to connect with Janine.'

'So why you?'

'Why me?'

'Your number was written on the pad by the phone in her room. You've told us she phoned you just before she was attacked, or at least it sounded over the phone as if she was being attacked. Why did she choose you? And what was she going to tell you that the murderer really, really didn't want you to hear?'

'I've no idea.'

'I'm sorry, but that won't do.'

He didn't sound sorry, she thought. She clenched her hands, letting the nails make white moons at the base of her thumbs. The reason that crouched in her mind was that Janine had been taking revenge. She had known some kind of trouble was brewing – pray God she hadn't known how bad – and she had wanted Eliza to be implicated.

It shouldn't have been a personal hatred, but it had been. She knew that too. There was no possible reason, beyond the accident of her discovering Harding's corpse. Perhaps that had been reason enough.

She would not have said this to Crane, but she could see she had to give him something. So she took a breath, and gave him instead an even-handed account of her encounters with Janine, first in Ken Thursby's office, then at the Mornington Arms. She told the truth, all of the truth, even if a part of her thought she was saying too much.

'So,' Crane said, half to the tape recorder, 'she said she was being bulled, and she said Harding had been having an affair.'

'She hinted at both. Those were the messages I got.'

'So who was it? This mysterious mistress?'

'I've no idea, none at all.'

'You're not going to tell me nobody knew except this girl who's now dead.'

'No, I'm not telling you that. I'm telling you I didn't know Harding well enough to have a sense who would know. Who his friends were, things like that. And whoever this mistress was, if there really was one, and I've no proof, none at all, it's just something Janine said – it couldn't have been anyone at RUS.'

'Couldn't have been?'

'I'd have thought. Things just weren't like that. I can't imagine any woman at RUS sleeping with Harding, except for Janine herself maybe, and we're not talking about her. Most likely it was someone in London. James said he didn't know of anyone, but he's not necessarily in a position to –'

'James?' Crane interrupted.

'James Connaught.'

There was a short fat silence. Crane said slowly, 'Connaught was with you last night.'

That wasn't a question. It must have been obvious. And the staff at the Mornington knew, would have known even before breakfast, that she had stayed in his room. Eliza winced.

'Now I asked you the day before yesterday about Mr Connaught, Miss Stannard, and you told me then that you didn't know him.'

'That's true, I didn't. I met him that morning, for the first time.'

'But you stayed in his room last night.'

This was invasive, it was unfair. 'That's none of your business. And it's got nothing, nothing at all to do with whoever killed Janine. Or Mr Harding.'

Crane leaned forwards, knitting the heels of his hands over the Formica. 'I'm not being nice to you, am I? You'll have to forgive me, Miss Stannard. The thing is, I want this crime solved, and I'm willing to step on a few toes to make my way to the solution. I'm sorry if I'm invading your privacy, but it's still a bloody sight better than what's happened to Janine Broughton. You think on that. You think on that poor girl laid out on the slab in the mortuary. You think on what she went through. You think on death. Then maybe you can think on giving me an answer.'

'All right,' Eliza said. 'I stayed with Mr Connaught last night.'

'Now let me tell you one reason I wanted to know that. I'm finding it bloody hard to fathom the social niceties, if that's what you call them, at RUS. You said that because of this all-encompassing enmity between the old guard and the newcomers, it wasn't possible for anyone who'd been at the civil service outfit to have an affair with Mr Harding?'

But Mr Harding was a toad, a beaver, a swine. To her. Not to Janine, however. Not to his wife. He was a forceful man, with money and power. Had been. She was experienced enough to know how little his ugliness would have mattered to some women.

She felt as if she had been twisted into a circle, and Crane was gleefully cramming her toes into her mouth. Through a full throat, she managed to say, 'I said what I thought, but maybe I was wrong. These things happen. It could have been someone at RUS he was seeing. I still don't know who.'

'Genevieve Bush?' he threw at her.

'God no! She hated him.'

'Some women find that a reason.'

'I can't believe it of Genevieve. She's happily married.'

'Miss Canning then, Crystal Canning?'

She shook her head.

'Please don't shake your head, Miss Stannard. We need you to answer for the tape.'

'No. I don't know. What sort of game is this? You want me to say it's possible? The honest answer is, *I don't know.*'

'How about the bullying, then? Do you know who was bullying Janine?'

'No.'

'David Summerfield? John Donaldson?'

'No!' She could feel her voice rising, feel her hands rising of their own volition to cover her ears, feel her body rocking on the hard chair, feel the screech of a voice that had to be her own shouting 'No! No! No!'

Through the siren scream, she was dimly conscious of both Crane and DC Joyce getting to their feet. A hand reached out to her – she could not have said whose.

No more.

26

When she recovered Crane was, to be fair, contrite. He hadn't meant to push her so hard, he said. It was nothing personal. They had been long days, long nights, for him as well as for her. He had misjudged it; he had not made enough allowance, he could see now, for what she had been through.

He left her with DC Joyce, who took her to the police canteen and got them both some more coffee. They drank it in a reasonably companionable silence. It was only once she had been escorted down to the main door that DC Joyce said, 'I'm sorry, but there's more we'll need to ask you. You do understand, don't you? We'll give you a ring – tomorrow, maybe. Go home and have a good rest first.'

Eliza said wearily, 'There's nothing else I know. I'm telling you the truth, I barely knew either Harding or Janine Broughton. I'm not the person who can tell you who murdered them.'

'I don't know anyone's going to tell us that, love,' DC Joyce said gently. 'Not straight out, at any rate. It's a jigsaw, you know, fitting little bits together. What doesn't seem important to you might turn out to be important to us. And to be honest, I can see why Inspector Crane's pushing at you. It's that morning when Mr Harding was murdered, mostly. When you look hard at your story, the timings you gave us, it doesn't add up. He thinks you're hiding something. So do I.'

'I probably got the times wrong when I told it to you. I wasn't at my best that morning.'

'Then you'll need to put them right, won't you?'

Easy to say, not so easy to do. No; she was being stupid, defeatist. It couldn't be so difficult to rethink it, to make the pieces fit.

DC Joyce said, 'Off you go now, love. Have a think about it on the way home.'

She did think about it all the way home, although not out of any sense of compliance. She walked the two miles from the police station. The cloudy mist had cleared and it was another bright morning. The city centre was crowded with shoppers and tourists, and there were kids playing on the swings in the

recreation ground on the hill. She walked past them like an
android, separate, encased in horror.

It doesn't add up, she thought. The bodies, the blood. The
times. The times, the bodies and blood. The unspoken words
echoed to the rhythm of her footsteps.

It was one o'clock when she got home. Her house still smelled
of curry. She threw the foil cartons in the bin outside, added the
congealed whipped egg and the salad, then went upstairs. She
took one of the (outdated) tablets the doctor had given her during
her split from Lewis, lay down on her quilt and slept, heavily, till
six in the evening.

The weekend spread like a rumpled sheet ahead of her.
Loneliness tangled with the creases. James had gone to London,
and he hadn't said anything about their meeting again.

And wanting him was still a terrible idea. What was worse, the
list of people who knew about the two of them had grown expo-
nentially. Phil. The police. Crane would ask other people about
her, she suspected, and quite likely let on to those other people. If
that put pressure on her, he wouldn't mind, in fact the reverse. He
would probably find it useful to subject her to their curiosity, their
disapproval.

She needed to be able to tell those other people, it's over. It was
a dumb thing that just happened at a terrible time. But I know
how dumb it was, and I've finished it. He's finished it. It's over,
over, over. Not that it ever quite started. A nothing, that's what it
was.

Turn to someone else, Eliza, she told herself. It would be a
lousy idea to spend the rest of the weekend alone. She needed the
quiet reassurance, the normality of old friends.

She had been working so hard, it was weeks since she had
bought tickets to a film or a concert, or planned a dinner party.
Sunday she was seeing Rachel for lunch as she did almost every
week, but that was her only weekend plan. In the months when
they had been seeing each other, she had always met up with Phil
on Saturday nights. Since their split she had done nothing more
than collapse in front of the television.

Who could she call? Not Rachel again. Alice and Peter had
plans, she knew; Joanne was in France. Mitchell and Val? Mitchell
would talk about RUS and the murders. Almost everyone she
knew worked at RUS, or had done. And the murders sat so large,

there was no pretending they had not happened. The thing was to live with the knowledge, somehow.

She went into her office and stared at the answering machine. James had taken the tape, he'd given it to the police. Her tape, from her machine, with Janine's screams on it.

Think on that girl on the mortuary slab.

Sluggishly she opened her desk drawers, found her spare tape and slotted it in. She dialled Mitchell's number. He was slow to answer, so it was a relief when his familiar voice came on the line. He had been in the garden, he said.

'Mitchell, I know you and Val most likely have plans for tonight. But I'd really, really appreciate it if you could fit me into them.'

'Well ... some people are coming over here for a drink. I wasn't going to ask you, because Lewis and Kate will be there.'

Oh. The things you don't talk to your friends about. She had known, in a theoretical kind of way, that Mitchell and Val had continued to see Lewis after her split from him. Why should they not? Lewis was a work colleague and a friend, just as much as she was. She might have wished people would side with her when he left her for Kate, but she was realistic enough to know that was asking too much. Not that she ever had asked it, she would not have let herself appear that visibly needy. But Mitchell had never mentioned seeing Lewis to her, as far as she could recall. And he had certainly never, but never, invited her and Lewis to his house at the same time.

As for Kate – she could not remember when had last seen Kate.

She could, she supposed, tell him all about Janine, play on his sympathy, and hope he would be so shocked and concerned that he would tell Lewis and Kate to clear the field for her. But that would have been cheap, she reckoned. Blood was – was blood. Janine's death was shocking, but she was not going to pretend it was a personal loss to her.

So could she face seeing Lewis and Kate?

Maybe she could, she decided. No, definitely she could. It was five years now, and both their lives had moved on. The wounds had scabbed over, then faded to pink puckers. She had seen Lewis not infrequently at RUS – up to when he had left the company a few weeks earlier – and survived it without trauma. Kate was an inoffensive little mouse. It might mystify her why Lewis had picked her, but she did not have to hate the woman.

'I'd be happy to see them too.'

There was a short silence, as if Mitchell wasn't sure he believed her. But he had little option but to take what she had said at face value. 'Any time after eight, then. There's cheese but not supper, if that's OK.'

'Great. Thanks ever so, and thank Val for me too.'

She flicked the answering machine back to on, and padded barefoot into the kitchen. The fridge contained a hard lump of cheddar, half a carton of Utterly Butterly, the remainder of the bagels and Philly she had bought a couple of days earlier, the broad beans, and three eggs. She surveyed her cupboards, found a tin of ravioli she could not recall buying (it was not the kind of thing she ate as a rule) and heated it. She grated cheese, and made a cup of tea. When she had finished the ravioli she ate a browning banana and a couple of chocolate digestives. It was not a comforting meal. The thought of making another trip to Tesco filled her with weariness. Tomorrow.

The phone rang once. Her answering machine broadcast a feedback-laden version of Phil's voice. She did not pick up the receiver, did not take in his words.

She thought about Inspector Crane. She thought about the timings that didn't satisfy him, and didn't satisfy DC Joyce either. The timings that were so stupidly, obviously wrong. She thought about Harding's corpse and the red blood on his shirt. She thought about Pat Shorten and his friends in the pub, discussing the murder as if it were a game of Cluedo or an Inspector Morse book. It occurred to her that her attitude had not been greatly different. About Janine's murder, though, she did not feel the same.

There were links, there had to be. But did that mean the same person had killed Harding as had killed Janine? She had no idea. But if it was different people, did that mean that more than one person had been involved from the start? The Orient Express type thing James had mentioned? She couldn't imagine even one person at RUS would plan a murder, let alone a whole raft of them.

But there were some people who knew things she did not know herself. Loads of them, probably. No one would put her in the top division of sleuths and gossips and networkers. Nor did she want to become someone like Hugh Worning, a diligent collector of contacts and info.

Howard Nkolo was a better template. Howard, who had discovered the body with her. Howard, who hadn't talked to her the day before, even though he must know as well as she did why they had, absolutely had to talk.

She went into the study and picked up the phone book. It took her some time to find his number: he was not someone who was part of her social circle, someone whose house she visited, and whom she asked back to hers. She kept a finger on the page as she dialled.

'Hello, it's Eliza. You need to know this.' She guessed he hadn't heard yet about Janine, and she was right, what she told him came as a shock. Nervously, she cut into his expressions of astonishment and sorrow. 'Yes, yes, I know. Later. The thing is now, the police are looking hard at me. They let me off this morning, but they made that clear. They don't believe what I told them about Thursday morning.'

'You did hear what I told you to say before I went in?'

'Yes, and I didn't mention that at all. But it doesn't add up, and he knows that.'

'Shit. I don't want to be seen with you.'

'Howard, you're surely not –'

'It's not me. I didn't kill him, you idiot. But there are things none of us want the police to know.'

'So help me sort out another story.'

'I will, I will, but –'

His buts didn't make much sense to her. And he seemed no keener to talk with he than he had been the day before. But by the time she rang off, she had his agreement to meet with her at eleven on Monday.

27

Mitchell lived five miles out of the city. Nominally his house was in a village but in reality it was in a sprawling rural area that shared the name of a hamlet a mile off. There were no other houses in sight. It was a wide-fronted, low-ceilinged cottage with two front rooms either side of a short fat passage, two central chimney pots, and doors on the back wall of each room leading, one to a narrow set of stairs, and the other to a large but scruffy kitchen and scullery. At the side was a black-painted wooden shed-cum-garage, and behind the house was a row of outhouses including a semi-functioning toilet. It made an L with the main house, shadowing a herb garden which Mitchell's wife Val kept in pristine order. Eliza had loved it since she had first come there nine, maybe ten years earlier. She never entered the garden without feeling a sense of calm seep over her.

As she came round the side of the house she saw the group sitting at the far side of the herb garden, on two wooden benches and a couple of folding chairs that had been set out around a slatted table on a small paved area. She recognized them all. Kate, Lewis and Jez were on the longer bench, Mitchell and Jez's wife Maggie on the shorter one. Val had one chair, and the other was empty. For her, she assumed. It was no wonder she was the last to arrive, it was pushing half past eight.

Beyond the group on the terrace, the gnarled old stems and new pale shoots of a rambling rose swarming over a cane archway were etched against a sky that was shaded from a thin blue to a radiant orange-red. There was an orchard beyond, and a pond beyond that before Mitchell and Val's land gave way to fields.

She could hear the sounds of their talk and laughter, hear too the faint noise of a television game show. The back door was open. Mitchell and Val had sons of eight and six; they were obviously indoors watching.

It was a still evening, the first that year when it had been possible to sit out after supper, but it was barely warm enough. Eliza had put on jeans and a thick denim jacket over a grey alpaca sweater. The garden smelled of spring, of damp earth, very faintly of thyme and lilac and lavender.

The empty chair rocked on an uneven paving stone as she sat on it.

Kate said, 'Good to see you, Eliza.'

'Nice to see you too, Kate,' she said politely. Kate was sitting neatly upright against Lewis' habitual sprawl. There was barely room for the two of them and Jez on the bench, but it seemed to Eliza a typical pose for Kate, not one prompted by the squash. There was something prim about Kate. She was wearing a white blouse with white embroidery around the wide round collar, and a denim pinafore. Her legs were bare, her sandals peasant-style brown leather. She did not look cold, but surely she was. Her straight dark hair was tied back in a ponytail.

When Lewis had taken up with her, Eliza had felt particularly enraged by what she had seen as the studied youthfulness of Kate's appearance, as well as by her actual youth. She had then been only nineteen. At twenty-four (or was it twenty-five now?) she still looked barely sixteen. In time it had come to enrage Eliza less, she accepted it as Kate's chosen style; although she wondered sometimes how it fitted into the dynamic of her and Lewis's relationship. Since she so rarely saw them she had little idea of that relationship, but her impression was that it was very different from what she and Lewis had shared.

Her eyes drifted to Lewis. He was a loose-limbed, broad-shouldered man, with big hands and feet and leonine hair swept back from a steeply curved brow. He moved slowly, spoke slowly – but frequently – and nursed a ferocious temper. He was thigh-to-thigh with Kate, his arms spread along the back of the bench, his left hand brushing Kate's upper arm. He met Eliza's eyes and said 'Hi,' but she had a sense that he was looking at her rather than engaging with her. There was none of the old spark between them.

'Red, or dry white?' Mitchell asked.

'Can I be fussy and ask for the white I brought?'

'Sure. We're not proud.' Mitchell and Val had no great interest in food or drink, and invariably provided Sainsbury's cheapest. As Mitchell was uncorking her Chablis, Eliza turned her attention to Jez. At least he provided a subject for conversation that did not involve the murders.

'So, one day of liberty. How does it feel?'

'Like a Saturday,' Jez said dryly. He was a slight man with neat features, slicked-back hair and frameless rectangular glasses. She had never seen him in denims; the navy-blue pinstriped suit he was wearing looked like the ones he wore to work, except he had taken off his tie. 'Ask me this time next week.'

'You don't have another job lined up?' Kate asked.

'No. Unlike your husband I'm not in great demand. I've no idea what I'll do next. Is that scandalous of me?'

'Sad, I'd have thought,' Kate said.

'But you don't understand. You don't work at RUS.' Kate was a library assistant; Lewis had met her over the counter in the music section.

'He's glad to go, Kate,' Lewis said lazily.

'Are you, Jez?'

'Am I, Eliza?'

She was not surprised to be appealed to; Jez had always played his audience carefully. 'In the circumstances,' she said.

'Go on.'

She turned to Kate. 'Jez is clever, and impatient with fools, and ambitious. It's three years or so since he last got a promotion, and he wants another one. Now things have shaken down at RUS after the takeover, and he could see it wasn't about to happen. Maybe it wouldn't ever have happened, the new management don't like left-wing argumentative types. So he decided to take the money and move on.'

'Touché,' Jez said.

'You asked.'

He inclined his head.

Kate said, 'But you don't want to leave, Eliza?'

'Why, do you think all that applies to me?'

Lewis said, 'Most of it.' Jez and Mitchell both laughed, and she felt herself redden.

Val said softly, 'That's not fair, Lewis.'

'No, it's not unfair,' Eliza said. 'I ...'

'You what?' Kate prompted.

An impulse made her tell them the truth. 'I wouldn't say I was anything like Jez, and I don't think I've reacted to the takeover in the same way he did, but I don't know that I fit in the new RUS either. I was thinking of something the police said, actually, when they interviewed me a couple of days ago. Inspector Crane, did you meet him?' (She addressed this to Mitchell.) 'He's pretty sharp. He was asking me what Howard Nkolo was like, why I thought he'd reacted as he had to Harding's murder, that kind of thing. He kept trapping me into admitting that I was reading my own motives into what Howard had done. Which I did, I suppose, because Howard and I are alike in ways that we're not like Harding or Donaldson or the rest of them.'

Mitchell said, 'Did Howard do much?'

'No. That was almost the point, that it was trivial things. All we did was find the body and phone the police. It was a dead end in their enquiry, but obviously he wanted there to be more. Only there wasn't. But there are universalities and there are differences, times you know why people did what they did and times you don't. This is starting to sound like a grade C essay in GCSE philosophy. I'll shut up.'

'No, tell me,' Lewis said. 'What's the difference between you and Jez?'

Jez said, 'As if you don't know. I can be nasty and Eliza doesn't know how.'

Mitchell said, 'I was about to say, six inches.'

'Six! You might flatter me and say eight.'

Eliza said, 'I'd have said, money.'

Jez paused in mid-gesture, leaning forward, his wineglass poised as if he had been about throw its contents over Mitchell. He grinned; first at the assembled group, and then specifically at Lewis, who grinned back at him. Eliza had the uncomfortable feeling that under the joking, she had missed something. She shouldn't have spoken; she should have let Mitchell's old joke close the conversation. Anyway it had come out wrong. She had meant the redundancy money, but she had somehow implied that Jez was over-fond of money generally. Actually that wasn't true. Jez was at heart an old-fashioned Marxist who despised capitalist values. He was ambitious, but not in the way of Hugh Worning, say. Money was not what he wanted most.

Nor was redundancy. She knew without asking that he hated it.

'How true, my dear,' Maggie said. 'We haven't drunk to the money yet.'

Jez sat back. 'Oh, we have, Mags. You haven't, Eliza. You missed my do yesterday.'

'Sorry about that. Never too late, though. To dosh.' She raised her glass, and the others followed.

'How much?' Kate asked.

'You rude little girl. A hundred and seventy thou, just over.'

'Christ.'

'No, the government,' Mitchell said.

The awkward moment had gone, defused by Mitchell's lightness, Kate's unselfconscious naivety, Jez's sardonic humour, or some mixture of them all. They were laughing, Maggie leaning over to say something to Val, Lewis listening to Jez, Mitchell reaching for wine and water to refill the drinkers' and drivers' glasses. Saturday night, almost as it used to be. No, as it never was, but as memory made it. Or perhaps rather as it had been and still could be, when the goodwill that had always been strong between them blotted out the undercurrents of ambition, betrayal and pain.

So Eliza thought, suspended for a moment outside it. The odd one of the seven, coming alone. She was still not used to it, she never would learn to prefer it.

Only Val mentioned it. Coming back from a foray to the house to put her sons to bed she said, 'So you haven't got back with Phil.'

'No, I won't do that.'

'I'm sorry.'

'But I'm not. It's my choice, Val. It wasn't a sudden thing, it had been brewing for ages. I knew I wasn't in the right place and I couldn't go on.'

'You always seemed fine to me.'

'In company we were, I guess. It's not that we quarrelled, it's more that it wasn't enough. I never felt like half of Phil and Eliza. And we never lived together, you know.'

'Maybe not, but that's not the be all and end all of a relationship, is it? I'd have thought it'd be rather nice to live alone and just have someone to go out with occasionally. Couldn't you try to find a way of ...?'

It surprised her. It was so far from her own ideal that she found it difficult to believe it was Val's. Of course Val was married. When you had a husband, it was natural enough that you would dream not of more commitment but of a degree of freedom. But Val and Mitchell were so perfectly matched that Val couldn't honestly wish them semi-detached, could she?

Maybe what she had imagined ...

No; she didn't want to explore that path. She needed to believe in Mitchell and Val's happiness, even if it was a comfortable illusion.

'No,' she said. 'I'd hate that.'

'I'm sorry. Still, maybe someone else will come along.'

Val didn't sound as if she believed it, Eliza thought. She was half-tempted to tell her about James, but that hardly seemed a relationship to boast about. Anyway with Val across the table from her she couldn't whisper, and Lewis, who had been caught outside the conversation as Kate talked to Mitchell, would have heard what she said – just as he had clearly heard the exchange about Phil. She glanced at him, and for an instant she thought he would say something, but he did not.

It was almost a relief when they moved on to talk about the murders. The talk that in the office, in the pub, had been bitter with cynicism was mellowed not only by the shock of Janine's death but by the night, the country smells and sounds, and the presence of three women who had never met either of the victims. Maggie was deeply religious, Kate a born innocent, and Val in her solidly practical way a considerate woman. They spoke of it simply, as a human tragedy, and Eliza welcomed the opportunity to follow their lead. There was something soothing in expressing plain pity for Janine, younger than any of them except Kate, and now never to grow older. Mitchell and Lewis also managed a gruff sympathy for Harding, although Jez remained sardonic, even vicious. It was tough on the man's wife; that was the most he would say.

Eliza said, 'I didn't know he had one.'

'Oh yes. Not that she came up to Costhorpe, he had other games to play up here.'

'An affair?' She was immediately alert. Jez might manoeuvre, but he did not lie; he would not have hinted it unless he knew something.

'What, was the Beaver shafting someone?' Mitchell asked.

Maggie said, 'Mitchell.'

Her sharp tone brought about a short silence all round the table. Jez said, 'Sorry, Mags. I shouldn't have mentioned it. Defaming the dead and all that. It's only gossip, anyway.'

Mitchell said, 'Nothing's only, when it comes to –'

Lewis's voice, lazy but firm, cut across his. 'True. It all matters, but this is not the time for it. In case you didn't take it in, Lizzy's had a hell of a time. Let's give her a break and change the subject.'

Surprised – no, not quite surprised – at his intervention, Eliza turned to her ex-husband. His face was expressionless, as it often was; Lewis was not a man whose thoughts you could read. But he was a man who read others. And though he was no Hugh Worning, no questioner and meddler, he was a man who picked up on gossip. It occurred to her that he probably knew far more about the situation that he had told anyone. Indeed, the police had probably not even asked him.

Val said, 'Oh God, Lizzy. Nobody meant to make it worse for you.'

'You didn't,' Eliza said, her eyes still on Lewis.

'Were the police hard on you?' he asked.

She picked her words carefully. 'It's no fun, being questioned. I wish I hadn't become involved, obviously. But really all I could do was tell them the bare facts. I arrived at the office, I ran into Howard, I picked up my papers and went to the meeting room. There's nothing they'd really want to follow up on in that.'

'End of subject. Would you like a brandy?' Mitchell asked.

'No, I'm all right, honestly. Nothing worse than a bit shaken.'

'Well, if it's not brandy time it's coffee time,' Val said briskly. 'Indoors, I think. I don't know about anyone else, but my shivers are down to being bloody cold out here.'

'Yes, let's go in,' Jez agreed.

They got up, and began to collect together the glasses and bottles. Val led the way in, Kate and Lewis headed after her, and Eliza paused by the table, hands full of empties, watching them.

And seeing what she had not seen before. So that was why Kate was wearing a pinafore.

'You're pregnant.'

She said it thoughtlessly, then bit her tongue; it sounded abrupt. In fact it sounded worse than that, it sounded Sabatier-sharp. Kate and Lewis both turned to her.

'You didn't know?' Kate asked.

'No. I noticed you weren't drinking, but I assumed it was because you were driving.'

'She is,' Lewis said. Eliza met his eyes; but after a split second he shied away.

Damn him, she thought. Damn Mitchell too, come to that. Had neither of them thought to warn her? Or even Val?

No; calm down, Eliza. Those happily with children, or those

who had never wanted them, would never really understand what it meant to face the prospect of having none at all. All those years when Lewis had said, let's wait a little longer – only in retrospect could it be read as meanness to her. It had meant what he said, that he wasn't ready. Indeed, with her perhaps he never would have been ready. But that wasn't a wish to spike her agenda, only an intention to follow his own. And now she was nowhere near the centre of his universe, and it probably had not occurred to him how painful this would be to her.

She couldn't show the ache, not in front of him, not in front of Kate. She made herself crank out the words of congratulations. She asked Kate how she was feeling, had she been sick in the mornings, when it was due. July the tenth, Kate said: three days after Eliza's thirty-eighth birthday. She was not embarrassed, she gave no sign that she realized it might hurt Eliza to learn this. Eliza supposed she had given it no thought at all. Kate had been unapologetic about taking her husband, so why should she apologize for having his child?

Val rescued her. 'Lizzy, d'you mind helping me in the kitchen?'

'Oh; sure, Val.' She turned her back on Lewis and headed for the kitchen door.

28

They stood side by side in the old-fashioned kitchen, waiting for the kettle to come to the boil. Val talked about Max and Billy, her sons. They were at a difficult age, she said, rowing with each other all the time, and Billy was suffering from bullying at school. She described the petty torments and jibes, Billy's thin arm dragging on hers on the way to school and the tears on the way home that Max mercilessly teased him about. They discussed how Billy, a slight boy with Mitchell's ginger hair, might be taught to fight back. The subtext was blatant but it was what Eliza needed. A dream was a dream; real life, everyone's real life, was a sea of petty problems islanded with moments of pleasure.

By the time the coffee was brewed she was able to face being in the same room as Kate. She avoided her and Lewis even so, going over to sit by Jez. She had half a mind to press him further about the Beaver and his mysterious love life, but Jez by then was half-drunk, and full of arch comments that irritated the hell out of her. She told herself it was not her business anyway. The police would find out. She should leave it to them.

She stayed till past 11, drinking coffee and helping Maggie and Mitchell demolish most of a chunk of blue brie. Mitchell played some of the music he loved, sonorous epic symphonies by Bruckner and Mahler. The heavy sway of it remained in her head as she drove back to the city.

Lights shone from most of the grey-brick houses in her street; to her surprise, even from her own. She hadn't closed the study curtains, and as she looked through the window from her parked car she could see that the open door to the hallway formed a trapezium of yellow warmth. It gave the illusion that someone was there, that there awaited the simple, lost pleasure of turning the key and calling out, 'I'm home, darling,' of drinking coffee and dissecting the gossip, of sliding into bed alongside a warm male body.

When she had lived with Lewis – not in this house, which she had bought after their split – he had always made them leave lights on when they went out. To deceive burglars, he had argued, but she thought now that psychology had played a larger part.

Her father had never in his life left a house lit up, indeed they had had a couple of rows about it when her parents came to stay. Dad had called it extravagance, but then there had been a warmth between her and Lewis that she had never sensed in her childhood home. Before it had all gone rotten.

It had been a slip, no more, but she should do it more often, she thought. Spoil herself. Not grope for the hall switch, but walk into a space that felt prepared for her. Perhaps her unconscious had planned as much, knowing that tonight she was too raw to face returning to a dark and silent house.

She locked the car quickly, shivering slightly as she moved from its warmth to the chill night air, and let herself quickly into the house. More coffee. No, camomile, she had had too much caffeine. No, coffee: she deserved it. The electric fire. Boz Scaggs or Lyle Lovett, or maybe Marianne Faithfull on the stereo.

She kept her jacket on and went straight through to the kitchen. The sitting room light was on as well as the hall light. As she came to the doorway she reached in to flick it off. It reminded her of her answering machine; would James have phoned? She would make coffee first then check, she decided.

She was just putting back the coffee jar on the shelf when she heard a sound behind her. A door closing. She sensed the change in the light, as it shut off the hallway.

Her body jerked, as if an insane puppeteer had pulled all her strings at once.

'It's only me,' he said even before she had turned round.

'Phil!'

'So he didn't come back with you.'

Her heart was high in her chest, bouncing like a rubber ball against its cavity. It was only Phil, but she could not have been more terrified if it had been a black-masked stranger with a gun.

'Or did he? Is he in the study?'

'W-what are you doing here?'

He took a step towards her, and she jerked again, backing hard against the kitchen counter.

'You're scared,' Phil said. He was still approaching. She was shaking all over, unable to speak. Even his normality, his cream polo top and his tan slacks, the heavy black frames of his glasses magnifying his eyes, seemed terrifyingly exaggerated.

'Don't be afraid,' he said. He reached out and touched her and she twitched away from him. 'It's only me.' He reached out again with both hands, as if to draw her into his embrace.

It was enough to squeeze a motive force into her shaking limbs. She slid under his arms, wriggling past him, running for the door. Dimly she heard him call out 'Liz!' and his footsteps as she fumbled with the handle of the door he had closed.

He reached her before she could get it open, slamming a hand past her, high on the door. She could feel his body behind her, close behind her, see his other hand which he had set on the doorframe at handle-height. Panting, she froze, as if to move an inch would be to invite him to touch her.

'I'm not touching you,' Phil said from behind her. 'Liz, please. You know the last thing I'd do is hurt you.'

Her tongue filled her mouth. She had consciously to draw in air and take a few shallow breaths before she could manage to speak.

'Get away from me.'

'I'm not touching you,' he repeated. 'There's nothing to be afraid of. I just came in to wait because I need to talk to you.'

He hadn't just done anything. He had come into her house, her space, while she wasn't there. He must have been waiting, in the dark – no, in that light she had found so cruelly enticing. In her sitting room, where she couldn't see him from the road. He had planned this.

'Liz,' Phil said again.

Another breath. She managed to say, 'Please move away from me.'

'Of course, if you want me to. There's no need, though. It's only me.'

There was a need, but she dared not articulate how bad it was. She forced herself to stay still, her eyes on his hand on the doorframe, until she saw him move it, and sensed him drawing back.

Even then it was some time before she could bring herself to turn round. Phil had retreated only as far as the dining table at the corridor end of the room. He was half-sitting on it, his hands on the edge. He looked pale and worried, but otherwise just like the normal Phil.

'OK now?'

Another breath. 'You really scared me.'

'That's obvious.' He gave a sort of laugh. 'Oh Liz, you really are on edge these days.'

'Can you blame me?' she said in a near-whisper.

'No. No, of course I don't blame you.' He pushed himself off the table, and had taken a step back towards her before the hand she raised instinctively stopped him. 'I think it's absolutely understandable, after the terrible things that have happened to you. But that's why I came, because you need help, you need support. You're not well. You shouldn't be here on your own, you need someone to look after you, and I'm the person to do that. I'd do anything for you, Liz. You just have to relax and let me take over.'

Never, she thought. She dared not say that to him. She said, 'How did you get in?'

'Mrs Dawson next door gave me your spare key. She's worried about you too, she read about it in the paper, Mr Harding and then the poor girl yesterday. Oh my God, when I think about it, that stupid bastard taking you there. Liz, you do know I had nothing to do with that?'

She nodded.

'That's good. Of course you know that. You know I'm not a violent man. I shouldn't have gone off. I tried to tell you then, he's no good for you, you need to be with me. But I took you by surprise, it was all too sudden. And you don't know everything, you maybe thought, he's rich or successful or whatever, but things are coming right for me now, and you'll see, I'll do just as well as he will. Afterwards I could see you didn't have a chance to choose me, because you didn't know all that. Then that terrible business happened, and that idiot, that insane idiot dragged you into it, and I thought, now she'll realize. She needs me now, Liz needs me now. I'll make up for everything. I just have to have a chance to tell you everything and make it all up between us. So here I am. Why don't I make us a nice cup of tea, and we'll have a sit down for a few minutes and you can get it all off your chest.'

She could have cursed Mrs Dawson. Of course she knew Phil, had seen him around often enough, but to give out the key when she herself wasn't there .... She would have to find someone else to leave her key with, she would never trust Mrs Dawson again.

Concentrate on Phil. Think. She had to last it out until she could lull him off guard. Then she had to run for the study, which had a bolt on the door, lock herself in and phone for help. She didn't feel she could cope with talking him into going. She needed the police to make him go.

'Tea,' she said. He'd have to move farther away to make it.

'That's better. That's a sensible girl. You know it really, you know I've got nothing to do with all these dreadful things. It's all got muddled in your mind but you know you don't have to be afraid of me. I'll make the tea. Oh, you've boiled the kettle.' It had clicked off and was gently emitting steam. 'I'll tell you what, you sit down here. I'll brew up, then we'll take the tea through and drink it in the sitting room. It's all right, I won't touch you. Here, this chair's for you.'

He was speaking with the exaggerated care of someone talking to a hysterical child, and moving around as he did so, taking a chair, angling it to the table, and gesturing at the seat like a furniture salesman. He never took his eyes off her for more than an instant. She didn't want to sit, but she reckoned she would still be able to get to the door once he went over to the kettle.

She hadn't bargained for the way he held the chair for her and tucked it back in under the table, or for the way her legs seemed to collapse as soon as she sat on it. There was a precious moment, as Phil was crossing the room and reaching to the mug tree, when she did not manage to move.

Still time. Phil was talking again. 'Of course it's understandable, it's all understandable. You being so shaken. I just need to help you put it all straight in your –'

Now. She did not try to be silent, she did it at a scramble, scraping the chair back, throwing herself at the door, scrabbling for the handle, hearing his 'Liz!' as she slammed it shut behind her. Two steps to the study door, and through into darkness. She had it shut behind her and her hand was on the bolt before she felt the rattle of his hand on the handle.

Smoothly home. It wasn't a heavy bolt, she would have to pray he didn't try to force the door. She reached a trembling hand for the light switch, and blinking as it killed the darkness, grabbed the phone.

Phil was shouting 'Liz! Liz!' through the door as she dialled. The operator was maddeningly slow putting her through, and once the police controller came on to the line it was a moment before she could collect herself enough to give her address and explain.

'So it's your boyfriend, love?'

'No, no. Ex-boyfriend. He broke in. I'm scared of him.'

'He ever hit you before, love?'

There was silence now through the door. Eliza held her breath for five seconds and listened, but there was nothing. She turned back to the receiver. 'He hasn't hit me now. I just want him to go. I need you to make him go.'

'Now calm down, love, and let's do this slowly. Whereabouts are you? Is this man right with you?'

Saturday night. 11.30, or maybe nearer midnight. Too many troubles and too few police. They wouldn't come quickly, and what could she say when they did come? A cool part of her brain knew she had fallen over the edge of hysteria. It could imagine an endless half-hour, hour even, sitting hunched in the study waiting for the police to arrive while Phil argued patiently through the door. It could envisage the humiliation, the police categorizing her terror somewhere below the average drunk driver in importance, and eventually dragging themselves round to sort out a domestic, only it wasn't much of a domestic even, because he hadn't hit her.

'Sorry, forget I phoned.'

She put the phone down, and listened to silence. Phil had a point, she thought. It wasn't that she was terrified of him: heaven knew, there was no one less scary than Phil. It was the circumstances, the corpses, the blood, her unconscious mind telling her she too was in danger. She was afraid, but not of Phil. He had misjudged it hopelessly, but that was all she could reproach him with. His intentions had been good, and hell, had she given him a shock with her reaction.

But she still wanted – no, needed – him to go. She didn't want him here, in her house, her space. She didn't want to talk to him. She didn't want to get sucked back into a relationship with him, she didn't want him to look after her, she didn't want an argument with him about James. Perhaps it wasn't something she could call the police to do, but she had to make him go.

She wondered wildly if he had left while she was on the phone. No, of course he hadn't. Dogged Phil had never known when to quit. And nor would he leave if she were to ask him again now. He would be determined to 'make it up with her' first.

Not the police, then, but if someone came, someone who could make it all seem normal, maybe they could persuade him to leave. She would ring someone and ask them to come round and make him go.

She wanted to ring Lewis, but she knew she couldn't. She couldn't ring Marshall, Jez, or anyone who knew Phil from RUS. Phil had been humiliated enough already, she didn't want this to get round the office. Who else did she know?

She reached for her address book and flicked through the entries. Finally she rang Edward Derbyshire, her elderly neighbour on the opposite side to Mrs Dawson. She woke him. She apologized. She asked him, with many more apologies, if he would please, please, put on some clothes and come around to her house and ring the doorbell. Edward was a practical man, and even when sleepy, capable of recognizing urgency. It would take him a minute or two, he said.

When she had rung off she listened again. He had to be there.

'Phil?' Her voice sounded strained and awkward to her.

'Liz. Liz, please.' She could tell that he was standing right by the door. 'This is ridiculous, I just want to talk to you. Please come out, Liz.'

'Phil, listen to me. My neighbour's coming round. When he rings the bell you need to open the door and let him in. Then I want you to go. I want you to put my key on the hall table now and I want you to go.'

'We have to talk, Liz.'

'All right, we have to talk some time, but I can't talk to you now. Phil, if you won't agree I'll call the police.'

'Good God, there's no need for that. Look, I'll leave right now. I'll ring you in the morning, OK?'

She wanted to say no. 'OK.'

'Right. I'm putting the key on the table now. It's just next to the blue and red vase. I'm going now. Won't you come out and say goodbye?'

She couldn't bring herself to. She listened to the click of the front door, and a moment later, to the doorbell ringing. Moving slowly, as if through water, she unbolted the study door and went to let in Edward Derbyshire.

29

It was a night of sweats and dark shadows and noises in the street that made her jump. She was afraid to sleep because she was afraid of her dreams. She rose at six, took a long bath and drank two cups of strong real coffee. She dressed in Levis and a violet cashmere jumper, and tied back her hair with a white ribbon. She looked up the numbers of locksmiths in the Yellow Pages. She wanted a heavy deadlock for her front door and another for the back. Several claimed to be 24-hour, but the first number she tried produced an answering machine, the second an irate sleepy woman. Too early, obviously: maybe after 9 she would have better luck.

The house was clean. She could not remember when she had last had nothing to do. There was an overflowing in-tray waiting for her at St Jude's House, but she would not have gone there. She felt too jumpy to settle to lacemaking or patchwork. Exercise would be pointless, since she was meeting Rachel at the gym at midday. She thought of decorating her back bedroom. She wondered if she was going insane.

She defrosted her freezer instead, attacking the encrustations of ice with a table knife and a hairdryer. It was 8.40 by the time she had washed the ice down the sink, packed everything back into the freezer and mopped up the floor. She went round the corner to the newsagent, collected an *Observer* off the pile, and was looking into the chiller display, wondering whether she could face bacon and eggs, when a voice said 'Eliza.'

It was a spruce-looking Edward Derbyshire, holding the lead of a blood-coloured dachshund. Eliza went into another stream of apologies, which he cut off with a slicing gesture. 'My dear, there's nothing to be sorry about. I'd noticed you were looking peaky recently, and I'm putting last night down to tiredness. Right?'

'Right,' she weakly agreed.

'Now Hubert here and I are going to make you let us treat you to breakfast.'

She was grateful, and said so. They haggled gently over who would pay for the bacon, and Edward let Eliza win. They walked back slowly, behind the little waddling dog, to Edward's house, a mirror image of Eliza's with fading cream-painted rooms and Thirties varnished wood furniture. Eliza sat at the table in his hi-tech white kitchen – revamped with his retirement lump sum, he explained: his wife when alive had always refused to change anything, but for himself he had welcomed the luxury of it – and listened to the news and *Letter from America* while her host busied himself with grill and saucepan.

They talked about the weather, about dogs, about cars. They did not talk about what had happened the night before. Nor did they talk about the murders. He didn't read the local paper, and Eliza supposed he had no idea of her involvement.

They were on their second slices of toast when the doorbell rang.

'I'll answer it,' Edward said. 'If it's your young man, shall I tell him you're not here?'

She was tired of explaining that Phil was not her young man. 'Please.'

When he had disappeared down the corridor she turned to her half-drunk orange juice. She would have to talk to Phil, she thought. Not at home though, please God, and not quite so soon. Maybe they could arrange to meet in a quiet pub. What could she say that would be unambiguous without being brutal? Why hadn't he already got the message? She had over-reacted enough the night before, you would think he might have realized by now that his attentions were unwanted.

'Eliza, I'm sorry.'

She swung round to see Edward Derbyshire dwarfed by two police officers. Inspector Crane was in front, looking like a stern Nazi in a black leather jacket, with Detective Constable Joyce, in jeans and a thick green jersey, behind him. Hubert the dachshund yapped at their ankles.

'Oh,' was all Eliza could manage to say.

'You know we wanted to talk to you again, Miss Stannard,' Crane said.

'Yes, but I told Constable Joyce there's nothing else I can tell you.'

'We'll be the judge of that, if you don't mind.'

Was this harassment, she wondered? Was there a point at which she could refuse to help them? Even if this was it, she could hardly make a stand in Edward Derbyshire's kitchen. Since she could read the worry on his face she turned to him and said apologetically that she would have to go. Fearing he would think it was connected with the incident with Phil, she explained that they were detectives on the team investigating the murder at St Jude's House. Crane stirred himself to add that she was not in any way a suspect, it was just routine enquiries, for which she was grateful.

'Thanks for breakfast,' she added. 'It was lovely.'

'We must do it again some time. My dear, I worry about you. That dreadful business, I hadn't realized you'd been involved. It's enough to upset anyone, especially a lady living on her own. Feel free to call on me if you need some company. You know where I am.'

'That's so kind of you. You're right, it's been a hard few days.'

Crane was waiting, not impatient but implacable, so she said no more. On the doorstep she asked Crane, 'My house?' and he said, 'If we may.'

It would be less awful than going to the police station again. She showed them in to her living room. It seemed small with the two police officers in it, less cosy than usual. Inspector Crane sat on her sofa, with DC Joyce next to him. Eliza took the button-backed chair by the fireplace. She remembered she had left her *Observer* next door. This wasn't the moment to go and collect it.

'I'm sorry about this,' Crane said, 'but it's important to be thorough in an investigation like this one. I want us to go again over the morning when you discovered Mr Harding's body.'

'I've told you it all, right from the moment I arrived at the office.'

'So you say, but it doesn't add up. You're lying to us, and I want to know why.'

Her head fell forward, on to her hand. She felt intensely weary. Hell, this was the last thing she wanted. She had expected to have longer, to be given warning, to be phoned and not have them turn up on her doorstep. She didn't feel composed and in control, and she hadn't got around to going over her story. She felt alone, stupid, incompetent. And it was so pointless anyway. Crane was going to launch in and batter her down, and OK, he'd get a buzz out of catching her in a fib or two, but he wouldn't end up any nearer to catching his murderer.

She said slowly, 'I've tried to be helpful, and I know I haven't been. I know you want to make some kind of breakthrough, but I can't give it to you.'

Crane said slightly more kindly, 'Don't worry about break-throughs. Don't worry about what's relevant. Don't try to do our job for us, we'll decide what's relevant. Just tell us everything.'

But nobody tells anyone everything, she thought silently. It's not possible to tell everything. We tell a story, that's all. She did not want to be part of this story.

It was unavoidable, she knew, but all the same she couldn't think what to say or how to say it. Crane let a silence drift by. Then he said in a low voice, 'I think it's more real to you, now Janine Broughton's dead as well. I think at first you couldn't take it in, the fact that someone at RUS had actually done this terrible thing. But you know now that they did. I don't mean you know who, because I don't suppose for a minute that you do, but you've absorbed it. You've had time to appreciate that there's a dangerous murderer out there. You've had time to accept that catching that murderer takes precedence over everything else. Doesn't it?'

She looked up. Crane met her eyes. He too looked tired, she thought. She guessed he had barely slept since the investigation began.

In a sense she trusted him. She believed he was doing an honest job in the best way he knew. That was naive of her, she supposed; a programmed response. Although he didn't have an uniform he was so much a copper. She had an impression of him as infinitely dogged and calm and persistent; or maybe she was confusing him with Phil. He was not Phil. He had a sharper temper, she had seen that already. He was cleverer than Phil. He would solve the case. He would bulldoze their pathetic barriers, lay waste a lot of lives, and get his man.

'I'm scared.'

'No wonder. It's a frightening business, getting caught up in something like this. We're trying to make it as safe for you as we can. I don't think you're a very likely target for this man, but for what it's worth, I reckon you'll be less of one once you've told us everything you know.'

At that moment, it seemed a thin reassurance.

D C Joyce said gently, 'You'll be much safer when he's caught.'

'But I can't help you find him.' It was almost a cry.

'Maybe you can. Just tell us what you know.'

Easily said, not easily done. Her silence filled the room.

'Why don't you make some coffee, Carol,' Crane said.

'I'll make it,' Eliza said, half-rising.

'No, you'll sit here. She's used to strange kitchens, aren't you, love?'

'I won't mess anything up,' Carol Joyce said. She set off to the kitchen, and Eliza turned back to Crane.

'Let's start with what we know,' he said. 'You arrived at St Jude's House at just before 6.30 that morning.'

'I guess so. It's not clear in my mind. You want a nice tidy one-dimensional account, but it wasn't like that. It's more like a crazy kaleidoscope.'

'Don't play games with me. Is that is true or is it not true?'

'It's true.' She was half-listening for the sounds of Carol in the kitchen. She knew she was not concentrating enough. She felt tired, so bloody tired. On impulse she looked up again, and met Crane's eyes. 'It's not that I'm afraid of retaliation or anything,' she heard herself say. 'It's the repercussions. For other people, mostly. What frightens me is that if I mention anyone, anyone at all, it'll turn the searchlight on to them. They'll be your main suspect, and you'll go after them, and that'll hurt them. Even if they're not the murderer it'll damage them. I don't want to do that to anyone. It's not that I think you're out to frame anyone, it's …'

'It's that you want to be in control. A part of you dares not leave it to me. But I can be objective where you can't.'

'I know,' she whispered.

'Let me tell you one thing which you already know. This was planned. It wasn't someone suddenly losing their head, it was someone who set it all up. They intended to kill Patrick Harding, and they intended to get away with it. They didn't make any stupid mistakes, they didn't leave any forensic clues, and they took the trouble to give us plenty of suspects. They must have had a motive, but they know that many other people also had motives, some of them good, some of them bad, but all of them motives that could have led to murder.'

Eliza nodded.

'I can well believe they've laid false trails. We've already unravelled a few of them. And knowing that, we're not going to latch on to the first person with opportunity and motive and say, it was you.'

'It's easy to say that.'

'But it's true. It's a little – only a little – like a crossword clue. There are plenty of words that seem to fit, but there's only one word that's right. And – do you ever do crosswords? – when you find it, you know it's the one.'

'People get clues wrong.'

'True, sometimes.' Carol Joyce came back with a tray of coffee. She had used the real, not the instant. Its pungent aroma filled the room. Crane went on, 'But the more dense the grid, the less likely that you can pass the wrong word off as the right one. Follow?'

'It's not a bad analogy.'

'So I want everything. I want a brain dump. I know, believe me, that this is costing you a privacy you cherish, but I must have it.'

She knew he was right, but even then she hesitated.

Inspector Crane stood up. He took a cup from the tray DC Joyce had put on the floor, and brought it over to her. He stood above her, cup in hand, then he squatted down till he was on a level with her, eye to eye. 'I must have it,' he repeated.

'I'll try,' Eliza said.

'You must. Because let me tell you something else you already know. That cool controlled killer has lost control now. Something went badly wrong. He had to kill again, and the second time it wasn't planned, it wasn't clinical, and he did leave clues. Not obvious clues, no nice clear fingerprints, but enough. He knows that. He knows we'll get him. He's in a corner, and he's desperate. He has nothing to lose, and he'll kill again if he thinks it'll help him. That's why I want him now. Today. Before it happens.'

He'd spoken steadily, holding her eyes. She felt a chill slide down her spine like a pastry brush dipped in cold water.

'You can't trust anyone,' Crane continued. 'Because you don't know who it is. Shield anyone and you could be shielding a killer. Be alone with anyone, and you could end up dead. Tell anything to anyone without telling it to us, and you could be condemning someone else to death.'

It was true, and it was terrifying.

'Except for us. It might be an unfashionable kind of thing to say, but I'm going to say it all the same. You can trust the police.'

30

Arriving at 6.28 was a given. She had parked then, and walked through the shopping precinct and under the ring-road underpass to St Jude's House. She had met Howard Nkolo on the steps. There had been no one else in sight.

They had walked together through the reception area, into the lift lobby, and gone together up to the second floor. He had told her about the security guards being given their notice. She told this to Crane and Joyce, who had surely known it anyway. They had seen no one else, except the guard at the desk. Was it Bill, or was it Stew? Crane asked her yet again, but she had nothing to add to what she had told him before. The fact that he kept asking bothered her, though. This had to mean that Howard had said it was Stew. But she was sure now that it had not been.

She had gone to her desk and collected her files. She felt as if she had been in a rush, but probably it had taken longer than she had first suggested to Crane. She had been flustered, angry too. Bloody 6.45 meetings. She had hung up her coat, and seen a dark mac in the cupboard. Whose? He made her concentrate, made her offer up names. Ahmed wore a coat like that sometimes, so did Russell, so did Fred. Martha had worn one once or twice, her boyfriend Tibor's, Eliza thought, which he had lent to her when it was pouring. It hadn't poured that week, as far as she could remember. It wasn't a distinctive coat. Surely this murderer was not one to hang his coat in her section's cupboard anyway.

She had seen no one in room 2B, although the fact that lights had been switched on had suggested Genevieve and Mitchell were in. Most likely by then they had been waiting for the Beaver in the rooms designated on their emails. She didn't know for sure.

Waiting for the lift, she had seen someone in the room at the far side of the lift lobby, room 2A. It was definitely a man, not a woman, but she didn't know who it was. Crane told her which men with desks in 2A had been in the office at that time. It could have been any of them, or it could have been someone else entirely. She couldn't say.

The lift had taken ages. That implied someone else had been using it. There were two lifts in the main lobby, but one was often out of action. She couldn't recall if it had been in service on Thursday morning, only the wait. She didn't think a lift had gone down past the second floor while she was waiting for one to take her up, but she couldn't be sure. Definitely no one had got out of a lift on her floor. She must have waited more than five minutes, she said.

'But you still got to the meeting room before Nkolo?'

'Er – yes.' Could she change that? No, she couldn't.

'He didn't have to wait for the lift. He went straight up to the fourth floor after you first met him.'

'If he says so. Maybe he took a while getting his papers together. He works on the fourth floor, round the corner from the meeting room. He must have gone to his desk first.'

It sounded thin. This will get Howard in trouble, she thought. But she didn't know what he had said, or come to that what he had done. Why had he not got there before her?

Or perhaps he had done. She said slowly, 'You were asking me that last time. If I'd read him right. So maybe I didn't. Maybe he found Harding first, then he thought, hell, I'll be a suspect if I call the police, so I'll let someone else find him. So he went back round into the L of the room, and watched while I went into the meeting room. Then when nothing happened –'

'You think he set you up?'

'I don't want to think so.'

Crane let that remark hang in the air. Then he said slowly, 'And it's not true, is it, that you didn't immediately realize the man was dead.'

'Actually it is. That's absolutely true.'

And she still couldn't believe what Crane was suggesting. She didn't think she was so very bad at perceiving other people. She thought Howard had been as surprised as she had been.

'And what happened then?'

'Well – this is where I didn't tell you absolutely everything.' She didn't dare look Crane in the eye. 'But only because I didn't really think it was relevant.'

'You'd better tell us now.'

She did. She told about Howard turning to her and saying, 'I have a feeling we're in the shit.'

'*We're* in the shit?'

'We're here, aren't we?'

'We'd better scarper then.'

'I suppose that's what the rest of them've done.'

'I suppose so.' She bit her lower lip. The sharp pain was what she needed. Bloody hell, she thought. Had Genevieve and Mitchell seen this and done a runner?

'Come on, let's go.'

They bundled up their files, opened the door and went out into the open empty space of room 4B.

'God,' Howard said. He subsided against the meeting-room wall. 'Do you think we've left fingerprints there?'

'I don't know. Most likely. Howard, we're going to get in worse shit if we run off.'

'No we're not.' Howard elbowed himself upright and set off for the lift lobby. Eliza followed. He headed for the stairs, then stopped without going through the swing doors at their head.

'I know. Let's say we thought the meeting wasn't in 4B1, it was in 3B1. We go down to 3B1 now. We wait ten minutes, a quarter of an hour. When it's around 7 there'll be lots more people around. We come back up when there's someone here, say to them, we wonder if we got the room wrong, go in, and … take it from there.'

'Are you sure it'll work?'

'What can go wrong?'

'I don't know, but I don't like it. I think we should phone the police now.'

'He's dead. He won't notice 15 minutes.'

'Yes, but …'

'Oh damn. All right. But we do this together.'

'I wouldn't leave you.'

'I'd bloody hope not. OK, let's get it over with.' He had just turned back towards 4B when the swing door crashed open, catching his shoulder. He dropped his files.

'Sod it,' Hugh Worning said. 'Sorry about that, rushing too much as usual. You all right?'

'You idiot.' Howard bent to pick up his files.

Eliza said, 'God, Hugh, you've shaved.'

'And you're the first – no, the second of 99 people who're going to tell me so today. Actually I already know. What're you doing up here?'

'We might ask what you are,' Howard said.

Sandie Masters came panting up after Hugh. She was a plump woman who worked in IT, with fair hair cut in a thick fringe and a fat plait hanging down her back. 'Hi, you two. Seen the Beaver?'

'Yes, he's not up here, is he?' Hugh asked.

'Bloody stupid,' Sandie said, 'but we had a meeting with him and we both seem to have got the room wrong. We've been waiting in different rooms and when we came out to see what was going on we ran into each other. You're not looking for him too by any chance, are you?'

Eliza stared at them. Howard took her arm with his file-free hand and guided her through the open stair door, forcing Hugh and Sandie to back on to the narrow landing at the stairhead. They stood there in a huddle. Behind Sandie's head was a poster, fishes in an artificial-looking ocean, or maybe it was supposed to be a well-decorated fishtank, and the caption, 'In a sea of choices, we must all be sure to fish for quality.'

'Look,' Howard said, 'something absolutely appalling has happened. You don't want to be involved, honest. And I swear Eliza and I haven't done anything wrong, anything at all. But if I were you I'd piss off down to the first floor and look for the Beaver there.'

Hugh said, 'You'll have to tell us a bit more than that. What's up?'

'He's dead, that's what's up. He's fucking murdered.'

'Christ, are you sure?'

'Very sure. Now go. You don't want to know.'

'Hugh, let's go.' There was rising panic in Sandie's voice. She started down the stairs, her pigtail swinging. Hugh stared for a moment at Eliza and Howard, then he turned and followed her.

Eliza said slowly, 'I thought we wanted witnesses.'

'Damn it, so we did. I'm making a complete muck of this. Come on, let's go and phone the police.'

31

She stopped. Inspector Crane was sitting on the sofa, unmoving, as he had been throughout the bulk of her account. DC Joyce's biro scratched across her pad for a moment more, then stilled.

'That's it,' Eliza said. 'Honest injun. If you check with Hugh or Sandie they'll confirm it.'

'It's not in their accounts,' Crane said.

'Of course it's bloody not. But it's what happened.'

Silence. She wasn't sure if he believed her. She said after a moment, 'I wouldn't have held back anything that'd really help you, but none of this does, surely. You knew Hugh and Sandie were in the office, and it's not as if they saw anything.'

'I don't know if it helps yet.'

'I feel a fool. You do understand?'

'Yes, but that doesn't matter.'

Actually she felt worse than a fool. She felt shallow, callous, vile. Her original account had scarcely painted her or Howard as heroes, but this one showed them in a meaner light. She had thought it might be a relief to admit to her earlier fibs, but it was not.

Crane said, 'You're sure it was Worning and Masters you saw?'

'Yes. We talked to them.'

'And no one else.'

'No. I didn't recognize the man in room 2A, and I didn't seen anyone in 2B, or in 4B.'

'I see.' Inspector Crane got heavily to his feet. 'I do appreciate –' he had begun, when the phone started to ring.

'Shall I answer it?' Eliza asked.

"If you like.'

She didn't like any of this. She wanted the police officers to go, she wanted to be alone. At least neither of them followed her as she went through to the study.

It was Rachel, checking that Eliza was still on for the gym and lunch. Sure thing, said Eliza. She had put down the phone and gone back into the hallway when it rang again.

This time it was Phil.

'Liz, look, I'm sorry about last night.'

She shouldn't have answered it. She should have put the answering machine on. It was stupid, but she had begun to shake.

She said as evenly as she could manage, 'So'm I. I know I over-reacted, but I don't you want you ever doing that to me again.'

'I won't. But we have to talk, and you have to stop pushing me away.'

The two didn't seem to her synonymous. She didn't want to do either. Better to get it over with, though. 'All right,' she said. 'I'll meet you at say, 7 this evening in the Queen's Head.'

'There's no need for that, I'll come over to your house.'

'No.'

Phil did not reply immediately. She was about to say that it wasn't negotiable when he said, 'All right, if you insist. I'll be there at 7.'

32

The police left soon afterwards. Crane was distant, Eliza thought, with no trace of his earlier professional sympathy. She thought he believed that what she had told him now was the truth, but he wasn't grateful. At best he was satisfied that he had been proved right and she had been proved guilty, albeit of no more than fibs.

Her house felt violated. She tried the locksmith again, and to her relief he answered, and came over promptly. He fitted strong deadlocks and better-quality bolts to her front and back doors. By 11.40 he was done, so she was just about on time to meet Rachel at the gym.

They went back afterwards to Rachel's house. It reeked of clean and calm. Eliza wanted to feel clean and calm herself, but she didn't. The workout had amplified every strain and bruise, and her brain was still clogged with horrible knowledge and equally horrible possibilities.

She hadn't actually implicated Hugh Worning or Sandie Masters, she told herself. It was obvious to her that they hadn't killed Harding. She had condemned them to another bout of questioning, that was all. Howard too, but that was largely his fault – first for talking her into telling that tidied-up version, then for being so elusive. Crane would tear him off a strip; or maybe it wasn't Crane who dealt with him, it was some other copper. Howard would survive, though, he could take care of himself.

'Relax,' said Rachel, and she did her best. While Rachel was making a salad she wandered round the ground floor, a glass of Fitou in her hand, remembering. Each holiday they had had together – there had been seven or eight, since they had both been divorced – she had bought a picture with flowers on it, and Rachel had bought something for her house. A beaten copper pot from the Gambia that sat in the hearth in her living area filled with a burgeoning Boston fern, a wall-hanging from Bali in the alcove above the television, a pair of black iron candlesticks from Bermuda on the mantelpiece. Memories, good memories.

She ended up in the kitchen area as Rachel was taking the cassoulet out of the oven for its final check.

'You remember, buying that casserole in Bergerac?'

'Mmm. And you bought that splashy painting with the fig tree, the one you've got over your dining table, in that fortified village, remember the name?'

'Lalinde, was it?'

'Where the restaurant with the great cheeseboard was, and those guys on the motorbikes who chatted us up.'

'God, we had fun.'

'We still do.' Rachel sprinkled a handful of cheese-and-bread-crumb mixture over the beans, chicken and sausage, and returned it to the oven. She sat on a high stool. Her house was open plan, retaining elements from a renovation in the 1950s including a breakfast bar which separated the kitchen from the downstairs living area. She picked up her glass of wine and twirled it between her fingers. 'So who is he?' she asked.

'How can you tell?'

Rachel narrowed her eyes. She was in black today, narrow-cut trousers and a long clinging tunic top. Her hair was loose, hanging flatly to her waist. 'I think I could have told just from being with you,' she said. 'Although things aren't normal with you, obviously. But to be honest I didn't need to. Phil phoned me this morning.'

'What a surprise.'

'Someone from work, was about all I got from him. Someone I don't know, which means someone new I suppose.'

'It would do. You know everyone old.'

'Pretty much.' Rachel put on her wistful look. 'Though it's getting to be ancient history now. Our era's gone. Everything will have changed, except in our picture of it. We're all bloody flies in amber, suspended in time, not moving on. Sorry for the diversion, I didn't mean to get grouchy. Do go on.'

'You've every right to be grouchy,' Eliza said. 'You're the casualties. Anyway, yes. He's not actually with RUS but he's a man I met at work.'

'Known him long?'

'No. We met Thursday.'

'Thursday – what, last Thursday?'

'Yes.' Three days, Eliza thought. It felt longer.

'You can't hardly know him,' Rachel said. 'Phil made out it was this great affair, that he'd finally worked out the reason you finished with him.'

'No. I wasn't seeing him when I was seeing Phil, and it had nothing to do with Phil and me finishing. It came afterwards.' She tried to choose her words. 'It's ... I don't know what it is. Circumstances and attraction throwing us together. It's all happened so fast, and it's not settled or anything. I don't even know if it's going to continue. It's a bad time in my life – well, you know some of that. I guess I plunged right into it because I needed to have someone there for me. Not just you or my other friends, but someone to touch, someone to stay the night with me. That's not an excuse, but it is an explanation.'

'Does it need an excuse?'

She looked at Rachel, and Rachel looked back. A good friend, who would listen, who would try to advise if invited, who wouldn't condemn. Who also wouldn't understand. Hell, you can't have everything.

She said, carefully, 'Does sexual desire need an excuse? No, not in my book. It's a natural instinct, it's part, the best part, of being alive. Does acting on it need an excuse? Not in itself; but I suppose yes, if it hurts someone. I don't think I've hurt anyone yet. I've used some spare time in his life, I haven't stolen it from anyone else. If he'd not been with me he'd have been alone. I'd have been alone too, and I needed not to be alone. But that was last week, strange times, and it doesn't apply on into the future. He has a relationship in London, and children. I know that's a bad game, you don't have to tell me. I'd like to think I'd never press him to leave his kids. I think that'd be wrong; no, I know just as well as you do that it'd be wrong. But I can't imagine managing to control myself into only wanting whatever he could spare. I need a partner, not the unused corners of someone else's partner. What I'm afraid will happen is, I'll fall in love, I'll want more, we'll both know I can't have more, we'll end it, and I'll be wrecked.'

'So you're not in love now?'

'God, Rachel, I'm not sixteen. Three days? Do me a favour. I do feel ... a real connection with him. But it's new, it's so new, I barely know him. You know what it's like at the start of an affair, when you haven't yet figured out what it'll be that makes it not work. Euphoria. I'm high on him. But he's not a part of my life, not woven into it the way you are, or Mitchell and Val, or any of my old friends. Love's too large a word for it. And I think if we ended it now, I could handle it. I'd just be left with the memory of great sex.'

'Great sex!'

Rachel sounded so incredulous that she had to smile. 'Yeah, great sex. I'll have the memory of that forever.'

'And you think that's valid?'

'It'll be no less valid if I never see him again. It's important to me. It'll be a memory as … as real to me as that casserole is to you.'

Rachel laughed. Eliza felt disconcerted; she had taken care to present a sunny picture that she had kidded herself, for a moment, Rachel might empathize with. But she realized almost immediately that Rachel's reaction was a characteristic one, and not intended to be hurtful.

'Sorry,' Rachel said, once she had regained her equilibrium. 'I know you didn't mean it to be funny, and it isn't really, you'll have to put it down to embarrassment or something. I feel like a colourblind man in a tropical garden. Not that I'm agin sex, but I can't imagine feeling like that about it. A part of me's jealous that I can't understand what you're raving about, and a part of me's relieved, because I see all the havoc it causes.'

'I'm well aware of that. A part of me is jealous of you.'

'Quits then.'

'Quits.'

Their glasses clashed across the Formica. They drank.

Rachel said, 'Maybe I should advise you to end it now, but I'm not going to. I have the sense you couldn't handle it. You're probably right, you need this guy – that is, assuming you're definite you don't want to go back to Phil. Phil'd be safer, but you knew that without my telling you. Of course he's heartbroken.'

'Phil's been a pain, worse than a pain.'

'I had that impression. He rang this morning, and he was going on about how I ought to get you to forgive him.'

'Did he tell you what he'd done?'

'Not really. There was a lot about some great new opportunity at work and maybe this other guy was richer but it might not be that way forever; but that's not about forgiveness, is it? D'you want to tell me?'

'I think I want to tell you it all. Going light on the mucky bits, if they'll fatally embarrass you.'

'Seems reasonable. I'll dish up first, then you can.'

She sat and watched as Rachel neatly, efficiently finished dressing the salad, found knives and forks, retrieved two warm plates and a warmed French stick, and finally drew the cassoulet out of the oven. She dished it up with her usual precision.

They ate, and Eliza talked. She told Rachel the entire story, from her first encounter with Howard on the step to her final interrogation by the police. Rachel listened in silence, nursing her wineglass, and when the cassoulet was eaten, picking sometimes at a hunk of dolcelatte and a bunch of purple grapes. The afternoon sun faded outside the window.

When she stopped Rachel slid off her stool, and went to fill the kettle. She switched it on, then came back to the counter.

'You're a very loyal person, aren't you, Lizzy?'

'I hope we both are.'

'True, but I don't think I'd realized before how deep it went. You know the old test, your friend or your country? You'd betray the country without a single qualm.'

'Oh, with plenty of qualms.'

'All right, but no doubts what you'd choose.'

'No. No doubts.'

'Are you still in love with Lewis?'

'A part of me always will be. At least, he can still hurt me: he proved that yesterday. Are you still in love with Peter?'

'I hate the bastard.'

'That's what I mean.'

Rachel gave a crooked smile. 'So we're not healed till we become indifferent, is that what you're saying?'

'Maybe we don't become indifferent till we're dead. I don't know I want indifference. I want to move on. I think that's a part of why I wanted James, because I thought he'd help me move on. I mean, it'd have been better if he was properly available, and it's not as if a screw's a substitute for sharing your life with someone, but I sensed he'd ... have an impact on me. Even if it ended in heartbreak it'd be a different heartbreak. It'd be one more step into the great unknowable future.'

'Sounds great,' Rachel said in a voice which implied the opposite.

'No, not great, but it'll have to do for now.'

33

She checked her answering machine when she got home. It was 4.42. Phil hadn't phoned again, but James hadn't phoned either. It made her feel bleak. She wished she hadn't told Rachel about him: not because she minded Rachel's knowing, but because the telling had made him bulk even larger in her mind.

It was insane of her to imagine it would continue. He didn't need her emotionally as she needed him, and if he wanted sex while he was in Costhorpe, there were far less fraught and complication-prone ways of getting it. Domestic life in London would have brought him to his senses by now. She had to put him behind her, to find some other, safe, emotional prop to get her through this. Anyway, she told herself firmly, there wasn't really anything to 'get through'. The horror was behind her. There would be no more of it, or at least none that affected her so closely: even the most unfortunate person could hardly stumble over three corpses in succession. Neither the Beaver's absence nor Janine's would have any significant impact on her daily life. The only thing she was waiting for was the arrest of their murderer. If it was someone she knew, it would greatly upset her. But even so, it wasn't James, it wasn't Rachel, she couldn't seriously imagine it was Mitchell. It wasn't her parents or her sister or her grandmother. Told it was – John Donaldson, say, or Hugh Worning, someone she knew about as well as that – she would be a bit shaken that they were capable of such viciousness, but she wouldn't be terminally wounded.

So the usual remedies would enable her to survive. Patchwork, lacemaking, lectures on archaeology, trips to the gym, drinks with friends, etcetera. Cut down the excess hours at work, bring those back into her life, and she would get by.

With this resolution made she took a half-finished patchwork cushion cover out of the chest in her bedroom, a Rose of Sharon design in red and green on a cream background that she intended to give to Val, and spent the rest of the afternoon working on it. She felt much calmer by then, almost ready to face Phil again.

But she didn't really expect that the meeting with him would solve anything. She was right. They spent a sterile hour in the Queen's Head. She told him as firmly as she could that she wanted no more than casual friendship from him. He told her that she was emotionally in no condition to change what he regarded as the status quo. She had been nervously anticipating a flood of jealousy over James, but Phil had apparently decided to rewrite the past. He made out that her attempts to finish with him all postdated the Beaver's murder, and were a result of her mind being temporarily unhinged by shock. As for the incident with James at her house, it might as well not have happened.

At the time they seemed to her bizarre tactics, but later an explanation occurred to her. Phil actually knew no more about James than he had deduced from that one brief encounter. He had had no joy in trying to pump Rachel for information, and he hadn't asked anyone else, perhaps because of embarrassment, or perhaps simply because he hadn't known who to ask. Possibly he didn't even know James's name; certainly he didn't mention it. Equally certainly he didn't know James had another relationship, or he would have made use of that knowledge, she felt sure.

He went on again about opportunities at work, but he wasn't specific, and when she asked him what they were he became evasive. She didn't press: it might have given him the illusion she would have felt differently if he were better off.

He would have repeated his argument all night, but after two drinks she insisted on leaving. He made a token protest, then gave in. He could see she was tired, he said. He'd see her again soon, right?

'I'll be around,' she said. It was just about enough to satisfy him, without committing her to anything.

He had parked his Land Rover in the Queen's Head carpark and she refused his offer to walk her the short distance back. She watched him drive off, then went home alone.

It was not quite dark, but even so she found herself hesitating on the doorstep. She felt weary, and depressed, and not a little vulnerable. She didn't relish entering the empty house. As she was weighing the keys in her hand, Edward Derbyshire and his dog emerged from next door.

'Evening, my dear. Fancy a walk? Hubert and I are off for our regular twice round the park.'

'Sounds lovely, but I couldn't face it right now. It's been a long day. Maybe tomorrow after work?' She could act on her resolutions and leave the office early.

'Fine. I'll be sure to remind you.' He squinted across the low wall between the two pathways. 'Everything all right?'

'Yes. Sorry. I'm just being ... nervous, I guess.'

'No need to be sorry. What can I do to help?'

Would it be storing up problems to lean on him? She couldn't see it. He had made it clear he was lonely and keen to be useful, and he was not the kind of man to presume or intrude. And if she was to do without James, she needed all the sources of small-scale support she could muster.

'I hope this doesn't sound stupid, but would you mind coming in with me? Just to make sure the house is empty.'

'Of course. That's not stupid at all, it's a very sensible precaution.' He hopped adroitly over the wall, reaching back to scoop up Hubert and deposit the stumpy-legged dog on her step. 'Hubert's not the fiercest of guard dogs I'm afraid, but if there's anyone there who shouldn't be, he'll make damn sure you know.'

Once in, he took charge with military firmness. 'Come on, Hubert,' he announced, unclipping the dog's lead. 'Reconnoitre.' They checked out all the downstairs rooms as Eliza stood, half-embarrassed, half-amused, in the hall, then he asked if she would like him to check upstairs.

'Please. This is really kind of you.'

'No trouble. Stairs, Hubert.'

Hubert took them at a waddle, and Edward followed. Eliza stayed in the hall, watching them as they set off down the landing.

'Eliza?'

The voice at her back jerked her spine rigid. She gasped.

'Sorry, I didn't mean to frighten you.'

He had. He was James. She took a breath, then another, deeper, and turned to him. It was James as she hadn't seen him before, in navy chinos and a navy V-necked sweater, worn over a grey shirt. They were preppier clothes than she would have guessed he'd wear in his time off. He looked younger, tousle-haired, less commanding. He was holding a bunch of irises in florist's paper.

'I'm sorry. I'm so on edge, I'll be jumping at shadows next.'

'No wonder,' he said gravely. 'It's all my fault, I should have phoned. I just got back to Costhorpe, and I thought I'd come straight over.'

A call of 'Back, Hubert. This way,' came from the top of the stairs.

'Oh. You're not alone.'

'It's my neighbour,' she said hastily. 'I'd just come home and I was uneasy about going into an empty house. Mr Derbyshire offered to check it out for me.' He didn't know about the Phil incident, she thought: he would probably think her crazy for asking her neighbour to do that. But she didn't want to tell him about it.

'I guess I've chosen a bad moment. Do you want me to push off?'

'Oh no, not at all.'

'Watch out.' She turned to find Hubert slithering down the stairs towards them. He scuttled past her and made straight for James's ankles. James bent smoothly, and straightened again with his hands round the dog's middle section. Four small legs and one stumpy tail paddled madly at thin air, accompanied by a frenzy of yelping, and the faint, sweetish smell of the irises. He smiled at the dog. 'Now mate, calm down. Is this your bloodhound?'

'He's mine,' said Edward, following at a more sedate pace. 'All clear upstairs,' he told Eliza. 'Er, did you …'

'Oh. Edward Derbyshire, James Connaught. Everything's fine, Edward.'

'I'll be pushing off then. You're still on for tomorrow?'

'I hope so, work permitting. Give me a shout when you're about to go, if it won't put you out.'

'I'd be delighted.' He turned to James. 'Nice to meet you, Mr Connaught.'

'Won't you stay for a cup of tea?' James asked. 'I don't want to push you –'

'You're not. Hubert and I were on our way out anyway. We'll meet again, perhaps?'

The half-question went unanswered. Eliza and James stood in the hallway and watched as Edward reconnected Hubert's lead and the two of them set off down the street, weaving half-figures-of-eight round the beech trees.

It was James who closed the door. It left them standing just as they had on his first visit, on either side of the lit hallway.

'Nice neighbour,' James said.

'He is. I hadn't seen much of him up to the last day or two. He's a widower, lonely.'

There was an awkward silence, then they started to speak at the same moment. Eliza felt herself flushing.

'Tell me if you want me to go,' James said again.

'No. No, I don't.' What she wanted was to not feel on edge and awkward with him, but that wasn't on offer. 'I just …. You took me by surprise.'

'I should have told you what I was planning. It was my daughter's sixth birthday yesterday, so I had to be there. I though you'd realize I'd be back this evening.'

'You don't have to explain yourself to me.'

He said, slowly, 'I think I do. Shall we sit down or something?'

'I guess. I'll take those, shall I?'

He handed her the irises, and she went through to the kitchen and ran a couple of inches of water into the sink before propping them in it. Then she returned to James, who was waiting for her in the hall.

He followed her into her sitting room. She headed for the button-backed chair, but he caught her hand, and drew her instead with him on to the sofa. Their knees clashed. He took her by the shoulder and guided her back against the cushions. He kept her there for a long moment, holding her eyes, then bent his head. His lips touched hers briefly; withdrew; came back, and they kissed at length. Her hand crept round his shoulder, but when he drew his head back he carried his body from hers as well, holding her almost at arms' length.

He said in a deliberate voice, 'You know and I know that I might not have come back. But I have.'

And for that moment, it was enough.

34

This time he was more gentle.

When they were done, James helped her strip the damp bedclothes and remake the bed with crisp dry sheets. She went downstairs and made them coffee. They took a bath together. They lay in her bed and talked. Tell me about your room, he said, about your house, about your life. She told him, I moved in here four and a half years ago, when I had to make a fresh start in my life. I bought the house because I loved the bathroom with its white tiles and its big white tub and that deep windowsill for my plants. I threw myself into making it mine. I bought postcards and stapled on samples of paint and fabric. I stripped off wallpaper and heat-gunned the doorframes. I painted, I papered, I sewed.

I wanted my bedroom to be a soft room, with cushions and lace, a room full of memories and hope. I made this quilt when I was seventeen. I crocheted the lace on the dressing table in the first year I worked at RUS. The cushion on that chair was made by my grandmother. The flower pictures I bought in a thrift store on Cape Cod. I was on holiday with my friend Rachel. The sun was shining and an icy wind ripped off the Atlantic. The shop was cold and smelled of damp. They had black frames, but I threw those away and brought them back loose in my luggage.

His fingers traced concentric circles on the skin of her shoulder. 'I like your house,' he said. 'I like you, Eliza.'

'Your turn. Now tell me about you.'

There was a space. She thought he would refuse. Then he said, 'When I was eleven I broke my left leg. I've the scar still, here, under my knee. They plastered it from ankle to thigh, and for weeks I didn't go to school. I sat at home and read Sherlock Holmes and Georges Simenon, books my father had had since he was a boy. I remember them sawing off the cast. I wanted to keep it, but they threw it away.'

'You didn't go to boarding school?'

'No.'

'I thought you would.'

'My family aren't rich.'

She wanted him to say more, but he would not. He said instead,

'Can you set your alarm for early – say, half-past five? I'd like to go in with you to St Jude's House tomorrow, while it's deserted. I want you to show me the way you usually come in, the way you went on Thursday, and all the rest of it.'

He meant to stay overnight with her, then. She hadn't dared to ask him. They would have at least this night together.

She slept pressed tight to him, in the Z of his body, his hand loosely on her breast, his breath warm on the back of her neck. The alarm at 5.30 was brutal. She woke heavy-headed. It did not seem strange that James was there. There was no time to shower, but she washed, put on lipstick and taupe eyeshadow, and dressed in a navy suit she often wore to work. It was too warm for a winter coat, too cool in the early morning to do without. She found a Liberty wool square in her drawer, blue and purple peacock feathers, and knotted that round her shoulders.

He was ready faster. He stood watching her brush her hair.

'I'll drive,' he said.

He drove his Merc as he had made love to her, with possessive pleasure. They went first to the Mornington, where she waited in the car while he went into the hotel. He emerged in his business suit. Then to St Jude's House, where he parked in one of the coveted places on the forecourt. It was still labelled 'P S Harding'.

It was four minutes to 6, and the building was in darkness. They got out of the car in unison and stood by its doors. She glanced at James. He was looking at the entrance, his mouth set in a narrow line, his expression unreadable.

'What do you want?'

'Walk me round the outside. Talk to me.'

'What shall I tell you?'

'Whatever comes in your mind. I want it all.'

'A brain dump.' It was Inspector Crane's phrase.

'That's right.'

She took a step forward. 'We're too close, almost. You can't take it all in from this angle.' They were practically under the parapet that jutted out over the main entrance and the steps in front of it. 'It's an ugly building, you don't need me to tell you that. Sixties brutalist architecture. Bloody concrete and whatever these panels are, a filthy sort of green I've always thought.'

'Cheap.'

'Not particularly, although it looks it. It's strange to see it dark.'

'It's early.'

'Yes, but it was never dark in the civil service days. When I started here there were shifts for the computers, 24 hours, and there were guards on the door all the time, day or night. I'd drive past, and there'd be lights on. I don't think there were always people there, it was just that the lights weren't turned off, they weren't that fussed about environmentalism then.'

'When did you start here?'

'1988. I'd joined RUS in London. I met Lewis there – Lewis Stannard, my ex-husband – and we transferred up to Costhorpe together when they moved the bulk of RUS up here.'

'Your ex-husband's at RUS?'

His voice was level. He was not looking at her, he was staring at the darkened entrance lobby.

'Was. He took the money back in January.'

'And?'

'Oh, Lewis is all right. Saleable. Back at the start he was an executive officer like me, but he drifted into something you could pass off as good experience for private-sector marketing. It's difficult to explain if you don't know, about generalization in the civil service.'

'Assume I know.' His voice had become more curt. 'Is he still in Costhorpe?'

'Of course. I saw him on Saturday, actually. He's married again.'

'Of course?' he echoed.

'You know, Costhorpe, graveyard of ambition? People get used to life here. They don't tend to leave.'

'So I've heard.' He moved forward. 'So you go in here.'

'Depends which way you're coming. If you come from the ring road and the underpass, you'd cut round the side of the A wing and go in this way. From the town centre it makes more sense to use the west door.' She followed him up the shallow concrete stairs that led to the heavy glass doors. They peered together through the glass. There was a light somewhere inside the building – she couldn't see the source – and in the dim glow she could make out the new reception area and the desk behind which Bill had so briefly held sway.

'Up till last month this reception area wasn't here,' she said. 'It was an open lobby through to the lifts. We'd go through and flash our passes.'

'You all have passes?'

'Yes, with our photos on, mostly appalling photos, they take them in bulk using some kind of instant machine. Of course the guards knew us all anyway so it was pretty routine, we'd have to get them out but we'd flash them from six feet away, ten feet, you know the kind of system.'

'And if you left?'

'Fired or quit, you mean? You'd hand your pass in, I suppose. I've never done it.'

'Does Lewis still have his?'

She turned to look at him. He didn't look back, he was staring with apparent intentness at the pale oak desk, the coffee table spread with a stack of pamphlets advertising RUS services and Friday's copies of the *Financial Times*, and the low upholstered chairs. She said slowly, 'Lewis left me. It hurt a great deal. Nowadays we manage to be polite, but we're hardly intimate. I wouldn't have a clue whether he kept his security pass.'

'And this was five years ago.' He still did not turn to her.

'Just over.' He had remembered what she had told him the evening before. 'It took us almost a year to finalize everything and sell the house. Since then there have been half a dozen men. Some only lasted a couple of dates, Phil lasted almost a year. In case you were wondering, I'd told him very explicitly that we were through before I ever met you.'

'I wasn't asking you that.'

But you wanted to know, she thought. She turned and began to walk along the side of A wing, away from the forecourt parking area. She did not look back, but she knew that James was following her.

He reached her at the corner of the building.

'Note the sign,' she said. 'A tasteful orangey red. They've hardly changed it from the sign we had when we were a government agency, continuity they say, though it looks like tight-fistedness to us. The standard joke's about the silent T.'

'I don't get it.'

'Think about it.'

'Let's go back to the entrance. What would have happened if you'd forgotten your pass?'

'You'd be in the shit. They didn't let you in without one. Even if you dashed down from the office to the shopping centre to get a pair of tights, you'd have to show it when you came back in. If you left it behind it your boss would have to come down and there'd be hell to pay.'

'But if, say, and this is only an example, if your ex-husband had left RUS and then he wanted to come back into the building for some reason, could he get past the security guard?'

She gave him a sharp glance.

'Lewis wasn't a director but he was a senior manager, and he's a dominant personality. RUS isn't a very small company but it used to be a tight community. You know it's the biggest employer at Costhorpe. Three generations of some families work here. Everyone knew Lewis and everyone knew when Lewis left. He had a big leaving do at the Brown Cow. Afterwards he couldn't have pretended to the security guards that he was still on the payroll and he'd just forgotten his pass, because they'd all have known it wasn't true. If he'd kept the pass for some reason, and I can't see why he should have done, he still couldn't have fooled the guards that he still worked here. That goes for all the senior managers, all the directors. We all knew all of them. We do know what happens here, even though aren't any staff newsletters any more.'

'Aren't there?'

'The staff who edited them were all fired.'

He glanced at her. You gave me that one on a plate, she thought. She thought for a moment that he would make some self-justifying comment, but he did not. 'Show me the other ways in,' he said.

'Follow me.' They went in single file, Eliza leading, round the side of the building that looked onto the ring road. There was only a locked fire door at this end of the long stretch of concrete and green panels. She pointed out what James had surely deduced, that the building was in the shape of an L, with the turn just after the west door at the far end of the wall. The main entrance was in the middle of the long section, with the A and B wings either side of it, and there was only a goods entrance on the outer side of the short projection. Then at the other side of the short section was the walled-off area, the other side of the forecourt from where they had arrived, that they called the Courtyard.

The west door was similar to the main door but there was no step leading up to it, and the reception area on the far side of the glass was smaller.

'Same thing here,' Eliza said. 'You know, this is the first time I've ever seen it without a guard on duty. They were told on Wednesday that all but one of them were being made redundant. Friday was their last day. Apparently from today we get women manning the reception desks. Girls, rather. I didn't know the hours had been cut down as well, but it's the sort of thing they wouldn't bother to tell us. You know, come in at 6.30 and find the building locked against you, ho ho.'

'The doors'll open at 7 am. It's the new security rules, no one's allowed into the building before then. There hasn't been time to circulate staff with the info. If anyone comes early this morning, they'll just have to come back again later.'

'You could have put a notice on the door.'

'Summerfield could, I'm not in charge here. Did you often come in at 6.30?'

'No, but a few people did. Since privatization, not before.'

James frowned. Then he said thoughtfully, 'So the guards were given their cards on Wednesday.'

'Downsized, made surplus to requirements, reorganized out of existence, liberated to pursue a new career. Choose your euphemism. I think so, yes. I found out when Howard told me first thing Thursday morning. Gossip moves fast at RUS, and Howard told it like it was fresh news. Anyway, that's the style: managers get the immediate escort to the door, cannon fodder get a couple of days to grumble.'

'Would you have expected them to retaliate?'

'That's a bloody awful question.'

'I know. Tell me.'

'Then, no. I mean, no one expected murder, if it was retaliation which is hardly proven, but I wouldn't have expected even minor sabotage. About 400 people at RUS have been made redundant in the last six or seven months. Apart from a few near-the-knuckle messages on the email system, I'm not aware that anyone's retaliated. True, things have changed. It goes on and on, and that doesn't help. These are people who thought they'd come through, the ones who're getting the piece of paper now. They've every reason to put a bomb under the bloody place, but it's not the sort of thing they'd do.'

'Someone killed Harding.'

And Janine. She couldn't believe it was – oh, what the hell.

Whoever she thought of, she wasn't able to believe it could be them.

James stepped back and stared to left and right. 'There are two other entrances?'

His coolness grated, but she made no comment. 'That's right.' She ducked down Narrow Street and took him round the remainder of the building, showing him the second fire door, then the goods entrance, which faced away from the roundabout, giving onto a small yard that blocked off the end of the street. 'This one's always been locked at night.'

'And Allen Mark has a list of keyholders, right?'

It occurred to her that if he knew this, then he had already known most of what she had been telling him. 'Yes,' she said shortly.

He went up to the door and pushed it. Nothing gave. He turned back to her. 'What's on the other side?'

'I can show you when we go in. That passage leads down to the main door, and there's a passage off it that goes into the Courtyard. Then there's a set of stairs over to the right.'

'So there are three sets of stairs altogether?'

'Yes, and two banks of lifts.'

They retraced their steps, since the remainder of the perimeter had no path around it. The sky was lightening. James took a bunch of keys from his trouser pocket.

'Am I to take it the 7 o'clock rule doesn't apply to us?'

'It doesn't apply to me. You're with me.' He unlocked the door and opened it just wide enough for Eliza to slip through. He followed her, bent to lock it again behind them, then turned to her and smiled. 'All ours,' he said.

There was something eerie about the silent reception area, something claustrophobic about the locked door. But she was not afraid of James, he was her talisman against fear. She felt invigorated, more than angered, by his brute refusal to edit or disguise his views to please her. She had not edited or disguised her views either. He had not pretended to like them, but he had not criticized her for displaying them. This added up to a kind of intimacy. She could have called it love. She smiled back at him.

He reached for her hand. 'We've got about three-quarters of an hour before anyone'll disturb us. Allen Mark said, don't use the lifts.'

They did not switch on any lights. She led him in near darkness through the echoing lobby, along a corridor and into the cavernous space of the Courtyard. It was open to the sky, and chilly in the early morning. In the half-light that percolated down they could make out the gaudy hut-like refreshment kiosk at the far end, the rows of steel and Formica tables with chairs upended on them, and the flower beds that ran along the walls. In the middle of the yard was another bed with a few prickly bushes and a couple of spindly birch trees that rose up as far as the second-storey windows. It was a garden of sorts, where no birds flew.

'Very pretty,' James said sardonically.

'There's a plan to roof it over. I think they got permission, but they didn't do it. I suppose they thought, after privatization, when we all become part of the rich extravagant private sector ...'

He ignored this. 'Is it used much?'

'It's freezing most of the year. It gets hardly any sunlight. The chairs give you red stripes on the backs of your thighs and the acoustics are bad. I bring visitors here sometimes, there isn't a proper entertainment budget any more so we can't take them to a restaurant, not even a pub or wine bar. The snack bar does one hot dish each day, plus sandwiches and rolls. You can eat for a couple of quid, and that can be charged direct to your cost centre, at least so far it can, it'll probably change when they realize we're doing it. Or they'll fine us for exceeding the budget. And we've been known to hold meetings down here in an emergency when all the meeting rooms are booked.'

'You can drop the propaganda, it's wasted on me. Anything complaints you have can go to Summerfield. Shall we go back inside?'

She bit her tongue, and led him diagonally across the Courtyard to a small door set in the side wall. 'This is the way to the goods entrance.'

It was locked. James took out the keys and tried a couple before he hit on the right one. They went through, and again he locked it behind them. It brought them into a narrow corridor which opened out on their left to a small lobby with a staircase leading up. This time he led and she followed, up to the inside of the glass doors. He bent to look at the steel lock. Eliza said, 'The mail room and the print room are down that way. Of course the printers were fired, so it's not really the print room any more.

Now the police are using it. There's no lift from this lobby, don't ask me why. It's not far to the west door and the lifts there. You go down through 1D, that room, to get to it. The smoking room's just on the right down that way.'

'Let's take a look.'

The doors to 1E, the former print room, were locked, and the glass had been covered with paper sheeting. James tried them, then looked at his watch. 'No matter. We've only about half an hour left before other people come in. Show me where you work, then we'll go up to Janine's office.'

'Janine's desk. She didn't have an office of her own, any more than I do.'

'Whatever.'

He had come to her desk before, but in the immediate aftermath of Harding's murder, and she assumed he had not taken in any details. She led him back to the main lobby and up the stairs. There was a low-level security light in the stairwell, enough for them to see by. 'Quality posters,' she said tersely as they reached the landing. 'Plastered everywhere, to spur us on.' She didn't pause for him to look. 'This way.' She went quickly through the lift lobby and into 2B, waving a hand to her left. 'All this is my section. There are six people working for me, and three sections like mine in this area. Genevieve Bush and Mitchell Jones head the other two. Genevieve's patch starts the other side of the slightly higher purple partition. I have this desk, Helen's next to me, then there's Martha, Russell, Mary and Jo around that open space, and Tom's desk on the other side of the low partition.'

'One computer each.'

'That's right.'

He wandered over to the desk she had indicated as hers, and picked up the topmost file from the stack in her action tray. His eyes scanned the list of initials and dates on the cover. 'OS01, what's that?'

'It's the internal mail address, to me. Office Services Manager number 1. In the civil service days they never addressed anything to us by name, it was all by position number. It's changed now.'

'I'd hope so.' He flicked through the contents, stopping to glance at a couple of letters and memos. She knew the file, it was a boring project. James seemed to agree. He put it down and peered at the blank screen of her computer. 'Do you use email much?'

'More than we used to, but not a lot. Mostly for internal stuff, it's a quick method when you want to circulate lots of people at once. You understand how it works?'

'I've made enquiries, I don't pretend to be a computer buff. It seems it's difficult or impossible to disguise which machine a message comes from. They all have individual addresses on the network, and there's an operating system which keeps track of that kind of thing.'

'So I understand. Which means the messages that were sent about Thursday morning meetings came from Janine's computer.'

'Janine's desk is up near Harding's office, I assume?'

'Yes, in 4A. I guess we can take a look.'

35

Janine's desk was not hard to find. The directors' secretaries all worked in an open-plan section, while the wall that looked onto the ring road was divided up into private offices for the directors themselves. All the old RUS staff had nameplates on their desks; only Janine had been a newcomer since the takeover. Ergo, the desk with no nameplate had to be hers.

James reached over and took a sheaf of papers from the topmost tray of a blue plastic stack. It was well past dawn now, but several of the vertical cream blinds across the windows were shut, and although it was possible to make out the headings it was impossible to read normal-sized typescript.

'Switch on the lights.'

Eliza went back to the door to find the switch. By the time she returned he was halfway through the pile, flicking papers to the bottom, pausing to speed-read one or two. 'Yes, these are addressed to Harding,' he said, glancing up at her. 'I'll have to get a temp in and have her go through this stuff.'

'There's no need to get a temp. There are women in the company you could redeploy.'

'A temp.' He said it firmly, dismissing her proposal. He dropped the memos back in the tray and looked around. Janine had worked in an area about six feet wide and ten deep, stretching from the central aisle to the windows, on the side overlooking the main entrance and the directors' carpark. There were few tall buildings in Costhorpe, and the window, its blinds set to open, provided a view that stretched as far as City Hall and St Philip's church. Her desk faced outwards to the aisle. It was L-shaped, with the end that held a computer, laser printer, fax machine and filter coffee machine angled against the partition that separated her area from Crystal's. Above the desk, the partition had a poster of sheep in a field and a sheepdog nipping at their legs, captioned 'Quality is a team being steered in the right direction', and a calendar from an office equipment supplier. May's photo was of fields of rape and an unidentifiable green crop, shot to resemble a three-dimensional checkerboard. A Little Pony plastic toy, slightly battered, sat between the fax machine and the coffee machine.

There were low cupboards arrayed along the wall behind the desk, all with shuttered fronts. A narrow gap between the end of the desk and the wall of the room provided the only access to the workspace. James slipped through it, paced to the window, turned and retraced his steps as far as the typing chair.

'There's nowhere to hide.'

'That's the hazard of being a secretary. They have to intercept visitors, and if you can't see them they can't see you.'

'True.' He swung round again and tried one of the cupboard fronts, shaking the shutter to confirm that it was locked and not merely stubborn to open. He tried a second with the same result, gave up, and turned his attention to the computer. 'This is the same model as yours?' he asked Eliza.

'A bit newer I think, but there's a generic similarity.'

'Can you use it?'

'I should think so, in theory at least. You want me to get into the email system?'

'That's right. See what you can do.'

She came round the desk and took the solitary chair. James leaned over her shoulder as she turned on the machine and waited for it to go through its start-up routine. She could sense his warmth, feel his breath on her cheek.

Her own computer used Windows; Janine's had Windows 95, which was not familiar to her. Made clumsy by the awareness he was watching, it took her a moment to identify the logo for the diary and mail utility. To her relief the screen that came up next was one she recognized. There was an 'Enter password' command in its centre. She swung round to James.

'Password,' he echoed.

'It comes up automatically, there's no way of avoiding it. Well, if you're a whizzo systems programmer I dare say there is, but not for the likes of me.'

'So you can't go any farther.'

'I wouldn't say that yet. Some lateral thinking's required.' She surveyed the surface of Janine's desk. An A4 desk diary lay open on the deskpad. There was a document holder next to the computer screen with a scrawled memo held in place by a grey plastic arm. Otherwise the only papers were in the blue trays. Janine seemed a tidy worker, albeit she had gone home unexpectedly on Thursday and never returned. Dead. It was hard to comprehend. Violently killed. There was no sense of violence in the office. She imagined Janine leaving. Crying. Had she made Crystal wait while she shut down the computer, or had someone else done that after she had left? Or was it not true that she hadn't returned? Perhaps she had come back at some point, after she had been quizzed about the memos, to check whether there was any trace of them on her system? If so, when? Who had quizzed her? Had they too done what Eliza was doing now? She had no answers to any of these questions.

Password. She focused on a short row of dictionaries, A4 binders and other volumes. At one end was a Costhorpe telephone directory and Yellow Pages; at the other, next to the steel bookend, a small manuscript book with a matt sky-blue cover. She reached for this, saw alphabet tabs as she opened it, and ran her finger down to the Ps.

'What are you doing?' James asked.

'Checking under P for password.'

'You must be joking.'

The look she returned him was deadpan. 'There are about twelve different computer programs on the network in this office, not counting all the non-networked ones, the word processors and spreadsheets and anything else special Janine might have used. I use five of them in my job – no, six now I need the nominal ledger to do my budget projections. They all have passwords which all have to be changed on different frequencies, and the systems won't let you just renew the previous one. It's a nightmare. OK, you're not supposed to write the passwords down, but it's like PIN numbers – you can remember one but not half a dozen. I keep in my head the password that locks my confidential files, assessments of my staff and so on, but the rest are in my little book. It looks like Janine had the same problem – and the same solution.' She'd turned to the second page of Ps – the first was full of addresses and phone numbers – and she flattened the book at the page-spread in triumph.

'She could have disguised it,' James said.

'Why? There won't be anything hugely confidential in her emails, nobody would send anything supersensitive that way, and there's a lot of hassle involved in a password nobody else knows. If she were off sick anyone who picked up her work would be left tearing their hair out every time a password screen came up.

With hindsight you can say she should have been more careful, but ask around the office, and you'll find she was only doing the same as everyone else.' As she spoke she was running her finger down the list. 'Here it is. Cromwl01. Eight-digit password, mixed alphanumeric as required.'

'Our Chief of Men.'

'Historical allusions? Radical ones? Can't see it from Janine. Maybe her mum lives at 101 Cromwell Road.' Eliza turned back to the screen and typed it in. The hard disc whirred and the screen changed. She pressed a couple more keys and brought up a list. 'That's her incoming mail.'

'We want her outgoing mail. Specifically, a dozen memos arranging meetings at 6.30 last Thursday.'

I know that, she thought silently. She said, 'There's a list that tells you which messages you sent, if they were read and when.' She was pressing keys as she spoke, focusing on the screen. 'But you can delete messages from the list if you want to. If they were sent from here they've been deleted. There's no sign of anything sent on Wednesday afternoon.'

'Damn. The machine was in use according to the IT department. Is there anything else you can try?'

'I'm not an expert, James. I'll see if she's saved the text anywhere.' She opened Windows Explorer and scrolled down the subdirectories. Conscious of James breathing over her shoulder, she opened up half a dozen files with cryptic names. They were all memos from Janine or from Harding, and none of them had anything to do with meetings on Thursday. She sat back with a sigh. 'That's about the limit of my capabilities.'

'How long would it have taken to send twelve emails?'

'It depends how fast whoever it was could type, and how well they knew the system. They might have typed in one message and edited it to create the others, or they might have done it from scratch twelve times. That wouldn't have taken much longer, they were only two-line messages. Say, at a minimum fifteen, twenty minutes? Maximum –'

'It'd take me an hour, I should think.'

'Or it would have been possible to type them in Word on a different computer, save them on a disc and read them into this programme, but the interface isn't good, and for short memos it'd hardly be worth it.' She swung round to James again. 'On a Wednesday afternoon ...'

'Between three and five.'

'Did the police tell you that?'

'Yes. It was one of several things they told me in confidence, but I can't see any harm in your knowing. I think everyone who's interested has worked out that much by now.'

Everyone who's interested. Until that point she had almost taken for granted this bizarre expedition. Now she wondered at her acquiescence.

'Are we doing this with the police's blessing?'

He frowned at her. His eyes narrowed into small chips of blue-black in the artificial light. He said slowly, 'No, but we're not disobeying their instructions either. To the best of my knowledge the police have already checked over this computer, dusted for fingerprints, looked at the email programme, whatever. I simply wanted to see for myself.'

'So you're ... investigating.'

'I have an interest in knowing what's going on,' he said. 'As do we all. I've no reason to distrust the police investigation, but the angle I'm coming from is different from theirs. I don't think it inconceivable I'll come across something they've missed. If so, I'll pass it over to them, if that's what you want to know.'

It was and wasn't. It was not that she expected the police to find out what they had done and be angry. Nor did she expect anyone else to find out. There was no clear reason she could articulate for her unease. Bullying, she thought. Investigating. James could not have been the bully who had threatened, then killed, Janine – at least, he certainly couldn't have killed her – but someone was. James was not the only person making his own enquiries, indeed most likely many people were. All of them had motives both simple and complex. Like James's, like her own. The killer knew, in a general way, that they were doing these things.

She glanced back at the computer. James was right, she thought: this small piece of the logistics was worth investigating. She said slowly, 'Wednesday afternoon. Janine was out of the office, I know because Mitchell told me he'd checked, and I think Mr Harding was at the same meeting. What about the rest of the people in this section?'

James answered her readily, which was not something she had

taken for granted. 'True, Janine and Patrick were at one of the series of client seminars, meet the new management. Frank Mills and Marjorie Bergman were there too, and two of the other secretaries. You know there are four secretaries in total servicing the directors.'

She nodded, although she wouldn't have been sure of the number if asked.

'David Summerfield was with me from 4 till 7, in a meeting room, 4B8, and he brought Crystal along to take notes and so on. John Donaldson, Andrew Banning and Gerald Young were in London, so for most of the afternoon this area was deserted. One secretary did come back early from the seminar, Mary something?'

'Mary Austin.'

'That's right. She doesn't remember anyone passing her desk after 4.30, but she can't speak for earlier. She didn't strike me as a dynamic lady, but I assume she'd have noticed if anyone was using Janine's computer while she was here.'

'I think she would. You're right, she's not particularly lively, but she's not blind or stupid.'

'So in summary there was a window of opportunity from 3 to 4.30, although I doubt anyone could have worked at this desk in absolute confidence they wouldn't be seen. I think the police are asking what everyone in the building was doing at that time, but I imagine it'll be difficult to rule out a great many people. Except for the directors; none of them could have sent the emails, or any of the secretaries in this area except for Mary.'

'I see.' She thought of her own Wednesday afternoon, the usual mixture of meetings, sessions at her computer, phonecalls made and received, trips to the loo and to get coffee. She could have gone missing for twenty minutes without anyone wondering where she was, as could almost anyone in Office Services.

James said, 'It's 7 o'clock. Can you turn this machine off?'

'Oh. Yes. We'd better be going.' She swung back to the screen and went rapidly through the computer shut-down routine, returning Janine's index book to its place while she waited for the disc drives to finish whirring. James stood watching her. She flicked the off switch and stood up.

He reached out and put a hand to hers. 'Thank you for that.'

'It's OK.'

'Is it?'

She widened her eyes in query. 'You're a strange mixture,' he said. 'I have the sense sometimes that you trust me, you're at ease with me, and then at other times it's as if you switch off, you're somewhere I can't get to. I suppose there's no reason you should trust me, you barely know me.'

'I do trust you.'

'Why?'

'Intuition, I suppose.'

'You mean sex.'

'I guess I do.' She smiled. 'Sounds bloody insane when you put it like that.'

'Chemistry. Leaping flesh.' He smiled too, a wide and warming smile that included his eyes. 'We know how fucking unreliable it is, but at the same time it matters so much.'

To you too, she thought? She could still barely believe she was special to him; that the way they were together was as extraordinary to him as it was to her. But he had sought her out from the start, and at every opportunity since. He had as much to lose as she did, perhaps more. The timing, the circumstances were terrible. A murderer was on the loose, they needed to be alert at each second. And yet a touch, and they were consumed by fire.

He was still smiling. His free hand drifted up to touch her jawbone, her chin, tilt her head up to his. He said in a husky voice, 'I want you right now.'

She wanted him too. Her entire body was responding to his touch. God, they were insane. It was only hours since they had made love. She hadn't showered since the last time the night before. His sweat was still on her body.

'As we were saying,' she said unsteadily, as he bent to kiss her forehead, 'this is not the most private of places.'

'True.' His hand brushed aside her scarf, the lapel of her jacket, and touched her breast. 'We'd better go somewhere else.'

'Where?'

'Hell, I don't – yes I do. The office I've been using, the one over there.'

She supposed he meant Ken Thursby's old office, which was only a few feet away. 'God, would you …?' Eliza whispered.

'Wouldn't you?' He didn't need an answer or at least not a spoken one: her body was answering for her. She did not resist as he drew her past the end of Janine's desk and across the aisle into the unused office.

She had never made love in the office, never. Not even a kiss in the stairwell, let alone what James was doing now. He kicked the door shut behind them and guided her backwards as far as the desk. She felt the hard edge of it at thigh-level, slipped onto it, sitting, reached her hands up to James's shoulders and her mouth up to his.

His mouth was hot on hers, his tongue insistent. She felt him pull up the hem of her skirt and slip a hand under it. His fingers traced circles on her skin through the sheer nylon of her tights. She was turning to liquid under his touch. He ran a forefinger along her crotch, lingering for an instant on her clitoris. Her breath drew in at the intensity of her response. It was like a small orgasm in itself.

'Get these damn tights off,' he whispered.

'James, if anyone ...' she half-protested.

'And your panties.'

They shouldn't. They had to. Just quickly. Just to feel him in her, to be one with him, to ease the ache, to come herself and feel him come.

This was way out of normality, this was somewhere wild where no rules applied. No one would come. Things fell apart. Death row. Danger, sex and danger, danger in the air, invisible as radiation, a whisper calling from round the next corner. Do this now, for you cannot trust in tomorrow.

She finished pulling her down her tights, stepped out of her panties and shoved them into the pocket of her jacket. Sex, death, scandal, all the untameable things. Wild sensation. She brought her bare feet up around his thighs, her knees to his buttocks, as he came into her.

She had expected him to ram her, but he did it slowly, measuring each centimetre, laughing into her eyes at the sheer raw intensity of it. His hand was on her thighs, holding her in position. She took in a sharp breath as his thighs came up against hers. She was aware of the full length of him inside her. The cream walls, the noticeboard, the fake-oak door of Ken Thursby's office came into focus and blurred into chaos.

She could feel her body squelching against his as he slowly thrust in, withdrew, thrust again. Her tissues seemed to swell against him, she was wet but tight, hot, pink fire. He moved his hand, finding her clitoris again. The intensity was too much, she could feel herself losing the last shreds of her control, she was on the edge of screaming. She was clutching at his shoulders, her buttocks clean off the desk, her body clenched around his as her orgasm built and began to explode.

He froze, clamping a hard hand over her mouth. His other hand pushed her back down on the desk. His penis slipped out. Her eyes widened.

He loosed his hand and put it to his lips. Ssh.

She could hear it now, as the thunder in her head faded. Voices outside the door to the office, male voices, indistinct through the chipboard of the partition.

She did not think he spoke, it was his hands that told her what to do, and she obeyed, silently slipping down from the desk, bending to grab her discarded shoes and following him, barefoot, round the big executive desk. He pulled her down to the floor, both of them sprawling at the back of the desk. It was poor cover: the desk had a modesty board at the front and anyone looking inside the room would not see them, but they would not be hidden from someone who came closer. There was nowhere else, no large cupboards in the room, not space for them both in the central hole of the desk.

Insane. Even more insane than what had gone before. Christ, to be caught like this, bare legged, bare assed, with the smell of sex heavy on her. Had they got time to move? She could sit on one side of the desk, surely, he on the other, they could pretend he had called her in to discuss –

No time; the click of the doorhandle. A voice, now clear and recognizable.

'No, he's still here. I'd rather he wasn't, but what can I say?'

'More of a hassle to Summerfield than to you, I guess.'

'True, but – Shut the door, Hugh.'

She was pressed tight against the foot of the desk, the smooth pale oak hard against her shoulderblade, and her face against the shoulder of James's suit. The beat of her heart, of his, seemed astonishingly loud in the quiet room. She was trying to breathe deeply, silently, but the air was sticking in her throat.

The door clicked shut.

'But if it wasn't for him it wouldn't be Summerfield, I assume,' the second man said.

'He sure wouldn't be my choice.'

'Nor mine. Was it Connaught put him in then?'

'That's about the length of it.'

'And is he telling you what's going on?'

'David? I don't think he knows, to be honest. The police aren't talking much, and when they do, if they do, it's to Connaught.'

'So it all comes back to bleeding Connaught. And he's not talking, I take it?'

A very short silence.

'Don't get me wrong, Hugh. I'm not on bad terms at all with Connaught. I wouldn't want you thinking he's passed me by, because that's not how it is from my angle. He's holding his options open, if you ask me. He's put Summerfield in as night watchman, not as the opening bat. I'd guess he's planning to look us all over more carefully before he makes a permanent recommendation to the Saturn board.'

'Which is where we come in.'

'That's what I wanted to talk to you about, yep.'

'Well, I must say I'm glad, Frank. These last few months have been bloody frustrating. I did think they'd look at the talent they'd got before hauling in all these outsiders. If Andrew Banning were brilliant I wouldn't mind so much, but to be honest I think he's a fucking disaster. Complete waste of space. I've so many ideas, I've got the record to prove I can bring them off, and can I get Banning to listen? Or Harding for that matter.'

'Oh, Harding's no loss, we all know that. He never was a good choice. It was all done in such a rush, that's what it comes down to. They didn't expect to win with their bid and they were caught with their pants down when the Chancellor said, here, take it. I think Saturn see that clearly enough now. Continuity, that's what it needs. Reassuring the old customers, then starting to build up the –'

'Yeah, that'll be my strategy as commercial director.'

Another short pause.

'Director?'

And another.

'You surely knew that was what I'd be looking for, Frank.'

'But you're young for it, Hugh. What are you, thirty?'

'Thirty-one, and I wouldn't say that was out of line these days, MBA and seven years' experience.'

'For a main board director ...' Frank's voice faded.

'OK, in the civil service I wouldn't have got it, but this is the private sector. It's what you need, a bit of youthful dynamism to round out the team. Think about it, Frank. You and me, with Donaldson and Young to back us, and maybe Bergman too. That'd be a board majority, and ...'

'Oh, I'm thinking.'

So was Eliza. Her leg was cramping up, she was thinking about that too, and how long this conversation was likely to go on, and whether Hugh and Frank would come nearer to the desk. They hadn't switched on the light, and it sounded as if they were still near the door.

'Any danger Connaught wants the job for himself?' Hugh asked.

'I've been wondering that, to tell the truth.'

'What's he make at Saturn, d'you think? A hundred K?'

'More, I'd guess, but he could write his own ticket here. I don't think he'd want to be a hands-on MD, though, he's got too much on in London. I'm working on sounding him out, seeing if he's interested in a deal that gives him a board position. I'd rather not, obviously, it'd unbalance things with his position at Saturn, but if that's his price I'll think hard about paying it. And if he doesn't play, I've other contacts at Saturn as well. Don't you worry, I've covered the angles, Hugh.'

'I'm sure you have.' Hugh's voice changed. 'You've heard the gossip, of course?'

'Gossip. Hell, there's so much, Hugh, I'm not sure which bit you –'

'Eliza Stannard.'

'What?'

Hugh's voice reeked of self-satisfaction. 'It's true, I kid you not, Connaught's fucking her. Rachel Morecambe told me last night. She had it straight from Eliza, you know they're best mates.'

'Well.' A particularly plump silence ensued, then Frank went on, 'Thank you for that, Hugh. Never hurts to have an ace or two in reserve. He's married, is he?'

'Live-in girlfriend in London, apparently. And a couple of kids.'

'Well, the sly bastard. At a time like this!'

'Makes you think, doesn't it? With Harding not yet in his grave, and that poor girl.'

'Terrible, terrible. The girl especially.'

'To be honest that was a relief in its way. When Harding was done for I was in the office, you know they questioned me? But I've an alibi for Friday night, so I'm in the clear now. I thought you'd like to know.'

'Oh. Yep. Me too, of course. Tell you the truth, even with two of them killed I can't see it as an inside job. Someone from London maybe, jealous wife or ...'

'I'd be surprised, but you never can tell. Course, I don't want to think it's anyone we know.'

'Can't believe it is. Well I must be getting on, Hugh. It's been useful, this talk, though.' There were a couple of heavy footsteps.

'We're on the same side, Frank. And you won't forget what I said.'

'Course not. I'll keep in close touch.'

The door opened. The voices grew fainter. It clicked shut.

James was the first to stand up, dusting himself down and pulling up the zip on his still-open fly. 'All clear,' he said. 'You'd better get dressed.'

'I am doing.' The panties and tights she pulled out of her pocket looked grubby, although they had been clean that morning.

James said, 'We can't go for five minutes or so, we'll have to give them time to move away. Sit down and fill me in. Frank Mills I recognized, but who's Hugh?'

So much for empathy, Eliza thought bitterly. She felt dirty, depressed, betrayed. God, Rachel! What had she been thinking of? And the squalidness of it all.

'Eliza, are you OK?'

She rolled up the second leg of her tights. and cast a slightly resentful look up at him. He had only had to zip up his fly, and once more he looked immaculate, although slightly grim, understandably she supposed. Mr Connaught in his position of power with his hundred K, with the peasants plotting behind his back and slimy gossip about his sex life starting to slither round the office.

'I'll live,' she said.

'Will you?' As she scrambled to her feet he reached out to take her arm.

'Why, d'you think I'm next on the death list?'

'That's not what I mean. It's not what you meant, is it?'

She didn't quite meet his eye. 'I can't say I'm feeling at one with the world. And before you say it, I appreciate this isn't too super-duper for you either.'

'No, it's not. It's a shitty situation. I'm rather inclined to ask who your best friend Ms Morecambe is, for starters. But I was planning not to, at least not right now, because the last thing I want is for us to argue.'

'So you need me as your little trusty to get you through this.'

It sounded resentful; it was. It must have taken him aback a little, because he didn't reply immediately, leaving the words to hang on the still air.

'Yes, I do, actually,' he said. 'I had the impression you need me too.'

Her eyes went to his. A quick retort died on her lips.

She said slowly, 'We don't always get what we need.'

'How true. And what we take we can't always afford. We both know this was a mistake and we shouldn't have done it. This morning, the whole affair come to that. It's bad timing, it's too fast, it was prompted by a lot of shit in my life, most of which you don't need to know about, and I suppose by about the same in yours. But there's no point being sorry, and no reason to be sorry for what's good about it, which is not only sex. I think trust is worth having, and I hope we still do have it. And mucky though this particular situation is, I think what we learned – or at least, what I learned – this morning was worth hearing.'

'It was all news to me too.'

'Good. Not that it's any great surprise that everyone's jostling for position, or that half of them want to cut me down. I'm not so easily beaten, actually.'

'I can believe that.'

'Good.' He gave her a slightly forced smile. 'At least they didn't find us. Now I think we'd better get out as soon as the way's clear. Go home, take a shower and have some breakfast. I'll phone you later. OK?'

It was verging on patronising, and she was tempted for a moment to refuse. Rationally, she couldn't afford the time to go home. She was too far behind with her work, and getting more behind every day. If she stumbled at work, if she fell, she knew James wouldn't pick her up. She didn't hold that against him, it was just how things were.

But he had a point. At times like this you did what you needed to do.

'Sure,' she said. 'The other man was Hugh Worning, by the way. He's in Major Sales, dealing with particularly large projects, hence his coveting Banning's job. You might know him by sight, five-eight or so, dark, slightly overweight, used to have a short beard but he shaved it off under pressure from Harding. Conniving bastard but he can be charming.'

'You think.' He smiled again, thinly. 'No; I shouldn't second-guess you, this is your world. D'you want to see if it's clear to go?'

'Yes.' On impulse she reached up, and pulled him down for a kiss. He acquiesced; he held her for a moment.

'Take care,' he said.

'And you.' She went to the door and slid it open a crack. The corridor was empty. She left without looking back.

36

Inspector Crane rang when she was just out of the shower, and drying her hair. 'I tried to get you at work,' he said. He sounded resentful that it should have taken him two calls.

Eliza didn't answer.

'I want to talk to you again.'

'There's nothing else I have to say.'

'But there's more I have to ask. I did appreciate what you told me on Sunday. I think we're a bit closer to the truth, but we're not there yet.'

Eliza said nothing.

'The timing, you see. We're still out on the timing.'

'I don't think so,' Eliza said.

'I do. Think about it, because I'll be coming to your office this afternoon. And I'll keep at it this time till you tell me everything.'

37

At least she already had a time fixed with Howard. She would have to update him on what she had told the police on Sunday (assuming they hadn't updated him themselves), and maybe he could help her plan a strategy for this next accursed bout with them.

She intended to phone him as soon as she got in, but was distracted by the sight of the rest of her team all standing round Helen's desk.

'What's up?'

Helen swung round. 'You're late this morning.'

'True.' The resentful note in Helen's voice irritated her: Helen was a reliable worker but she always made everything seem so hard. Eliza dumped her briefcase on her chair, unwound her wool square and draped that over the back. 'So what's this about?'

'You haven't heard? About Janine Broughton?'

'Yes; yes, I have. Dreadful, I agree.'

'I think they ought to close the office.'

'They won't do that. Not again, not after closing it a day for Harding. For the funerals, maybe.'

'I don't mean as respect, I mean for safety's sake. There's a lunatic at large. We have to be protected!'

'The police are here. You've plenty of company. Realistically you're probably safer in the office than you would be at home on your own, Helen.'

'You never understand.'

'Maybe not.' She sat down and reached to switch on her computer. 'Back to work, please, everyone. We'll have a team meeting at 9.30 and discuss any issues you want to raise then.'

Mary, Jo, Russell and Tom obeyed. Eliza did not look at Helen, although she was conscious of the younger woman's eyes fixed grumpily on her. Finally Helen shrugged, and turned back to her own computer. Martha picked up the spare in-tray they used as a tea tray. She drifted across to Eliza.

'Yes, coffee please. The usual,' Eliza said without looking up from the screen.

Martha said, 'Eliza, you're being a pain. It's not like you. I mean, we're upset, we're all bloody upset. The Beaver, that was like too gross to believe, but Janine I knew. She was only a few years older than me, and she's dead.'

Even Martha, who was as resilient as they came. Eliza sighed inwardly and pushed back her chair.

'I'm sorry,' she said. 'I've got a lot on my mind. You're right, I could have handled that better. I do appreciate that everyone's really cut up by this, me included for what it's worth, but I meant what I said to Helen. I think it's best to work on through it.'

'Got to make sure the surviving shareholders get their bloody bonuses.'

'For us, not for them. As a way to cope with it. Does that make sense to you?'

'I want to do something, something to recognize the fact that there's a woman dead. Maybe you can just switch the computer on and go into boss mode, but I can't function like that.'

None of us can, Eliza thought. Boss mode. All it means is, I have to worry about you and you don't worry about me. She tried to push James, Rachel, Crane and the rest out of her head, and come up with something to appease Martha.

'I'll tell you what, has anyone organized condolence cards? Would you and Helen like to do it together, for the team? Come to that you could ask Mitchell and Genevieve, maybe they'd like you to do it for the whole department.'

'For him and her?'

'I don't think it would be on to do it for just one of them. You can take the money out of petty cash, and Personnel will know who to send them to. All right?'

'Yeah. Yeah, we'll do that.' Martha set off with the tray.

Eliza sat for a moment watching her. Small consolations, she thought. She thought of James. What's good about it is not only sex, so he'd said. We also have trust, of a kind. Was there more? Was there love, his love? He had not yet used the word to her, or she to him come to that. It had not been a relationship character-ized by candlelit meals and whispered nothings. Two people were dead. This was not on the same scale of significance, but still it mattered.

He would phone. Later. She trusted him to phone.

Meanwhile, she had to finalize her appointment with Howard. She rang him and suggested she book a meeting room. If anyone asked, they could say it was a budget discussion. If he would much rather, they could go out of the office and meet in the café on Ham Road, but she didn't particularly want to do that because it would take longer, and she was so bloody behind with her work.

She was taken aback when Howard said no to both. He didn't want them to fake a budget meeting because no one would believe it, he said: Summerfield had put the budget revisions on hold. Anyway there was no point in meeting now. She had already done the damage.

He didn't sound like the familiar easy-going Howard she knew. He was as close to anger as she had ever known him. It angered Eliza in return. If he had been given a tough time on Sunday it was largely his own damn fault. She hunched her shoulders and brought the receiver closer to her mouth.

'Look, Howard. I know you're pissed off with me because I didn't keep to the story, but I didn't have any sodding choice. The cops didn't believe it. I warned you I was going to have to change it. They'd had me in twice and they told me they were coming back for another go. If I'd had my way we'd have swapped notes before they got to me, then we could have sorted something out. It was you who wouldn't break your bloody weekend.'

'Bloody's the word for it,' Howard said.

'Mine too, for what it's worth. I'm not going to cry for you, if I cry for anyone I'll cry for Janine. Now I need to swap notes with you about what we both told them, and I need to sort out what I'm going to tell them next, because they're coming back this afternoon.'

'So we head for some meeting room and stick a label on the door saying "Conspiracy in Progress".'

'Any better ideas?'

Silence. She had almost begun to wonder if Howard had put the phone down and walked off, when he said, 'All right. I'm sorry, Lizzy. It's not really you I'm angry with, but you don't know what it's like. No one thinks you did it.'

And they did think Howard did it? Really thought it? It shook her.

'I'm sorry,' was all she could think to say.

'And I am not, not going to give them any more reason to suspect me. I'll tell you what we'll do. I'll head down to the smoking room around five to 11, and you can drift in about 11. It'll most likely be empty, and if it's not we'll have to play it by ear.'

'Howard, I don't smoke.'

'You do now,' he said grimly.

38

The team meeting was subdued. Everyone seemed on edge. Eliza talked them through a long memo from David Summerfield about the new security arrangements. Everyone was to sign in on entering the building and sign out on leaving it. If they left their desk during the day, they were to fill in a slip saying where they were going. If they left the office they were to sign out formally. Unless they were leaving for lunch, they were to indicate precisely where they were going, who they were meeting (if anyone), and for how long they intended to be there.

Helen wanted more. She didn't want ever to be in a meeting with just one other person, she said; not till they had caught whoever had done it. Eliza argued that there weren't many two-person meetings anyway. That was all the more reason to agree, Helen said. Martha and Jo supported her, and eventually Eliza agreed that if any were proposed, they should be discussed with her and the arrangements changed if at all possible.

As they were breaking up Martha held her back. 'Eliza, I forgot. Does not being alone apply to business trips too?'

'Why, what d'you have planned?'

'I've got a meeting in Bristol tomorrow with the Vehicle Inspectorate guy. You remember we agreed I'd go down on my own and discuss their requirements, and you'd negotiate the deal by phone afterwards?'

'Oh. Yes, I remember.'

'But it's not ideal, is it? They weren't at all happy when we said it'd just be me coming down. It was only because you were too busy to come with me.'

'I was, and I still am. It's a hell of a way, Mattie. Four, five hours by car, or a sod of a train journey.'

'All the more reason to not go there alone.'

Martha's fears about the murderer were genuine enough, no doubt, but Eliza had a sense the younger woman was playing on them. She had made it clear from the start she was reluctant to handle the VI meeting on her own, and she was not the type to put up and shut up. She couldn't honestly claim there was a great security risk in taking the train on her own. It seemed unlikely that she was a target for the murderer, and if she were, he would surely not pick a crowded station to do the deed.

Martha said, 'Come to that, it'd do you good to get out of the office. You're looking tired, y'know?'

Even though she knew Martha had said it for her own reasons, Eliza was moved. For an instant she thought of escaping to Bristol and avoiding Inspector Crane in the process. God knew what he would think if she did that.

She said slowly, 'I wish I could, but it's just not on. There's no way I can get out of town at the moment. Tell you what, if you can persuade one of the others to come with you I'll authorize that.'

'Helen's the only one who knows the VI people, and she'd drive me mad.'

'Mattie, for God's sake. We're under all kinds of pressure at the moment. It's not my priority to set you up with your favourite travelling companion.'

'I can tell. Don't bloody bother then.' Martha hesitated for a moment, as if she was expected an immediate apology and change of heart. Not getting it, she turned on her heels and stormed off.

Eliza thought for a moment of going after her, but common sense told her to leave it. Let the girl grumble to someone else: they would soon put her right about the realities of life. She had to learn that she couldn't act like a spoilt child in the office.

It was just past 10. Time she got some work done. She dug in to her backlog, finishing off the Wigan proposal, signing off circulars and approving expense claims. She was checking through the DRMS proposal that Helen, conscientious as always, had prepared over the weekend when Mitchell came over to her desk. He leaned heavily on the edge, and blinked at her from behind his glasses. He looked a wreck, she thought, but then Mitchell always had a shaggy, hung-over air about him.

'Lizzy, do you know where Genevieve is?'

'I haven't seen her all morning. I'm snowed under here, and I've hardly had a chance to talk to anyone. Why, do you need her for something?'

'No, but Ahmed and Emily are worried because she hasn't come in. She's not down to be out in the diary, and she's not in the London office because they've phoned.'

'There are a dozen other places she could be.' She glanced

down at the file in her hand. Helen's proposal brought problems
enough, it was apparent the profit margin on the deal was far
too small, but at that moment it seemed infinitely more appealing
than what she knew was coming.

'I know. And I know if it wasn't for what happened last week
we wouldn't think twice about it. But.'

'Has anyone phoned her at home?'

'I was hoping you would.'

'Mitchell, couldn't you do it this once?'

Mitchell blinked again. 'If it was only one phonecall, but I
have a feeling it won't be. Women's stuff, maybe, and ... .
Lizzy, I dare say you don't want it dumped on you, but I do need
to dump it. Donaldson's not around of course: when is he ever?
Marjorie Bergman's in London as usual, and you know we don't
have a personnel person in the department any more, so there's
no one else. I can tell you're busy, but you can't be harder pushed
than me. Donaldson's been on to me already this morning. You
know I lost that MoD contract last week.'

'No one blames you for that.'

'God, you must be joking. Who else do they blame? Their
bloody selves?'

'But –' she began; then stopped. Mitchell wasn't one of life's
worriers. If he was in a funk, he probably had good reason to be.

He went on, 'That was the biggest job the MOD had coming
up, but now there's another one that's decent sized, worth having,
and Donaldson's made it clear enough that if I don't wrap it up
I'll be on the next list.'

She wanted to say, no you won't. But she couldn't. She remembered the comments Donaldson had made to her a couple of
weeks earlier, when he had called her in for a meeting that seemed
vaguely designed to replace the three-monthly reviews they had
had in the civil service. All of them were performing below par,
he had said. In fact she wasn't the worst, but that didn't mean she
could be complacent. They weren't just missing the new targets,
they were making less than they had last year. OK, morale was a
mud-puddle, OK, half their best staff had gone, but they had to
deliver or they would be out their ears. It's not just down to me,
Eliza, he had said. It's not even down to Harding, it's Saturn Trust
who will pull the plug. And in case you think I'm sitting pretty, if
we don't get near those targets I'll be the first to go.

Yes, she had thought silently, with a half-million payoff.

'OK,' she said to Mitchell. 'If Genevieve has screwed up, although I can't imagine it, I dare say she'd rather get me on the phone than Ms Bergman. Leave it with me.'

'Bless you, Lizzy.'

'Blue skies follow the grey, and all that. If you really need help putting this deal together, let me know and I'll send Helen over. Oh, and Saturday evening was great.'

'Glad you enjoyed yourself. I thought you did, but Val wasn't so sure. She reckoned you were upset about Kate, you know, being pregnant. It never struck me you didn't know, or I'd have said something when you phoned.'

'I was surprised, that's all.' She had no right to load Mitchell with her miseries. 'It's ancient history now, me and Lewis.'

'But you still like the bastard, don't you?'

'That's one word for it.'

She thought Mitchell was about to go, but he hesitated, then said, 'It's not all blue skies there either, Lizzy. Don't tell him I told you, but this exciting new job's more like a hope, you know?'

It pulled a string inside her. She had always agonized over Lewis's disappointments. He was by nature a crazy optimist, and had regularly been crashed down by hard reality, even in the dear old civil service, even in the easy-going 1980s. He would find it no easier to survive in the open seas of the Nasty Nineties.

'I won't tell,' she said, and Mitchell gave a weak grin before departing.

Sighing, she turned back to her desk, and leafed through her index book for Genevieve's home number. She and Genevieve were not on visiting terms for all their friendliness in the office, but she had noted it down a couple of years before, when Genevieve had been laid up with a broken ankle and she had been overseeing the other woman's section.

She didn't really expect anyone to answer, thinking it more likely Genevieve had forgotten to tell Ahmed about a late-arranged meeting. But on the eleventh ring the receiver was picked up.

'Genevieve?'

There was silence on the other end of the line. 'Genevieve?' she repeated.

'Who is that?'

'Eliza, Eliza Stannard from the office.' She tried to sound upbeat, but she had a depressing premonition of more tears, more tantrums. And from Genevieve, who had always been so briskly reliable.

'Oh. Oh God I'm sorry, Eliza. I know I ought to be there.'

'It's OK.' It wasn't really, these days, but what else could she say? 'What shall I tell them?'

Silence again. Eliza said as patiently as she could, 'I'll have to say something, Genevieve. Are you feeling sick, a stomach upset, or do you have a touch of flu?'

She heard what sounded like a stifled sob. A moment's silence again. Then Genevieve said brokenly, 'You can tell them I'm falling to bits.' Before Eliza could respond she had put the phone down.

39

She would have to go round to Genevieve's house, she supposed, but there was no time before her meeting with Howard. Lunchtime, maybe: then she would be able to leave the office without filling in one of the security forms.

First, the smoking room. The prospect depressed her. Not only would she be stuck amid the fumes for ten or fifteen minutes, it didn't seem to her a particularly good ruse for ensuring their meeting would not be noticed. She had never been a smoker, and she had never been in the smoking room. There were those who claimed this last bastion provided the best forum for gossip in RUS, but she had been happy to pass on it. Any regular who came in while she was talking to Howard would surely wonder at her presence.

There were plenty of deserted areas in St Jude's House these days. Why couldn't they find a quiet corner at the far end of the ground floor from the police, say?

She said nothing to Helen or Martha, and after some thought, filled out her 'Employee Leaving Workstation' form to indicate she had gone to the photocopier. If anyone questioned her, she would be able to say she had done that first, then – well, it would depend where they found her. She took a couple of expenses forms with her, copied them, detoured to the stairs and went down. The smoking room was on the ground floor, close to the post room and goods entrance. She slowed as she approached it. It was seven minutes to 11, so maybe she could catch Howard before he went in.

She peered through the fluted glass of the door. He was already there. She could just make out a vertically sliced image of him, on his own, sitting in a chair, knees spread, arms resting on his thighs, leaning forward as he took a drag of his cigarette.

She had never seen Howard smoking before. He looked sleazier, she thought, almost furtive.

'Come in, it won't kill you,' he said as she edged the door open.

'I don't know, the fumes in here. You forget so quickly, the whole office was like this once.'

'A relic of the past like booze at lunchtimes.' Howard shrugged.

'True. Howard, I still think it's stupid to meet in here. Can't we go and talk in 3C, say? No one'd notice us behind the cupboards.'

'No. Absolutely not.'

'I think you're wrong.' She sat down next to him, in another of the battered easy chairs that were set around the sides of the charmless room. 'And I don't have any fags.'

'So have one of mine.' Eliza waved the pack away, but he persisted. 'You've got to smoke in here. It's not arsenic, you won't drop dead. It might even do you good. You're all strung up, you're far more likely to die of a heart attack than anything you'll get from this.'

Reluctantly she took one. They were Marlboro Lights, the gold and white pack pale against his dark hand. It reminded her of something. The picture solidified in her mind: a small round table, a paperback ...

'Janine smoked these,' she said as Howard reached in his jacket pocket for his lighter. She bent to catch the flame, took a mouthful of smoke and blew it rapidly out. It felt strange, hot in her mouth.

'What?'

'Janine Broughton. She was a Marlboro smoker.'

He shook his head. 'Was she? Poor kid.'

'She used to come down here, did she?'

'The smoking room? The Beaver's secretary? Not bloody likely.'

'She must have done if she smoked.'

'I never saw her here. She probably went outside. That's what some people do, stand outside the west door.'

True, she had seen them sometimes, sad huddles of addicts – but not Janine. It nagged, and something else was snagging at the hems of her mind too, but she couldn't place it. Anyway, time was short and there were things she needed to say.

'Howard, before someone comes.'

'Me first. One thing you ought to know, I checked it out, and the police told me the papers on the conference room table confirmed it. Harding really had wanted to talk to you and me about the budget.'

'About the budget!'

'Yep. Donaldson set it up, apparently. He thought it would boost morale if we knew that top management were really interested in the budget. So Harding was going to call the section leaders in one by one, for a series of pep talks about the importance of the budget.'

'It would boost what!'

'I know. A novel definition of morale. But as Donaldson told me, there's nothing more important, nothing, than the budget. Quote.'

'Words fail me.'

'Me too. So, your turn. I guess you've told the police something that's going to get someone in shit?'

'Hugh and Sandie. Not too much shit I hope. For you or for them. They were on the list anyway, people who were in the building. I'm sorry, but the police were pushing, and I had to tell them.'

'And are you sorry about telling them you got here at 6.28?'

She hadn't expected that. She recoiled from his vehemence. Then she said slowly, 'Yes. Very sorry. I did it without thinking, right at the start of that first interview with them.'

'So how've you explained the time we took?'

'I haven't. That's why they want to see me again this afternoon.'

'Brilliant.'

'How've you explained it?'

'I said we met at the main door at about a quarter to 7.'

'Oh.' It didn't take much thought for her to realize she wouldn't be believed if she gave the same story at this stage. That 6.28 had been too precise. 'Did Bill back you up?'

Howard took a drag, stabbed out his fag end in the ashtray on the floor by his feet, then turned to her. 'It was Stew on the door when we came in that morning, not Bill.'

'I'd thought it was Bill. If I got that wrong it wasn't deliberate. The police have been on about it, and I told them I wasn't sure.'

'You are sure. Get it? Stew Harker.'

But she had a clear memory of Howard saying 'Good morning' to someone he had referred to as Bill. She knew too that the man on the desk that morning had been the man everyone had called Bill in the Brown Cow. She frowned. She was sure Howard was lying, but it seemed worse than unwise to tell him so.

The cigarette was warm between her fingers. Its smoke curled up around them. Howard stood as if to leave.

'Wait.'

He turned to her. His face was expressionless, shuttered. 'What?'

'I'm thinking.'

He did not sit again, nor did he move. Eliza was thinking now about the timing, the timing that Inspector Crane had been so sure didn't work. Of course he had been, because she knew very well it didn't work.

She knew when the gap came: 6.28 at the carpark; say, 6.30 at the outer door; 6.33 or so when they had separated, with the lift at the second floor. Then it must have been about five to 7 when she had pushed her way into room 4B1 – late, as she had told his silent body – to find the Beaver. Part of the gap that had worried Crane was filled by the meeting with Hugh and Sandie, but this part wasn't. Even though she had pretended she had got to the room earlier, she knew she hadn't.

Howard hadn't asked her what she had been doing in those twenty minutes or so, and she hadn't asked him. It was longer than it took to get to a desk and collect papers for a meeting you were late for. She knew that, and so did he.

'So?' Howard demanded.

Eliza said slowly, 'I'll have to tell them something about why I took so long. I mean, not just change it to a quarter to 7.'

'Yeah. Tell them your watch stopped.'

'What have they said to you, Howard?'

His expression did not change. He said in a flat voice, 'They've said I have a motive because Carla was made redundant. I had an opportunity because I was in St Jude's House that morning. They say I lied about when I arrived even though Stew backed me up, because you told them something different. They say it's enough to charge me if they want to, and it's only because they want more proof that they haven't done it yet.'

'And what have you said?'

'What I told you. Plus, of course, it wasn't me.'

'Do you know who it was?'

His eyes opened wider. 'No,' he said.

Eliza said, 'I don't believe you.'

'Thank you.'

'Well, hell, Howard. I know you're lying!'

Howard took a step back towards her, and bent down so his face was close to hers. She sensed the alien warmth and smell of his body. 'Well, hell, Eliza, I know you're lying too,' he said.

'I'm not lying.' She took his expression, and amplified quickly, momentarily afraid of what she saw. 'I'm just not telling them everything.'

'So you know who did it and you're leaving them to dump on me.'

'No! Of course I don't know who did it!' She edged out of the chair, and backed a step from him. 'Jesus, I wouldn't hide it if I knew that!'

'Wouldn't you?'

A 'No!' took shape in her throat, but it didn't get as far as her lips, because at that instant the door opened. She and Howard jumped farther apart.

Frank Mills stepped in. Dapper, alert as a sparrow, he was wearing a mid-grey suit with faint dark stripes and a red brocade waistcoat. He looked at the two of them. Eliza couldn't help wondering if he had paused outside the door before opening it, and how much he had seen. Heard, even: she and Howard had both raised their voices by the end of the exchange. His expression gave no clue.

Howard took a couple of steps towards the door and Frank. Frank, moving aside, said, 'Morning all. We don't often see you in here, Eliza.'

'I don't often come in here.' She forced a smile. 'Overstressed. In need of calming my nerves. You maybe even caught me yelling at Howard just then, and when did anyone ever do that?'

'So Mr Nkolo kindly provided some nicotine.' Frank beamed at Howard, who stood as if he was calculating the soonest acceptable moment to quit the room. 'Can't criticize. The more of us there are, the harder it'll be for them to finish us off.' He sat down, crossed his legs, brought out his cigarettes, then added, 'I wouldn't sign up to the weed if I were you though, love. If you're feeling overstressed you ought to take some time off. Get a sick note – depression, exhaustion.'

'I've too much work on for that, and someone's got to stay here.'

'Why d'you –' Howard began, but Frank cut in.

'And you're not the type to give in, are you love? Sit down again.'

Howard gave them both a narrow look. Then he said shortly, 'I'll see you later, Eliza,' and darted out of the room.

Damn him. Now he had gone, she couldn't, not without exchanging a few words with Frank. Who had been handed her picture on the Ace of Hearts that morning, she recalled uneasily.

'Handy you're here,' he said lightly. 'I could just do with a word.' He patted the nubby blue tweed arm of the chair next to his.

Hesitantly, she took the chair. Frank smiled encouragingly at her. 'Another fag?'

'No thanks.'

'Ah well.' He slipped the Dunhills back into his pocket. 'I've been meaning to talk to you for a while. How's it going?'

'Work?' Presumably he didn't mean the murder investigation. 'So-so.'

'You're too modest. That's your trouble, you haven't changed your style yet. Great worker, lousy self-publicist. In the civil service you could get by without selling yourself, but you can't do it now.'

'I'll bear that in mind.'

'I've always thought you had loads of potential. Ted Hawley thought so too. I know he gave that coordinator job to Jez Barnard, but it was a close-run thing, you know.'

That had been three, nearly four years ago. He had never mentioned it to her before. She saw what was coming, and couldn't think how to head it off.

Frank went on, 'It's never too late, though. In fact this isn't a bad time, because with Harding out of the way, tragedy that, a real tragedy, there're going to be changes for sure.'

He had spoken with all the sincerity of a double-glazing salesman. Eliza said 'Mmm?'

'And this time we're going to take charge of them.' He leaned so close she could almost count the grey hairs brushed across his bald patch. His sharp blue eyes held hers. 'I'll let you in on something, Eliza. I reckon I made a hell of a mistake when I advised the board not to put in a bid for RUS.'

Eliza said warily, 'Maybe you did, Frank.'

'But I'm not making it twice. So I'll tell you now, I'm putting together a little group of good people, really good people, who're interested in working out where we go from here.'

'I see.' She still couldn't see a way out.

'A blueprint for the organization, you might say. We're working on something to take to the Saturn Trust. Things haven't gone well these last few months, I don't need to tell you that, do I? So what we've got to do now is re-establish their faith in us. Saturn

Trust first, to secure the funding for another year or so, then the clients, the workforce, everyone. Even the unions.' He chuckled. 'No, really. It'll be a complete proposal, realistic budgets, sales projections, everything. And key people.'

'Really.'

'I'll tell you something else. Of course, all this is in absolute confidence.' His eyes held hers again. His voice fell to a near-whisper. 'When I started this I pencilled in John Donaldson.' He sat back, and smiled. 'Oh, you can laugh, Eliza, but I like to think I gave the man a good chance. Ought to do that with anyone new, don't you agree? But I've heard a bit of feedback here and there, and tell you the truth I've been having second thoughts. It seems no one who works closely with him is that impressed.'

In spite of herself, she admired his adroitness. 'You've been planning this for long?' she asked.

Frank's gaze narrowed. He said without a noticeable pause, 'Of course. I've been reviewing the situation ever since the privatization, and before, needless to say. It's not something that's been prompted by Harding's death, though obviously that's given some extra impetus to it.'

'I see.'

'So now's the moment to firm things up and make a definite move. Not for a day or two, obviously, David Summerfield's doing a valiant job of tiding us over, and I wouldn't be so tasteless as to drop it on James Connaught's desk before the funeral. But I'm ... to be honest, I'm looking at ways I can give him an indication what's in the air.' At this he did pause, expectantly. Eliza said nothing, and he went on quite smoothly, 'Then as soon as the timing's right, I'll present him with the whole package.'

'I see.'

'So. Are you with us?'

She would have liked to say no, but self-preservation prevented her. She had made an enemy of Frank once before – years before, when he had made a pass at a conference, and she had not only turned him down, but made sure several people knew of her outrage. Their reaction had told her she had been wrong to tell them, but it had been a long time before she had brought herself to acknowledge that she had made a bad mistake.

Office politics had never been her forte. They were Frank's, of course: that was what had carried him so high in RUS. And he had favoured people with the same style, brown-nosers like Hugh Worning. Plus anyone else who could be useful to him. She wasn't so dense that she didn't realize why he was talking to her now. A cool part of her wondered how far he would go. Would he actually offer to nominate her as director of Office Services? Did he really believe she would take it as genuine admiration for her talents? And another interesting question, what would he do if she then split with James?

She said cautiously, 'I'm flattered, Frank.'

'Don't be.' He reached over and patted her knee. 'It's what you deserve. Tell you what, we're having a little get-together down at the Jugged Hare tomorrow at eight. Nothing formal, just a chat, rather like the old Pipe Club. You've heard of the Pipe Club?'

His condescension stuck in her throat. She made herself nod.

'It'd be great if you could make it. All right with you?'

'I'll see what I can do.'

'Great. That's great. Well, I must be getting on my way, and so must you, I expect.'

'Yes. Yes, I guess I must.'

They stood up together. They left together. 'Toodle pip,' said Frank as they parted in the corridor.

40

She thought about Howard on the way to Genevieve's house. He had seemed genuinely outraged at the police's fingering him for the murders; the more so, she thought, because there was a possible element of colour prejudice. It didn't sound as if the police had much in the way of evidence. She told herself she shouldn't take it for granted he was innocent, but even so she couldn't believe he was guilty.

But he obviously knew something; he had seen or done something in the missing quarter-hour. He had asked her to lie: at least, that was what it amounted to. And lie about several things, which she couldn't readily put together. The timing. The security guard. Hugh and Sandie.

She didn't want to lie. Mind, she didn't want to tell the police the things she hadn't yet told them, either.

In short, she was in no position to handle another interview with Crane that afternoon. It had been naive of her to think talking to Howard would make it easier. It had made it more difficult.

She hoped, without believing, that seeing Genevieve might show her a way forward.

Genevieve lived in an inner suburb of Costhorpe, in a tree-lined street full of large early Victorian houses set in huge gardens. She had once confided to Eliza that she and her husband had tried to get permission to sell off the garden for a building plot, but it hadn't been allowed. The character of the area would be affected, the planners claimed.

The character struck Eliza as soporific. At 1 pm there were no cars driving down Hazel Grove, and none parked by the road as they were in her own street. No mower or weeder could be seen in the fiercely tidy gardens, no child called out, no one strolled past walking a dog.

She pulled up her old Lotus on the gravel drive, and sat for a moment inspecting Genevieve's house. It was grey brick. A fine wisteria grew up the shallow porch and sent its tendrils round the first-floor windows. The lawn at the front had at its centre a magnolia tree in bud.

The doorbell was the old-fashioned kind, with a lever you had to pull. Eliza could hear it echoing inside the house. She glanced across at the garage. The door was shut, so she couldn't be sure if Genevieve's car was there.

She had told no one she was coming. Mitchell hadn't come near her for the rest of the morning, and she had said only to Ahmed and the rest of Genevieve's team that she understood Genevieve wasn't feeling well. She hadn't told Genevieve she was coming either. She had no illusion she would be welcome. Genevieve was in her way a very private woman. She would resent Eliza's having seen a glimpse of her pain, and would find it unendurable if it became public knowledge.

The timing of her breakdown couldn't be a coincidence. But Eliza couldn't believe ... hell. She knew this 'no one I know' stance was an inadequate response to the horror of two murders, but all the same it was her response. And it was surely, surely not Genevieve.

After a minute or so she heard footsteps, and an indistinct figure materialized in the shadows behind the frosted glass of the door. The door creaked open slowly, as if it was rarely used, and Genevieve peeped round it.

She was in a dressing gown, or perhaps rather a negligée, a filmy garment of pale silk splotched with pink and peach-coloured blooms. It looked faintly grubby. Her hair was mussy, her face had the puffiness of tears long indulged, and her eyelids were swollen and pink.

'You didn't have to come,' she said without opening the door any wider.

'Would you rather someone else had?'

There was a silence. Somewhere long off, a dog barked.

'Oh shit, you'd better come in.' Genevieve pulled the door wide and stood aside.

'You're on your own?' Eliza asked as she came into a shadowy but attractive hall. A bowl of narcissi, browning at the edges, sat on a polished mahogany table under an imposing staircase that turned at right angles, squaring off the space.

Genevieve gave her an odd look. For a moment Eliza thought she was about to cry again. 'Too bloody right,' she said instead. 'D'you mind the kitchen?'

'No, sure.'

Genevieve led them through. The kitchen was a huge room, with a green Aga set between two old pine dressers displaying china with a faded maroon border pattern, and a broad window, its ledge lined with pots of geraniums, looking across the lawn to a clump of firs and a high wooden fence. Copper pans gleamed from a ceiling rack. There was a pine table with wheelbacked chairs set round it, still half-laid for breakfast with one used plate and knife, an open pot of apricot jam, a butter dish, and a bread-board holding the end of a bloomer and an overflow of crumbs. A portable radiocassette player, a couple of white-enveloped letters and a copy of the *Morning Record*, seemingly unopened, sat at one end.

Genevieve headed for a Lloyd Loom chair with a faded patchwork cushion in the corner by the Aga, huddling into its seat in a way that told Eliza she had been sitting there all morning. Eliza took the nearest wheelback. Genevieve was not looking at her, and did not appear on the verge of further speech. 'Shall I make coffee?' Eliza offered.

Genevieve didn't answer. More irritated than concerned, she took this for assent, filled the kettle on the Aga and set it to heat. She sat down again. Genevieve sniffed.

'You don't have to tell me anything,' Eliza said.

Genevieve sniffed again.

'I haven't said anything in the office, except you're not well. I didn't tell anyone in the department I was coming, so I won't have to say anything when I get back.'

Silence.

Eliza tried once more. 'Have you seen a doctor? Apparently they're very good at giving certificates for stress. You barely need do more than mention RUS, they all know someone there, and they know how bad it is.'

Genevieve said, 'I can't stay here.'

'Everybody'd understand, I'm sure. So many people have –'

'I'd go berserk,' Genevieve said in a louder voice. 'You might as well know. Malcolm's left me.'

The middle-aged women's epidemic. Nothing to do, thank God, with the murders. Disastrous for Genevieve, clearly, but a fathomable disaster. Eliza hid her relief as best she could and said, 'I'm sorry, Genevieve, I'd no idea.'

'He said he'd sue for adultery.' She fished a crumpled tissue out of a pocket in the negligée, blew her nose, and looked across at Eliza. 'He can do that still, can't he? I bet he would, the bastard. Kick 'em when they're down, that's Malcolm.'

At least she seemed to be regaining some energy. Good strong anger at the errant Malcolm. With luck that would carry her through the ordeal. But – adultery? Genevieve?

'So …' She was thinking aloud. 'There's nothing going with your lover, then? I take it he's I married?'

'My lover's dead.'

Someone else dead?

No; it was more simple and more complex than that. In the lake of her astonishment, an island of comprehension firmed up. It couldn't be; yes, it could be. It was.

Genevieve was saying bitterly, 'He wouldn't have known, I swear he wouldn't, I'd been so careful. Never here, always where no one would see us. And when you told me what had happened, I thought, I can live with this. I can get through it. If I keep busy and don't look down, I'll be all right. Just keep swimming and you won't drown. I lasted right up to the weekend. Then when I got home Friday night, and Malcolm was late, he's always fucking late, and the house was so empty, just walking round the house, the kids gone, only Malcolm to wait up for, and I felt myself going crazy. Completely crazy. He found me crying and I told him, plain told him, I hate you and I can't bear it.'

She was crying again, runnels of silent tears oozing down each cheek. Genevieve, always so chic, looked suddenly old.

The kettle hissed. Eliza got up to make the tea. She was glad to have something to do, hunting through tins on the dresser for the teabags and sugar while Genevieve sat in her chair in the corner, rocking slightly, clutching the scrap of tissue, and crying. She found a half-used carton of milk in an almost empty fridge. She brought a mug over to Genevieve and took her own back to the table.

They sat for some time. It was a charming room, charming house come to that, thought Eliza, but so large and so empty. She had imagined Genevieve's marriage was a happy one. Not that Genevieve had said anything, now she looked back: perhaps only because she appeared so capable, so in control. She hadn't seemed the woman to have got it so wrong. Or perhaps it was her own reluctantly unmarried woman's tendency to see sunny scenes behind everyone else's closed curtains. Partnerships like Mitchell and Val, Lewis and Kate, even James and his unknown partner in London, were icons for her, but all of them were flawed, most likely, to those on the inside.

Genevieve and the Beaver, though. The best she could think was that in time it might come to be comprehensible to her. She wanted to ask Genevieve how, why? Does Malcolm know who it is? I guess you won't tell, but might he?

Other questions crowded in. Genevieve was on the suspect list: she had been in St Jude's House on the fatal morning. She had seemed so confused, uncomprehending even, when she had heard what had happened. It made a kind of sense now. But what had she thought when she had got Harding's email? What had she done when she had waited in an empty room and he hadn't come?

She had made a phonecall, Mitchell had said. To whom? Not Harding, presumably. She wouldn't have known where he was; and most likely he was dead by the time she placed the call. Janine was an obvious choice, but she wouldn't have been in the office so early. So, who? And why had she gone back to her desk as if nothing had happened? Had she really known nothing? Had she made no more attempts to find the right room, but simply given up? It must have been, what, half an hour, forty minutes even from when she made the call to when Eliza herself came in and told her what had happened.

She doubted she would ever find an opportunity to ask these questions.

Genevieve stood up, crossed the room, tore a piece of kitchen wipe off a roll fixed on the wall, and blew her nose again. 'What a bloody wreck I am,' she said. A fat black cat slinked in and headed for a dish of food by the back door. Genevieve ignored it, and it ignored her.

Eliza looked inside herself for sympathy, and didn't quite find it. The Beaver, for Christ's sake! She settled for briskness. 'You'll survive, Genevieve. Women do.'

'Easy to say, but it never seems that easy when you're trying to do it. Oh shit.' She opened a cupboard under the sink and threw the piece of wipe in a bin. 'I think part of it's bloody exhaustion,' she went on. 'I've been working till I drop, well haven't we all, and the thought of selling the house and dividing up the china and negotiating over the stocks and shares is like a sheer cliff ahead of me. And I don't want to lose Malcolm. Or maybe I do, maybe subconsciously I did when I started it. He's a pain but he's what I've got, what I know. What I had.'

'He might come back,' Eliza said.

'I doubt it. I know him.'

'Then you'll have to get through it. We'll help you.'

'No, but thanks for the offer.' She tore off another square of wipe, blew her nose again and went to retrieve her mug of tea. She remained standing, leaning against the warm bulk of the Aga. She sipped it in silence for a minute or so, then said, narrowing her eyes on Eliza, 'I couldn't bear it if anyone knew. That he left me, yes, but not why.'

Eliza said, 'I won't tell.'

'Thanks. You're a good mate, Eliza. I suppose you find this incomprehensible, how could I fall for him and so on.'

'I do a bit.'

'So do I sometimes. But it happened, and once it had happened, strangely it worked.' Her pixie-like features contorted into a frown. 'I'd almost forgotten what it was to be happy. Getting on with it, yes, but not happy. And he gave me that. I'd gather round with you lot and say, he's a bastard, and I wasn't fibbing, I could understand it, I even thought it sometimes. But at the same time I loved him for making me happy.'

There was nothing Eliza could say. Perhaps Genevieve, brisk pragmatic Genevieve, realized as much. She said after another moment, 'I don't suppose I'll be happy like that again.' Then she rallied, shoved the wipe in her pocket, and said, 'Anyway I'll do the sensible thing and get a sick note. I'm sure you're right, Doctor Singh'll oblige, bloody wreck like me. Sorry to load more on to you, Eliza. You can leave a lot to Ahmed though, he's come on well.'

'He's a good lad,' Eliza agreed.

41

Getting on with it, but not happy. It sounded all right to her, Eliza thought as she drove back to St Jude's House. If only they could all go back to when life was like that.

She had been gone less than an hour, but that was long enough for the housing of her monitor to have been papered in yellow Post-its, mostly in Helen's neat handwriting. '12.30 Howard Nkolo rang. He's looking into it but don't ring him back.' 'Phone Sandra in IT. Mon 12.40.' 'John Donaldson wants you in his office at 2.30.' And in Martha's writing, larger, more angular, with a wry cartoon face in the corner of the sheet, 'Eliza pls phone Derek Madison at the VI.'

Oh Mattie. Doubtless Madison would insist that she came down to Bristol; doubtless he had been encouraged to insist that. Maybe she would go down to Bristol. What time was Crane likely to turn up? He hadn't said, as far as she could recall.

Postponing the inevitable, she went down to the snack bar and bought a takeaway ham and coleslaw French stick and a cup of decent coffee. Munching at her desk, she made some notes for Helen on her draft proposal. Her first judgement was borne out by closer examination: it was no good, for all the evident work behind it. Helen had used the old RUS form, and hadn't amended the profit calculation. Donaldson wouldn't pass it. Helen was right if she thought the client wouldn't accept a higher quote; so, she would have to fudge it. Why did she need everything spelling out? The woman had no political sense at all.

'Back to me before you send it to Donaldson,' she finished, and dumped the file on Helen's desk. Then she went through her emails. There was the usual stack of junk circulars and a dozen that needed attention, mostly demanding reports and announcing meetings, either from David Summerfield or copied to him. Night watchman or not, he was clearly busy knitting himself into position.

Ahmed came over as she was deleting the rubbish, and told her Genevieve had just rung in to say she was feeling unwell and had made an appointment with her doctor. She would phone again after seeing her, but they shouldn't expect her in for a day or two.

A small relief. Eliza offered to give Ahmed whatever help he needed, and agreed she would spend an hour later that afternoon going through his team's work-in-progress sheets. That would be after she had seen Donaldson, but maybe she could lean on him to provide some cover himself. It seemed to her a reasonable request, albeit she didn't think he would do it. Whatever the man did – she had little idea – he always made out it was too important for him to involve himself in the day to day crises of his department.

Her phone rang. It was an impatient Madison. Not happy about seeing only junior staff, couldn't help wondering if they were wasting his time, obviously not an important project to them, and with all these disturbing events he had read about in the paper maybe it would be better if he placed the contract elsewhere. Christ, they couldn't afford to lose the VI. It was one of the few contracts that actually made a good profit. She reached for the stress phone and squeezed the yielding red plastic. Not at all, Mr Madison. You're one of our most valued clients. I'm sorry if Martha hasn't been able to satisfy you, she's normally very reliable. Oh – that's all right then. Glad to hear she's been looking after you, but if you'd like me to be at tomorrow's meeting too, then of course …

Martha appeared as she was putting the phone down.

'That was Madison,' Eliza said.

'Oh. He rang this morning, in a shitty mood. I'd fixed with Helen to come down with me, and I told him we'd both be there, but he wasn't happy.'

'So I gathered. I had to tell him I'd come down. Have you booked for Helen?'

'A room for tonight, yeah. Not a train ticket, 'cos she was going to drive us both.'

'Then I'd better drive. I've got to see Donaldson and sort out Genevieve's team, then we'll go straight after that. With luck we can be in Bristol for a late supper. You've got your overnight stuff here?'

'Of course.'

'I'll need mine. We'll stop off at my house on the way. Where's Helen?'

'Mitchell's borrowed her for something.'

'Oh. Tell her I'm going instead of her when she comes back, Matty, and don't make it sound like she's failed. I've got to see Donaldson now.'

42

Donaldson wasn't helpful, but Ahmed was, and by a quarter to four Eliza and Martha were ready to leave the office. Helen pursued them to the door of 2B, begging Eliza to listen to messages and give instructions. Can't see how to rework the DRMS proposal, I know I calculated the profit properly. You didn't phone Sandra back. What do I do if Summerfield calls about the budget figures?

It annoyed her all the more, coming straight after her meeting with Ahmed. 'Cut it out, Helen,' she said finally. 'If there's anything urgent you do it as best you can. Otherwise it can wait till Wednesday. Or if it can't wait and you can't handle it, go to Donaldson.' She practically hustled Martha down the stairs to get away from Helen's 'But Eliza, I was told to tell you …'.

She hadn't seen Crane. She hadn't told Helen what to do if he appeared. Better, she reckoned, to make it seem she had forgotten in the pressure of work.

Martha was cheery. Whoopee, no St Jude's House tomorrow, she said as Eliza unlocked the Lotus. Restaurant food tonight, you'll let us go somewhere decent, won't you, Eliza? And I love your car, did it cost you a fortune?

'The insurance does,' Eliza said shortly. 'Mattie, do me a favour. I've got a splitting headache and I'd be really, really grateful if you didn't talk for the next hour or so.'

'I'll map-read.'

There was no need, she knew the route to Bristol, but she agreed for the sake of peace. Martha buried her head in the AA Atlas, and although she made a few comments about the pros and cons of dodging the M25 as they were sitting in Costhorpe's rush-hour jam, was by her own standards quiet. She even agreed to wait in the car as Eliza went into her house and packed, and by 4.15 they were on the dual carriageway that led south.

The traffic was steady, the day still clear, the car purring like an old lion. There was time to think. She had been both relieved and disturbed by her meeting with Genevieve's team. It was good that their urgent work was up to date, Ahmed was well in control and they would not need too much of her attention, particularly since Donaldson had made it plain he would neither

assist himself nor permit her to share the load with Mitchell.
(Mitchell hadn't exaggerated, it sounded like he was going down
like a bad stand-up comic.) What worried her was the contrast
between Genevieve's team and her own. She had always known
in a general way that Genevieve was the most efficient of the
three sector managers, but it hadn't mattered much in the old
days. They had all been regarded as doing well, and they had all
had their triumphant projects as well as their occasional disasters.
Now it was like the old poster of the men on the stepladder, trying
to climb out of the floodwater. Mitchell was neck-deep, she was
waist-deep, and Genevieve was barely dipping a toe in the murk.
When the waters rose a foot higher, not everyone would still be
breathing.

This took her thoughts to Frank Mills, and the invitation to his
pseudo-Pipe-Club meeting. She was curious to know who else he
had signed up, but she was also uneasy. For one thing, she didn't
want to see Frank Mills as the next chief exec; for another, she had
no doubt he had approached her in the hope of buying influence
with James. A clean promotion, with Frank as ultimate boss, she
might have lived with, but this deal was something different. She
would be hard pushed to look Genevieve in the eye if she leap-
frogged to a promotion over her, and she couldn't even begin to
imagine lobbying James on Frank's behalf.

Shit. She hadn't told James she was leaving Costhorpe. A filling
station was coming up, so she flicked on her indicator and slowed
the Lotus.

Martha jerked out of her reverie. 'Out of petrol already?'

'No, I need to phone someone. Sorry about this.'

She got out of the car so Martha wouldn't be able to listen
in, and rang St Jude's House, assuming he would still be there.
Instead she had a frustrating conversation with one of the new
receptionists. There was no Mr Connaught in her staff phone
directory. The office was closing shortly, all visitors had left for
the day, and if he wasn't a member of staff he wasn't in the office,
madam. No, the receptionist couldn't phone anyone to check; no,
of course she couldn't leave her desk. Eliza gritted her teeth and
asked to be put through to Crystal Canning.

'Oh, Miss Canning. That's all right, I think she's still here. Just
a moment.' There was a space filled with a snatch from 'The
Dying Swan', then Crystal's soft voice came on to the line. She

confirmed rather more convincingly that James wasn't in the office, and offered to take a message.

'Is he at the Mornington, as far as you know?' Most likely, Crystal agreed. 'I'll phone him there.' She had to go into the filling station and top up her mobile, then she tried another switchboard. The result was the same, though: no James.

They hadn't actually arranged to meet that evening. But he had intended it, surely? Eliza left a message at the hotel – just that she had been called away on business, and would be back Tuesday evening – and returned to the car and Martha.

'Can I talk now?' Martha asked once they were back on the road.

'OK. I had a couple of Solpadeine while I was packing, they've done the trick.'

'That's good.' From the corner of her eye she could see Martha nodding, her brown curls bouncing. 'I had a couple myself this morning. Saturday and Sunday, I had two really bad nights. Tibor made me cocoa but I kept on waking up and going aargh. And now Janine, that's even worse.'

'You knew her, you were saying this morning? I mean, not just casually.'

'We weren't best mates, but we were on chatting terms. She used to know Tibor's brother Marek, back in London. We had her round a couple of times.'

'I'd no idea.'

'Why should you?'

'No reason. Do the police know that, Mattie?'

'Know what?'

'That you and Janine were friendly.'

'What's it to do with them?'

'They want to know everything about her, to build up a picture, you know.'

'God, I wouldn't talk to the police.'

The younger girl's vehemence surprised her. She tried to explain to Martha that talking to them wouldn't get her in trouble, but Martha was adamant. If the police asked you questions you had to answer them, but no sane person offered them information for free, that was her philosophy. As for it helping them solve the murder, that was plain stupid: more likely it would send them careering down the wrong path. She wasn't alone, that was how everyone had played it. You too, Eliza.

There was too much truth in that for Eliza's comfort. But she couldn't admit it to a subordinate, so she said stiffly, 'I told them everything I thought would be useful.'

'Did you tell them about the Beaver and Genevieve?'

Her hand jumped on the steering wheel. The Lotus's light steering responded, and she had to concentrate for a moment on correcting its course.

'How the hell do you know about that?'

'Janine, obviously. You haven't told them, have you? Of course you haven't. You can just see them thinking, broken love affair, middle-aged anguish, crime of passion ...'

Her hand jerked again.

'Watch it, Eliza. Oh. I mean ... you did know?'

'I – no.' Martha wasn't that gullible. 'I knew about the affair, but ...'

'But not that they split.'

'No. When was this?'

'I don't know all the details. Just, Janine told me last week that the Beaver was in a pig of a mood because they'd had a big row and it was all over. God knows how it even started, a repulsive little Napoleon like him. I suppose you have to be less fussy if you want to carry on getting it at Genevieve's age, but Christ, I could never get it on with a man who's five foot four and going bald.'

The casual arrogance of youth. Eliza let this pass. 'Did anyone else know?'

'I never thought. Probably not, if you didn't. Janine didn't spread news around much, and Genevieve wouldn't have said, would she? Before, she probably thought they'd get back together, and afterwards she'd have had to keep mum because of the cops and their one-track minds. Imagine the little lights going off in their heads. Even though it couldn't have been her. I mean, as if you'd go berserk with a broken heart over the Beaver.'

Other people's passions are always incomprehensible to some degree. You could go berserk with a broken heart over the Beaver; or at least, Eliza had believed that lunchtime that Genevieve had done just that.

But hell, she had misread the entire situation. She had thought beforehand that she understood Genevieve – only the Genevieve she had thought she knew had been calm, happily married, immune to emotion, a woman she would never have confided in about James, because she had never categorized Genevieve and herself together in that guilty subclass of sexual pirates. Then that Genevieve had been wiped off the board, and she had seen a Genevieve distraught with grief, a Genevieve all too like herself, another woman who had been seduced by the enemy. Now that Genevieve too was dust on the chalk eraser, and she saw – what?

That Genevieve had lied to her was hurtful, but understandable. If Martha could see the need to keep silent about the break-up, Genevieve herself would certainly have seen it. That Genevieve was capable of such dissembling was a new realization, however. So the woman she had encountered that lunchtime was one with capabilities totally unknown to her. What had Genevieve's real feelings been? It could be that she had been grieving over the ex-lover killed by someone else, the quarrel that would never now be made up, a phase in her life that was over forever. But there was another possibility: that she had been driven to collapse and despair in the aftermath of a sequence that had gone from passion to betrayal to agony to fury. A killing fury, her own killing fury.

Genevieve couldn't – no, she couldn't say that. She had thought Genevieve couldn't, but now she didn't know. Passion could uncover dark urges in people that they hadn't even known themselves existed. And someone had killed Patrick Harding.

But someone had also killed Janine Broughton. The passionate fury of an ex-lover was hardly the explanation for that crime. Unless Janine had … no. Eliza couldn't believe Janine had supplanted Genevieve, it didn't fit with anything she had seen or heard.

It was just about imaginable that an ex-mistress – this ex-mistress – had killed Patrick Harding, but Eliza could think of no matching explanation for the second, more frenzied killing.

Until Martha said calmly, 'Anyway, nobody's going to ask me about Janine or any of this, because nobody knows about it, now that Janine's dead. Except you and Genevieve, and neither of you will tell on me, will you?'

43

Suspicion is a hardy perennial. Once planted, it tends to spread.

It spread that evening and that night, looping black tendrils through Eliza's mind. Through the drive through dusk and beyond to Bristol; through the hunt for the hotel, the check-in, through the supper that Martha insisted they ate together. It was too late for the hotel restaurant, so they ate at a curry house round the corner. Martha drank lager. Poppadoms, pickles, tandoori chicken, prawn pathia, vegetable biryani, coffee, terror.

It was another long dark night.

If it were Genevieve. She tried to reconstruct the events, but it was no use, she didn't know enough. She couldn't say, no it can't be; she couldn't say, yes it is. Only that there was a possibility, a motive, the appalling truth that the minds even of those we think we know have depths we cannot fathom. Touch us one way, and we explode in orgasm; touch us another and we flower into anger. Red anger, the blood before the eyes, the moment out of control, the knife in the hand, the slow horrific coming to one's senses and realizing what has happened.

If it were Genevieve, would she tell? If it were Genevieve arrested, protesting her innocence, the case in court with the worms of doubt wriggling through it, the conviction, the black despair of a woman sentenced to rot for life. Could she live with that? My colleague is a murderess. My colleague is maybe not a murderess, but the jury believed it; I helped to put her away.

Or if it were Howard. Howard, who she knew had also lied to her.

In her mind she was waking in a different hotel room, and the nightmare imagine on her retina was of a woman sprawled on a bed, her neck encircled with a collar of blood.

She needed to tell; she could not tell. Perhaps Crane would come, and seduce it all from her. The coward's way. It was done, but not by me.

She did not sleep at all.

44

The grey morning light brought a sense of proportion. She showered, drank instant black coffee from a sachet in her room, sat on her bed and tried to meditate.

There were arguments, good arguments, against her terrified imaginings. Harding's murder had been no crime of passion. It had been planned, prepared for. Surely if Genevieve had been driven to murder she would not have done it like that; or so soon. Affairs end, but they can rekindle. No woman of Genevieve's age would destroy all hope within days.

Another thing: it was unlikely anyone would be convicted in error. As James had pointed out, Janine's killer had left forensic traces. The police would surely check them against their suspect before bringing charges, and even in the unlikely event that they did not, defence lawyers would.

Unease remained, even so. Perhaps it was not Genevieve, and not Howard either, but she could not believe both killings were the random acts of a psychopath, and nor did she accept Frank Mills's thin argument that most likely the answer lay in Harding's life in London. She felt sure the killer was someone involved with RUS, someone she knew.

She thought, too, about Janine's words, captured on the answering machine tape the police had taken. Why, why had Janine chosen her to call? And not picked her at random, but looked up her number and written it down on a pad? What had Janine been about to tell her, before someone had silenced her for ever? If it was Genevieve, Howard – hell, whoever it was, it was hard to imagine that she was the obvious recipient of the information that nailed them. But it could not only have been spite or revenge that caused Janine to pick her. There had to be some reason, one that she had not yet uncovered.

She felt sure, too, that the killer would be found. There might be a sizeable number of potential suspects, but there were not too many for the police to sift. Two murders justified whatever effort was necessary. If everyone who had ever worked for RUS had to be DNA tested, the police would do it.

Then it would be over. A part – an unknown, unmeasurable

part – of her life would be changed for ever. And she would change with it, in ways that she sensed and dreaded.

She and Martha had agreed to meet for breakfast in the restaurant at eight. It was barely seven. She went for a walk through the deserted streets of central Bristol, then returned to the slab-like hotel. Martha was waiting for her in the lobby, looking young and lively in a green trouser suit.

Eliza drank three more cups of black coffee and dismembered a croissant. Martha ate a full English, sausages, fried bread and all. She bullied Eliza into doing what they had not done the evening before, reviewing the proposals for the VI and planning their tactics.

Their tactics were good, and Martha, at least, presented them well. With Eliza as back-up, her nervousness was gone. She did most of the talking in the meeting with Madison. She was vivacious, charming, persuasive. She soon uncovered the fact that Madison had been blustering when he had threatened to take the contract elsewhere: he was used to working with RUS, and not anxious for the hassle of switching to a different contractor. He liked their proposals. They came to terms without difficulty, and by lunchtime were back on the road to Costhorpe.

Eliza was still feeling weary and woolly-headed. She hadn't heard from James; not surprising, since she hadn't left a contact number at his hotel, or indeed with anyone in Costhorpe. He had her home number, but there was no reason to think he had her mobile number, which she had avoided giving out to people in the office. She hadn't tried to phone him again: there had been little time, and her mood had not been right. Also she was uncomfortably aware that Inspector Crane would be looking for her. He had not gone as far as tracing her through Martha's Tibor, but he would almost certainly have made enquiries. It was more than likely he had asked James where she was. James would not have been pleased.

'You're worried, aren't you?' Martha said, shortly after they had joined the M4.

'Observant of you.' It was only half-ironic.

'Is it about Genevieve, her not telling you she'd split up with Harding? I can see now I was awfully tactless last night. I didn't mean to crow, me knowing and you not. I know you're a good friend of hers.'

'It'd have been easier if she'd told me, but I can see why she didn't. No, it's not that. It's just... all the obvious things.'

'Like what?'

Eliza glanced at the younger girl. Martha briefly met her eye, before she turned back to the road. Eliza felt a rush of fondness for her. She had proved on the whole to be a good travelling companion; in a small way they had become friends. But only in a small way, and she meant to take it no further. She had not forgotten that Martha was her subordinate, or the limitations of Martha's judgement and discretion. However much she wanted a confidante, she did not have a suitable one in Martha.

She said carefully, 'The obvious means the murders, surely. It's impossible to get away from them. A part of me doesn't want to know who this murderer is, and a part of me wants to know it very badly.'

'Do you know?' Martha put the question in her usual breezy tone.

'No. Do you?'

'No idea. I mean, yeah – I hope it's someone vile. John Donaldson not Howard Nkolo, you know. But I wasn't there, I haven't a clue. You're closer to it.'

'That doesn't mean it's down to me to investigate. In some ways I want to do what you're doing, tell the cops nothing, and in some ways …. Maybe it's just that I'm older. I didn't grow up thinking of them as the enemy.'

'You smoked dope, didn't you?'

She smiled to herself. 'Yes. You're right. What that did to our attitudes.'

Martha settled back, and they drove on in silence. Eliza broke it only once before they stopped to eat. 'Tell me,' she said. 'Did Janine smoke?'

'Smoke cigarettes, you mean? Why d'you ask?'

'I need to know.'

'I don't think so. I never saw her smoking.' A pause. 'No, I'm sure she didn't.'

45

As they were leaving the motorway services after lunch, Martha asked if she could switch on the car radio. If you like, said Eliza. It was tuned to Classic FM. Martha asked if she could retune to Virgin, and Eliza said no. 'Jesus,' said Martha. 'Sometimes you seem so middle-aged. Not even my parents listen to that crap.'

She switched it on anyway, at low volume, and they both listened in silence until the news headlines at two. Eliza turned up the radio so she would hear them clearly over the whine of the car engine.

It was the second story.

'A third unnatural death within a week has shattered the recently privatized RUS Group, formerly Regional Utility Services. Computer manager Philip Curtin was found dead at his home this morning. Police have refused to confirm whether they are treating the death as murder. RUS chief executive Patrick Harding was killed last week, and on Friday came the death of his secretary Janine Broughton. Both these are the subject of murder investigations.

'At the EC Summit in Brussels...'

There was a click; Martha had switched it off. Eliza's hands were white on the steering wheel. Phil. Oh my God, Phil.

'Shivering fucking sardines,' said Martha. 'D'you want to stop?'

She managed to say, 'It's the M4 for Christ's sake.'

'You can stop on the hard shoulder.'

'It's not an emergency.'

'It bloody feels like one to me. Jesus, I'm shaking.'

'So am I.' Martha was right, she was not capable of driving on. She indicated, slowed, veered from middle lane to slow lane and on to the shoulder. The Lotus jerked to a halt. It was an effort to move her hands from the steering wheel, put the gears to neutral and switch off the ignition. Her body felt cold, her head as if it would explode. God, Phil. It was all she could think.

'Give yourself five minutes,' Martha said. 'We can't really phone from here, it's so noisy. But when you've got it back together you can drive off the motorway and find a layby.'

Sane advice. Five minutes. It was too long, and not long enough.

The traffic was zipping past, the slipstreams of lorries licking at the car. They could not get out. There was no immediate way of finding out more.

Dear God. Who would murder Phil?

'I'm really sorry, Eliza,' Martha said. 'I know it's a bloody inadequate thing to say, but I do feel for you. I mean, you loved him I suppose.'

'Yes. No. Thanks.' She reached out and touched the girl's hand. It felt warm. She supposed it was just because her own was so cold. Like Phil's. Phil was dead. She couldn't believe it.

'D'you want me to drive? I will if you like. I'll go slowly.'

'No, I need to have something to do. But I've got to know what happened. We'll stop at the next services and phone from there.'

46

She asked for Mitchell, then it occurred to her as his extension was ringing that she should have phoned James. Although it was too much to load on him. They had had so little time, and so much had weighed it down. She couldn't cry, couldn't not cry, over the phone to him about Phil. Mitchell was a sheepdog in comparison; she could bury her head in his fur, and he would let her weep.

'Lizzy, where are you?' was the first thing he said.

'Halfway down the M4. I'm with Martha, we had a meeting with the VI in Bristol. It's not a secret, it's in the diary, for Martha anyway. I only went at the last minute.'

'You should have told me. Helen hasn't been in today, and nobody seemed to have a clue where you were. The police are asking for you, and that guy from Saturn, James whatsit, and Howard Nkolo.'

Howard Nkolo. The Marlboro Lights smoker. There was a web of thoughts she had pieced together in the car: some facts she had recently acquired, some she had had for a while but not previously fitted into place. Some possibilities that she had been unable to face – but facing them was now unavoidable. Three deaths. The Beaver, Janine, now Phil. The unfolding tragedy wrapped round her like a badly-made patchwork, the raw seams digging into her bare skin.

'I'll get to the office this afternoon, maybe by six. Mitchell, I have to know. What happened to Phil?'

'There's only rumours, no one's certain. You sure you want to know?'

'I have to know.'

There was a pause. Then Mitchell's voice, crackly over the line, indistinct against the chatter of the service area forecourt, said, 'What I heard was, he was found hanged. I think there's a note. The word is it might not have been murder. But don't take it as gospel, it's only what I've heard.'

'What do you mean? How can it not have been murder?'

'Suicide maybe; at least it's a possibility. Lizzy, are you OK?'

'Are any of us OK?'

'I mean, to drive. D'you want me to come down and fetch you?'

'That's kind of you, Mitch. It's a bloody long way, though. I reckon I'll stay in one bit till I get back, and Martha's been great. She'll take over if I need it. I'll see you at sixish, OK?'

'Yes, sure. Take care.'

'Oh – can you check on Helen? I worry.'

'Jo did, she's home sick.'

'And one last thing, give me James Connaught's extension.'

'I'll transfer you. Have you got enough credit to last?'

'Just about, I reckon.'

The line went blank. She stood there waiting, just outside the entrance to Burger King and W H Smith. Through the glass of the lobby area she could see Martha hopping from one leg to another, her arms wrapped round her body. As if it was cold. It was cold, inside them. Martha looked pinch-faced, uncertain, absurdly young.

'Eliza?' It was James' deep voice. She had been nervous almost of talking to him, but she knew immediately she needn't have been. Whatever there was between them, trust if he didn't want to call it love, anyway, it was still there.

'Yes, yes I'm here. Did you get my message yesterday?'

'It didn't say where you were.'

'I'm sorry. I'll be back in Costhorpe around six, and I'll come straight to the office.'

'I'll have to tell the police that.'

'Uh-huh. James, what happened? Was it suicide?'

'They're not certain, but it looks like it. I know there's a note addressed to you.'

'Can I ask you something?'

'Yes?'

'Will you stay with me while I talk to them?'

She didn't hear a reply, and for a moment she thought he wouldn't give one. Then he said slowly, 'If you need me to. I'll see you then.'

'And tell them one thing now.'

'Can't it wait?'

'I want them to know now. When I went to Janine's room, that morning before it happened, there was a packet of cigarettes there, Marlboro Lights. And an ashtray, dirty: someone had been smoking. From what I've heard Janine didn't smoke.'

A short silence. Then James said, 'Who do you know smokes Marlboro Lights?'

'Lots of people, it's a popular brand isn't it? I'm sure there're lots of people.'

'Lizzy, who?'

He sounded impatient. He knew her, she thought. He could read her mind. She said quickly, 'Howard Nkolo', and put down the phone.

47

Martha drove much of the way, torching the Lotus, almost lost in the clean dangerous pleasure of speed. Eliza barely noticed. She had thoughts but as yet no feelings, only an awareness that her mind was changing, inevitably, unpreventably, hollowing out a deep well labelled horror in which everything else would fall. She knew that telling herself she was not guilty was no defence against feeling guilt, and that the guilt would bring her nightmares.

At 5.30 they were back in Costhorpe. Martha drove to her own house – Eliza's suggestion – then left Eliza to go on alone to St Jude's House.

She had to find enough composure to talk about it, because Crane would demand that. He had to explain it and he wanted the explanations to come from her. But even in this pre-horror state she had no real explanations to offer. She had not anticipated this at all. Phil had always seemed to her a man whose thoughts contained his feelings. He had his own view of the world, unbalanced as it had become over the last few days, and never failed to hold on to it. He had been solid and steady even in his obsessiveness. It was inconceivable that he should have cracked like Genevieve. She had never seen him shout or weep. He had been hurt, yes, but in an everyday kind of – hell, that was unfair. She knew she didn't want to be the cause of this, just as she knew that failure to love was no crime to compare with murder. But pain was pain; it didn't follow league tables, it didn't bear any standard mathematical relationship to its causes.

She parked in the multi-storey, left her case in the car, and walked alone through the underpass and up to the main entrance. The evening was fine, the sky still clear. It did not surprise her to see DC Joyce standing in the reception area, close by the counter as if she had been chatting to the receptionist. They fell into step without talking.

Once they were in the lift DC Joyce said, 'You were close friends, weren't you? I'm sorry.'

The humanity of it surprised her. 'Thanks,' she said.

She did not ask where they were going. They emerged on to

floor 4, and turned into A wing, going past the secretaries' desks
and into Ken Thursby's old office.

Inspector Crane was there, and so was James. Her eyes went
first to James. He did not smile. He met her look steadily. What
she read into his look – what she perhaps needed to read into it
– was that he would give her support. He didn't pretend to understand what had happened, and he would not respond to it in any
way that mirrored her. But she had his trust; he was there for her.

They had been waiting for her, clearly, but they were not ready.
There were only two chairs in the room, one behind the desk and
one in front of it. The men had been standing. Carol Joyce busied
herself finding two more chairs. None of them offered to help her.
When she had them arranged they all sat, Inspector Crane in the
executive chair, Eliza in the visitors' chair, DC Joyce and James in
the chairs she had brought in. DC Joyce was right behind Eliza
near the door, but James was sideways from her. She had only to
turn her head to see him.

He had not spoken to her. None of them had said more than a
couple of words.

Inspector Crane leaned forwards across the blond oak desk.

'Right,' he said. 'This time you will help us with our enquiries.
I'm going to get the truth out of you.'

She had been taken aback by his aggression at previous encounters, but it had not forearmed her. She shivered. After a moment
she managed to say, 'You have to tell me first. What happened. Is
there a note? Mitchell said he thought there was, a note addressed
to me.'

'Miss Stannard, you're misunderstanding.' Crane said coldly.
'What we're engaged in here is a murder investigation. Two
people have been killed, Patrick Harding and Janine Broughton.
We've also just learned that Philip Curtin is dead, but under
circumstances that lead us to suspect it's suicide. That's a sad
thing, I agree. I don't mean to disparage it, and in due course
we'll need to know what you can tell us in connection with it, but
it's not our priority at this moment. Right now my priority is the
murders, and my concern is to make you tell me the truth about
the Thursday morning when you found Harding.'

The Thursday morning. Howard. Lies. She had almost forgotten
what she had told James over the phone.

'Have you arrested Howard Nkolo?'

'He's not been charged with anything, not as yet, but he's in custody at present, helping us with our enquiries.'

'I see.'

'Do you see, Miss Stannard? What you should see is that we've wasted four days on this enquiry, four days in which a second person has been killed, largely because you lied in your evidence to us.'

'That's not true!' She said it instinctively, angrily; then bit her lip.

'What's not true? That you lied?'

But it was true. She didn't even take refuge in the thin distinction she had used to excuse it to Howard.

'You've lied to me twice now,' Crane said. 'It's intolerable, it's a criminal offence, and I'm having no more of it. This time I want the truth, and all of the truth.'

And this time she would have to tell it. She hadn't been conscious of changing her mind, but she knew now that she had been coming to this realization for some time. She knew more: she knew Crane was right, and that she had done wrong.

'I will tell you.'

'You're damn right you will.'

'There was ... some time. When I got to the lift, after picking up my papers.'

'No, don't start there. We'll have it all, thank you. You can tell us first why you told us Bill Downs was on the reception desk.'

He was being too aggressive; she felt he should have realized she had surrendered. She dared not say so. She knew too that he had written a story in his mind, and that he would be angry if what she had to tell didn't match it. When. This part clearly didn't match his story.

'It was Bill. I'm as sure as I reasonably can be. I mean, I've never known all the guards by name, but I remember Howard calling him Bill that morning. He's the elderly one, with the grey hair and the Norfolk accent. Howard told me afterwards it was Stew, Stew Harker, but I think he was lying. I think it was Bill.'

'Say that again. You think Nkolo was lying.'

'Yes.' She raised her head and confronted Crane. 'I don't think he did it, though. Honestly I don't. I think he's covering up something, for someone, but I don't know who and I don't

know what. He hasn't told me anything. But I can't believe that
Howard's a murderer.'

Crane stared at her. Then he said in a gentler voice, 'I know you
can't. Leave that to us. Just tell us the truth.'

'I am doing. We arrived here at the office just like I told you,
at the time I told you, I got to the carpark at 6.28 so it was a
couple of minutes after that. We got in the lift together. I got out
at the second floor and went to get my papers. Then I didn't see
Howard again until I got up to the fourth floor, and that was
quite a bit later. Maybe fifteen minutes.'

'Fifteen minutes.'

'About. That's why the timings were out. You were right about
that. We didn't take that long phoning the police after we found
the body, the missing time was after we split up and before I went
into the meeting room. And Howard came in a few minutes later,
just like I said.'

'So what did you do in this missing time?'

'Nothing that had anything to do with the murder, I swear. I'd
have told you if I'd thought I'd seen anything useful, but I was, I
am, sure it isn't. What's useful is the time. I can see that now, but
the thing is, I didn't want to tell you what I'd been doing. And I
was wrong, and I'm sorry.'

'Miss Stannard,' Crane cut in. 'Tell me what happened.'

'Yes; yes, I am doing. I got back to the lift lobby and I had to
wait for a lift to come, and while I was waiting I saw someone
in room 2A, on the other side of the lift lobby. He was down
towards the end of the room. I couldn't make out who it was, but
I know there was someone there. There must have been, because
it was when he'd disappeared behind the cupboards that another
man came out into the centre aisle and headed my way. I don't
think he saw me straight away, but he didn't have much choice,
there's only one way out of 2A and he obviously wanted to get
out of there before the other man saw him.'

Crane said, 'Let me have this clear. There were two men in
room 2A.'

Eliza nodded. 'That's right. One I only saw in passing, but the
other one came into the lift lobby. We talked.'

'In the lift lobby.'

'No, at the top of the stairs, on the landing behind the swing
doors. He didn't want to be seen.'

Carol Joyce said, 'Who didn't want to be seen, Eliza?'

She swung round with relief: there was no hard suppressed anger in the woman's voice, and it made it easier to say, 'Lewis. Lewis Stannard, my ex-husband.'

She had known it wasn't what they expected, but she was still surprised by the intensity of the astonishment that filled the room. She turned back to Crane. 'That's why I didn't tell you, because I knew you didn't know Lewis had been there, and I didn't want him to get caught up in all this. He didn't have anything to do with the murder, he couldn't have, because he wasn't on the fourth floor, he was on the second floor and then he went downstairs and out of the building. Harding must have been killed when we were talking, so I'm his alibi, I guess. I can prove he didn't do it.'

Silence. A disbelieving silence. It sounded thin even to her, which annoyed her, because it was the absolute truth as she knew it. She went on, 'I know why he was there, because he told me, and it wasn't anything at all to do with Harding. He'd come in to get a database, names and addresses that he needed for some job he was getting. Sorry, I ought to explain. Lewis used to work at RUS, but he was made redundant in January. This was a list of people he'd dealt with when he was there, and he'd forgotten to take with him when he left. I mean, obviously he shouldn't have taken it with him, strictly speaking, but he might have done, only he didn't. Then later he realized he could really use it, so he thought he'd come back in to get it.'

There was a moment's silence. Eliza wondered if it had made sense to them. She thought she had been clear but she didn't trust in her own mental state at that moment.

Crane said slowly, 'You're telling us this was industrial espionage.'

'That's an awfully hard word for it. I'm telling you I know it was wrong of him, but not appallingly, shockingly wrong. I mean, I knew he'd be in trouble if people found out, but I didn't think he was that wrong to do it. I didn't want him to be found out. Do you follow?'

'Sort of,' Crane said.

'The thing is, the whole takeover was wrong. It was corrupt, rotten, everyone knew it. All people pulling strings and connections and nothing open or honest and nobody asking us or saying anything to us. Then when we were taken over it was worse, it was vile, they acted like we were fools, all of us. They threw lots of us out, they threw Lewis out. He'd been there seventeen years. He was good too, he worked hard, he was brilliant at his job. It meant everything to him.'

'So he had reason to be angry with Patrick Harding.'

She had known this would happen. It was at the core of her reluctance to tell them. 'Yes. That's true, but like I told you, he didn't kill him. He was bitter enough to bend the rules, to go in and get these addresses he wanted. But not angry, not bitter enough to kill Harding.'

Crane's face was shuttered. She knew what his thoughts would be behind it, but she couldn't think of anything else to say that would help Lewis.

After a moment Crane said, 'How did he get in? Did he tell you that?'

'I didn't ask, but I'm pretty sure he had a key to the goods entrance. He wouldn't have involved the guards if he could avoid it, he was friendly with them and they might have agreed to let him in, but he wouldn't have wanted to ask them. He used to have a key in the days we were married. Lots of people did. Lots of people still do. Everyone at RUS knows that. And I suppose you knew it? I mean, that you couldn't be sure exactly who was in St Jude's House that morning, because there were so many people who could have sneaked in using their keys.'

'The directors,' Crane said.

'Not only them. Lewis wasn't a director. Other people picked up keys one way and another, copied someone's for some reason, or Allen Mark lent them one and forgot he didn't get it back.'

She thought Crane would push her on this, but perhaps he saw that there was nothing more she could say. Or perhaps he had known: as she had said, it was no secret, and it had been in plenty of people's interest to tell the police their list was probably incomplete. He turned to DC Joyce. 'Carol, you'd better get this man brought in. Lewis...'

'Stannard,' Eliza supplied. '40 Regent Road, Costhorpe.'

'Now?'

'Yes. Nip outside and phone down to the incident room.'

Carol Joyce went out, leaving Eliza, Crane and James in the room. Eliza didn't look at James. She said, 'Lewis must have taken several minutes doing his printout. He had to print it all out because the computer discs are protected, he couldn't have run one on his own computer, so it was no good simply copying the disc. There's a programme that unprotects them but Lewis wouldn't know how to run it. He had the printout in his bag when I saw him.'

Crane looked expressionlessly back at her. He said, 'I'm aware this is hard for you. Now go home and leave us to do our job.'

She knew she couldn't do that yet. It took a moment for her to remember why.

'I need to see the note first. The note Phil Curtin left.'

48

'That's Curtin's handwriting?' Crane asked as he held out the envelope. It was grey, Basildon Bond it looked like. She remembered his writing her a note once before on the same type of paper. She slid her finger under the flap, broke it open and withdrew a single sheet of matching paper.

'Yes.' Her eyes focused on the words. Phil had written in blue biro. His writing was small, neat-looking but not easy to decipher. He had dated it in the top right-hand corner, Monday April 20th.

> *'Darling Liz,*
> *I've been wanting so much to talk to you and at the end there isn't that much to say, only that I'm more sorry than I can begin to explain. I never meant any of it to happen, and believe me I had no idea how it would turn out. But it's done now, and there's no way to take back the things I've done wrong. Only this is left, because I can't live with it. There seems to be nothing for me now, no happiness, no hope, so the best thing is to end it all. Think of me kindly sometimes, but don't grieve too hard for me.*
> *I loved you more than I can begin to say.*
> *If there is an eternity, you'll be in my thoughts for all of it,*
> *Phil'*

She read it twice. James reached out a hand, and she gave it to him. He read it through and passed it to Crane, who was the last to read it.

Carol Joyce slipped back into the room. Crane looked up at Eliza. 'So?'

'It's what Phil would have written,' Eliza said. 'I wish it wasn't. I wish he'd written to his mother instead. I suppose that's ungrateful of me, but it'll be so hurtful to her. She's a widow, and he's her only child. He lived with her till he was nearly thirty. Or if he'd mentioned her even. He could have addressed it to me but written something I could have showed her, something to make it easier.'

'There's no way to make it easier when something like this happens.'

Eliza disagreed, but she did not say so.

James said, 'What is it that he regretted so much?'

'I imagine he means what happened last Saturday night.' She recounted the incident briefly. 'I was terrified,' she added. 'Probably more terrified than it deserved, but I was off balance, and he took me completely by surprise. I guess Phil was pretty shaken when I went supernova. He hadn't meant to upset me, I knew that even then, he just judged it hopelessly wrong.'

Crane said, 'Are you certain that's what he's referring to?'

'What else could it have been?'

'That's something I'd like to know.'

Eliza stared at her hands. She frowned.

'There's nothing else, between us, and I can't think that there was any other problem in his life. He had no money worries: he wasn't the type to get into debt, he didn't gamble, and I can't imagine his job was ever at risk. In fact the opposite, he'd been hoping for a promotion.'

'He'd been what?' James echoed.

'He had hopes of something. That's all I know, but it must have been reasonably definite, because he told my friend Rachel as well as – Oh.'

'What?' Crane demanded.

'I can see now.' She glanced at James. 'You know Frank Mills has been planning to make you a proposal for him to take over as chief exec with a new team in place behind him. He's even spoken to me. I think he reckoned I'd put in a good word for him with you. Phil always got on well with Frank. I guess Frank had talked to him and offered him something senior on the IT side.'

James showed no reaction. Crane said, 'Did this fall through?'

'Not that I'm aware, though you'd have to check with Frank. Unless you …'. She glanced at James.

'I've done nothing,' he said.

Crane said, 'It doesn't sound like a reason for suicide. What about Curtin's private life?'

'There's nothing that comes to mind. His mother was a trial sometimes, but he was very patient with her. I'm sure there was no other woman. He was hung up on me.'

'But was he hung up enough to kill himself because of that Saturday night?' Carol Joyce asked.

Eliza said slowly, 'I think maybe he was. There was something self-dramatizing about Phil. He wasn't one for heavy rows, but he had a self-pitying streak that he'd play on sometimes. I can see it in this note. I don't mean to speak ill of him, but you need to understand. To me it's all out of proportion, but when I ask myself, could that have been why he did it, the answer I come to is – yes.'

Crane said, 'I have to ask you this. Did he know Harding or Janine Broughton?'

'No,' Eliza said. 'Except in so far as everyone at RUS did. Again, that's as far as I'm aware: I can't be certain because I haven't seen much of him since we split up. But he never mentioned to me having anything special to do with either of them, and I didn't get the impression he was particularly cut up about them dying. He was saddened, obviously, as we all were, but not –'

James interrupted her. 'But you've just told us he was upset. He was acting irrationally. There were two incidents at least, the one you've just mentioned and the one when I encountered him.' He turned to Crane and summarized that.

Crane said to Eliza, 'This wasn't typical behaviour for Curtin?'

She didn't like the way the conversation was going. She said carefully, 'It wasn't, no. He was normally a very steady sort of man. It's true, I'm sure, that he was affected by the murders. Everyone was, and Phil maybe more so than average, but that's not because he was caught up with Harding or Janine, it's because he thought I needed support and I wasn't prepared to take it from him. I can't believe there's more to it than that.'

'How well did he know Howard Nkolo?' James asked.

'He knew him at work, but they weren't close either. They didn't work in the same department, they didn't have similar interests or lifestyles, and they didn't socialize outside the office. If you're suggesting they plotted Harding's murder together, that's absurd. It's the last thing I'd believe. It's simply not conceivable.'

'And one more question. Did Curtin smoke?'

Crane seemed to have let James take over. She glanced at the policeman before she answered. 'No, never. He was very disapproving of people who smoked.'

'Maybe it was Nkolo then.'

'What was Nkolo?' Crane asked.

'I'd been thinking. This room. When we came in here on Thursday, it smelled of tobacco.'

'That's right,' Eliza said.

'When was this?'

'Early in the morning, after Harding's body was discovered.' James turned to Eliza. 'This room wasn't being used, officially, but I dare say it was used unofficially. What I'm envisaging is someone unplugging Janine Broughton's computer and bringing it in here on the Wednesday afternoon.'

'And smoking a cigarette while they sent a dozen emails,' Eliza said slowly.

'That's about the size of it.'

49

Crane told Carol Joyce to send down to the incident room for a computer expert. He told Eliza and James they could leave. Eliza had thought James might prefer to stay, but he said nothing. He followed her out of the room and between the partitions to the lift lobby.

It was about seven o'clock. Eliza supposed she was tired, but she was strung too tight to be able to sense the fatigue. Phil, Lewis, Howard: their disasters felt like her own. And someone, soon, would be charged with murder.

They took the lift together and went through the reception area together. Eliza paused at the top of the concrete steps, supposing she should say something before leaving James. She didn't want to say anything. She had no resources left for countering his anger.

'I'll go straight home. I'm done in.'

James said, 'Are you angry with me?'

Her eyes went to his in surprise. But it was he who was angry, surely?

He didn't appear to be. He showed no signs of fury, and none of cold cynicism. He looked like the kind of businessman who emerges from the rubble of an earthquake with his suit immaculately pressed and concise orders for his secretary on his tongue. She could see he was tired, but he was not overwhelmed by his tiredness.

'I …' She had no idea what to say. 'No. I've no reason to be.'

'Huh,' James said. 'Then why …? I mean. I'm not under the illusion that you're itching to commemorate Curtin's death by going to bed with me. Do you imagine I'm good for nothing else, or …?'

'No!' It was so far from the reaction she'd expected from him that she didn't know how to handle it. She reached out and touched his shoulder. 'You ought to be angry.'

'Ought I?' He frowned. 'I see.' He put his hand on the side of her waist and propelled her, not ungently, down the steps. At their foot he stopped again. 'So. Is this because I don't understand your protecting your friends from the police? Or because I'm speechless with shock that your ex-husband tried to purloin some files from the organization that sacked him? Am I supposed to think that the moment Harding was found dead, you'd have thought to yourself, one of my best mates must have done this? Or is there something else I've missed?'

'No. That's pretty comprehensive. I'm sorry. I don't mean to underestimate you.'

'But you –' He stopped himself. 'You wanted me there.'

'I know.' She moved slightly, farther into the warmth of his body, not sure whether this was what she wanted or not. 'I suppose what I want is the kind of relationship I don't have. I mean, something ... with time behind it. That can handle this. I'm not saying you can't. But ...'

'But I'm a stranger to you, and so are you to me.' He spoke thoughtfully. 'There's no buffer of old tolerance, that's true. And no assumption that we're stuck with each other. We're very different people, and we've acknowledged right from the start that we're on opposite sides, if there are any sides in this. We've been honest with each other, I think. There are things you haven't rushed to tell me, but I haven't exactly rushed to tell you about my personal life. I know what you mean, all this is too much to bear, but here you are and here I am and so far I'm bloody glad I found you here. I don't know that I could have handled it without you.'

She knew she couldn't have handled it without him. Her head fell slowly on to his shoulder. His arm folded round her. They stood like that for a long moment on the steps of St Jude's House.

Eliza raised her head. 'Thank you,' she said.

'What now?'

'I think ... I go home on my own. If you don't mind being on your own.'

'You're sure?'

She nodded. 'I need some time alone. I need you too, but not right now. I'm sorry.'

She was conscious of him looking intently at her. 'Don't be,' he said eventually. 'That's honest. I like your honesty. Phone me when you're ready to see me.'

'I will.'

50

She ran a deep bath and tipped into it the remains of a bottle of horse chestnut bath essence. She clambered into the greenish water and sat amid the pungent smell of the fumes rising off it, staring at the green plants and white tiles, until the water was cool around her. She got out, skin wrinkled, wrapped herself in a large white towel and went into her bedroom. The bed was still unmade, as she and James had left it on Monday morning. She transferred her body from the towel to a fold of duvet, and lay there, shivering, telling herself to sleep.

She was too tired to sleep. She was too shaken to sleep. Phil was dead. Howard was the most likely suspect for sticking a knife in the Beaver's chest and slashing Janine's throat. That second murder had happened because they hadn't solved the first soon enough. She had held up the police by not telling them everything, therefore, she had played a part in causing the second murder. James might think it forgivable, but it didn't feel forgivable to her.

How could it have been Howard? She couldn't reconstruct any kind of story that allowed for Howard killing Harding in the fifteen minutes between her leaving him in the lift and her seeing him again on the fourth floor.

She needed to talk, but to whom? Perhaps she had been wrong to send James away. What she hadn't said to him was that she was afraid of wading in deeper, when she knew he was committed elsewhere. If they came through this and then he ditched her: that was what she wouldn't be able to handle.

Or if they came through this and he didn't ditch her: perhaps she wouldn't be able to handle that either. There was something in her response to him, something that she couldn't disentangle from all the vileness of the murders, and she was aware that she was afraid it would still be there once the murders had been left behind them.

James was a stranger, but he knew things about her now that no one else did. These were not things she could confide to Mitchell, or to Rachel. Last of all Rachel, after that casual betrayal she had learned of in Ken Thursby's office. She had a vague feeling she would forgive it in time, but she couldn't follow James's example and find it instantly understandable and excusable.

At any rate there was no point pretending she was about to fall asleep. It was nine o'clock. She got dressed in an old soft duck-egg-blue jersey two-piece, went down to the kitchen and made a cup of coffee. She made a toasted cheese sandwich too, and thought as she ate it that it would ferment her nightmares.

She thought about Phil's mother, a small talkative irritable woman. Maybe she should phone her; but she was so tired. Mrs Curtin would probably blame her for Phil's death, and was perfectly capable of saying so. Eliza didn't trust herself to be diplomatic.

Perhaps she could write instead. It would be better than silence, safer than the phone. The newsagent was still open, it was always open. She slipped on her pumps, found her bag and went round the corner. She leafed through the In Your Time of Sadness cards and moved on to the Any Occasion section. Finally she settled on a view of Costhorpe Cathedral from Wanswick Heath.

She came back home and sat at the table in her kitchen, staring at the card. The painting was by Crome, it was in the Castle Art Gallery, she and Phil had looked at it together. She knew the view it portrayed: they had walked down that hill overlooking the city, along the broad cobbled streets of the Close, past the cloisters and through that door in the south transept. They had stared at the echoing heights of the vaulted stone ceiling together. Was Phil religious? He had never mentioned God to her, not when they were in the cathedral and not at any other time that she recalled. What had he put in his note? Inspector Crane had taken it back, so she couldn't check the wording. 'If there is an eternity' – was that his phrase?

There was an eternity, and it was here and now. She could barely believe in his death, that he had tied the noose, put his head through it, jumped off the chair or whatever he had used, and was now a corpse. Of the three tragic deaths at RUS, his was the only corpse she had not seen. Perhaps she should ask to see it, then she would know it was true. But what was true? She did not want to face this truth, any more than she wanted to face a truth that told her Howard Nkolo had killed a man then sauntered back to joke with her.

She should find a pen, write something. What could she write? I did not love your son, although he hoped I would, and sometimes so did I. I hate him now because he has implicated me in this death, he has given me guilt which I cannot bear, he has brought death back to my room where it hovers in the corners, like a spiderweb that will smother me with its sticky strands if I stray too close.

The phone rang.

She did not move. No need, the answering machine was on. The ringing tone ended. There was a click, a silence in which she knew her message was playing, another couple of clicks, then a male voice boomed out of the tiny speaker in her study.

'Eliza? It's Frank Mills. I'm at the Jugged Hare. You remember that little get-together I mentioned? I guess you couldn't make it. Phil Curtin I suppose, terrible business. Terrible, terrible business. But I'm sorry you didn't get here, because there are a few things we need to talk about. I wondered if there was any chance I could pop round now. It's what ... a quarter to ten. We've finished here, and I'm in the city. I don't want to leave it, because things are moving fast. It wouldn't take long, so if you're in .... If you come back in before 11.30, say ...'

She had stood up without conscious thought. It was someone, someone to fill the void, to make her not alone, for a moment or two at least. Someone who wouldn't blame or criticize. Frank was a realist, who more so? He had done his share of conspiring, kept his share of secrets.

She picked up the phone as Frank was saying, 'I'm not at home so you can't call me back, but I'll maybe ring you again in –'

'Frank? It's me, Eliza.'

'Oh. Oh, you're there.'

'Yes, yes I'm here.' It sounded inane. It occurred to her that she didn't want to see Frank after all. If he had been James, or Lewis, or Mitchell or Rachel; but it was Frank Mills. She had never liked Frank Mills. What had she been thinking of?

Frank said, 'So if I could just take ten minutes of your time.'

'I don't know, Frank.' She groped for suitable words. 'It's been a long day, and I'm really off balance. To be honest I'm not in any state to think about RUS.' She paused. 'I'm sorry.'

'You're on your own?'

'Yes.'

'God, you shouldn't be on your own. That's terrible, on your

own after something like this. Tell you what, I'll bring round
some brandy. I won't take long. Just give you some company, and
maybe throw an idea or two by you, but you don't have to give
me an answer right away. No obligation, you know.'

'It's kind of you, but I really don't –'

'I'm not far away. I'll be there in ten minutes.' He rang off
before she could protest.

She barely had the energy left to curse to herself. Hopefully
he would see it was useless, she thought, and leave more or less
immediately.

She went back into to the kitchen and rinsed her greasy plate
under the tap. She put the kettle back on. She couldn't imagine
drinking brandy with Frank Mills. He had never been to her house
before. As for sitting with him, sipping companionably while he
outlined his proposal to her, the prospect made her feel sick. How
would he approach it? These are the people I've lined up, this is
what I'm bribing them each with, this is the one I'm planning to
replace Phil with, now we want you to go to James Connaught
and tell him it's a done deal?

All she wanted at that moment was to be gone from RUS, to
know she would never have to walk through the door again. She
envied Rachel, for all her empty despair, envied Ted Hawley and
the rest of them. Jez, Lewis, they had all gone. She should follow
them, she thought.

Oh God, Lewis; Lewis in custody. She was sure he would be
released, and quickly most likely, but there would be publicity,
since dozens of reporters were now following the case. People
would remember he had been involved. People would get to know
why he had been in St Jude's House. Most bosses wouldn't, in
public at least, take the practical attitude James had taken. Lewis
would lose all chance of that job which Mitchell had said wasn't
as firm as he had made out, and of any other job come to that.

Bloody Lewis. Poor Kate.

An impulse made her go back into her study and pick
up the phone. She could at least tell Kate he wasn't a serious
murder suspect. There would be time, surely, before Frank
arrived. It would be a good thing to do, and she needed to
feel she had done some good. She flicked through her book
for their number, and dialled before she could think better
of it.

Kate answered on the second ring. 'Lewis …?' Her voice quivered with naive hopefulness. How little the girl knew. Maybe that was what Lewis had wanted, Eliza thought with sudden clarity. Not an equal partner, but someone to protect, someone who would look up to him, who wouldn't have to forgive his failings because she wouldn't even recognize them.

It was not her voice Kate wanted to hear. Knowing that, she spoke gently, easing Kate through surprise and embarrassment and towards relief; although it would at best be a temporary relief, before the impact of what Lewis actually had done rebounded on them. Perhaps she wasn't really being kind to Kate, but just rubbing ointment into her own sore conscience.

She had an urge to say, tell him I'm sorry I told the police, and ring off, but that was not Kate's agenda. Kate was tearfully aggressive, confused, demanding. What do you mean? How can you have seen Lewis? What did you say, what did he say? Eliza was caught in the thorns of it when the doorbell rang. It was a strange irony, probably the only time in her life she was glad to have Frank Mills turn up.

'Hold on, Kate. There's someone at the door.' She could hear Kate's high voice continuing unabated as she set the receiver down on the desk and went out into the hall.

Frank was wearing a navy mac, an uncharacteristically drab garment for him she thought, and heavy for a warm April night. He was carrying an Oddbins bag. 'Evening, my dear,' he said.

'I'm just on the phone, Frank. Come in. Why don't you wait in here?' She opened the door to the sitting room, and reached through to switch on the light. 'I won't be a minute.' She returned to the study. 'Kate? Sorry about that.'

'Eliza, this isn't making any sense. How can Lewis have been at RUS? You know he left –'

A shadow fell over her shoulder.

Her hand went up to her mouth as she span round. The telephone fell from her other hand.

God, she was edgy. It was only Frank. He had followed her, damn him, instead of waiting. He never had bloody known how much space to give people. 'You shook me,' she said awkwardly. 'I said I wouldn't be a minute.' She reached down to pick up the receiver. At the same moment Frank reached for it. Their heads clashed.

She snatched the receiver, giving Frank a small shove. Only a small one, but he stumbled, tripped on the edge of the rug, and slid gracelessly to the ground, feet in front of him, landing hard on his plump backside.

A tiny incident, but it was enough to further unnerve her. It occurred to her, belatedly, that at this time it was not a good idea to be alone in her house with a man she was not close to – a man whose ruthlessness she had seen displayed all too recently. And no one knew he was there.

She brought the receiver up to her mouth and said loudly, over the tinny sound of Kate's voice, 'Frank Mills.'

'Eliza! Eliza, what's –'

'Frank Mills is here. I've got to go, Kate. I'll see you soon.' She put the telephone down.

Frank had recovered from the slip. He got clumsily to his feet. He brushed down his mac. Then looked at her, his eyes expressionless.

'Why did you do that?'

So someone would know. She said, sharply, 'I could ask why you reached out for the phone. My phone.'

'Who was it calling?'

She felt fairly sure he wouldn't have recognized Kate's voice. Had she given the name? No matter if she had, it was a common enough one. 'No one you know, an old friend in London. Shall we go back into the other room?'

'If you like.' He turned and headed towards the sitting room.

Eliza followed him. 'I saw you brought a bottle. I'll get some glasses.' Frank did not answer. As she went through to the kitchen, she told herself to calm down. It was not credible, it really was not credible that Frank Mills intended her harm. But she had no idea what he wanted from her. What had he said, some things he wanted to check on, or something like that? She did not imagine this was entirely about fleshing out the kind of job he might offer if he managed to worm his way back to the top job at RUS. He might mention that as a sweetener, but he had to have some other agenda. She supposed he was asking around about the murders, like all too many people, worried at the situation, hoping to make some kind of a breakthrough.

And it was true that she was an obvious person to ask. For her sins, she was at the middle of everything. Not investigating, not exactly, but wanting answers all the same. To why Janine had chosen her to phone, for instance. There had to be a reason, one she hadn't yet come to.

Maybe if they shared information, they would both end up in a better position.

She opened the kitchen cupboard and took out two Paris goblets. Brandy was not her usual drink, and she had nothing more suitable to drink it in. She got a small bottle of soda water from a second cupboard, and carried all three items through to the sitting room. It looked drab and unwelcoming in the flat light from the central fitting; usually at night she lit a standard lamp and a spotlight over the CD player. And the whole house smelled like a funeral parlour, from the three lots of flowers in their vases.

Frank had taken off his coat while she was in the kitchen. He was wearing a navy single-breasted business suit and a navy waistcoat with a white windowpane check. The coat he had draped over the arm of the sofa wasn't the coat which had been in her section's cupboard at St Jude's House. That had been black, while Frank's was a mid-navy with a slight sheen to it.

She put down the glasses and the soda water on the coffee table. 'I'm sorry I've no ice. I haven't got round to making any recently.'

'No need, love, I'm not an ice man.' Frank sat down heavily on the low sofa, and reached for the Oddbins bag. He brought out a bottle of Sainsbury's own-label brandy. It was a full bottle, although he hadn't bought it in Oddbins, obviously. He had to break the seal. Leaning forward, he poured two generous glasses, pushed one across to Eliza who was still standing, and took a swig of his own, neat. 'Mind if I smoke?'

'Actually, yes.' Eliza took her glass, filled it to the brim with soda, and retreated to the button-backed chair. He smokes, she thought. Not Marlboros though. What did Frank smoke? She couldn't remember.

'So it's been a hard day, love.'

'Pretty hard.'

'Terrible thing about Phil Curtin. So difficult to understand too.'

'Yes.'

'He left a note, I heard?'

'Yes.'

'Explained it, did it?'

Of all the things he might raise, Phil's note seemed about the most unlikely. Was this a bizarre attempt at smalltalk before he turned to whatever it was that he really wanted to know? It was all she could think. And there was something crass about Frank, it was almost conceivable.

That didn't alter the fact that she had no desire, less than no desire, to discuss Phil's forlorn suicide note. She said warily, 'It said he was sorry, mostly.'

'Oh. Of course you had to wonder ...'

'Wonder what?'

'Well ... you know. With the murders.'

'You think *Phil* was the murderer?'

'Oh no, love. No, of course not. No one could possibly think that.' He let out a bark that was maybe intended to represent a laugh. This did not improve the situation.

Eliza, rapidly become more irritated than edgy, said sharply, 'It really is none of your business. But what he was sorry for was nothing to do with RUS, it was all about Phil and me. So if you're imagining this was some sweeping confession that's going to clear the boards so the rest of us can all just get on with life, then I can only say you're wrong.'

'I'm sorry,' Frank said, and he almost sounded it. 'I didn't mean to offend you. I'm sure it's a coincidence. I mean, it happening right now. Anyway, the police will check him out, won't they? And we'll all know for certain before any time at all.'

Check him out? She had to turn the phrase over before she took in what he meant. Forensic tests, it had to be.

Everyone knew that the police had said there was no forensic evidence to do with Harding's murder. No sign of the weapon, no fingerprints, no convenient hairs or fingernail clippings, nothing. It occurred to her for the first time that because they had all been told this, though most of them had had it at third or fourth hand, it did not mean it was true.

And Janine's murder had been different. She had seen enough to know that it was probably the case that the murderer had left some traces then.

This was not small talk. This was not even a clumsy, not even an unbelievably dumb, attempt to console her. This had to be what Frank had come to ask her.

And it had to mean he really believed it could be Phil who had committed the murders.

Astonished – too astonished to hide it, though she could not see why she should in any case – she said slowly, 'This is insane, Frank. Phil's no one's idea of a murderer.'

Frank took another gulp of the Sainsbury's brandy. 'I'm sure you're right. Eliza, I'm sorry. I haven't handled this well, have I? I just feel, you know, we need to cross the i's and dot the t's. I mean, the other way round. I mean, it's not like the police are telling us everything. It's all bloody Connaught, he's the only one they seem to talk to. So we have to stick together, don't we? All us old guard.' He tried a smile. 'Share notes. Make sure no one gets shafted.'

Bloody Connaught. So this was on his agenda too.

'If you imagine James Connaught tells me what the police tell him, then you're totally wrong.' Again, she added silently.

Frank gave her a narrow look. Surely, surely, Eliza thought, he will not be jerk enough to tell me he knows about me and James?

He wasn't. He shrugged. 'I wondered,' he said. 'That's all. And I had a sense, just a sense mind, that you get on pretty well with him. Of course, he's not seeing anything we haven't all seen. Like I was telling you earlier, I reckon we're getting to a phase when openings are going to come up, positions on offer, and this time around they aren't going to ignore everyone who knows what really goes on at RUS. All the stars, the good old people with lots of experience. You're one of them, Eliza, no doubt about that. I've got you on my list, dear. You're definitely on my list.'

'This is hardly the time to think about that.'

Frank's eyes narrowed again. 'It's not the time to *do* anything, love. Not yet. But that doesn't mean it's too soon to think about it.'

She felt too disgusted to reply.

'So, I just wanted to – keep the channels open. And tell you how sorry I am. About Curtin.'

'Thank you.' She assumed he had not got whatever he had come for, but she sensed too that he knew he would have to give up, at least for a while.

He hadn't mentioned Howard Nkolo. It surprised her. Surely

someone would have told him they had Howard in custody? But if they hadn't, she didn't want to tell him herself.

'Nice place you have here,' Frank said.

'Thank you. I like it.'

They drank in silence, Frank as fast as was compatible with politeness. As soon as his glass was empty he got to his feet.

'I'll leave you to it. It's getting late, and I know you're done in. I hope you didn't mind me coming over.'

She could not think of an answer she could give to that.

'Tell you what, give yourself a bit of a rest in the morning. Take it off and come in at lunchtime.'

As if he had the right to boss her.

'I'll see myself out.'

'Don't forget the bottle.'

'No, keep it, love.'

When he had gone she bolted the front door, double-locked the new lock she had had fitted on Sunday, checked all the window locks and the back door. She put a chair under the latch of the bedroom door when she went upstairs.

Still she could not sleep.

51

It was while she was driving in to work the next morning (at eight, although she had been awake since 6.30) that Eliza realized she would leave Costhorpe. It had the oddness that such realizations often do, as if she couldn't imagine why she hadn't thought it sooner. What was there for her in Costhorpe? Her family weren't there. (Her parents were in Andover, her sister in Sydney.) She had no lover there. She had friends, but almost all of them were linked to RUS. They were Lewis's friends anyway, most of them. She might be over the pain of breaking up with Lewis, but she still had no desire to spend the rest of her life in a city which was inhabited by him, Kate and their children. She was not particularly likely to find another life partner in Costhorpe, where the social scene was small and all too familiar to her. As for RUS, it was depressing even to catch sight from the ring road of the green-grey bulk of St Jude's House.

It felt as if the only secure place left to her, the only one where she really belonged, was the narrow interior of her Lotus. If I've come to this, she thought as she parked it, I've already left it far too late. Perhaps I should just pack my bags and drive off.

No; that had the shine of a fantasy, and the police, for one, wouldn't allow it. But the more she considered it, the more she thought it would make sense to leave RUS behind her – and leave James behind too. They had walked too far down a road that led only to the quarry's edge. She needed to turn back before she reached the precipice.

She could resign immediately, and leave as soon as her notice was up. Surely the police would have finished with her by then.

The decision brought an uncharacteristic spring to her step. She sailed past the babe on the door, and in the lobby, looked with amusement, almost, at the image on her identity card before putting it back in her purse. Eliza Stannard, age thirty-seven, one-time civil servant.

She had a little money in the bank; she could sell her house. She could go to the Greek Islands, to Goa, to Bali, to Patagonia. On the other side of the heavy glass doors, an entire world awaited her.

She took the stairs, not the lift. On the second-floor landing the Quality poster loomed at her in the dim light. This one was a racetrack, with a Ferrari (or so she supposed, it was not a great likeness) hurtling into the middle distance. 'Head for the chequered flag of Quality', the caption read. On impulse she lifted her briefcase and hefted it, metal-reinforced corner forwards, at the Ferrari's exhaust pipe. The glass shattered satisfyingly, cracks radiating to each side, a large triangle falling out and on to the floor tiles. No one had seen. She left the glass where it lay and went on to her desk.

'Morning, Mattie. Hi Helen, hi Russell.' She was the last one of the team to come in. She dropped her bag, shook off her suit jacket, rolled the sleeves of her grey jersey top as far as her elbows and took a sheet of headed paper off the pile by the printer.

'Oh I'm so glad you're back, Eliza.' Helen couldn't wait any longer. 'There are so many crises you can't begin to imagine.'

'I can.'

'We didn't think you'd be in today, after what happened. I'm awfully sorry, it's such a tragedy. He was an ever so nice man.'

You would have suited him well, Helen, Eliza thought. And you would have loved him back. How perverse human beings can be. You're not entirely unlovable, but Phil didn't love you, nor has anyone else as far as I know. Helen's was not a life she envied.

They batted to and fro a succession of little eulogies. Phil deserved it; they were all true. In his small way he had been a good man. Eliza thought, I must go to his funeral before I leave.

Helen wanted her to take in a dozen messages, give advice on a dozen projects. 'Later,' she said. 'There's something I want to do first.'

'But Eliza –'

'Cool it, Helen.'

She wrote out her resignation by hand, dated it, signed it, put it in an envelope and addressed it to John Donaldson. He wasn't a boss she would regret leaving, she thought as she sealed it. She carried it to his office, which was empty. His desk was almost bare. There were not many bare desks in RUS, except for those whose occupants had left. She would never know now what he did with his days. She propped the envelope on his computer keyboard, leaning against the screen. She wondered briefly if he ever switched on the machine. Possibly not.

She could fetch coffee for the team, she thought as she headed back again. It was a chore she took on all too rarely. She picked up the tray from by the fax machine, then she stopped dead. Howard Nkolo was standing by her desk.

Marlboro Lights. Did he know who had told them?

'Howard.' She tried to make her voice sound natural. 'You're OK?'

'About as OK as anyone can be after ten hours of questioning.'

'God, ten hours.' She could see its marks on him, in the deeper-than-usual bags under his eyes and the grey tinge to his chocolate skin.

'I've got to talk to you.' Howard grabbed the tray, pulled it out of her hands and put it down on the desk, and taking her arm, steered her briskly towards the conference room, and through the door, which he shut with a clunk behind them.

'Lizzy, tell me this. Did you think I did it?'

'To be honest, Howard, I don't have a fucking clue what I think any more.'

'Well, thank you.'

'I don't want it to be you. I don't want it to be Phil. Frank Mills as good as told me last night he thought it was Phil.'

'What the hell were you doing with Frank Mills last night?'

'I don't know.' She sat down, heavily, on one of the chairs round the limed oak table. This was not the conference room the Beaver had been killed in, but it was its twin, alarmingly similar. 'The cops brought in Lewis too. I don't want it to be Lewis. I told them I'd seen him here that morning.'

'You what?'

'I did, I saw him here. I don't think he killed Harding. I can't see how he can have done. And I saw you here, and I know you haven't told me what you did in that missing quarter of an hour, and I don't think you killed Harding either. But someone bloody did. And it had got to the stage where I had to tell them the truth, all the truth, and let them work it out from there.'

'Let me tell you. One, there's forensic evidence pointing to Janine's killer, and that cleared me. It wasn't me, and the police know it, and in the end they had to stop making out that even if I didn't kill her I killed Harding, and let me go. Two, it's true I went to the Mornington to see Janine. I smoked two cigarettes in her bedroom eleven hours before she was murdered. I wanted to see what she knew, because they'd made it clear I was suspect number one, and I wanted to find a suspect number two for them. She didn't fucking know anything.'

He had bullied her. Howard Nkolo, easy-going Howard. Howard Nkolo the murder suspect.

'Three,' Howard went on. 'In that quarter hour before you turned up on the fourth floor I was with Stew Harker and Jack Lines.'

'You what?'

'They're my alibi. Or I'm theirs. Or if the police don't believe us, we're all the murderers.'

'Stew and Jack the security guards?'

'That's right. Now you and I and Stew and Jack are going to get together and work out who the fuck it was who killed Harding, because it sure as hell wasn't us.'

'So it wasn't Stew on the door.'

'No, it wasn't Stew on the door. But you think I'd have told the cops that?'

'You could have told me that.'

'You might have told them. I should have straightened it out before we first talked to the cops, but I didn't think of it. Then afterwards I thought, you don't know the guards all that well, so you got confused. Best not to explain or you might give something away. Best just to let them think you got confused. And what I did do was, I said to Carla, if the cops come for me again, tell the guys to make themselves scarce for a while. Which they've done. I know where they are. So we'll go and join them now, and see if we can get this damn thing cleared up once and for all.'

52

'But Eliza,' Helen wailed when she realized Eliza was about to leave with Howard. 'You haven't even heard your messages.'

I've been an awful boss recently, she thought. Helen had some cause to be frustrated. 'So tell me them quick.'

Helen did not like to be quick, but she did her best. She had no ability at all to set priorities, so she stuck to the order she had written on her notepad. Donaldson wanted some figures, as always. Derek Madison had faxed through a draft contract. Both those could wait, Eliza said. Mitchell wanted Helen to spend the next week on his MOD proposal; was that all right? It was. Lots of people wanted to see Eliza urgently. Frank Mills had asked her to phone as soon as she came in, Hugh Worning and Sandie Masters had left the same message, and James Connaught had been insistent too.

She had no intention of talking to Frank, Hugh or Sandie, but the message from James made her pause. It was as likely as anything, though, that he was chasing on Crane's behalf, looking for Stew, Jack and Bill. He would have to wait.

She said so, and picked up her bag. 'Eliza!' Helen's despair was penetrating. 'You've got to fill in a form if you go out of the office.'

'Sod the forms.'

Helen's face began to crumple.

'Oh shit. Howard, where the hell are we going?'

'Out,' said Howard.

She grabbed a form. 'E Stannard,' she scrawled. 'Time: 8.30. Reason for leaving the office: Personal Crisis. Destination: unknown.'

53

Howard fleshed out his account of the morning of Harding's murder as they were walking into the city centre. As she had assumed, he had taken the lift straight up to the fourth floor when she left him. He had dashed to his desk to collect the files he had left ready the night before, then headed for 4B1.

'But I didn't get there,' he explained. 'I ran into Jack and Stew in the main office. It was Stew's shift on the desk that morning, and most of the time he was down there. Everyone who came in before 6.25 saw him, but there were fifteen minutes or so, from about 6.25 to 6.40, when Bill took over from him.'

'I'm confused. What were Jack and Stew doing on the fourth floor?'

'Looking for the Beaver.'

They had almost reached the Technical Institute. She stopped dead in the road. 'They were what?'

'Remember, they'd just had their cards. They knew Marjorie Bergman wouldn't change her mind, but Stew reckoned if they begged the Beaver to think again they'd have a chance. None of them could hack the redundancy, so they agreed it was worth a try. Bill came in to cover for Stew while he did it, because he was the one with a free shift but he's no talker, and Stew and Jack went up to look for Harding. They didn't plan to kill him, only to talk to him. They weren't being devious about it, they didn't try to dodge me.'

'And they found him.'

'They hadn't found him when I first saw them. They knew he'd come in, because he'd passed Stew on the door, but they'd been to his office and he wasn't there.'

'No wonder, he was in 4B1.'

'Yes, as we know. So they said to me, any idea where the Beaver is, and I said, why, and they told me, and I said, he's in 4B1, maybe on his own, I'm not sure, and tell you what, I don't think it'll do any good but I'll keep back Eliza when she comes up and give you five minutes to put it to him.'

It was the kind of thing Howard would do.

'So you waited by the lift?'

'That's right. I saw Stew and Jack go into 4B1, and I saw them come out a moment later, like pinballs hitting the cushion. God, you never saw men so white. When they got to me I said, Christ, he must be in a bad mood this morning, and they said, Christ, he's dead.'

'You're sure they didn't kill him.'

'Not a chance. They couldn't have. They'd no weapon, no blood on their hands, no time to do it. Someone else was there first, but I didn't see him, and nor did Jack or Stew.'

'Then what happened?'

Howard shrugged. 'I told them to hop it. I reckoned they could make out they'd never been up there. It's not busy on the doors at 6.30, so quite likely only you and I had seen Bill in the few minutes he'd been covering for Stew. I mean, now I know a whole stream of people had already come in, but I didn't know that then. I thought when they'd gone, their fingerprints might be on the door, so I gave it a wipe best I could, then I backed off to my desk so I could dump the tissue I'd used. I put it in my bin. Then I reckoned that wasn't good enough, so I took it out and I thought I'd burn it. Then I thought, dumb idea, what'll you do with the ash, so I crumpled it up and put it in the bin by the coffee machine. Then I thought, hell, they'd never find second-hand fingerprints on a sodding tissue anyway.'

'And meanwhile I came along.'

'Yeah. I thought you must be there by then, and I was kind of waiting for a shout. Not that I meant to dump you in it, Eliza. But there are worse people. I mean, no one ever thought you murdered him.'

And quite a few people thought it of you, Eliza added silently. So Howard really had been acting when he had come into the meeting room. He had known in advance what they would find there. She hadn't read him at all.

Howard turned down St Asaph Lane, then left down St James's Street. Eliza said, 'Jesus. Are they at the Mornington?'

'No, the church, the redundant one they keep open.'

'St James's,' Eliza said pedantically. Sanctuary, she thought.

St James's Street had the usual scattering of shoppers and tourists heading from the cathedral to the city centre or vice versa. As they approached the flint bulk of St James in its churchyard, they saw a couple of them head up the path. 'Damn,' Howard muttered. 'Come on.' He did the last fifty yards at a lick, and got to the couple as they were trying the door. 'I wouldn't advise going in there, folks. We've come to inspect a dangerous monument.'

'Oh, sorry, sorry.'

They waited till the pair had gone, then Howard knocked on the heavy door. 'Jack? It's me and Eliza.' There was a squeaking noise, the latch turned, and the door creaked open a foot, no farther.

'Come in quick.'

Howard slid through the narrow gap, and reached out a hand to draw Eliza after him. She blinked as she stepped into the echoing half-light. Jack pushed the door shut after her, and lodged a chair under the latch.

'You ain't brought a drink, have you?'

''Fraid not, but we'll sort this out and get you back home in no time. Hi Bill, hi Stew.' Howard's cheeriness had to be faked, Eliza thought, but he managed a fair show of it anyway, as he headed down to a huddle of chairs at the far end of the north aisle, under the lectern. After a second, she followed him.

Bill and a plump, heavy-jowled man whom she assumed was Stew were sitting there, hunched in donkey jackets. They and Jack looked strange without their uniforms.

'Fucking freezing in here,' Stew said.

'Too bad. It's none too bloody warm in the police station either.'

'So what's happening?'

Howard told them, briefly. 'So we want what you know. Every last little thing you know.'

'Don't know anything much,' Bill said.

'It doesn't have to be much,' Eliza said. 'Give us every little thing.'

The guards looked at each other. And trust us, Eliza added under her breath.

'If she thought you were the murderers,' Howard said, 'she wouldn't be here.'

'Or you neither, I suppose.'

True. It was irrational perhaps, and she was past trusting her instincts, but she did not feel any sense of danger. As a silence grew she glanced around her. The walls were full of dusty monuments. Nathaniel Bolingbroke, twice mayor of this city and attorney at law. Giles Etherington, greatly respected as a surgeon. Mostly men, she thought. Dangerous monuments.

'So,' Bill said. 'We did this list of who we saw. Twenty-three of them, I make it. Never had such a busy time before seven before.'

'Mostly before you took over from Stew,' Howard prompted.

'Thass right. Just you two came in during the next ten minutes or so. Then Stew came back, and told me what had happened, and I scarpered.'

Twenty-three. That was all those Pat Shorten had listed, plus a couple more. People not quite in the loop of gossip, perhaps. Or ...

Eliza said, 'Did you see Frank Mills? Or Phil Curtin?'

'Not then. Why'd you ask?'

'No real reason.'

'I wouldn't say I remember everyone,' Stew said, 'because there's so many each day. But Mr Mills I remember, because he stopped and talked to me when he came in. It was just after I got back down and took over from Bill – say, 6.45, 6.50. He said he was sorry about the redundancy, and asked if I'd got any plans.'

Howard said, 'Did he often talk to you?'

'Sometimes. Not often.'

'Tell you one thing,' Jack offered.

They all turned to him.

'When we got up to 4A, when we were looking for Mr Harding. We went to his office first. There was a light on and an umbrella in the corner opened out to dry. You could tell he'd been there but he wasn't there then. So we looked in the other offices, but the only one that looked like someone had been in was Ken Thursby's old office, and whoever it was wasn't there. He hadn't left the light on but his coat was flung over the chair nearest the door, and it was wet from the rain.'

'And you remember the coat?

'Of course I do. A blue raincoat, dark blue with a sort of shine to it.'

54

Proof they did not have; but they had a story now, a story that made sense to them all. Frank had a motive, in his fury and humiliation when he had lost the chief executive's job, and his silent determination to get it back, and punish the man who had taken it from him. Was it enough? They reckoned it could have been.

'He must have been planning for months,' Howard said.

'Eight. Eight months.'

And he knew St Jude's House, knew RUS, well enough that he could work out exactly how best to do it. First, wait till there was an afternoon when the executive suite would be empty, or close enough to empty that he could lure the last person or two out of it. An afternoon when Harding would be in Costhorpe, and planning to stay there till the next day.

Then send the emails, to muddy the trail. To ensure there would be so many suspects, almost all of them people who had been loud in their hatred of the Beaver, that the police would never be able to work out which of them had done it.

He could not have done that himself, of course. He had to have – he did have – a solid alibi. He had enlisted someone else, or perhaps even several other people, Eliza thought wildly. The Orient Express type thing that James had mentioned might not be so very far off the truth after all.

So he had sneaked in early, through the goods entrance, most likely – anyway, through an entrance well away from the main lobby. He had gone up to the fourth floor, left his damp coat in Ken Thursby's old office, perhaps smoked a cigarette to calm himself. Then when it was around 6.30 he had tracked down Harding, and –

She still could barely believe he had intended murder. Perhaps it had all gone wrong? He must have meant to confront Harding, present him with a coup, blackmail him even, but murder?

'Oh Eliza,' said Howard. 'Don't kid yourself. He knew what would happen.'

And he had known, they all agreed, what would happen afterwards too. It wasn't likely that anyone would see him, or realize who had done it – except for his accomplices, whoever they might be. But if they did see anything – if the old RUS people like her had seen anything, then he must have reckoned that they would cover for him.

Frank would have found it impossible to retrieve his coat. None of the meetings he and his accomplice had fixed were for the fourth floor, so he had surely expected it to be quiet, but instead he could only just have missed running into Stew and Jack, and Howard as well. So he must have left without it, sneaked back the way he had come, waited a few minutes, then driven up to the directors' carpark and made a very visible entrance.

He had worn no coat when he greeted Stew in the lobby, in spite of the drizzle. He had been rumpled when she had seen him a few moments later. Uncharacteristically rumpled, for Frank. Even that tiny piece of evidence fitted.

But had she seen it earlier? No, none of them had. No one from the old RUS, the civil service RUS, had really wanted to believe it was one of them. And given a hint of evidence, most of them would have wanted to do what she had done herself, quietly dismiss it, let things be. They would close ranks, slide like a river past the stony death of this loathed man who had come to boss them all, and on into the future under Frank Mills.

'Fucking Frank Mills as boss again?' Jack said. 'Those London guys wouldn't have settled for that, would they? Hell, I wouldn't even vote for that meself.'

'No,' Howard answered slowly. 'But Mills most likely kidded himself they would.'

Yes, that was believable. Eliza knew how James had perceived him, but she knew too how Frank perceived himself. She knew about the deals that people like Hugh Worning – and most likely Phil Curtin too – were willing to make. There was no future for them under those London guys. But with Frank back in the top seat – they would have settled for that.

But who could have sent the emails?'

'Cigarette smoke', Eliza said. 'That's what made me sure it couldn't have been Phil.'

'But that doesn't prove it. The smoke could have been from Frank, later on. The next morning, or even that night, after he came back.'

It could have been. There were plenty of other people it could have been too.

'Tell you this,' Stew said. 'Whoever it was, Janine Broughton was on to them.'

Eliza said slowly, 'Must have been.'

'And she would have told you, Eliza, wouldn't she? Because it was you she rang.'

True. Eliza's number had been on Janine's pad, and it had not, presumably, been written down there in the few minutes after the murderer came to her room. Janine must have planned to tell her earlier, gone as far as finding out her number, then decided not to call it. Then when someone came to her room, she had made a rash – a fatal – decision to pick up the phone.

'Phil Curtin', Howard said on a breath.

There was a horrible logic to it. But Eliza said instinctively, 'It can't have been.'

'I bet you it was.'

55

They spent an hour, perhaps more, in the chill of St James's, mulling it over. Making plans, and dismissing them. Frank had been careful, very careful. They had a story, but only the thinnest of evidence. They needed more. But Frank was – well, he had not been quite so careful at Eliza's house the night before, but he was no fool, even so. It would not be easy to trap him now.

In the end they agreed that Howard and Eliza should go back to RUS and chase the few other leads they had, while the guards continued to hide from the police. Eliza and Howard would compare notes at four, unless they made a dramatic breakthrough earlier, and Howard would meet the guards again at six.

She would ring Genevieve first, Eliza reckoned. She had to know whom Genevieve had phoned, and what the other woman had seen. Howard was to talk to Hugh, and she was to talk to Sandie and again to Mitchell. Most of all she wanted a reason – a reason that did not involve Phil – why Janine had chosen her to phone in those desperate last minutes. She doubted Genevieve or Mitchell would supply her with one. She could not think of anyone who might. But surprises might come. Look at Martha's revelations about Genevieve and the Beaver: she had never seen that one coming.

Phil didn't smoke. She clung to that. But the others were right, Frank must have been in Ken Thursby's office the following morning, and he could have smoked a cigarette then.

No, it still didn't make sense to her. Frank, yes, she could almost believe that. Phil – involved, that was clear, but surely no murderer. And someone else? Someone who had sent the emails, and treated themselves to a fag while doing so?

She hoped, even if it was against hope, that it might also have been that someone who had murdered Janine.

She and Howard walked side by side back to St Jude's. It hadn't been Howard, at least, Eliza reminded herself. The forensic evidence proved that.

And would probably prove before long who it really had been who had attacked Janine.

They flicked their passes at the girl on the reception desk from the standard ten feet off. Eliza was taken aback when she called out in return. 'Miss Stannard?'

'Yes? You go on, Howard.'

The girl smiled. 'It's the hair that I recognized. You've lovely hair.'

'Well, thank you.'

'I was to tell you as soon as you came in. Mr Connaught wants you, he's in room 4A4, you know the office?'

'Yes, I know.'

'I'll phone and tell him you're on your way. No need to wait, you can go straight up.'

He hadn't left a note in her in-tray this time. This was official. He might have learned about her resignation, she thought. Or perhaps Crane had asked him to ask her more questions.

At the door to the open-plan section on floor 4 she hesitated. The last thing she wanted was to run into Frank Mills. But she couldn't see him in the secretaries' area, so she slipped through the glass door and went rapidly to Ken Thursby's old office.

James stood up as she entered. He was alone. He had been working in this room, she saw: his laptop was humming on the corner of the desk, next to the unused computer that had been Thursby's, and the desk top was littered with files and papers. He looked serious, but not angry.

'You've been out of the office.'

'Yes. Yes, I have.'

'Where?'

She sat down in one of the chairs that had been left in the room from the night before, and he sat too. 'James, I'm sorry, but I can't tell you that. I think I know who murdered Patrick Harding. I'm trying – we're trying – to prove it. I'm not working against the police, but the people I'm working with won't work with them. I think it'll be sorted out today, one way or another. Will you trust me for that long?'

She couldn't read his expression. A silence, surprisingly long, unfurled and hovered like a smoke trail over the desktop that separated them.

'Oh Eliza.'

'I'm not trying to get the killer off. I want to catch them.'

'Eliza. I wish it wasn't me who had to tell you, but I thought there wouldn't be anyone you'd rather have it from. That's been done already.'

'You've got him? But – that's great. And it's not that I mind. I mean, if it had to be someone, I can live with it being Frank.'

'Frank?'

She was slow to take it in, but not that slow. And slow, but not that slow, to say, 'But it has to be Frank.'

James stood, walked round the big expanse of desk, squatted down so he was at her own level and took her hands in his. His hands felt warm, but there was no reassurance in his face. 'Then for your sake, I wish it had been.'

'Oh God. Not Lewis.'

'No. It's Phil Curtin.'

A heavy door clanged shut in her brain.

She said quietly, 'Janine. The forensics.'

'True. There's no doubt. A couple of fibres on Janine's jumper, which match a jacket they found in Curtin's wardrobe. And his Land Rover was seen near the hotel that evening. He must have gone straight there from your house. It only takes five minutes, as you know. He had long enough.'

'Then – did he send the emails?'

'I reckon he did it all, darling. The emails, killing Harding, killing Janine. And thank God, he ended by killing himself.'

Forensic evidence. No room for doubt. Phil on the step, calling out to her. The same man – the same man! – taking a knife to Janine. Why, why? He hadn't been planning to go to the Mornington, he had wanted to spend the evening with her. But she had thrown him out, she and James, and for reasons they would never entirely disentangle now, he had chosen to go to confront Janine instead.

'The emails – maybe,' she told him. 'Janine – I wish it wasn't so, but I can almost believe that. But I don't believe Phil can have killed the Beaver.'

'Why else would he kill Janine? Remember what she said on the phone. She knew, and she was going to tell you.'

'Knew about the emails', Eliza said doggedly. 'Knew who it was, but even then that didn't mean it had to have been Phil. It could have been Frank telling him to deal with her, to cover up for someone else.'

'I know how hard this is,' James responded. 'It'll take for while for you to come to terms with it.'

A while! It would take several lifetimes, Eliza thought blankly.

A knock at the door hardly penetrated her thoughts, and she was only dimly aware of Crystal coming in with a tray of tea. 'Do you want me to stay?' she asked. James said no, to Eliza's relief. He drew up one of the chairs Carol Joyce had brought in, and sat with her while she sipped the sweet hot liquid.

She put down the empty cup and put her head in her hands.

'I'll take you home,' James said.

'No. Not yet.' She looked up again. 'James, I do know what you've told me. And I do believe it, much as I don't want to. I believe Phil killed Janine, and I believe he probably sent the emails. He sent them because someone persuaded him to. Someone who smoked, because Phil didn't, someone who was in this room smoking that day, or maybe a day or two earlier, while they were planning it all. And I know who that was, and I know that it was that man, the man who persuaded him, who killed Patrick Harding.'

'Eliza –' James began, but Eliza went determinedly on.

'It was Frank Mills. I know you don't want to hear this, but I have to say it. It fits. Everything fits now. I have to talk to Howard. We've almost got enough to prove it. The police can find the rest, I'm sure. Howard and I ought to go to them now.'

'Eliza, no.'

'Yes. I'm going to get Frank Mills and I'm going to have him put down forever. No, don't stop me,' she added, as James took her arm to prevent her getting to her feet. 'I have to go to the police.'

'Sit down, Eliza. Calm down. Talk to me. I'll listen to you.'

But he was; no. He was right. It would cost her nothing to tell him first. He needed to know, and he would show her how to play it with Crane.

James's little computer was purring in the quiet room. There were faint noises coming through the partition from the main office, a dim buzz of traffic from the road outside. The two of them sat alone in the eye of the hurricane. James listened, and Eliza slowly, methodically went through the story she had worked out with Howard and the guards.

'You see,' she finished, 'even Phil's suicide note confirms it. I'd though it was all about me, about us, but it's obvious now that that was only a small part of it. It was the guilt of murder he couldn't live with. And he'd never have intended it to happen, I'm sure. He can't have known what he was getting into. I suppose Frank made out that he'd benefit out of it, that it was some way of seeing Harding off the scene, but I'm sure he didn't realize Frank meant murder. Think what he said, how he hadn't known how it would end.'

James said, 'It's not proof, Eliza.'

'So we don't have proof yet. We're trying. We'll find some.'

'You're making the assumption there is some to find.'

'There must be. There has to be. We can't let him get away with it.'

James stood up. He took a couple of paces away from her, and stopped facing the window. The long curve of his back confronted her, the hard set of his shoulders.

Eliza repeated it slowly. 'We can't let him get away with it.'

The face that he turned back to her was little more than a silhouette with the late morning light behind him. But his deep voice, cool, implacable, told her its expression.

'You're a realist, Eliza. I've seen that. Now think about this realistically. This organization, half this city, has been on the brink of collapse. The murders shattered everyone. Now the police have announced that they've solved them. The danger is over. They've got their man. And they are not wrong, Eliza, they have not framed an innocent man. They have proof enough to satisfy any court, although in reality it'll never have to, that Philip Curtin was a killer.'

He paused. 'Now what you suggest is that we go to them and tell them, and not only them, the employees here, the media, everyone, that they haven't actually got it right. You ask them to look for another man, and you ask that knowing that there is nothing, nothing, in the way of definite proof that would persuade a court to convict this other man. The case is no sooner closed than you want to open it again, and yet to open it isn't likely to achieve anything. Except rumours and fear and bloody chaos all over again.'

'Don't you want to avenge Patrick Harding?'

'He is avenged.' He met her eyes steadily. 'In all the damage this has done. And I promise you that Frank Mills will never, never, take his place at RUS. But I'm asking you to leave it at that.'

'What about justice?'

'Hell, the criminal system doesn't have much to do with justice. It's a device for keeping society in order. I honestly don't believe that society's going to be in danger from Frank Mills in future.'

'He could kill again. If you've done it once .... An elderly relative, maybe, or ...'

'You don't seriously believe that.' His eyes narrowed. 'We've been honest so far, so let's be honest now. I know you don't like Frank Mills, and I believe in your desire to see him punished. But let's not call that justice. It's much less abstract than that. You wouldn't be talking the same way if we suspected but couldn't prove that Lewis had murdered Harding, or even that Howard Nkolo had. To be honest, neither of us has been pursuing justice with single-minded fervour. I've been looking for a way to get RUS back up and running, and you've been looking for a way to feel safe without hurting your friends. Well, I've got it and you've got it. Now you're asking for more. And I'm telling you you can't have more.'

'I can go to the police without you.'

James said very softly, 'Don't do that, Eliza.'

55

He told her to go home, to take some time off, to give herself a chance to recover. He had been told about her resignation. She could hold to it or rescind it as she chose, he said. He didn't want to force her out, but he thought there was some sense in her going, and was willing to try to swing it so she got a redundancy payment. He thought their relationship would continue: he reckoned it would be easier if she was not working for a Saturn-owned company.

She didn't argue with him any further. She went home.

Rachel turned up on her doorstep at midday. 'No, don't send me away,' she said. 'Your James rang me. I know I've got to apologize, he told me what Hugh had done. What a prat. I dare say you're livid with me, but you need someone with you, Lizzy, and I guess I'm still the best one for it.'

'I can't imagine why you'd have told Hugh, of all people.'

'Of all people. I'm sorry. I don't know that this is the moment to explain, but for what it's worth, the explanation's the obvious one.'

'What obvious one?'

'Intimacy. Sex. All that. Shall we go to my house? I'll cook you lunch.'

They went. Eliza sat on the sofa and stared into space as Rachel busied herself making mushroom soup, fresh soda bread and fruit salad. She ate. Then she talked.

Rachel listened. 'I can't tell you what to do, Lizzy,' she said. 'But James is right, you're done in right now. And I think he has a point about the rest of it, to be honest. Do you really want to sweep lots of other people into the net? People we care about, you and me?'

People like Hugh, Eliza thought silently. Hugh was a smoker.

'It wouldn't help anyone,' Rachel repeated. 'It's time now to stop. To mourn. Well, kind of. Sleep for a week and see how things work out.'

She slept for a night, in Rachel's narrow spare bed. Then she went home. The house was cold. James's carnations smiled from the vase on her dining table, his irises from a yellow vase in her sitting room, her own carnations, browning now, from the brass Singalese bowl she had put them in – it seemed like a lifetime ago, though it was days, no more. The house still smelled to her of death.

There was no message from him on her answering machine; but then, he had said he would give her time.

But she should fill that time by learning more, she thought, with dull hopelessness. Time to stop? No. It was not that she wanted to avenge Harding, but she could not see how Phil could have killed him. There was a murderer out there. She did not want Phil blamed for Harding's death, even though it would make little difference to anyone now. She wanted the real killer found, and punished.

Howard had rung. She phoned him back. He wanted it too, that was clear from everything he said. He had tried everything, the leads he had set himself and once he had learned what had happened, the leads she had intended to follow up too. Genevieve had been bloody to him. I'm done with it, she had said. None of your fucking business who I phoned. But I'll tell you this, if I could implicate that bastard Frank Mills I'd do it, so you can read into that what you like.

He had taken the story of the raincoat to the police, and they had told him, we've solved the crime now. The incident room had been closed down. The news had been in all the papers.

Lewis had rung too. Eliza did not want to talk to Lewis.

Frank Mills had rung. She did not want to talk to Frank Mills either. What a relief it's all over, he said on the tape. I'm sorry to hear you've decided to take the money, Eliza. If you ever want to come back, we'd be glad to have you. And I'll give you a great reference, don't you worry.

56

Lewis rang again the next day. Eliza had been sitting on her sofa finishing the patchwork cushion for Val. She had been invited to Val and Mitchell's that evening, so she wanted to have it ready to take with her. Val wouldn't expect it, but that wasn't the point. She needed to do it.

All her friends seemed to have phoned with invitations, as if they had all been given the message she mustn't be left alone to brood. This time she answered Lewis, though with misgivings, and mostly to ensure he would not keep on calling.

'You rang Kate,' he said.

'Yes. Stupid, perhaps, but it felt right at the time. I feel so guilty for having told the police about you being at St Jude's House. I knew what chaos it would cause in your life. But in the end I had to tell them, I had to.'

Did she? she thought when she said it. Well, it had seemed at the time that she did.

And Lewis did not argue. 'I realize that,' he said. 'It was too much to imagine it wouldn't come out. It was my own bloody fault, I should never have tried to get that database.'

'Will it affect this job offer?'

'It's affected everything. Kate's not even speaking to me.'

'She'll come round.'

'You think.'

He seemed to be fishing for a sympathy she didn't want to give him. 'Well,' she said, 'I'm glad we talked. I'll see you around.'

'One thing,' said Lewis.

'Yes?' She had been about to hang up on him.

'You don't want to talk any more, I can see, but I need to make sense of it. How the hell was it Phil who went for killing Harding? I mean, he hated him, sure, we all hated the bastard. I hated him as much as anyone, but I'd never have gone as far as killing him. You knew Phil really well. Was that, you know, in him?'

'I hadn't thought so. To be honest, I don't think he did it. Janine, yes, I think he must have killed Janine. But that came after.'

'So who did kill the Beaver?'

'Don't quote me, Lewis, for obvious reasons. I still reckon it was Frank Mills.'

'Kate didn't tell me herself, but she told Val and Val told me. That when you called her, Frank Mills was there? It was weird, she said.'

'Yes. Weird it was. I kind of wondered then. You know Frank, he always has an agenda, but I couldn't figure out what this one was. Why would he want to talk to me? He went on about a job he'd offer me, but that was smoke, that wasn't his reason. But it's obvious now. He wanted to find out what Phil might have told me.'

'What Phil might have told you.'

'Yes. I don't think Phil was very far from telling me, except I never realized he had anything to tell. But he was in league with Frank, he must have been. Frank had the plan. He got Phil to send the emails, but I'm sure he must have killed Harding himself. Then somehow Janine figured out what had happened, or at least a bit of it, Phil's bit of it, and Phil – Phil panicked.'

'But Mills didn't panic.'

'Worse luck.' But he would have acted, she thought now, if she had given him the wrong answers. Killed her, even. 'No, he's clear, the bastard. He left no evidence, and nobody saw him. His raincoat, yes, that was in St Jude's at the right time, but it's not enough. We can't put Frank there much before seven o'clock. And the police and the RUS people, all of them want to close down the investigation now they've got Phil.'

There was a space. Then Lewis said in his slow drawl, 'You need to put Frank in St Jude's at the right time.'

'Yes. Half six, or a few moments before.'

'Shit. If only I'd known.'

'Known what, Lewis?'

'That the police needed to know what I never fucking told them. I saw him, you see. After I left you, after that row we had. I went down the back stairs, out to the goods entrance, and I was still fumbling to unlock the door when Frank bloody ran into me. He must have come down the other stairs, just after me. Down from –'

'The fourth floor', they finished together.

57

It tumbled into place, over the next few days. Frank never confessed. That would have been too much to hope. And although Eliza said she thought there might have been someone else too, someone who had smoked a cigarette in Ken Thursby's office, no one wanted to listen to her. But they listened to Lewis, listened to Jack and Stew. Checked the banisters of the stairs, the ones that Lewis reckoned Frank must have used, and found a couple of clear prints at the foot of them. The rumpled suit, the promises he had made to Hugh Worning, and to half a dozen others who came forward – belatedly, and swearing they had known nothing of what he had really planned. It added up to just enough evidence.

But perhaps not, or not originally, a plan for murder. Some of them were still convinced he could not have intended to kill Harding from the start, that he must have been meaning to stop short of that.

They dredged the river, just across from St Jude's, and found a knife.

Not intended it? The knife fitted Harding's wound. And his murderer had come armed with it.

Eliza would have chosen to leave Costhorpe, but she had to stay for the trial. There was no exultancy in it. Even those people who had cared for Patrick Harding seemed bleak and subdued when Frank Mills was found guilty.

The last day of the trial, she bought a ticket to Rio. No reason she had chosen Brazil, she said to Rachel; except that it was a long way away.

She stayed a year. It felt like long enough. By the last few months there were whole days when she did not think of any of it. Rachel sent her letters sometimes. She missed Rachel's wedding to Hugh, but she sent them a set of carved spoons she had found in a little shop just off the harbour. Amelia sent her postcards from Sydney, her parents wrote sometimes from Andover. It was not quite the end of the world; she was not out of touch.

She did not hear from James. She had told him, don't write, and in the end he had believed her. But when she came back and bought a flat in Finchley, she found a parcel from him among her things. Rachel had put it there, she supposed. (Rachel had had everything put in store for her, just as Rachel had sold the house in Browning Street.) At first it had been Rachel's line that James sounded like a bastard, she was well rid of him, but in seemed in time he had won her over.

It was a flower painting, Cape leadwort growing in a terracotta pot, done in watercolours, very precise, almost botanical. There was a caption underneath, in a spidery copperplate:

Plumbago auriculata or Cape leadwort, so named by the Romans, notably Pliny, because it was believed to be a cure for lead poisoning. Clusters of up to 20 pale blue flowers from spring to autumn. A narrow darker blue stripe runs down each of the five petals which flare from a tube. Protect from frost. Best grown in a container: once planted in open ground, inclined to spread.

She hung it on her living room wall, just along from the print of the bougainvillaea and a painting of an amaryllis she had bought back from Rio. She thought of him sometimes when she looked at it. He had left a message, his new address and a note to say he was sort of unattached these days, although he still saw something of Laura and his children. It was an invitation to contact him, but she didn't do so.

She didn't go anywhere she thought he would go, not that she had ever found out what kind of places he went, so it was a surprise when she saw him at Mickey's christening. It shouldn't have been, she realized almost immediately. Hugh was in charge now at RUS, an appointment that according to Mitchell had astonished people there only briefly, and of course James would be in close touch with him.

He was in a grey suit with a blue silk tie; he looked tall and elegant, but older than she remembered him. He was greying slightly. She had never asked his age, but she guessed he was then about thirty-five.

She had taken the train up to Costhorpe, so when he said he would drive her back to London, she said, OK. He had a new Mercedes, dark blue. She watched his hands on the wheel. She turned sometimes and looked at his profile. Once he reached across, and brushed his hand deliberately across her thigh.

He came in when they got to the flat, and they went straight up to her bedroom. The lovemaking was good; even great, except for a moment right at the end. As she felt her orgasm build within her she closed her eyes, then at the peak she opened them. Her vision was blurred, her lashes damp. But for a moment, only a moment, she had the illusion that the out-of-focus face she was looking into was not his but the Beaver's; the Beaver's as she and Howard had found him, with glazed open eyes and a faint yellow crust congealing around his mouth.

Afterwards they lay in her bed and drank Vouvray together.

She thought he would say, why didn't you phone me? But he did not. They talked mostly about Rachel and Hugh. Rachel was still at the Castle Arts Centre; she had just gone back from her maternity leave. The pay was lousy, but they weren't hard up, with Hugh doing so well. James made it clear that Hugh had been his choice. He had pushed the decision through straight after he had bullied Summerfield into quitting. He had seen something in Hugh, a ruthless streak (so he called it) which he liked.

'So,' he said, when it was time for him to go. 'When shall I see you again?'

Her body was damp from his, her limbs heavy, her breasts sore. Bullied, she thought, although that had not been a word he had used, and he had not at one moment been rough with her.

'You won't,' she said.

Also by Susan Curran

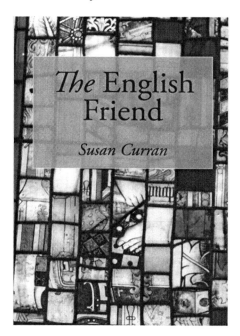

An illustrated biography of William de la Pole, first duke of Suffolk (1396–1450)

William de la Pole spent half his life fighting for the Lancastrian kings in France, in the later stages of the Hundred Years War. The war cost him his father and his four brothers. Taken prisoner, he lost a fortune paying his ransom – and gained two friends: his captor, the bastard of Orleans, and the bastard's half-brother, the famous French poet Charles of Orleans. Suffolk, also a poet, was to become Orleans' jailer. He spent the remainder of his life trying to bring about peace between England and France. It made him the most hated man in England.

This powerful true story of friendship, loyalty and treachery is the first full-length biography of an extraordinary man. Susan Curran uses a wide range of sources including contemporary documents and chronicles to bring Suffolk's story to life. The illustrations include photographs of the places Suffolk knew, and contemporary stained glass from England and France.

For more information on all Lasse Press books, visit

www.lassepress.com

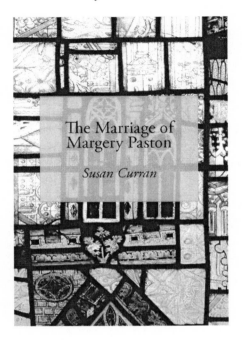

A true story of two lovers in medieval East Anglia

When Margery Paston announced that she wished to marry her family's land agent, Richard Calle, her mother and her brothers were appalled. They resisted the marriage so strongly that rather than let Margery follow her heart, they created a public feud which culminated in her being examined in public by the bishop of Norwich.

Richard was no shop assistant. He was an intelligent, well-educated professional man, perfectly capable of keeping a wife in the manner that might have been expected of Margery's husband. So why were her family so determined to prevent the marriage? Was it really because they believed it was socially beneath them, or were there other, better hidden reasons?

The book is illustrated in colour throughout, with maps, family trees and many photographs of East Anglian scenes, stained glass and other details of medieval buildings.

.

Lightning Source UK Ltd.
Milton Keynes UK
UKOW04f1519180315

248101UK00002B/46/P